LADY
LEFT

Also by Robert Westbrook

Journey Behind the Iron Curtain
The Magic Garden of Stanley Sweetheart
The Left-Handed Policeman
Nostalgia Kills

LADY
LEFT A LEFT-HANDED
POLICEMAN
NOVEL

Robert Westbrook

Crown Publishers, Inc., New York

AUTHOR'S NOTE

This is a work of fiction. According to unreliable reports, there exists a country somewhat south of California and west of Cuba that goes by the name of Nicaragua—though for those of us in the United States, this has always been a purely imaginary land, little more than a conveniently distant playing field for our right- and left-wing politicians to let off steam. Beverly Hills, of which I also write, is more shadowy still; I grew up in this place as a child, and years later must still occasionally pinch myself to see if I am real. As for the characters, incidents, and dialogues depicted in this book—they are also products of my imagination and are not to be construed as real. Where the names of actual persons, living or dead, are used, the situations, incidents and dialogues concerning those persons are entirely fictional and are not intended to depict any actual events or change the entirely fictional nature of the work.

Published by Crown Publishers, Inc., 201 East 50th Street, New York, New York 10022. Member of the Crown Publishing Group.

CROWN is a trademark of Crown Publishers, Inc.

Manufactured in the United States of America

Library of Congress Cataloging-in-Publication Data
Westbrook, Robert.
    Lady left / by Robert Westbrook.—1st ed.
       p.   cm.
    I. Title.
    PS3573.E827L3   1991
    813'.54—dc20   90-2251
                                                    CIP

ISBN 0-517-57131-5
Book design by Shari deMiskey
10   9   8   7   6   5   4   3   2   1
First Edition

This is for my mother, Sheilah Graham,
who arrived on these Hollywood shores
with little but courage and optimism—and succeeded
in creating a life for herself
equal to her imagination.

Contents

Prologue

THE BUNGLE IN THE JUNGLE

"DOOMSDAY!" SAID THE MAN FROM DISNEY. "WHAT WE'RE TALKING about here is a threat to every living creature on planet Earth."

There was a murmur of agreement in the room, for in Hollywood, when Disney spoke, people listened—and planet Earth was in big trouble these days.

"You'd think they'd feel guilty, for chrissake, cutting down all those trees," sighed Ziggy Ornstein, independent producer, who had a face as sad as that of a basset hound.

"My dear Ziggy, do you honestly believe Brazilians are *capable* of guilt?" asked a Beverly Hills hairdresser dramatically. "Cut down trees?" he cried. "My God, I knew this boy in São Paulo who'd cut out your heart and do a samba on your grave, if you let him!"

The studio executive hurriedly brought the discussion back under control. "There's no doubt about it—we're on a collision course with nature," he said pointedly. "By the middle of the next century, our air will be unbreathable, our rivers fouled, the forests bare, and the oceans will begin to rise."

He paused for effect. The speaker was in his early thirties, but looked older due to a premature loss of hair and the weight of global extinction upon his conscience. There were more than thirty prominent Hollywood figures gathered this evening in his spacious Coldwater Canyon living room, seated on creamy sofas and Bauhaus chairs, and some even cross-legged on handwoven Navajo rugs on the floor. Among the most notable features of this beautiful, $3.2-million home were its huge mahogany beams and seeming acres of polished hardwood floors.

"Last year an estimated twelve thousand three hundred and fifty square miles of Brazilian rain forest were burned to the ground— that's an area larger than the entire country of Belgium," he said. "Every *second*, even as we sit here, a patch of trees the size of a football field is gone forever."

"Wha'd he say?" whispered a young movie star to the actress on his left. The movie star was at this meeting because his agent said it would be good to appear interested in things besides getting laid and driving expensive cars. He'd been distracted by the girl's neatly crossed legs.

"Beats me," admitted the actress, whispering back. "To tell the truth, I was practicing lines."

"Hey, look—why don't we have dinner afterwards?" suggested the movie star smoothly. "That way we could practice lines together."

The executive gave the actress and actor each a stern look—the chances were neither would be working for his particular studio in the foreseeable future.

"*Why* should we care if they bungle the jungle thousands of miles away? I'll *tell* you why!" he said—and he went on at some length about carbon dioxide and the greenhouse effect that was changing the global climate and how if it got much warmer the polar ice caps would begin to melt, and if that happened we could all kiss Malibu good-bye and start building our beach homes in Nevada.

"But what can Hollywood do to help?" asked record producer Rip Beasley, with an almost saintly expression on his face. Rip had a Louis XIV hairdo, with thick black curls cascading down his shoulders. He had arrived tonight in a BMW convertible with a tie-dyed top, and was dressed in surfer shorts, Gucci loafers without socks, and a white dinner jacket. In Hollywood, you could get away with such attire as long as you were successful, and Rip had been nominated for Grammys two years in a row now—though that final prize still eluded him. It was a grave disappointment, naturally, and despite his flamboyant life-style, he went about town with the manner of a man misunderstood.

"Let me tell you something," said Rip. "I was with Madonna at the benefit we put on at the Brooklyn Academy of Music. We got a gigantic response—I'm sure you remember what a *monster* evening that was. Everyone was there—Christie and Billy, Calvin and Kelly Klein—but the Brazilians gave us the fucking cold shoulder. Now, I'm not looking for gratitude, but a little appreciation *might* have been in order."

Katherine Hall, actress and longtime activist, shook her head at all this idiocy. "Look," she said, "the Brazilians are saying we've blown our scene—ruined our environment, cut down *our* forests, in

3

order to enjoy our so-called high standard of living. So how can we blame a poor Third World nation for trying to develop its resources and be just like us?"

"Like always, everything comes down to money," said Ziggy Ornstein with a sigh.

"Exactly—and that's where *we* come in," said Rip. "Whad'ya say we do another really monster benefit—maybe a Global Rain Forest Awareness Day, with live TV satellite coverage around the world? There could be spin-off rights for a movie, a record deal, a book— you name it. And coincidentally on this very subject, I had Paul McCartney on the blower just yesterday morning. . . ."

What a roomful of jerks, thought Katherine Hall, whose friends called her Kitty. As far as she was concerned, the environmental movement had been a lot more fun before the so-called Great Awakening—that magical moment in the late eighties when Hollywood decided *en masse* and almost overnight to save what they generally referred to as planet Earth. Although this was not her home, Kitty had volunteered to provide tonight's refreshments, and she helped play hostess momentarily by refilling glasses of fruit-flavored Koala water and offering around a tray of braised-tofu appetizers served on whole-wheat crackers. At the age of forty-two, Kitty Hall was strictly health-conscious and the results were there for all to see: a strikingly beautiful woman who looked nowhere near her age.

Kitty glanced up to see her husband, Cory, come into the room. He was late, as always, and making a grand celebrity entrance— though he was, in fact, one of the few people here tonight who was *not* a celebrity. He came jogging into the living room dressed in old blue jeans and sneakers, a white T-shirt, and a brown leather flight jacket, waving and smiling at everyone in sight. There was something about him that made people wave and smile back, even though he was, strictly speaking, a has-been from the sixties—now only a professor at UCLA—and under most Hollywood circumstances a person to avoid.

"'How's planet Earth?" he whispered to his wife as he kissed her on the cheek.

"Don't laugh," she told him. "When those rain forests are gone, *you're* going to need your galoshes, buddy."

4

Cory grinned at her. He enjoyed giving his wife a hard time about having been involved in *every* liberal cause from the antiwar movement to the Great Malibu Sewer Debate. As for Cory, his credentials in left-wing politics were good enough that he could afford an ironic attitude.

Cory had a theory that Hollywood's Great Awakening was actually a strange by-product of the AIDS epidemic and would be over the moment scientists found a cure; meanwhile, people were afraid to be decadent, and thus had virtue thrust upon them. Cory often said he couldn't see much difference between the cocaine and self-indulgence Tinsel Town had given up and the activism it had embraced: Both were narcotics, a big, beautiful ego high.

"Get me a beer, and I'll love you forever," Cory whispered to a passing Mexican servant—a young girl who giggled, blushed, and hurried to the kitchen to do his bidding. Rip's idea to stage a massive new benefit for the rain forests had taken hold around the room, and various suggestions were being bantered about, as well as a possible list of stars who might wish to participate. This would be the sort of event that would not hurt anyone's career. Cory sat without further comment, smiled happily at the whole affair, and when the meeting was finally over, he followed his wife outside to the carport, came up behind her, and gently took hold of her breasts. He whispered one tantalizing word into her left ear: "Nicaragua!"

"No," she told him firmly, removing his hands.

"Why not?"

"God damn it, Cory—you know why. You're going to get us fucking killed!"

"Better that than sitting through another meeting like this one," said he.

The night was cool and damp, and carried a scent of the ocean mixed with the exhaust of a million automobiles. Despite the weather, Cory put down the top of his Jaguar XKE and drove too fast over Coldwater Canyon, coming back into Beverly Hills. Kitty had let her limousine go in order to ride home with her husband, but now she was having second thoughts.

"Slow down, for chrissake," she told him.

5

"I could drive this road with my eyes closed," he assured her. "Wanna see me try?"

"No!" she told him quickly, for with the slightest encouragement, Cory might do anything.

He laughed at her nervousness. "Keep an eye out for Rip Beasley," he said. "I've been watching him—the guy has to be an undercover cop—I mean, *no* one else would drive a tie-dyed BMW, not even in Beverly Hills."

"You're full of shit—you know that?" said Kitty, turning on the floor heater full blast to offset the rushing cold of the open car.

"My dear and darling wife," he said over the growl of the engine. "I promise not to pick on Rip anymore if you'll only come with me to Central America."

"Cory, are we really going to discuss your Nicaraguan fantasy? I swear to God, you come up with ideas like this, I hardly believe you're an adult."

"What you mean is, no one gives a damn about Nicaragua anymore—it's not the chic cause this year, like banning fur coats and saving the rain forest."

"You know damn well I'm not like that. Slow down, Cory, *please.*"

They were cruising over the top of the hills, flying down the narrow and twisty road toward the flatlands below. "Look, I'm talking about a way to get our hands on enough money to get rid of that Violeta Chamorro woman and put the Sandinistas back in power," he said. "Don't you see how beautiful this is going to be? It's a God damn Ollie North in reverse! It's the perfect revenge!"

"Darling, the whole idea's utterly fantastic. First of all, what you're proposing is practically extortion—I'm certain it can't even be completely legal."

"Legal!" he cried to the half moon above his head.

"Sweetheart, you want to be a martyr, you go ahead. But you can count me out."

"Do you know what your problem is, Kitty? You've become respectable. That's right—I mean, when the hell did leftist politics become a black-tie affair? God save us from limousine liberals!" he sighed.

"Cory, those were important people tonight. They control movie studios, television programming—they can get the word out to the public. They can really change things—we're not playing at student revolution anymore, this is the big time."

"Christ! Give me a break, Kitty! Next year I guarantee it—all of your Hollywood friends will be into something new, like saving pandas in New Zealand."

"Darling, there *aren't* any pandas in New Zealand," she told him.

"*That's* what I mean!" he shouted. She smiled at his histrionics. Cory, whatever his faults, at least was never boring.

"Look," he said, "I've been a leftie a long time now, Kitty. Back in '67, '68, it wasn't any black-tie affair, I can tell you that. I remember a meeting with Malcolm X in a little Harlem storefront—we had these white college kids and black radicals trying to sit down together. I mean, *that* was a meeting! I wasn't sure who was going to kill us first, the Muslims or the cops breaking in."

"So you're saying it has to be dangerous to get your rocks off? Is that it, Cory?"

"Let me tell you something—you want to change the world, you have to be a revolutionary, and revolution and respectable just don't mix. You can't have it both ways."

"Slow down," she told him one more time, reaching for a cigarette. Smoking was something she generally did when she was angry.

"Look at yourself, Kitty—you've become bourgeois. You're not even an actress anymore—you're a God damn *corporation*, for chrissake! Middle-aged!" he told her angrily. "Middle class!"

This got to her—middle-aged was something she worried about recently. "I didn't say no to Nicaragua," said Kitty defensively, "I just said I want to think about it."

The Jaguar came out of the hills and skidded into a left turn on Sunset, barely making the light. Unfortunately, the speed limit here was a sedate thirty-five miles per hour, and in his rearview mirror Cory noticed the flashing red light of a BHPD patrol car wanting him to pull over.

"Swell!" said Kitty. "Just what we need!"

Cory glanced over to his wife and flashed a rakish smile. "Hold on, darling."

"Cory, you *wouldn't!*"

He would, and he did. He pushed the gas pedal to the floor and the Jag leaped forward like a thoroughbred horse just given its head. Behind them, the black and white police car turned on its mournful siren and came after them in pursuit.

"God damn you, you crazy motherfucker! Stop this car!" Kitty screamed. She was furious. Cory just grinned at her.

"Loosen up, honey. Have some fun for a change."

Cory floated a right turn off Sunset, raced through a quiet residential block, downshifted into third, and made a hard left onto Whittier. The police car was twenty yards behind them at the turn, but it was no match for the Jaguar on the straightaway. By the time Cory got into fifth gear, the patrol car was half a block behind them. The powerful engine reverberated down the canyon of sleeping houses—mansions and palm trees flew past in a blur.

They were going a little over eighty miles an hour when they came to the first cross street, Lomitas. Cory slammed on the brakes, downshifted, and barely made the turn.

"This is it, you bastard! I'm going to divorce you!" Kitty screamed.

Cory didn't pay her any attention. He revved the engine and sped eastward on Lomitas for two blocks, narrowly missing a Mercedes at the intersection on Bedford. He saw the flashing red lights in his mirror and cut right on Camden, scraping against the side of a parked Bentley. Kitty screamed and closed her eyes.

He was gaining distance on the patrol car. By the time Cory made a fast left onto Elevado, he couldn't see the red lights in his mirror anymore. He sped across town, not stopping at stop signs, flying over the speed bumps at Rodeo, Beverly, Canon, Crescent Drive—a left turn onto Rexford and they were nearly home.

"The door!" he shouted to his wife. "Get the garage door!"

Kitty hit the remote-control button beneath the dash, and the garage door began swinging open, the lights coming on, just as Cory pulled into the driveway.

"Close it!" he cried, as the Jag drifted home. The garage door slid shut safely behind them, and in a moment they heard the sound of a police car—siren screaming—racing past their home and then disappearing into the distance.

Kitty was breathing hard. For a moment he thought she was

going to scratch his eyes out—but then she laughed crazily, giving vent to all the stored-up adrenaline of the chase.

"Admit it, you enjoyed that, didn't you?"

"No," she said, but they both knew she was lying.

"Sex and revolution," he whispered, putting his hand on her thigh. "That's what it's all about, Kitty. You and me."

"Just don't get us killed down there—okay?"

"Live dangerously," he said, "and you'll be forever young." This was an appealing theory for an aging movie queen, so appealing that she let him take her right there in the garage, making love in the bucket seats like teenagers—rocking against the gear shift, feet dangling out the window, both of them hoping the maid would not wake up

"You got to face it, Kitty," he told her when they were getting dressed. "You and me, babe—we're just too wild for Beverly Hills."

Part One

ON EVERY RIM, A
LITTLE SALT

1

THE JET PLANE CHARTERED BY THE HOLLYWOOD COMMITTEE FOR
Justice in Nicaragua climbed into the night sky above Orange
County, banked left over Long Beach, and headed south.

The high-pitched engine whine changed abruptly to a lower fre-
quency. The fuselage shivered as if it couldn't quite stand the strain.
Nicky Rachmaninoff, in seat 13B, involuntarily clutched the hand
of his ex-wife, Susan, in the next seat over. Were they going to
crash? Like the fuselage, he also could not stand the strain.

When it came to flying, Rachmaninoff was not an optimist. He
knew it was only the force of constant worry that kept the plane in
the air. A single lapse of concentration and you could hit wind shear
(whatever that was) or some more tangible object, such as a sea gull,
or a private plane buzzing about the air lanes, the pilot probably
drunk and having acrobatic sex with his secretary at twenty thousand
feet.

Rachmaninoff was a large man with patient hands, which were
sweating slightly at the moment and folded neatly in his lap. He
retained some traces of having been handsome in his youth, but
now had a battered look to him, as if he had been tossed by storms
emotional and physical. Air travel left him with a dark and desperate
look in the eye.

"Exciting, isn't it?" asked Susan Merril from seat 13A.

He managed a pale and sweaty smile. Susan laughed at him,
which was not good—for when beautiful women laugh at you, it is
one more cause for alarm.

Fortunately, it was not a long journey from John Wayne Airport
in Orange County to Sandino International—which was how this
particular group of Americans still referred to the airport in Managua, though the Sandinistas were no longer in power there. Probably John Wayne would not be pleased with his close proximity to
a has-been left-wing bandit, Cesar Augusto Sandino, but there it
was—a crowded hemisphere.

"This is going to be *such* a good trip!" Susan told him, not for the first time. "Good for all of us."

"Of course it will," said Nicky, not at all convinced. In "all of us" Susan was including Tanya, their fourteen-year-old daughter, who occupied seat 13D, across the aisle by the window.

"I'm going for a soda at the bar," said Tanya.

"Hold it!" Nicky told her urgently. "The seat belt light is still on!"

"Dad! For chrissake, *other* people are moving around."

"Honey, as you get older you'll find that other people generally don't know shit from Shinola," said her father. "You have to start thinking for yourself."

Tanya flashed her green eyes, then retreated beneath shaggy blond hair that had a way of falling over her face whenever she wanted to hide. She was dressed tonight in a faded denim jacket that was several sizes too large, and faded jeans that were several sizes too small. The pants had cost over a hundred dollars at Saks in Beverly Hills. The first thing Tanya had done with them was shred the knees with a knife so that her bare skin stuck out and she could look like a starving child of Appalachia.

"Look, Dad, the seat-belt light just went off," she told him now. "So I think I'll go stretch out on a couch in the back."

"A couch in the back!" Nicky repeated ominously.

Unfortunately, this was no ordinary plane, but a flying pleasure pit, an old 707 that had been converted for the use of touring rock groups—Elton John had reputedly used it last—leased out by a company that called itself Air Albatross, which Nicky knew was not a good omen.

The Rachmaninoff family was ensconced in what had once been the first-class section of the plane, but behind them—where tourist had been—was now a mock Beverly Hills living room: sofas, white leather armchairs, coffee tables, a bar, and a stereo system big enough to knock them out of the sky. Nicky was certain God had not intended living rooms to fly.

"Listen, dear," said Nicky to his daughter, "I think you should just stay in your seat and keep your belt loosely fastened. You never know when we might hit an air pocket. Out of nowhere, we could drop a thousand feet."

"Am I dreaming this?" asked Tanya, coming out from behind her hair. "For God's sake, if this plane was safe enough for Elton John, it's *probably* safe enough for me to walk around in—don't you think?"

He smiled at her innocence. "Honey, rock stars are killed in airplanes all the time—Buddy Holly, the Big Bopper, Richie Valens, Otis Redding, Rick Nelson. . . . There are more, if only I could remember. They all became careless and started walking about without their seat belts on."

Tanya gave up. The young were no match for the sheer oppressive force of middle age. Susan squeezed his hand in a way that was meant to be reassuring.

"Relax, darling. You're on vacation."

"Sure," he said gloomily.

Susan returned to the book in her lap, the autobiography of a Sandinista guerrilla during the last violent years of the Somoza dictatorship. Susan was an actress, but she was trying hard to change her image from blond goddess to concerned political activist. In the past year alone, she had become an active friend of whales and dolphins, an avowed enemy of nuclear weapons and power plants and those who wished to deface lovely Malibu with unsightly off-shore oil rigs.

Nicaragua was one more cause in a world gone mad, and Susan was dressed for the occasion in khaki pants and a tan safari jacket, looking very much as if she had just stepped from a Banana Republic window. With her long blond hair, long legs, and flashing blue eyes, she would undoubtedly give new meaning to jungle chic.

Nicky had been left behind by his ex-wife's sudden rise in the world. He and Susan had been divorced for more than twelve years now, and it wasn't until after their marriage was over that she had begun her transformation from housewife to Hollywood star—quite to his surprise. It was disconcerting, really, almost rude in fact, for someone you thought you knew—a perfectly ordinary person—to turn around and become famous on you. Going to Nicaragua together was definitely experimental. The trip was Susan's idea—it would be good for Tanya, she said, good for the three of them to be together. And besides that, Susan was between husbands at the moment, which left Rachmaninoff with a vague feeling of alarm. He wasn't at all certain what the sleeping arrangements would be.

"God, Somoza—what a fucker!" cried Susan, eyes blazing, looking up from her book. "Do you know what he used to do? He'd have his national guard hang people by their toes and beat them with sticks."

Nicky shook his head. "If I was a dictator and wanted to torture people—I'd tie 'em to a chair and make 'em watch MTV."

The plane made a small dip. To be on the safe side, Nicky tightened his seat belt to the point where he could barely breathe. Suddenly it hit him—he knew without any doubt that this trip they were taking was a very big mistake. *A family excursion to Nicaragua!* Rachmaninoff had allowed himself to become seduced by fine liberal sentiments uttered in the perfect safety of Beverly Hills living rooms—but there was a quasi-war going on down there, for chrissake! Nicaragua was the sort of place in which violence could break out at any time.

"Tell you what," he whispered to Susan. "I'll pretend I'm having a heart attack. We'll get the plane to turn around and drop us off back at John Wayne."

"Nicholas Rachmaninoff! I absolutely *don't* believe you! We've been all through this. Nicaragua is going to be lovely, and it's going to be as safe . . . as safe as going on a trip to downtown Los Angeles!"

Nicky trembled. As safe as downtown L.A.? This was worse than he feared.

2

NICKY AND HIS FAMILY WERE NOT ALONE ON TONIGHT'S SPECIAL AIR Albatross flight to Managua. There were thirty-five passengers in all—Hollywood writers, directors, actors, and lawyers. There were a radical Beverly Hills hairdresser, two musicians, three producers, four agents trying to be hip enough to attract new clientele, a journalist from *Rolling Stone*, as well as wives, girlfriends, husbands—

and in Nicky's case, an *ex*-husband who was busy keeping the plane aloft.

All together, they constituted the Hollywood Committee for Justice in Nicaragua, or simply the HCJN. Whatever else they were, half an hour out of John Wayne, the HCJN had managed to transform themselves into a flying cocktail party.

Nicky watched an alarmingly beautiful lady walking down the aisle their way. She moved with feline grace—she was worth watching, all right—her eyes smoky gray, her hair a lustrous brown, swept back from a Hollywood-perfect face. It was Kitty Hall, one of the organizers of tonight's junket, coming over to say hello.

"Susan! Well, we're off at last! Hello, Rachmaninoff," she added in her husky voice, leaning over Nicky to give Susan a kiss.

For a moment, Nicky had to hold his breath; there was a firm and shapely breast thrust into his face. He forced himself not to do anything rash.

The breast retreated, and Kitty was looking at him with an ironic smile.

"Well, Rachmaninoff, I'm impressed. Somehow I thought you'd duck out on us and go skiing at the last moment."

"I only regret I have but one vacation to give," he told her gallantly.

"Nicky's being *very* brave," Susan interceded on his behalf. "He's terrified of flying, aren't you, darling?"

"I'm more terrified of bloodthirsty *contras* and wild-eyed Marxists and loose cannons from the CIA," he admitted, "but then I'm just a working man."

Kitty smiled vacantly and turned to Susan instead. Nicky always had the impression she didn't like him much—held his profession against him, which was unfair, considering *he* wasn't all that wild about actresses, to be perfectly frank, but made a point of keeping an open mind.

"The last we heard, we're still hoping Danny's going to be at the airport to meet us," said Kitty to Susan.

Susan indicated this was several times better than swell.

"Danny who?" asked Nicky—he was lost in these Hollywood conversations in which no one had a last name. "De Vito? Danny Rather? Danny Schorr, perhaps?"

16

"*Ortega*," muttered Susan, embarrassed.

"Ah! Mr. Sunglasses."

The women gave him icy stares, then looked away. "Poor Danny," said Susan with a sigh. "He must still be depressed about his terrible loss."

It was many months now since the defeat of the left-wing Sandinistas in the Nicaraguan election, but the HCJN still felt it as keenly as a fresh wound.

"Yes, the United States finally did him in," said Kitty darkly. "Ten years of war destroyed the economy, and then they pumped millions of dollars into that lamebrained CIA bitch, Violeta Chamorro. And *that* is what Washington calls democracy in Latin America!"

This was familiar news, but it retained the power to make Susan distraught. "There are times, Kitty, when I'm truly ashamed to be an American."

"Well, I believe it's time to find the bar," said Nicky Rachmaninoff, without shame. The plane had not yet crashed, and he thought he might possibly chance leaving his seat. "Can I bring you something?"

The women declined. To keep figures like the ones they had, they must drink alcohol rarely, if at all. Only carrot juice and wheat germ could be allowed to pass such lovely lips. Nicky was tremendously relieved he was not a movie star himself.

He abandoned his seat and watched Kitty sink down into his vacant spot. He hoped he'd left it warm enough for her.

"Rachmaninoff's certainly in fine form," he heard Kitty remark.

"He *thinks* he's being funny," said Susan.

Now that hurt! Nicky made his way down the aisle. He thought he was being a pretty good sport about this, all in all, considering he had given up a nice bourgeois ski trip to the perfect snows of Taos, New Mexico.

The members of the Hollywood Committee for Justice in Nicaragua were wandering about, sitting on the edges of sofas and drinking and talking and carrying on as if they were safe on the ground. Near the bar, Nicky overheard Rip Beasley, the music producer, telling everybody about a new Ethiopian restaurant he had discovered on Melrose. Nicky had a feeling he was going to learn a lot on this trip. Up to now, for instance, he hadn't even known there *was* such a thing as Ethiopian cuisine.

"What can I get you?" asked the bartender.

Nicky considered his choices. Something strong, he wanted to say. A handful of Valium, perhaps. A parachute. He was about to settle for a triple Bloody Mary when he felt a strong, friendly grip on his arm.

"Nick-o-lass! Hey, amigo! I was worried you were going to back out on us, buddy."

It was Cory Heard—Kitty's husband. He always acted as if he and Nicky were special friends with some secret understanding between them—though in fact they had met exactly three times.

"So you decided not to go to Taos," Cory said with a chuckle, flashing a conspiratorial grin.

Nicky shrugged. "Well," he said, "this year Managua, next year Iran."

Cory laughed immoderately. He had wavy black hair and a boyish face—in his own way he was nearly as good looking as his wife, which Nicky found disgusting. Good-looking Hollywood couples were generally a very big pain in the ass.

"I gather Susan forced you into this trip, huh?"

"I'm trying to prove I'm not shallow."

"Uh, Nick—can I ask you something?" asked Cory, lowering his voice.

"Why not?"

"Are you carrying, *amigo?*"

"*Carrying?*"

Cory seemed a little put out that Nicky should be so slow on the uptake. "Hey, you know . . . a gun."

"Ah!" said Nicky Rachmaninoff, fairly certain he did not like this new conversational twist.

"Well?"

"Bring a gun on a tropical vacation? Surely you must be kidding."

"You brought no weapon at all?" Cory's smile was becoming a little strained.

"I decided I'd rely only on my charm and wit," Nicky confided. "But then, of course, I'm the sort of guy who can destroy a tank with a turn of phrase."

Cory tried to laugh, but there seemed to be something bothering him. "Look, can we go somewhere and talk?"

"How about right here?" suggested Nicky. "I was just about to get a Bloody Mary for my nerves."

"We'll try the front cabin," said Cory, taking him by the arm.

"Do you mean, er . . . where the pilot is?"

"Sure, it's quiet in there."

"Listen, Cory . . . *not* the front cabin. Please."

"Come on, Nick. This is important."

Cory led the way up the aisle. With his charisma, everyone wanted a word with him as he passed through the plane, a moment of his time. Cory smiled back, waved, gave them each the impression they were central to his thoughts, and kept moving. His charm was like a Plexiglas shield.

"Cory, please, we *can't* go in there," Nicky pleaded as Cory rapped on the closed door at the front of the plane.

"Nick, relax. These guys are friends of mine—Air Albatross is like Loose City, if you know what I mean."

Nicky was growing faint with terror. The door was opened by a young man with a mustache and a big smile.

"Hey, Cory!"

"How you doin', Bill . . . Pete, Chuck. Smooth flight, guys."

The guys laughed. There were three of them in the cockpit, lit by a hundred green glowing dials, looking barely older than college kids. Nicky could hardly tear his eyes away from the front window, which showed the blackness into which they were hurtling. The copilot pulled out a six-pack of Budweiser from under his seat.

"You guys wanna beer?"

"Sure," said Cory. "Nick, how about you?"

Nicky felt his legs going weak. Someone stood up to give him a seat. Nicky eased down into the seat with a long sigh.

"Guys," said Cory to the crew, "I want you to meet one of my favorite people—Lieutenant Nicholas Rachmaninoff, chief homicide investigator for the Beverly Hills police."

3

"YOU LOOK PALE, NICHOLAS—ME, I LOVE FLYING," SAID CORY HEARD, nonstop. "I love soaring up into the air, free of the earth, leaving all the sordidness beneath me—hey, did I tell you, I got my helicopter license six months ago? Now *that's* the way to go, amigo. Total freedom! In the next century, I'm convinced we're all going to have our personal chopper, just like the family car is now. Anytime we want, we'll be able to get aboard and fly."

Cory had entirely too much energy and enthusiasm. As far as Nicky was concerned, helicopters were even worse than planes—much worse—and it was an unfortunate hazard of being a modern policeman to suffer this intolerable mode of transportation all too often.

"Would you like to hear a story, Nicholas?" asked Cory.

"Actually, no—I would not," muttered Nicky Rachmaninoff.

Cory smiled indulgently and began his tale anyway. "Once upon a time there was a dictator—" he began. Rachmaninoff groaned and tried to stand up, but Cory held on to his arm.

"Once upon a time there was a dictator, and the name of this dictator was Anastasio Somoza Debayle. A fancy name, but this was a fancy guy. He held absolute power over an insignificant little pisshole of a country called Nicaragua that would have had little importance to anyone outside its borders except for the fact of its close proximity to a big important country called the United States.

"Now, Anastasio Somoza Debayle was actually the third member of his family to rule Nicaragua, after his father, Anastasio Somoza Garcia—who was assassinated by a poet in 1956—and his brother, Luis Somoza. Little Anastasio, or Tachito as his friends called him, cared for two things above all others—Money and Power—and in pursuit of these goals he was successful beyond his wildest dreams.

"Now, Nicholas, when we in America talk about *rich*, it's difficult for us to completely comprehend a land without income tax, in which one is constrained only by the limits of one's greed. Little

20

Tachito gathered his country to his breast—omnivorously. He owned fifty percent of the actual real estate of Nicaragua outright. He owned the national bank. He owned the national airline. He even owned the national Mercedes-Benz concession, so that he could make a profit from those of his subjects he had not sufficiently fleeced who could still afford a luxury car.

"Tachito grew and grew. Sometimes unexpected gifts would come his way. In 1972 there was a terrible earthquake that destroyed most of Managua and killed many thousands of people. The international community was kind enough to send him a hundred million dollars in relief aid as well as food, medicine, and building materials. Tachito was delighted with such generosity. He promptly deposited the hundred million dollars into his personal bank account and sold the food, medicine, and building materials at greatly inflated prices. And so Tachito was a happy man, certain his subjects loved him greatly, and those of his subjects who *didn't* love him, of course, kept very, very quiet for fear they might be taken quickly out into a field and shot.

"Now, as much as Tachito loved Money and Power, there was one thing he hated with equal fervor—and that was communism in any form. Even the mention of something as mild as socialism gave him indigestion for days. For this reason he was greatly beloved by Washington, and whenever Tachito wanted another fifty million dollars or so, all he had to do was get on the phone to the White House and say two terrible words: *Fidel Castro!* It was like a magic formula. Fidel Castro, *Abracadabra!* And more money would come pouring in.

"As time went by, little Tachito grew richer and fatter and eventually he took an American mistress. Perhaps Tachito was lulled to sleep by his many years of uninterrupted greed, because he became sloppy and made a very grave mistake, Nicholas: he came to believe the United States would never let him fall from power in a left-wing insurgency. And so he grew careless, and he made another terrible mistake—can you guess what it was?"

Nicky stared at Cory in silence for nearly half a minute. Despite himself, he could not resist the urge to solve a riddle. "It has to do with the money, doesn't it? Somoza didn't get his money out?"

Cory clapped his hands together, delighted. "You got it, amigo!

21

Or, to be perfectly correct, he got *most* of his money out, but not all. When the guerrillas started gathering in the mountains to overthrow his regime, he did not become alarmed soon enough. He didn't take proper precautions. When the end came in 1979, it was fast and furious and there was a lot of confusion in Nicaragua, as you might imagine. On July seventeenth, in the middle of the night, with the Sandinista revolution pressing hard against him, Anastasio Somoza Debayle hid himself in the presidential limousine and drove to the airport with a truck following close behind carrying the coffins of his father and brother—Somoza One and Somoza Two. The news media made a lot of this at the time; it was a ghoulish and memorable image to think of this deposed dictator flying to Miami in the presidential jet with two coffins, like he was Dracula or something. But, Nicholas, this wasn't all sentiment—there was a lot more in those coffins than his relatives."

"Money?"

"There was supposed to be, at least. But here's the big rub. In all the confusion of the final days, Somoza's soldiers *dug up the wrong two coffins!*"

"You're kidding me."

"No, I'm not. And you know how much money we're talking about got left behind? A billion dollars! And it's still there in Nicaragua, Nick, hidden underground."

"Come on, Cory—a billion dollars, that's unbelievable."

"You think so? Actually, this was only a small part of the fortune; believe me, Somoza had plenty of bucks left over to while away the hours before he was assassinated by a car bomb in Paraguay a year later."

"Now that the Sandinistas are out of power," said Nicky, "I bet Somoza's relatives will appear out of the woodwork quick as little bunny rabbits and claim what's theirs."

"No they won't, and do you know why? Tachito was a very secretive man, and the few people who knew the location of this hidden fortune are long dead."

"But I suppose *you* know where this money is buried?" Nicky sighed.

"Almost," said Cory dreamily. "And what I don't know, I'm going to find out in Managua—with *your* help, amigo."

"Not me," said Rachmaninoff. "I hate treasure hunts."

"Listen to me, Nicholas—I'm an expert on Nicaragua, I've been studying this little country for *fifteen* years! I've been down there countless times, both before the revolution and after. I know what I'm talking about—Somoza's lost fortune is just sitting in the ground, waiting for us."

"Aren't you rich enough, Cory? Whad'ya want to do—move from Beverly Hills to Bel Air, or something?"

Cory stared at Nicky like he was nuts. "It's not for *me!*" he cried. "Whad'ya think—*I* want the billion dollars for *myself?* I'm going to give the money to the Sandinistas, of course. Don't you understand what the United States did to Nicaragua? We shattered their economy, we crushed their revolution, and unfortunately it all comes down to money. A billion dollars, my friend, will bring the Sandinistas back from the grave—and, Nicky, as Americans, we *owe* them this chance. Don't you see? It's a matter of retribution."

"At least it's not a matter for the Beverly Hills police," said a thankful Rachmaninoff. "So let me just wish you all the luck in the world, and I—"

"Not so fast, amigo. There are a few problems for us to take care of before this retribution can come to pass."

"Cory, I wish you would stop saying 'we.' "

"Nick, let me put it to you straight—I think there's a CIA agent on this plane, disguised as one of us. Those guys have been following me around for years, and if they get wind of this money, they're going to cause some serious shit to happen. Can you dig it? Some of these CIA dudes would go totally apeshit at the mere thought of the Sandinistas getting their hands on a billion dollars and Creeping Communism spreading north toward Disneyland—and to be perfectly frank, Violeta Chamorro and her right-wing cronies would not be too thrilled about it either. Are you beginning to understand why I asked if you brought a gun?"

Nicky rose tenuously from his seat to discover that his legs still functioned. "You're beginning to scare the shit out of me, Cory."

"Nick! You're one of us, I know it! I've talked with Susan about you—she told me you used to demonstrate for civil rights back in the sixties, for chrissake. Maybe we were in the same riot together.

23

Tell me something honestly, Nick—don't you feel like a ship-wrecked sailor, marooned in the nineties without a cause?"

"With me, it's more a feeling of flying at thirty-seven thousand feet with a bunch of lunatics at the controls and a madman talking into my ear."

Cory smiled indulgently. "Please, Nick, promise me you'll think about it, at least. I'm positive Nicaragua is going to make a believer out of you again—the Sandinista revolution was everything you once thought was beautiful. It was innocent, Nick—and the United States crushed it—like stepping on a God damn bug."

Rachmaninoff sighed. "Let's get something straight, Cory. I'm not looking to become a believer again, not in anything. What I am, I'm on vacation, and if you want to find me the next ten days, I'll be at the hotel swimming pool, dangling my toes in the water and drinking whatever passes for a margarita down there."

Cory laughed unexpectedly. "You're telling me you're going to Nicaragua for a kind of tropical *vacation*, Nick?"

"Sure," Nicky replied defensively. "Susan assured me it would be almost like going to Hawaii."

Nicky Rachmaninoff returned to the rear of the plane, trying to imagine why Cory Heard should find the idea of a tropical vacation in Nicaragua so hilariously funny.

4

THE AIR ALBATROSS JET TOUCHED DOWN HARD, BOUNCING ON THE runway a few times before taxiing toward the terminal. It was not the smoothest of landings, but Nicky Rachmaninoff felt his body relax for the first time since leaving John Wayne.

Outside the window, Nicky had a quick glimpse of a squadron of World War II–era aircraft, old bombers in decorative brown-green camouflage colors. There were also more-lethal-looking Soviet attack helicopters, and jeeps mounted with machine guns. The buildings in the distance were low and desolate, surrounded by loose rolls of barbed wire.

"Boy, what a dump!" said Tanya solemnly, her nose pressed to the glass.

"This is a poor country, Tanya," her mother said testily, "but that doesn't mean it's a dump. It's time you learned there are places in the world, young lady, where not every family has a Rolls-Royce."

"Mom, *honestly*! I mean, believe it or not, even *I* have friends whose parents can only come up with a Mercedes."

Susan gave her daughter an icy stare.

"That was supposed to be a joke, Mom. You know—ha, ha."

"*I* got it, dear," Nicky told her. He didn't have many theories about child-raising, but he felt it was important to encourage a fledgling sense of humor. "That must be the Club Med over there," he added, nodding toward the dilapidated main terminal. Tanya snickered. Susan looked as though she wanted to dump both of them.

The plane door opened, and the Hollywood Committee for Justice in Nicaragua began to disembark down metal stairs that had been rolled up to the side of the aircraft. A screenwriter from Malibu had been drinking so heavily he more or less slid his way down onto Nicaraguan soil, supported by his agent on one side and the railing on the other.

"Gosh, actual *stairs*!" said Tanya, awed by the primitiveness of this brand-new world. "Don't they have jetways here?"

"But smell that tropical air!" Nicky exulted, breathing in a great lungful. The night was hot and full of subtle foreign aromas, a mixture of jungle rot, jet fuel, and distant cooking all mixed together on a humid breeze that seemed to slap them in the face. It was like walking into a big armpit, thought Nicky—though he did not say so for fear Susan should find him shallow.

At the foot of the stairs, Cory and Kitty were already on the tarmac, giving a small speech to the world's press, who had managed to come tonight. Beyond the throng of reporters was a semicircle of soldiers armed with automatic weapons. The soldiers appeared absurdly young and not very menacing. They were grinning and bobbing up and down in line to get a good look at the celebrities coming off the plane.

"The United States' treatment of Nicaragua has clearly been one of the most despicable events in American history—or *anyone's* history, for that matter," Kitty Hall was saying to the gathered reporters. Though a small woman, she had a stadium-sized voice. "I'd like you to picture for a moment the outcry there would be in our country if ever a hostile foreign government—say Libya, for example—gave thirty million dollars to one of *our* presidential candidates! . . ."

Kitty had more to say about what she called the rape of Nicaragua, but the American press had their own ideas of what was news.

"Kitty, can you tell us if there's any truth to the rumors of trouble in your marriage?"

"Kitty, look this way, please . . . smile!"

When the Rachmaninoff contingency reached the tarmac, a small group of reporters broke off from the Heards and came over to immortalize Susan Merril's arrival in Managua. Susan flashed her most radiant smile, but then seemed to remind herself consciously this was *not* a Hollywood premiere. She narrowed her eyes, cocked her pretty head slightly to one side, and managed to look ever so thoughtful.

"Mr. Merril, could you move in closer to your wife and daughter for a photograph?"

Nicky smiled, ever agreeable. "Whatever," he said.

"*Dad!* Tell him your name isn't Mr. *Merril*," Tanya huffed.

"It's okay, dear. *I* know who I am. That's the main thing."

Tanya let her hair settle over her eyes, going into a serious hiding mode just as the cameras began to click.

They made their way through the gauntlet of reporters toward the main terminal, where they came to a large hall with water-stained walls of peeling plaster. The press was not allowed inside here, Nicky was relieved to see. At the far end of the room, two officials sat at their desks, flanked by soldiers with machine pistols, waiting to give everyone's passport a good hard look and collect sixty American dollars from each arriving tourist. Right wing or left wing, everyone lusted for the American dollar.

Susan moved ahead in the line to have a chat with the liberal producer, Ziggy Ornstein. They were talking about doing a movie together; whilst protesting U.S. involvement in Nicaragua, there was no harm in making a few deals on the side. This left Nicky standing alone with Tanya, who quickly buried herself in a copy of

Rolling Stone. Not far ahead in the line, Kitty and Cory were telling Rip Beasley that, yes, it was a pity Danny Ortega had not managed to come to the airport—but perhaps he had more pressing business. Rip, with his Louis XIV curls cascading down his shoulders, appeared a little put out by the nonappearance of the country's ex-leader, who clearly needed all the help he could get if he was ever to return to power.

"I mean, *I'm* busy too," he pouted. "You think *my* time isn't important? I should be in a studio right now, making an album!"

Nicky tried to remind himself he was on vacation and that for the next few glorious weeks there would be no cops, no homicidal maniacs, just himself and his family and a foreign country to see from his hotel window.

"This sure is going to be fun," he said hopefully to his daughter.

"Dad, for chrissake, you know damn well you *hate* to travel," said Tanya, not looking up from her magazine.

"Now that's not quite fair, dear. Just because I enjoy a certain routine in my life . . ."

"I'll meet you on the other side," Susan called back in line, going through passport control with Ziggy and his family. In a few moments it was Nicky's turn. He gave his passport to a fat man in combat fatigues who spent a long time examining Nicky's photograph from every angle.

"They never do you justice, these passport photos," Nicky observed. He was trying to be friendly, do his bit for peace and understanding between nations.

The official looked at Nicky with fierce concentration and then back and forth to the photograph several times. He didn't appear happy.

"*Momento, señor, por favor,*" said the official, adding something fast to the machine-pistol-wielding soldiers at his side. Nicky didn't like the way they all looked at him with a new predatory interest. The official stood up, took Nicky's passport into another room, and closed the door behind him.

"What's happening, Dad?" Tanya asked impatiently, looking up at last from *Rolling Stone.*

"Not much, honey. The usual bureaucratic paper-shuffling. Same the world over."

The passport official came back escorted by two more soldiers, each of whom carried an automatic rifle. He said something to Nicky in an operatic flourish of language. Nicky didn't know a word of Spanish, but it sounded serious.

"He wants you to go with him," Tanya told him. Her expensive private-school education was at last bearing fruit—she could speak a foreign tongue, if not completely her own.

"Is there something wrong with my passport?" Nicky asked, trying to hide his alarm.

"*El pasaporte de mi padre esta en regla,*" Tanya said with some authority. "*Qué quiere con el?*"

The official spoke rapidly, rolling his r's and gesturing angrily.

"Dad, he's saying you've got to go with him immediately or there will be big trouble. *Por qué?*" demanded Tanya, giving the poor official a smoldering look.

Without further warning, the soldiers took Nicky by each arm and began to lead him forcibly toward the closed door. Tanya tried to follow, but a third soldier blocked her way.

"Dad!" she cried. "*Adónde esta lleverado mi papá?*"

"It's okay, munchkin," Nicky called over his shoulder. "Just a little friendly mistake, I'm sure."

"Dad, I'll get the American Embassy! I'll get you out!"

"Don't worry, I'll be—"

He didn't manage to finish the sentence. The door leading from the main hall was slammed behind him. Nicky was led through a long, bleak corridor, then pushed into a small room that was empty except for a single wooden chair. There was a bare lightbulb suspended from the ceiling, and one small window high up on a peeling wall, far above eye level. The window had bars on it. Nicky knew that was not a good sign.

5

HE WAS STRIPPED AND SEARCHED. HANDS AGAINST THE WALL, SPREAD your legs; it was the same the world over. When mankind shared common customs like these, it hardly mattered that they spoke a different tongue.

Nicky had no concealed weapons except his devastating wit—which he decided to keep to himself, feeling he might have need of it later. The soldiers were hardly more than boys, and they were surprisingly gentle. Eventually they returned his clothes and took him to their leader.

Their leader was waiting in a narrow office with a high ceiling that had an old-fashioned wooden fan overhead, slowly stirring the hot and sluggish air. The walls were a dismal shade of military green. Heavy metal shutters closed off the single window to the outside, just in case some fresh air tried to come in. Behind a battered wooden desk sat a military officer in his combat fatigues. He had a pistol on his belt and regarded Nicky sadly, as the two young soldiers waited smartly on either side of the door to prevent any escape.

"Lieutenant Rachmaninoff," he sighed. "Are you CIA? DEA? FBI? What exactly?"

"BHPD," said Nicky Rachmaninoff.

"And what devilish thing is this BHPD?"

"The Beverly Hills Police Department," said Rachmaninoff, hoping to put the right note of pride in his voice. For some reason he never quite understood, people generally snickered when he mentioned where he worked.

The officer simply sighed, more deeply than before. He was a handsome man with jet black hair and a very bushy mustache—handsome but weary, with dark, sad, romantic eyes. His uniform looked as if he had slept in it for the past two months.

"You are a policeman, then?"

"Alas," said Nicky.

"And why does a policeman travel with a bunch of left-wing lunatics who apparently wish to undermine our democratic election and bring back the hated Sandinistas?"

"You may not believe this," said Rachmaninoff, "but I'm here on vacation."

This admission brought a trace of a smile to the sad man's lips. "You are right—I do not believe you. I think you are here in some fiendish capacity to cause trouble in my country. I think you are some kind of lousy *contra* in reverse. Maybe you are a nostalgic revolutionary, eh?"

"A *what?*"

"You feel sad for the revolution that is gone forever—oh, I know your type! And let me tell you something—we are tired of you *yanquis* coming down here like Nicaragua is some sort of Ping-Pong ball for you to hit back and forth—right wing, left wing, Democrats, Republicans! It's crazy, I tell you! Why can't you just leave us alone?"

"I'll leave you alone," Nicky promised. "You have my word on it."

The military officer gave one of his tremendous sighs and began shuffling through a stack of papers on his desk. "Your wife is with you? She is Tanya Rachmaninoff?"

"That's my daughter," said Nicky. "Now you tell me what kind of leftist troublemaker comes here with his daughter? My wife is Susan Merril—you should find her on your list somewhere."

The officer looked up sharply. "Cassie O'Day! *That's* your wife?"

He was referring to the TV role that had made Susan famous, "Cassie and the Cop," in which she played a scatterbrained house-wife who solved a weekly crime. The point of each episode seemed to be to get Susan Merril into a bathing suit as often as possible.

"Susan's my *ex*-wife," said Nicky, to set the record straight. "You, er—get 'Cassie and the Cop' down here, do you?"

"You think we don't have television? Do you take us for ignorant *campesinos?*"

"Not at all," said Nicky hurriedly.

"You claim to be nothing more than a policeman on vacation, yet how can this be? How can a mere policeman be married to a famous television star?"

"*Used* to be married," Nicky reminded him. "That's the key to understanding my particular domestic puzzle. When I knew Susan, she was in fact a lovely nobody, and frankly that's what I encouraged her to remain. I told her wealth and fame were only a hindrance in the search for Universal Truth, but she wouldn't listen to me."

"So she left you to become a great star?"

There was a dreamy light in the officer's luminous brown eyes. Nicky Rachmaninoff suddenly saw a way out of his present difficulties.

"I suppose you wouldn't like to meet Susan Merril, would you?"

"This can be arranged?"

"Of course!"

The officer gazed at Nicky long and hard, tapping the top of his desk rhythmically with a pencil. At last he seemed to make up his mind. He barked an order in Spanish at the two young soldiers at the door, who quickly turned and left the room, closing the door behind them. To Nicky's surprise, the officer moved stealthily around from his desk, leaned close to his ear, and began to whisper.

"Sorry about this foolish playacting—I could not talk freely in front of those soldiers," whispered the officer. "I am Major Ricardo García Aivas, Chief of Airport Security. Cory must have told you about me."

"Good God, no! You know Cory Heard?"

"Keep your voice down. Don't you understand? I am a Sandinista—we are on the same side, you and I," he whispered urgently. "At least I *was* a Sandinista before February twenty-fifth of last year. Now I must pretend to be something else while I wait and hope for the revolution to come again. There are many of us still in the army, of course. I used to be in charge of an entire battalion, but when Uno won the election, I was demoted to airport security—a mere policeman's job! Oh, sorry . . ."

"Listen, if I could find a better job, I'd go for it in a second."

"You must forgive me—I thought you must be a CIA agent infiltrating the HCJN! I was about to . . . well, we won't talk about that. Why don't we go meet your lovely wife?" suggested Major Aivas eagerly. "She will be worried about you."

"Ex-wife," said Rachmaninoff for the record, one more time. "And believe me, she gave up worrying about me a long time ago."

6

SUSAN AND TANYA WERE WAITING ON HARD BENCHES NEAR THE BAG-
gage area, looking dismal and exhausted in the harsh airport lights.
They both jumped up and ran to Nicky when they saw him coming.

"Darling, are you okay?"

"Did they torture you, Dad?" Tanya asked—a bit too eagerly,
Nicky thought.

"Only a small misunderstanding," Nicky assured them. "They
thought I might be dangerous. But I made a new friend I'd like you
to meet—Major Ricardo García Aivas."

The major was at Nicky's side, gazing at Susan with deep rapture.
At the sound of his name, he lurched forward and kissed her hand.
With ardor like that, Nicky was afraid he might get carried away and
swallow a finger.

"This is a very great honor," said the major, breathing hard.
"You will find you have many admirers in Nicaragua."

With great difficulty, Major Ricardo García Aivas managed to let
go of Susan's hand long enough to be introduced to Tanya. "You
are as beautiful as your mother," he told her.

Tanya giggled. Even Susan had a slight blush beneath her California tan. Nicky felt it would be worthwhile to take notes on the
effects of Latin charm on supposedly modern women.

"José, you are to come here, please," the major said briskly. A
young soldier stepped forward on command. He could not have
been more than seventeen, all arms and legs, a handsome but
gangly youth. He had raven black hair, high cheekbones, and al-
mond eyes. On his lip, a faint stubble was trying to grow up and
become a mustache.

"I want you to meet my son, Corporal José María Aivas," said the
major, stiff with pride. "I am placing him at your service during
your stay in my country. He will be your guide, your driver, your
translator—whatever you wish."

32

"But, Major Aivas, I can't let you go to all this trouble!" protested Susan.

"You must call me Ricardo," he insisted. "And truly, you will be doing me a great favor. You see, I am most anxious for my José to practice his English and become more educated in foreign ways. And for his part, perhaps he will make your journey here a little easier."

At the moment, José looked too goofy to make anyone's journey easier. He was dressed in combat fatigues that were too large. The buttons of his shirt were open in front to reveal a black Iron Maiden T-shirt underneath. The way he carried his Soviet-made AK-47 assault rifle reminded Nicky more of a kid with a baseball bat than a soldier. And there was more for a father to worry about: ever since José had stepped forward, he had looked only at Tanya, staring at her with haunted, moonstruck eyes. Tanya gazed back at him haughtily, but Nicky couldn't help noticing that her hair had magically parted from her eyes.

"Iron Maiden!" she said with the greatest disdain, gazing at his T-shirt. "Yuck!"

José was devastated. "You don't like the heavy metal, *señorita?*"

"*Not* Iron Maiden," said Tanya, very definitely.

They all began walking through the airport together, Nicky and Susan and Major Aivas in one line, with Tanya following at a slight distance—the young corporal shuffling along at her side like a big puppy.

"Do you always carry that gun?" Tanya asked.

"Oh yes, *señorita!* In my country, war can begin at any time. As for me, I am not afraid to die!"

Nicky always worried about people who were not afraid to die. At his side, Ricardo was telling Susan about some of the sights she must see in Nicaragua. "You and your family will come for dinner at my house while you are here—yes?" he inquired, and then added more softly, "You see, I am a Sandinista—I was with Ortega when he came down from the mountains in '79. We are most grateful for your help, *señora*. In Nicaragua, we have long known it is the United States government that is our enemy, not the American people."

Nicky had a feeling the major had never been in Orange County, but he kept his mouth shut. The airport was bustling with people, though it was past midnight by now. Whole families seemed to be hanging out just watching the planes come in and go out—maybe this was big-time entertainment in Managua. Outside the terminal building, an ancient Mercedes-Benz was waiting at the curb. At least the car had been a Mercedes at one time; now it was a strange hybrid of other models, with a fender that did not quite fit and a door that apparently had once belonged to a VW bug. The hood was green, the sides orange, and there was a large pair of dice tied to the antenna.

"This is my car," said José proudly.

"Wow! Totally rad!" cried Tanya.

The young corporal seemed uncertain. "*Rad?* What does this mean?"

"Radical," Tanya explained. "You know—cool."

José still appeared confused. "It is a good thing to be radical in the United States?"

Tanya giggled. "No, silly. Radical doesn't mean *radical.* You're kinda out of it, aren't you?"

José sighed. "You will have to teach me more about America. I am most eager to learn."

Tanya giggled again. Nicky couldn't help noticing that his daughter was doing a lot of giggling lately. José was going to drive them into Managua, but just as they were about to step inside the mongrelized Mercedes, another car pulled up beside them, a shiny new American station wagon that seemed wildly out of place at the Managua airport. A big-eared man wearing polyester slacks and a Hawaiian shirt stepped out of the driver's side and came hurrying over.

"Hi, Bob Arnold, U.S. Embassy," he told them. "I understand you folks had some trouble here."

"Nothing we couldn't handle," Susan said coolly. "Now, if you'll excuse us, please . . ."

The man from the U.S. Embassy smiled sheepishly. Besides having big ears, he wore a pair of thick glasses with heavy frames, which made him look nearly as goofy as José. "Look, Miss Merril, we're all a little concerned about your group coming down just now.

34

Why don't I give you and your family a lift to your hotel? It would give us a chance to talk."

"Thank you, but that won't be necessary," Susan replied. "Major Aivas has been kind enough to offer us a car and a perfectly charming chauffeur. We are quite able to take care of ourselves."

Bob turned to Nicky. "Lieutenant Rachmaninoff, please—I think we all need to sit down and have a good long talk."

"Are you coming, Nicky?" asked Susan, stepping toward the ancient Mercedes.

"I'm sorry," said Nicky to the man from the U.S. Embassy. "Personally, I'd be glad for a talk, but my ex-wife seems to think you're an imperialist warmonger reactionary slime."

"Amen!" added Susan Merril.

Bob Arnold could only sigh, get in his gas guzzler from Detroit and drive away. As a public employee himself, Nicky felt sympathy for a man in an impossible situation.

"What a jerk!" said Susan. "He has CIA written all over him!"

"He's just a prawn of the military-industrial complex," added Tanya, hoping to impress José.

"A *pawn*, dear," her father corrected her. "A prawn is something you eat."

Young José opened up the trunk of his car and moved aside a small army of empty beer bottles to make way for their luggage, which had been carried to the curb by a trailing squad of soldiers. Susan's idea of traveling light was four large Louis Vuitton suitcases. Tanya had three, Nicky a small duffel bag. Fortunately, the Mercedes had a mammoth trunk. When all the bags were inside, Corporal José María Aivas even had room to throw his AK-47 on top.

He was a most polite young man. José opened the rear door for Nicky and Susan and moved aside a soccer ball and a box of ammunition so that they could slide on in. When Nicky and Susan were settled, he closed the door after them, fixing it in place with a piece of baling wire.

Tanya stepped around to the other side.

"I'll ride up front," she said. "With José."

7

"DO YOU LIKE RAP MUSIC?" ASKED CORPORAL AIVAS OF TANYA RACH-maninoff.

"Some of it's okay, I guess. Wanna piece of gum, José?"

"Sugar-free?" he inquired. "Thank you very much. What about Madonna? She is one of my favorites."

"I like the way she looks, but her music sort of sucks."

"You look a little like Madonna," said the corporal suddenly. "Only much more beautiful."

"Christ!" muttered Nicky in the backseat. "We have to watch him seduce our daughter?"

"Sh!" Susan whispered in his ear. "Don't be an old grouch. Anyway, I think they're cute together."

Nicky peered out the window at the passing city in the night. Managua was the strangest city he had ever seen. From what he could see from the car, large portions of the town seemed to lie in rubble. Buildings without roofs stood next to solitary stone walls rising in the moonlight. It was rare to see two entire buildings standing side by side. They passed the skeleton of what had once been a multistory office building, whose ghostly beams now protruded into the sky. Amid the rubble was a sprawling shantytown, makeshift shacks built out of cardboard and cloth and odd pieces of wood, all leaning against each other, nestled among the ruins.

"I can certainly see why tourists flock here," said Nicky.

"You should have been here before the destruction, Señor Rach-maninoff," said José over his shoulder. "Managua, I'm told, she was a beautiful city once."

"The destruction—it came from the revolution, did it?" asked Nicky.

"No, it was—how you say?—the big quaking of the earth in 1972."

"Earthquake?"

"Yes, yes—many people were killed. Most of the city, she was destroyed."

"You remember, darling," Susan told him. "Bianca Jagger was going around raising all that money for relief. Didn't we go to a charity ball at the Beverly Hills Hotel?"

"That must have been one of your other husbands," said Rachmaninoff, without regret. "Anyway, Somoza stole all the relief aid you guys raised—a hundred million dollars' worth—and he sold all the building and medical supplies for his own profit."

Susan was impressed. "Nicky! I never knew you were so informed."

"Hey, just because I'm a cop doesn't mean I'm an ignoramus," he replied a bit stuffily.

"Señor Rachmaninoff is right," said José. "The Somoza family was crazy. They owned everything here, and they always wanted more."

"That's terrible!" Tanya cried passionately.

"See that building there?" José was pointing out the window to a pile of rubble. "That was the blood bank. We called it *casa de vampiros*. Blood used to be Nicaragua's biggest export."

"Blood bank?" asked Tanya.

"The *campesinos*, they go there to sell their blood. How else could they live? The *casa de vampiros*, she was run by Somoza and a man named Ramos. They bought the blood for very, very little, then sold it for much, much more."

Tanya was outraged. "But who would buy blood?" she cried. "I mean, that's gross!"

"Ah, it was your country that did this," José told her with a sad look. "At one time, twenty thousand liters of blood were sent to the United States every month. You were sucking us dry, like a vampire, no?"

Tanya could only shake her head. "Boy, this is maybe the sickest thing I've ever heard," she said gravely.

"You will see many incredible things here in Nicaragua," José promised the young girl by his side. "I will show you. I will take you to the northern frontier, where you can still see the monstrous things *la contra* has done with your tax dollars. Now these *contras* have turned into bandits who kill and rape the poor *capesinos*. Oh, it will make you very angry, *señorita!*"

"No way, José!" Nicky protested from the rear of the car.

"*Dad!*" cried Tanya, turning around.

"Nicky, you're embarrassing her," Susan whispered in his ear.

"Sorry," he told them. "I just had to say it once, you know. But there's no way, José, I'm going to allow Tanya to go near the frontier. And that's final."

The young corporal leaned closer to Tanya. "This 'no way, José' is some kind of joke?"

Tanya glared back at her father. She could really make her green eyes do fireworks when she was mad. "Dad," she said, "why don't you just mellow out a little? I mean, for chrissake, we're *supposed* to be having fun."

8

THEY WERE STAYING AT THE HOTEL INTERCONTINENTAL IN MANAGUA, a modern, air-conditioned pyramid sitting on top of a hill. The hotel predated the revolution, a relic of the Somoza era, and Nicky classified the interior decor as vintage Holiday Inn gone slightly to seed with Marxist meddling, not yet revived by the new whiff of market capitalism in the air.

Susan and Nicky had a top-floor suite with a balcony overlooking the strangely haphazard city below. The colors of the suite were creams and pastels. In the living room, one entire wall was papered with a motif of green palm trees and happy Indians working in sugar fields. There was a bar and a television set and, from the balcony, a view of Lake Managua, dreamy in the distance.

The sleeping arrangements were as follows: Susan occupied the master bedroom, with Nicky in a slightly smaller bedroom on the other side of the living room. Tanya had her own single across the hall.

The first night passed without event, though Nicky had rather expected Susan to come tiptoeing in to molest him. After all the pretty-boy Hollywood types and tycoons she hung out with these days, he imagined she must be desperate for the passionate embrace of a slightly overweight, slightly alcoholic, middle-aged cop. But Nicky's only nocturnal visitors were the mosquitoes that managed to sneak in past the air conditioning. Their bite was not so sweet.

In the morning, José came by to take Susan and Tanya on a tour of the city. They were going to visit day-care centers and military hospitals and a factory that made rubber sandals out of old tires. As fascinating as this was, Nicky wished them all the best of luck and he himself headed toward the hotel pool.

At last, true vacation! He had a new swimsuit for the occasion, with a tropical motif of blue-green jungle with yellow flowers. It was deliciously gaudy. To go with the trunks, he wore a yellow T-shirt with BHPD SOFTBALL LEAGUE printed on the back. Last of all, he had his rubber thongs, suntan lotion, dark glasses, beach towel, and a bag full of sleazy paperback novels.

El Gringo was ready for action!

"Una margarita, por favor," he called to the roving barman by the pool. It was challenging to speak a foreign language, but after a few tries, the phrase came rolling off his tongue in one fluid and salty flourish.

And what a day it was! The sky was blue, the sun like a ripe papaya hanging in the sky. The other guests of the hotel seemed to be spies, diplomats, journalists, and an assortment of international curiosity-seekers come to watch Nicaragua rebuild after its David-and-Goliath struggle with the United States. As far as Nicky could tell, he was the only one here who had come simply to get sloshed around the pool.

This was harder work than one might imagine. It took some time getting *really* comfortable—finding the right deck chair that was not too close to screaming children, but near enough to the pool to check out the more interesting bikinis. Nicky was no amateur. With careful experimentation he located the correct notch for the back of his chair—a height where he could be supremely comfortable and still have access to his margarita with one mere lazy motion of the hand.

There came a moment of near bliss, the euphoria of absolute

vacation. He was on his third margarita after a brief dip in the pool, a Raymond Chandler mystery propped on his stomach, feeling the warm glow of the sun bake down upon his body. His eyes were drowsy, and he let them close—why not? Two young ladies in the briefest bikinis were swimming laps in the pool, a soft, rhythmic sound. With his eyes closed, he could still see their lovely bodies. Somewhere nearby, a child laughed.

Paradise!

And then he heard a familiar voice, female—an actressy voice that cut right through the drowsy peace of the morning.

"It really pisses me off," she was saying. "For chrissake, even Abraham Lincoln suspended habeas corpus in the Civil War. FDR put American citizens of Japanese descent into internment camps at the beginning of World War II! So how can you have the nerve to criticize the Sandinistas for suspending some civil rights, when the United States spent ten years trying to overthrow their government?"

It was Katherine Hall, lecturing two American reporters over coffee and orange juice at a poolside table. Nicky half-opened his eyes to see. She was wearing a straw hat, big round sunglasses, and a sleeveless shirt. She looked as pretty as could be in the morning sun, but her voice had an unpleasant, self-righteous twang. What had made her so angry, Nicky wondered. After all, she had been born into a prosperous Hollywood family, raised with every advantage—her father one of the great film directors of the Golden Era, her mother a well-known Broadway actress. Why should a pampered kid from Beverly Hills turn into such a revolutionary?

She was truly lovely to look at. A rich person's face, thought Nicky—delicate, used to the best things money can buy. A pert little nose. Her hair cascaded over her shoulders from beneath the straw hat. Her legs were superbly crossed. . . . Kitty caught sight of Nicky staring at her, and stopped her discourse in the middle of a sentence. Even from beneath her dark glasses, Nicky could feel the force of her disapproval leveled at him like a gun. What she saw, he imagined, was a white-skinned imperialist lounging around a pool in a gaudy swimsuit, margarita in hand—a cop, a pig, a male chauvinist—probably everything she detested.

Nicky grinned and raised his margarita glass in a salute. She did not smile, nor did she wave back. With only a slight pause she continued her diatribe against the hypocrisy of U.S. foreign policy.

Nicky closed his heavy-lidded eyes. *Well, you can't get all the pretty girls,* he reckoned philosophically. Deep thoughts like this came with the advent of middle age. Three margaritas and the sun had put him into a drowsy euphoria that not even Kitty Hall's disapproval could fully destroy.

He was drifting when a shadow came between him and the sun.

"You look positively decadent, Rachmaninoff," he heard. It was Kitty. He smiled with his eyes closed.

"I need to speak with you," she said unhappily. She might as well have been admitting to a need for an appendectomy.

"Speak," said Rachmaninoff.

"Not here. Meet me up in my suite in ten minutes."

Nicky cautiously cocked open an eye. "Are you propositioning me, Ms. Hall?"

Kitty glared down at him, a storm cloud blocking his sun. "Grow up, Rachmaninoff. This is a matter of life or death!"

She turned and left him. For an angry woman, oh, what a lovely ass!

Nicky gathered his belongings and went back to his room to change. It was the Rachmaninoff motto *never* to deal with life-or-death situations dressed only in a swimsuit.

9

"HELLO, RACHMANINOFF," SAID KITTY HALL, LETTING HIM INTO HER suite at the Hotel Intercontinental. She tried very briefly to smile. It worried Nicky, her getting so friendly all of a sudden.

She had changed into a loose gray jogging suit. Normally, Nicky found that athletic clothing did little to enhance feminine charms, but in Kitty's case the formless material only stirred the imagination to picture the curves underneath. The rich brown hair was hanging loose and wild.

"Would you like some mineral water?" she offered.

"Don't you have anything to put in it?"

"Ice," she told him coldly.

The Heard suite was larger than the one Nicky was sharing with Susan. Kitty spent a moment getting his mineral water from a refrigerator beneath the bar, and Nicky watched her closely, hostess in action. She had great wrist action with the twist-off top.

"Isn't this nice?" said Nicky Rachmaninoff. "I always like a good cool drink whenever I'm about to learn something really juicy."

Kitty did not seem at ease. She sat down on a creamy sofa and lit a cigarette. A thin, nervous stream of smoke issued from her luscious lips.

"God, I hate cigarettes," she told him. "I feel like I'm killing myself every time I light up."

"Maybe that's the thrill. Of course, you could just say no."

"I can't. There's too much stress in my life." She was regarding him as an object of great scientific interest, this strange species sitting in her hotel suite: a pre-feminist cop, a true dinosaur of history.

"Susan once told me it took her ten years of psychoanalysis to get over five years of being married to you," she mused. "Ten years, Rachmaninoff!"

Nicky grinned. "Can I help it if women find me unforgettable?"

"Look, this is a mistake—I can see that. Maybe you should just leave."

"No, please, go ahead. After all, I'm here, I changed out of my swimsuit, I'm drinking your mineral water. . . ."

"Shut up a second, okay? Susan thought you might be able to help me with a certain problem. It's my husband, as a matter of fact," she added reluctantly.

It generally was, but Nicky refrained from saying so. He flashed a suave smile and tried to look like the kind of man a beautiful woman could confide in. Kitty stubbed out her half-smoked cigarette with an angry motion.

"How well do you know my husband?" she asked.

"Not very. We've met a few times. Years ago I read that book he wrote about student rebellion in the sixties. What was it called?"

"*Paisley Prose*," she told him, wincing slightly at the title—there were things about the sixties that were embarrassing to recall. "Cory was very young when he wrote that, Rachmaninoff. Twenty-one. Unfortunately, he never grew up."

"Ah, childhood!" said Nicky elegiacally. "To be young and irresponsible and have your parents foot the bill!"

Kitty lit a new cigarette and regarded him like a tigress about to jump its prey.

"Cory's up to something," she said. "I need to find out what it is."

"Up to something? Well, why don't you just ask him?"

"Our communication isn't so good right now. I thought maybe you could look into this for me."

Nicky took a sip of his mineral water. It was refreshing but lacking of some essential spirit. He tried a stock phrase of his profession: "Maybe you'd better start at the beginning."

"Well, he's been so depressed lately, you know. Six months back there was this article in *Rolling Stone* about the sixties—a kind of 'Where are they now' piece. Cory got mentioned, along with some other ex-student radicals who are now stockbrokers and lawyers and doing pretty well for themselves in a system they once despised. Cory was upset for days."

"He didn't seem so depressed yesterday," Nicky mentioned.

"That's the point—he's not. That's why I think he's up to something."

"Ah, well . . . marriage is difficult, and men will be boys."

"Not *that*, Rachmaninoff—or rather, Cory's *always* up to that. I mean, there's something about this trip I don't know about. He was on the phone a lot before we left, hanging up when I'd come into the room. Unfortunately, I know who he was talking to. A very wealthy Nicaraguan exile by the name of Octavio Morales."

Nicky looked up sharply at the name.

"I can see you know who Octavio Morales is," she said.

"He's one of our more unpleasant additions to Beverly Hills," Nicky admitted. "We suspect he launders money for the Medellin drug cartel, but no one has been able to prove a thing against him."

"He was also related to the ruling family down here before the revolution. Did you know his uncle was Anastasio Somoza Debayle?"

"How does Cory know a guy like that?"

"It's a bit of a story. They met in college years ago in New York—at Columbia. Cory was living off campus, somewhere on the edge of Harlem, where he spent most of his time organizing student protests against the war in Vietnam. Occasionally he even went to class, I suppose—and that's where he met Octavio, who at the time was most likely a nerdy little foreign student in suit and tie. They sat near each other in their Contemporary Civ class. The teacher, poor man, encouraged class participation and got more than he bargained for; Cory took the liberal side of every argument, and Octavio the conservative side. Between the two of them, I imagine hardly anyone else was able to get a word in. This was 1966, you'll remember, and some of these discussions got very heated.

"Anyway, after about six months of arguing every conservative-liberal issue to death, one day after class the foreign student in suit and tie comes up to Cory—who's probably wearing old blue jeans and sneakers with his toes sticking out—and he invites Cory for dinner. Cory says sure, he'd love to have dinner—he thinks it's a real lark. So that evening, an enormous black stretch limousine pulls up in front of Cory's apartment building on 122nd Street and ferries him down to the Plaza Hotel, where it seems Octavio Morales is living in great style in a suite of rooms overlooking the park, with his own personal butler, who has been sent from Nicaragua to take care of him.

"Well, Cory thinks this is a lot of fun. Radical though he may be, he's always been attracted to people with money—of that I can assure you! When he discovers Octavio's uncle is the fucking *dictator* of Nicaragua, Cory probably creams his pants. This isn't just money, it's power. And so the two of them, Cory and Octavio, go from being adversaries to great friends—an extremely weird friendship, but there it is. They continue to argue about politics, of course, all the time."

"Sounds like a marriage made in heaven," said Nicky Rachmaninoff.

"Well, they both got something out of it, I suppose. Cory took

Octavio around to all the hip places in New York, and Octavio had the money to pick up the bill. So they saw a lot of each other the last two years of college. A few times, Cory got himself arrested for various acts of civil disobedience, and Octavio showed up at the jail in his limousine to bail him out. It was handy to have a rich friend, I'm sure.

"Okay, so then college is over, they both graduate in '68, and as so often happens, the friends go their separate ways. Cory writes his book, *Paisley Prose,* and becomes a minor celebrity among the radical chic, and Octavio goes home to work for his Uncle Tachito. Maybe the first few years they write to each other occasionally, and then the letters gradually cease.

"Ten years go by. In the United States, the sixties are over in a big way, and Cory finds his fifteen minutes of fame come and gone. He goes back to school to get his M.A., then later his doctorate. This time around, he actually studies and he ends up teaching college, first at NYU and then later at UCLA. In Nicaragua, Octavio rises high in his uncle's service and starts to become very rich in his own right. Unlike his uncle, he is clever enough to see the end coming, and he manages to get out of Nicaragua with his wealth intact fully six months before the Sandinistas take power in '79. He moves to Miami for a year, and then New York and finally Beverly Hills, where all the gaudy money eventually gravitates. Cory and Octavio have no idea they are such close neighbors until one day they run into each other—literally—jogging down North Beverly Drive. There are hugs and cries of affection, and promises to see each other soon—but this time the friendship doesn't really pan out. Too much time has passed, and they are committed to very different life-styles. It's obvious Octavio has become some sort of narco-gangster, though exactly what he does for a living is a little vague. Once in a while, Cory and Octavio get together to play tennis and talk about old times—and that's about it."

"Well, that all sounds fairly harmless," said Nicky.

"You think so? All of a sudden they're talking on the phone a lot. They're real palsy-walsy again. One night last month, Cory comes to bed drunk at three in the morning, and when I ask where he's been, he says he's been doing the town with Octavio Morales. I don't like it, Rachmaninoff. I don't like it one bit."

45

Nicky shrugged. "Well, there's no law to keep a guy from hanging out with an old college buddy. But maybe this all has something to do with finding Uncle Somoza's lost loot?"

"How do *you* know about Somoza's loot?" she asked sharply.

"Cory told me."

"He *told* you?" Kitty repeated, standing up in alarm. "He told *you!*"

"People tell me a lot of things. What I believe is my own business."

Kitty ignored this comment, pacing over to a coffee table to find a hated cigarette. There was a worried expression on her face as she said yes to nicotine.

"What the hell is that bastard up to, I wonder?" she asked the four walls, blowing out smoke.

"Don't you trust your husband, Ms. Hall?" asked the mild-mannered policeman.

"Trust him!" she exclaimed. "*Trust* him! You have to be kidding. One thing about Cory, he's managed to go from college to middle age without getting one day older—mentally, that is. He's an absolute adolescent, Rachmaninoff—there's no telling *what* he'll do!"

"Ah, well," said Nicky soothingly.

"Look, Rachmaninoff," she said, "there's something strange going on here, I just know it—I think Octavio asked Cory to do him some kind of favor while he was down here, and I don't like it."

Kitty studied him for a moment, her lovely eyes narrowed in his direction as she sucked on her cigarette. "Let me tell you something. For the past two years, Cory's been absolutely broke except for the money he earns at UCLA, which isn't much. Actually, I cut him off *my* money because he was so damn irresponsible and I'm sensitive, you see, about men living off me. Then two weeks ago I opened up one of his bank statements by mistake and saw he had just made a deposit of a hundred thousand dollars into his account. The only way I can imagine he could come up with such a sum is through Octavio."

"Did you ask him about it?"

"Sure, several times—and Cory just gets all cute and hints at all kinds of fantastic deals and deeds he's about to perform—but he doesn't tell me a thing."

"Maybe there's nothing much to tell."

"What about the hundred thousand dollars, then? And there's something else," said Kitty. She paused, with an embarrassed look upon her Hollywood-perfect face.

"Yes?" said Rachmaninoff.

"I don't want you to think I *spy* on him, but—well, this one time I *did* listen in on one of his phone calls with Octavio, only because I was worried. I picked up the extension in the bedroom while he was in the den. . . ."

Nicky had to nod encouragingly. "Yes?"

"Octavio was talking about money. What he said was that if Cory did exactly as he was told, he would never have to worry about money again."

"Does Cory care about money so much? I thought he was down on materialism, and all that."

Kitty snickered. "Sure! That's why he lives in Beverly Hills!"

"Well, what else did you overhear on the phone?"

"They were talking about ways to get a big bundle of something over the border into the United States. Cory said why not sew it into the seats of the airplane, but Octavio said this was the first place customs people would look."

"Then what?"

"That was it. I think maybe Octavio heard me breathing on the extension, because suddenly he got very cautious and said they would talk about this another time."

"I see," Nicky said slowly. He was trying not to become interested, but he was professionally and personally a very nosy guy. "What do you think it's all about?"

"I think he's made a deal with Octavio Morales and he's not going to give Somoza's treasure to the Sandinistas at all—I think he's going to steal the God damn money and split it up with Octavio."

"Why should he give Octavio any of it?"

"The two of them have been in this together from the start, don't you see? Cory's an expert on Central America and he knows how to research something like this, but Octavio had all the important contacts—after all, he was Somoza's favorite nephew. I'm just hoping Cory will double-cross that son of a bitch and give the money to the Sandinistas like he told me."

47

"You'd better hope he *doesn't*, sweetheart," Nicky told her cheer-
fully. "You cross a guy like Octavio Morales, you don't live long
enough to enjoy your victory. Maybe they'll even kill *you* first, right
in front of him. These Medellin guys are real big on going for the
wife and kids while Daddy gets to watch."

Kitty had become very pale. "Won't you help me, Rachmaninoff? You could keep an eye on him. He's such a child, you know—
he probably doesn't even realize the consequences of what he's
doing."

Nicky stood up and put down his mineral water. '"Kitty, I think
what you need is a marriage counselor, not a policeman."

She glared at him. "So you're saying no, is that it?"

"That's it," he told her. "I keep saying this to people, but for some
reason no one believes me—you're looking at a guy who's on vacation."

"Christ! I should have known it! Well, go back to the swimming
pool, then, and all those margaritas you're sloshing down. You
know something, Rachmaninoff—you're pathetic!"

That hurt a little, and it seemed unfair as well. But Rachmaninoff's smile never faltered.

"Look, pussycat, why don't you come on down to the pool with
me—we'll hoist a few. Or are you afraid the extra calories might
ruin your sex appeal?"

Kitty's dark eyes flashed daggers. "You're a real asshole, aren't
you, Rachmaninoff?"

Nicky just grinned at her, from cheek to cheek.

10

FOR TANYA RACHMANINOFF, NICARAGUA WAS FAST BECOMING HER
favorite Third World country ever. On the morning tour of the
day-care center and sandal factory with her mother and José, she
had felt José's eyes upon her at every step. It was a brand-new feeling

to be bathed in male attention, as if she were on stage with a spotlight upon her, creating a kind of magic circle in which she was more beautiful and clever than she had ever been before.

When they arrived at the military hospital, Tanya balked.

"Mom, I know it would be really *good* for me to see a lot of blood and gore, but I'm not sure I can take it so early in the morning."

José rose to the occasion. "Perhaps Tanya and I can have a coffee while you visit the hospital, Señora Merril."

Susan looked at the teenagers and smiled. "Go ahead," she told them. "Why don't we meet back here in an hour?"

And so Tanya and José managed to steal some time alone. He led her across a dusty plaza where some old women were selling vegetables and live chickens. The day was becoming hot, and Tanya found her clothes clinging to her in a way that made her acutely conscious of her body.

"So what do you think of my country?" asked José.

"God, it's wonderful!" she cried with an enthusiasm that had nothing to do with the dusty plaza through which they were walking. They both laughed, though no joke had been made.

José took her to a small outdoor café, where they sat in the shade of a banana tree. She couldn't believe it, but there were actual chickens pecking around loose at her feet, and a rusted truck engine leaning up against the side of the building. She supposed this was what writers meant by *ambience*.

"Would you like coffee? Or perhaps a beer on this hot day?"

"A beer, I think," said Tanya with smooth nonchalance.

But would they really serve her? . . . *Yes, they did!* Now *this* was a civilized country where a young lady of fourteen and a half years could be treated with some respect! José and Tanya clinked their bottles in a toast. José's eyes never left her face. From the expression she found there, Tanya knew with utter certainty he must be madly in love with her.

He really was *very* handsome, she decided. And sweet too. There was something quiet about him, and strong. And sensitive.

"I bet you absolutely *hate* Americans," she suggested coyly, "after all the horrible things we've done to your country."

"Oh no—we love America. But maybe that is our national tragedy. We do not feel loved in return."

"Maybe America might learn to love you better," Tanya said gently, "if she had a chance to know you like I do."

José did not take the opening. Tanya was beginning to suspect men were not as subtle as women; he obviously thought they were talking about politics!

"It is my very big dream to go to California," he admitted. "I want to be a surfer at Malibu. I want very much to go to Disneyland."

"You wouldn't want to live there, José. It's all very shallow, you know. All people care about is money. Here you have something to believe in."

José gave her a funny look. "To tell the truth, we are all of us very tired of being poor. Even though the war is over, we still have nothing—no gasoline, no surfboards, no parts for our cars when they break down. You go into a store and it is a bad joke! All the shelves are empty."

"I see what you mean," said Tanya. "But it doesn't really help to have a lot of stuff. I mean, look at Beverly Hills—when you have everything, people just find new things to worry about, like their stupid diets and self-esteem."

José smiled at her. "What kind of car does your mother drive?" he asked.

"A Bentley," said Tanya, which was extremely embarrassing to admit.

"I don't know this Bentley—what is it?"

"Sort of like a Rolls-Royce," she said unhappily.

"Ah! Now *this* is what I dream about! A car like that, you could go to the beach whenever you want!"

Tanya couldn't quite figure José out. He was both more innocent and more mature than the boys back home. She found herself writing in an imaginary diary: *What a total enigma he is! Strong yet soft, foolish but wise. And here I am sitting in this little café drinking actual beer with actual chickens and a truck engine and looking into his enigmatic brown eyes. . . . Am I in love? Am I ready? . . . Yes! Yes! Yes!*

The bartender was an old man with a limp, and he came by to see if they wanted another beer. Tanya told him she'd prefer a cherry Coke—she was feeling a bit giddy from her one beer. The old man had no Coke at all—imagine that!—not cherry, nor caffeine-free, not even Coke Classic. So Tanya settled for a glass of water, but she was proud of herself for managing the entire exchange in Spanish.

"I like it when you speak Spanish," José told her, smiling with his eyes. "You learned this in school?"

"Partly . . . but mostly from my maid, Anna."

"You have a maid?"

"Well, she's gone now," Tanya said quickly, "but Anna was like one of the family. I mean, she practically *raised* me, since my Mom was always off doing this dumb TV show, 'Cassie and the Cop.' I really thought of Anna as my mother, if you want to know the truth."

"This must be nice, to have a maid," said José.

"I think it's disgusting—almost like owning a slave," Tanya said quickly, so he wouldn't think she was a terrible person. "Of course, I *loved* Anna," she added hastily. "Not that it makes up for keeping another human being in bondage—but for me, Anna wasn't a maid at all, really. For a long time she was my best and only friend."

There was a lot here she couldn't quite put into words. Tanya tried to tell José how Anna used to sing her to sleep with Spanish lullabies, giving her all the warmth and love her real mother was always too busy to provide. She tried to tell José how the first true crisis in her life was at the age of eleven when Anna gave notice and moved to San Antonio, Texas, to marry a man who owned a restaurant. There was all this and more, but she could tell from the amused look in José's eyes that he didn't understand, not really. Probably all this talk about "her maid" only made her seem to him like a spoiled rich girl.

It was really very frustrating not to be able to explain.

"Of course, I was glad for Anna when she was able to leave us and make a life of her own," she lied. (As a matter of fact, Tanya had been bitterly angry and had cried for days.) "She wrote me once—she has a *real* child now, not just a brat she was paid to take care of like me."

Tanya was not quite sure why she felt so close to bursting into tears. José was gazing at her more seriously, his brown eyes luminous and gentle.

"Will you come out with me tonight? I think I would like very much to see you."

"I think I would very much like to see you too," she laughed. A few of the tears that had been threatening managed to squeeze out the corners of her eyes while she was laughing. She was surprised to see that José was holding her hand.

"Of course . . ." She was about to tell him that, of course, she would have to ask her mother and father for permission, but after the near disaster talking about her maid, it was simply too embarrassing to admit she was not old enough to go where she pleased.

"Of course, what?"

"Just of course!" she told him, laughing. "Why don't you meet me outside the hotel, say about nine o'clock."

And so it was arranged. Tanya would figure a way to sneak out. Parents, after all, could be manipulated, but love in a tropical climate might never come again.

11

NICKY RACHMANINOFF RETURNED TO HIS ROOM TO CHANGE BACK INTO his swimsuit. He was not in a good mood. The memory of Kitty was irritating, like a pebble caught in his shoe.

Rachmaninoff, you're pathetic! she had said.

But *she* was the one who was pathetic—just a spoiled rich girl from Beverly Hills who was used to having everything her own way! Sure, she called herself a liberal, but *he* was the workingman, for chrissake—that was the real laugh here. Naturally, she was too much of a God damn movie star to understand that a workingman might need a God damn vacation after running around Los Angeles arresting people and getting shot at and having to deal with the media assholes and big-shot politico assholes and even more assholes from one end of the town to the other.

Coming back to his suite, he was unpleasantly surprised to find the door unlocked. He pushed it open to discover an elfin little man with big ears and glasses, sitting on his living-room couch. The little man was wearing an aloha shirt, and Bermuda shorts that revealed wobbly little knees. Nicky rather hoped this might be only a hallucination.

"Who the fuck are you?" he asked in an experimental tone. But the hallucination did not go away.

"Bob Arnold, U.S. Embassy. Remember? We met last night at the airport."

Nicky ignored him. He stripped off his clothes and walked naked into the shower. He returned ten minutes later to find Bob, aloha shirt and all, still on the living-room couch.

"What did Kitty want to talk to you about?" Bob asked.

"Who says she wanted to talk?"

"She went over to you by the pool and asked you up to her room. These actress types are so dramatic—you may remember, Lieutenant, she said it was a matter of life or death."

"Where were you, Bob? Lurking behind a palm tree? Or were you under my deck chair?"

"I was on the other side of the pool, near the restaurant."

Bob Arnold flashed a cagy little smile and brought out what appeared to be a small cassette player and earphones from a briefcase by his side.

"Looks like a Walkman, doesn't it? Actually, you put the earphones on and you can listen in on a conversation a hundred yards away."

"The CIA comes up with these nifty little gadgets, do they?"

"As a matter of fact, this is from Sharper Image. So tell me, Lieutenant—what happened up there in her suite?"

"Why so curious, Bob?"

"It's professional curiosity, Lieutenant. We've been keeping our eye on Kitty Hall ever since Vietnam. I'm sure you can understand why."

Nicky sat down in an armchair across from the spook in the aloha shirt and gave one long, weary sigh.

"Spill the beans, Lieutenant."

"You want to know what happened in her room, Bob? Well, okay—she opened the door and I noticed she was wearing nothing except a towel. 'Come on in, Nick, out of the cold,' she said in a silky voice. I stepped inside the room, and by the time I closed the door, the towel had coyly slid off her perfect body to reveal her taut, firm nipples and creamy thighs. One arm wrapped around my neck—a lovely little hand wandered between my legs. 'I can't stay away from you another moment,' she cried, working at the zipper to release my hot red engine of love from the imprisonment of pants. She wrapped her legs around my waist and I . . . well, you get the picture, Bob? I would go into further lurid details, but I'm not the kind to kiss and tell."

Bob Arnold's glasses had become slightly steamed. "Keep dreaming, Rachmaninoff. A lady like that wouldn't go for a cop. And you're old, Rachmaninoff—you'll never see forty again. You're not going to get women like *that* anymore, not on your salary."

Nicky sighed. These CIA guys really knew how to break a man.

"Anyway," said Bob, "you haven't asked why I'm here."

"That's because I'm hoping you'll go away."

Bob smiled. "The reason I'm here," he explained patiently, "is to take you back with me to the embassy compound. There's a secure call coming in for you at fourteen hundred hours from California. Wesley McGroder wants a word with you."

Nicky wiggled in his chair. Chief Wesley McGroder happened to be his boss, the head of the BHPD.

"What does McGroder want?"

"Gosh, I don't know, Lieutenant! Why don't we just go find out?"

12

THE UNITED STATES EMBASSY IN MANAGUA HAD ALL THE CHARM OF A concrete bunker. High walls protected the perimeter. On the roof, a tangle of strangely shaped antennae sent back deep secrets to Washington. Before the main entrance stood a concrete barrier to fend off unwanted trucks laden with dynamite.

"A great place for a paranoid schizophrenic," observed Nicky Rachmaninoff.

"We take security seriously," said Bob Arnold. "That's what it's all about."

Bob led the way through a security gate, past a Marine checkpoint, and into the compound. Once inside the main building, they entered an elevator that moved so quietly Nicky was not certain whether they were going up or down. The elevator opened out upon a windowless corridor that was unmarked by any number and gave no indication where they were.

Nicky was led from this windowless corridor to a windowless room whose walls seemed thick as a bank vault. In this room there was a big surprise waiting for him. Sitting behind a desk, with an autographed photograph of Nancy Reagan on the wall behind him, was a familiar pear-shaped face topped with an extremely flamboyant Louis XIV hairdo—little black ringlets of curls falling down his shoulders.

"My God, it's Rip!" said Rachmaninoff in astonishment. "Rip Beasley!"

"Welcome, Lieutenant," said Rip, rising. "I'm glad to meet you under true circumstances at last. Please continue to call me Rip, though of course that's not my real name."

"You're . . . then you're . . ."

"An FBI agent, as a matter of fact. I've been in deep cover for years, waiting for an opportunity like this to protect American society from the unfathomable dangers of Hollywood personalities run amuck."

"But you're a famous record producer!" Nicky protested. "Why, didn't you even win a Grammy last year or something?"

"I was nominated," Rip said with a small smile. "Music was my cover, a way to get on the inside track. It turned out I was good at my new trade."

"But what about all the money you made? Did the Bureau let you keep it?"

Again the small smile flickered across the pear-like face. "Oh, the government is always in need of more money—especially money Congress knows nothing about. What did we do with the profits from 'Shot of Love,' Bob?"

"Ethnic unrest in the Soviet Union," said the man in the aloha shirt.

"My God, you did *that?*" Nicky asked in astonishment.

"It's only rock and roll," Rip said modestly, "but we like it."

Nicky's legs felt weak and he slipped down into a leather arm-chair.

"So let's get down to business," said Rip, easing his rear end down against the edge of his desk. "I've been reading your file, Nick. Very impressive, I must say. *Very* impressive."

"Oh, I'm just your average cop, Rip. Battling the odds."

"No, no, Nick! Average you are not." Rip opened the folder and began scanning through. "For example, I see you're left-handed, Nick. Now that's *not* particularly average, is it?"

"Isn't it?"

"Generally, here in the federal government we don't believe in hiring left-handed people. I'm sure you can appreciate the reason."

"Well, no, not really, Rip. Actually, you have me there."

"*Too* creative," Rip confided. "Are you aware, Nick, that your brain function is the complete reverse of normal people's?"

Nicky sighed. "I've always suspected something."

"Well, you're a Capricorn, at least," Rip mentioned, glancing back to the file. "That accounts for your goatlike tenacity in catching criminals. Do you know your rising sign?"

"Haven't the foggiest," said Nick.

"You should find out, Lieutenant. Astrology is extremely important. It reaches right up into the White House, if you'll allow me to pass on a small secret."

"Surely not in the new administration," Nicky demurred.

Rip smiled at his innocence. "Do you think Nancy Reagan would have allowed George Bush to become President if he *wasn't* into astrology? Of course, as I'm sure you know, she still runs things from Bel Air."

"But George Bush . . ."

"Come on, Lieutenant, get wise! George Bush couldn't run an outhouse if his life depended on it. You should be able to tell that just from looking at the guy."

"Of course," murmured Rachmaninoff. He found his hands were sweating. A simple small-town cop had a lot to learn in these halls of power.

"Let's get down to cases, Nick. We're all a little concerned about Katherine Hall and Cory Heard, trying to figure out what they're up to down here. What do you think it's all about?"

"Gosh, Rip, it's just a fact-finding tour, as you know. A chance to see poverty and feel good about ourselves. It's really quite simple."

"I wonder," said Rip ominously.

It was at this moment that one of the three telephones on Rip's desk—the blue one—gave a discreet little beep.

"Well, well, right on time," said Rip, glancing at his watch. He gestured for Nicky to pick up the phone.

"Hello. That you, Lieutenant? It's me, Chief McGroder."

"Chief, what a surprise!"

"Er, you having a good vacation, Lieutenant?"

"Great, Chief. The swimming's really excellent, and I'm having all kinds of swell adventures."

"Well, that's grand," said the Chief. "Er, Nick—you've probably guessed I'm not calling you on a secure line at the American Embassy just to talk about swimming. What it is, Nick, I got a phone call this morning from Washington. I'm not at liberty to tell you who it was, but I want you to know this was a person pretty damn high up the ladder. Do I make myself clear, Lieutenant?"

"Oh yes, sir."

"Er, this individual asked me if you were a good American, Nick."

"What did you tell him, sir?"

"I said you were a patriot and a family man."

"Thank you, sir. I hope you mentioned I've killed a few people too, sir. I wouldn't want them to think I'm some sort of wimp."

"Lieutenant, shut up, okay?"

"Yes, sir," sighed Nicky.

"They want you to work for them, Nick. Just on a temporary basis."

Nicky glanced up at Rip and Bob, who smiled back pleasantly.

"What if I say no?" he asked, whispering desperately into the receiver.

Chief McGroder's voice became deep and grave. "Look, Nick, this is really quite an honor, both for you and the department. We can use these kinds of connections. Washington will owe us a few serious favors here."

"Yes, but Chief—what do *I* know about international intrigue, and all that shit? I'm just a homicide dick. And besides—*I'm on vacation!*"

The Chief's tone was getting hard. "Lieutenant, you are back on duty as of this moment, with a temporary assignment to the State Department in Managua. You will do exactly what they tell you. I am informed you are in a unique position to render service to your country, and you will do precisely that."

"Yes, sir," said a weary Rachmaninoff.

"And as for your vacation," said the Chief, softening a little, "maybe I'll give you three weeks when you get back stateside. What do you say to that, Lieutenant?"

"I don't know if I can stand any more vacation. It's too exhausting."

Chief McGroder chuckled nastily. "So do your duty, Nick. Make us proud back here in the hills of Beverly."

The Chief sometimes got eloquent like that. The blue phone went dead and the hills of Beverly were just a far-off dream.

Rip and Bob were gazing at him now with proprietary interest. Nicky Rachmaninoff had just become their new man in Managua.

13

WHEN NICKY GOT BACK TO THE INTERCONTINENTAL, THERE WAS A note waiting for him at the front desk:

N.—

Let's have a chat, amigo. Meet me in the lobby at 5 in your running clothes. We'll get in some jogging as we talk.

"*Jogging!*" Nicky cried in horror to the desk clerk. This was getting worse and worse. "What kind of yuppie bullshit is this?"

"I don't know, *señor.*"

"Neither do I," said Nicky mournfully.

Nonetheless, he appeared on time, dressed in makeshift running clothes: loose jeans, a pair of ancient Nikes, and a Local Motion T-shirt that his homicide squad partner, Charlie Cat, had brought back from Hawaii. The T-shirt had a picture of a nice palm tree swaying in the breeze; the jeans concealed Nicky's new toy, a .38 automatic strapped to his left leg in an ankle holster. Rip and Bob had assured him a personal weapon was quite the vogue in Central America these days, and that in a matter of this kind it was wise to be fashionable.

Cory was in the lobby, talking to a lady journalist who was gazing at him with huge and hungry eyes. It was unbelievable how well Cory did with the ladies—it must be his Peter Pan charm, thought Nicky. Cory laughed when he saw Nicky's makeshift jogging outfit. He himself was dressed in perfectly matched running attire: shorts, shirt, good lightweight running shoes and headband—all the same light cream color, with a dashing orange stripe on the sleeves of the shirt and the sides of the shoes.

"Well, Nick, here we go, amigo. No pain, no gain!"

Cory led the way, jogging out of the hotel lobby into the late afternoon. Darkening clouds had gathered over the city. Rain felt imminent. Nicky was drenched in sweat before he had gone a hundred feet. The sweat tasted salty, with a trace of lime.

The first part of the run was mercifully downhill. At the foot of the hotel they turned toward a noisy *barrio*, jogging along an uneven dirt road past shacks with palm-leaf roofs. Half-naked children gazed in astonishment at the two *gringos* from Beverly Hills passing through their world. Thin, scraggly dogs barked at their heels.

Nicky had to work hard to keep up. After fifteen minutes his heart was beating crazily and his legs felt like dead weights. He was sweating so much he could hardly see. Bottle that sweat, he thought, and some enterprising soul could open up a margarita bar. Finally Nicky had to stop, hands on thighs, to catch his breath.

"Come on, Nicholas! You can do it!" Cory called from ahead.

"Fuck you!" Nicky managed.

Cory laughed jubilantly. He was having a great time. Rachmaninoff was getting angry. He sure as hell wasn't going to let some yuppie Hollywood professor show him up—not if it killed him. He gulped a few breaths of air and got back in the race.

"You're out of shape, Nick," Cory chided when they were running side by side.

"I'm just finding my rhythm, so shut up."

Managua was a chaotic sprawl without apparent rhyme or reason to its design—not unlike Los Angeles in this way—but Cory seemed to know where they were going. They ran through a maze of narrow streets where the riotous growth of jungle and brightly colored flowers threatened to swallow the half-ruined buildings and shanty-towns, past a blur of open markets with pigs and chickens and old ladies yelling out comments that sounded vaguely obscene. At last they came to a small plaza with an ancient church at one end and an outdoor café at the other. Nicky didn't think he was going to last another moment.

"Let's take a rest," Cory suggested, slowing to a walk. Nicky was breathing too hard to answer. Cory took him by the arm and kept him moving across the plaza to the café. They sank down into metal chairs beneath an umbrella. The proprietor was a wrinkled old man who seemed apprehensive at the appearance of the two *yanquis*, but Cory spoke to him rapidly in Spanish until the man's face burst into a smile. Cory apparently had this effect on people. Nicky sat with his heart beating wildly, trying to catch his breath.

"I've ordered us some beer," Cory said, looking at Nicky with some concern. "Better replace some of those lost body fluids, amigo."

The beer was brought on a tray by a pretty girl. She had shiny black hair and milk-chocolate skin and a lovely shy smile.

"You wanna know the secret of politics?" Cory said when the girl had gone. "Right wing is about money, left wing is about sex. It's all the same old screw, but with a different slant—vertical or horizontal—you dig?"

"Not really," said Rachmaninoff, wishing Cory would stop talking like some hip young blood from the streets and be himself—an educated guy, supposedly, with a Ph.D. in political science and a house in Beverly Hills. Nicky had just enough strength to clink bottles and bring his beer to his lips. The taste was slightly bitter and very cold. He was beginning to think he might live.

"This is basic political philosophy, my man. Daniel Ortega is an intensely sexy dude—just ask any woman—but George Bush might as well be neutered," said Cory. "And that's the difference between left and right: Democrats get caught with their pants down, Republicans with their hand in the cash register. Sex and money! Teddy Kennedy, Gary Hart, these guys might have become President of the United States if only they had kept their zippers up. But what the hell. Personally I'm glad to be a left-wing sort of guy—what about you, Nick?"

"I'm somewhere in the middle, Cory, in some netherworld sex and money forgot."

Cory had a good laugh. "That's a very evasive answer, amigo, and untrue. Come on, what turns you on? What *tempts* you, Nick? Is it money? Is it sex? Do you want a place in the history books? I'm trying to figure out where you're at."

"I'm just a cop," said Nicky with a shrug. "No big deal."

"Come on, I'm serious—let's talk life philosophy. Let's get down to the nitty-gritty here."

Rachmaninoff felt a natural hesitancy to enter into such a subject with a professional bullshitter like Cory Heard. But Cory asked for it. "All right," said Rachmaninoff. "I call my philosophy

'Take out the garbage when the garbage can is full.' Or 'Do the shit that comes along as best you can.' It may not be very glamorous, but there it is."

"Interesting," said Cory, rubbing his chin. "Would you describe yourself as an existentialist?"

"I'm a garbageman," insisted Rachmaninoff. "The way I see it, a lot of people think up these very grand schemes of things—all kinds of fancy philosophies—but these are generally the very people whose personal garbage is stinking up the entire block. Get the picture?"

"In other words, 'Take care of thine own garbage and skip the rest'?" asked Cory, grinning from ear to ear. "You know, Nicky, I sure get a kick out of you—but this, my friend, is a worm's-eye view of the universe. Sometimes you gotta get up on a ladder and look around you some—you gotta do something big."

"Not me," said Rachmaninoff, shaking his head. "I'll stick with the worms."

"Nicky! What you're doing, you're thinking only as an individual! Ultimately this is very selfish—you gotta open your heart to the whole of humanity. You gotta go for the big time."

"Do I? Well, you tell me what good's an environmentalist, for instance, who smokes cigarettes? Or maybe a peace activist who comes home and screams at his kids? The way I see it, charity begins at home and physician heal thyself, sort of thing—and spare the rest of us your sanctimonious bullshit."

"In other words, you have to be perfect—is that what you're saying—before you can be involved in a cause?"

Nicky shrugged. "I'm just saying small's the only thing that counts. Take care of your family, give some time to the people around you, and you make the world a better place. Everything else is self-delusion, Cory—very dangerous stuff, as a matter of fact, in which monsters tend to be born. And speaking of monsters, if I were you, I'd go out of my way to avoid a particular Beverly Hills monster who goes by the name of Octavio Morales."

Cory's grin grew even larger.

"Ah-ha! Kitty's been talking to you, I see! Did she tell you Octavio Morales was Somoza's nephew?"

"I believe *that's* what she's worried about. She thinks maybe you've sold out the liberal cause, Cory."

"Come on, would I do that? Listen to me, Octavio's a very old friend of mine—the guy's extremely well connected to the Nicaraguan exile community, and I went to him to find certain people in Paraguay. As it happens, Octavio turned me on to a guy who was Tachito's personal secretary at the time of the revolution—and it was this secretary who gave me the final clue I needed to figure out where Somoza buried his fortune."

Nicky raised an eyebrow. "Hold on a moment. You're telling me Octavio Morales and Somoza's old secretary *know* about your little treasure hunt?"

"Hey, you think I'm stupid, Nick? If those guys knew about this money, they'd want it for themselves—right? So I made up a whole story—said I was doing research for a book, for chrissake. They swallowed it all the way."

Nicky sighed. He didn't have much faith that Cory could keep secrets. "Swell," he said. "We probably have a bunch of goons from Medellin keeping an eye on us now, as *well* as the CIA, the FBI, the *contras*, the Sandinistas, Uno, even the KGB, I imagine. Nice going, Cory. You're going to get us all killed."

"Relax, amigo. Octavio doesn't suspect a thing, and Somoza's old secretary is practically senile. This is going to work," said Cory with a wild glint in his eye. "Believe me, a billion dollars will put the Sandinistas back in power, and this time the revolution is going all the way. It's poetic justice, don't you see? The United States bought the election for Violeta Chamorro, and now we're going to buy it right back again!"

"Cory, this is nuts. The Nicaraguan election was fair and square. Can't you get that through your head? The Sandinistas *lost*—nobody wants them anymore."

Cory didn't seem to be paying full attention. "Do you know how Violeta Chamorro decides government policy? She's a mystic, for chrissake, worse than Nancy Reagan. The lady has seances where she consults God and her dead husband, asking for advice—and *this* is what we spent hundreds of millions of dollars to defeat the Sandinistas for! Look, Nick, I know deep down you're a revolutionary just like me. So why don't you just give yourself some more time. I bet you're going to end up having some square named after you. *Plaza de Rachmaninoff!* Maybe they'll even put a bronze statue of you in the middle!"

"Statues get shat upon," said Rachmaninoff sagely. "Can't they name a drink after me instead?"

Cory had decided the conversation was over. He was a man who could turn off as quickly as he turned on, and now his interest was elsewhere. He put some money down on the table and was getting up to leave.

"Hey!" he cried. "I'll race you back to the hotel. A hundred dollars says I get there first!"

"God damn it," cried Rachmaninoff. "This is like having a conversation with a six-year-old!"

But Cory was already taking off down the street. Nicky was beginning to see what Kitty had been talking about when she said her husband never grew up. "Betcha can't catch me, Nick!" he taunted, calling back over his shoulder.

"Yeah?" said Rachmaninoff. He finished his beer, and when Cory was out of sight he stood up leisurely from the table and flagged down a taxi.

"Bet I can, Cory!"

14

NICKY STOOD IN HIS SHOWER UNDER A STREAM OF COLD WATER, trying to decide whether Cory was a dangerous menace or merely a middle-aged kid having fun.

As a matter of history, Nicky happened to know that in the mid-sixties Cory had once led a protest march down to Wall Street with all the marchers wearing three-piece suits and carrying blank placards. In those days such an event was called a "happening"— and perhaps this Robin Hood lark was the same sort of harmless prank. Perhaps not. Nicky spent some time in the shower trying to convince himself he should be laughing—and yet the laughter did not come.

Another problem he had was whether to tell the boys at the U.S. Embassy about this. Unfortunately, the fact that Cory was hoping to infuse a billion dollars into the Sandinista party in a bid to return them to power was *exactly* the sort of thing they had in mind for him to report.

Well, screw the CIA! thought Nicky Rachmaninoff. And all the damn Hollywood limousine liberals with their tremendous egos and guilt, *and* Chief of Police McGroder for ending his long-awaited vacation in such a miserable way!

Nicky was bemoaning his lost vacation when he was startled to hear the bathroom door slowly open. He became very still and cautious, stepping back from the stream of water. Was it a murderous messenger from Medellin? A cunning criminal from the CIA? Nicky heard a soft footstep on the tiles—and then Susan slipped inside the shower stall alongside him. She was wearing nothing at all.

"I thought you might need some help working up a lather," she told him.

"Ah! Even with ten years of psychoanalysis, you still lust after my perfect body, don't you?"

"Oh, Nicky, you're a big old familiar bear, but I'm horny as hell. Do you mind?"

It wasn't the most romantic offer he had ever had, but it was certainly the best offer he had had all day. Nicky was no fool. He picked up Susan and carried her all wet and wiggling into her bed.

15

THE RAIN CAME DOWN. THEY LEFT THE WINDOW OPEN WHEN THEY made love because it was so wonderful to hear. Fingers of lightning electrified the night, illuminating the sleeping city for just a moment before fading away. They didn't have rain like this in Los Angeles. This was sheer tropical release.

Across town from the Hotel Intercontinental, Tanya Rachmaninoff gently disengaged herself from José's embrace. She had worn him out, poor boy—he had fallen asleep. It made Tanya think perhaps there *was* some truth in what her mother always told her: women were the stronger sex.

Tanya sat up in bed and reached for a cigarette on the floor. She could hardly believe she had actually *done it*—lost her virginity, a momentous occasion! Among her friends, hers had been the last to go—except for Bunky Baker's, of course, who was overweight and homely and might *never* get laid. Kirsten Cooleridge had been the first of her set, doing it at the age of twelve with the family gardener, and Tanya had always been jealous of her graphic accounts. Still, she had waited for something special, and something special had come at last.

Tanya found herself taking mental snapshots to store away, of José's bedroom and of herself lying naked in a strange bed in a foreign country with a hot tropical storm raging outside. This was definitely her idea of romance. A week from now, she would be back in boring Beverly Hills, where nothing exciting ever happened. The sense of loss was already upon her. Tanya knew she must memorize this moment, engrave it upon her heart forever.

José's bedroom was unlike any bedroom she had ever seen. There was no furniture, just a lumpy mattress on the floor, a wooden fruit crate for a bedside table, a candle in a rum bottle, and a patchwork of pictures cut out of magazines that almost seemed to be holding up the walls. In a sense, it was the bedroom that had seduced her. She had not planned to go all the way—not on the first date—but a mattress on the floor was much too romantic to resist, and besides, how else could she prove to José that she was not a snob?

Tanya began pleasantly daydreaming how she would tell her friends back home about this. She would say nothing, of course— why be so gauche as to recount the graphic details, as Kirsten had done? No, she would let her friends reach their own conclusions from the new grace with which she moved and the slightly tragic sparkle in her eye. Without saying a word, the most discerning members of the ninth grade would surely know Tanya Rachmaninoff was no longer a virgin.

"Who was it?" they might well ask. "A rock star? A poet? A young god?"

But Tanya would answer with only a mysterious and enigmatic smile.

She was blowing a thin stream of smoke across the room in a very pleasant reverie, when she heard some people come into the house from outside. José's mother had died four years ago during a *contra* attack, and now he shared the house only with his father, who was supposedly gone for the night. The house was small—hardly more than a shack divided into partitions by thin walls—and Tanya had a sudden realization that her present unclothed situation could become embarrassing.

Two men were moving about in the next room. They were speaking Spanish, but to her surprise they switched suddenly to English.

"Whatever happens, I don't wish to harm Daniel Ortega," said a voice—she recognized it as belonging to Major Aivas, José's father. The next voice she wasn't sure about.

"Listen to me, Ricardo—I have the greatest respect for Ortega. He should be put into a glorious retirement and revered as the father of modern Nicaragua. He is a poet, a beautiful man. But unfortunately he was never much of a politician, and he doesn't seem to have the stomach to be a soldier anymore."

Ricardo sighed. "He will not like this coup d'etat. You know that, of course—he still thinks the Sandinistas can come back to power through an election."

"He's fucking dreaming," said the other man. "Uncle Sam will kill him first. Now tell me about the junior army officers. Are they ready to do as we say?"

The two speakers were bilingual, and the conversation flowed back into a rapid Spanish that Tanya could not understand. She was just as glad. Lying in the darkness of the next room, Tanya was quite certain this was a conversation it would be better not to hear. She slipped down lower in the bed, snuggling against José for protection. He stirred and she soon felt a hand wandering up her leg. She took his hand firmly in her own—this was not the right time for *that*.

"Mm, my delicious darling . . . I fall asleep, I think."

"Sh! Your father's home. He's with someone—it's Cory Heard, I think."

José didn't care. He was ready for more love. He pulled himself up so he could lie on top of her, but he hadn't reckoned on the fact that Tanya was still smoking a cigarette. He let out a small cry of pain and pulled away.

"Oh my God! Did I burn you?"

"It's nothing," he assured her, wiping the ash from his arm.

"Let me see, José. Gosh, maybe you need a Band-Aid or something."

Tanya stuck the offending cigarette in the corner of her mouth and leaned over José to look at his arm. Unfortunately, the glowing end had been knocked loose by the collision. As Tanya was leaning forward, the fiery ash fell loose onto José's chest and continued rolling down his stomach all the way to his—

"*Yah!*" screamed José, jumping from the bed and brushing at himself furiously.

"God, I'm such a total klutz! Are you okay, José?"

"Not to worry," he told her—but there was an edge to his voice she had never heard before. "I think I have been in more serious danger in the war."

At this moment the bedroom door burst open and the two men came in. Tanya found herself kneeling on top of the bed without a stitch of clothing, with Major Ricardo Aivas and Cory Heard staring at her. She made a fast dive for José's sheet, putting it over her head and disappearing from view.

"This is positively the *most* embarrassing thing that's *ever* happened to me," she said again and again, like a mantra.

"They're gone now. You can get dressed, Tanya," said José. But Tanya wasn't coming out from hiding—no way!

"Why didn't you *tell* me your father was coming home?" she shouted from beneath the sheet.

"I didn't know. He was supposed to go to the north, you see, but then this meeting came up. But Tanya, please—it is not such a big thing. They have all seen a naked woman before, I think."

"Probably in *your* bed," she hurled at him. "But not *me!*"

José was at a loss. He approached the lump beneath the sheet and put a hand where he imagined her back must be. "Tanya . . ."

"Don't touch me!" she screamed.

"This is ridiculous," he sighed. "Well, please yourself."

When she heard him leave the bedroom, Tanya promptly burst into tears. She had not ventured very far along the paths of love before encountering its first thorns.

16

CORY DROVE TANYA BACK TO THE HOTEL IN A VW VAN HE HAD PARKED outside. The rain had stopped, and a full moon was sitting fat in the clear night sky. Nicaragua seemed to be a place of sudden and violent change.

Tanya lit another cigarette and coughed.

"You shouldn't smoke so much," Cory told her. "You'll regret it in a few years."

Tanya ignored him. She let the fringe of her honey blond hair settle over her eyes. Tanya was in deep hiding.

After a while, Cory pulled over to the curb and turned off the engine. Tanya could see the pyramid shape of the Intercontinental on a hill not far away.

"Why are you stopping?"

"I think we need to have a chat, Tanya."

She executed her coldest shrug.

"Look, honey, your parents are good friends of mine. Especially your mother," he said with a subtle emphasis.

Tanya glared at him. What a creep! As it happened, about a year ago she had come back from school early, due to a minimum day, and found Cory and her mom in bed. Personally, Tanya didn't care one way or another if her mom was screwing her best friend's husband—how boring, really! How utterly Beverly Hills! But as far as Tanya was concerned, one didn't talk about these things, and it was *très gauche* of Cory to bring it up.

Cory was looking at her hard. "Look here, honey, I want to make a little deal with you. Your parents probably wouldn't be too thrilled to learn about your budding sex life—so what do you say I don't tell them? Okay?"

Tanya studiously said nothing.

"You see, the thing is, parents have this selective amnesia—they forget the kind of things *they* used to do when they were young. Your father especially—he's not very realistic, is he? You're his little girl, I bet. Poor guy would probably blow his arterial valves if he thought guys were getting into your pants already—don't you think?"

"Would you please take me back to the hotel," Tanya commanded in a cold and haughty voice that wavered only a little toward the end.

"I will, sweetheart, I will. What I'm saying to you is that your father doesn't *have* to find out about this. We can both of us forget what we saw and what we heard tonight. You see what I mean?"

"I didn't hear anything," Tanya said quickly. "I was asleep."

Cory smiled. "Then there's no problem, is there? Next time we meet, we'll simply erase this entire event. I'll pretend I never saw you all cute and naked in young José's bed, and you'll pretend I was never even there, having a somewhat indiscreet conversation with Major Aivas. It will be like the whole thing never happened."

Tanya looked at him with utter loathing. But she had to admit he had a point. "Okay," she said, "this evening never happened. That's okay by me. But you sure are a gross slimeball, if I ever saw one!"

Cory laughed pleasantly. "Well," he said, "I'm just glad your mother doesn't think so."

17

RACHMANINOFF DECIDED THAT BEING BACK AT WORK WAS THE MOST relaxing thing that had happened to him since coming on vacation. Some people were just no good at lying around in the sun.

For the next three days, Nicky kept an eye on things. He went everywhere he supposed Cory Heard might go—to tours of jails and schools and all sorts of discussion groups with various Sandinista sympathizers. He sat in on a round-table discussion with the U.S. ambassador, a dinner with the editor of a leftist newspaper, and a meeting with a Catholic bishop to discuss something they referred to as "liberation theology." It was all highly educational, but Nicky had nothing unusual to report to his new bosses at the CIA and FBI.

Susan, for her part, was extremely impressed by her ex-husband's sudden interest in political matters, and at night she made sure he was liberally rewarded in bed.

"It's hard to believe this is really *you*," she told him, lying in bed together, her golden hair against his chest. "You've been so good the last few days, it almost worries me, Nicky."

"It's the least I can do, Susan, when I think of all the destruction the United States has wrought upon poor Nicaragua!"

"Do you ever feel guilty, Nicky? I sure do."

They were drinking Peruvian champagne. Susan leaned out of bed to the ice bucket on the floor, and refilled their glasses.

"Do you know what I *really* feel guilty about?" she asked, not quite daring to look him in the eye. "You're going to think I'm terrible. For a while last year I had an affair with Cory Heard."

"Did you? Well, he's an attractive guy, I guess."

"Nicky! His wife is my best friend!"

"Does Kitty know?"

"Are you kidding? She'd *kill* me if she found out—I can't tell you how utterly *devastated* by guilt I feel whenever I'm even near her."

They were quiet for a few minutes, sitting in bed side by side with their glasses of champagne and their thoughts.

"Well, why did you do it then?" Nicky asked at last.

Susan sighed. "My psychiatrist says I'm trying to compete with her, maybe get even for the fact that she always gets better roles than me."

"Come on, Susan—you're as big a star as Kitty Hall," he told her gallantly.

"I am not!" she cried vehemently. "*She* always gets the movies with the important social issues. Me, I'm still playing daffy blondes. It's just not fair, Nicky."

Nicky took Susan in his arms and stroked her hair. "If you want better parts, maybe you should screw your agent," he suggested, "rather than Cory Heard."

"Nicky, that's a *terrible* thing to say," said Susan, putting her arms around his waist and snuggling close. "Anyway, my agent's gay."

"That's a tough break," Rachmaninoff admitted.

"God, I hate her—Kitty, I mean. Just to give you an example, she's such a bitch about her one measly Academy Award, leaving it out on her breakfast table, for chrissake, like she's so terribly *casual* about it. And all the time, of course, she's hoping you'll eat your God damn heart out with envy."

"And yet she's your best friend," Nicky reminded.

"You know something? I'm *glad* I fucked her husband!" said Susan suddenly. "Even if he *was* a lousy lay!"

Nicky played with the lovely blond hair that was splayed across his chest like fallen sunlight.

"There, there," he soothed. "You see, you don't really feel guilty at all. . . ."

18

THE FOLLOWING MORNING, NICKY RACHMANINOFF SAT IN THE HOTEL bar drinking coffee, in a spot from which he could keep an eye on the lobby and watch the Hollywood Committee for Justice in Nicaragua come and go, passing through the hotel on their merry way to gather more facts.

Just when Nicky was getting bored, Kitty and Cory stepped out of an elevator. They seemed to be having a fight about something. Though Nicky couldn't hear the words, the body language was unmistakable. He found himself wishing he had a fake Walkman from Sharper Image like the big boys in the CIA, but then he was just a low-tech sort of guy.

Kitty and Cory soon went their separate ways—Kitty outside the hotel, Cory back to the bank of elevators off the lobby. In a moment, Tanya emerged from the elevator just in time to give Cory an unquestionably dirty look, and then she walked past the reception desk to meet José, who was waiting for her. Tanya and José sat down in a corner near a potted palm, and to Nicky's surprise, they too appeared to be having a fight. Maybe Venus was in Mars today. If Rip Beasley were around, Nicky would certainly have asked for an astrological weather report. He too might wish to avoid romantic entanglements.

It was fascinating, spying on people. Near him in the bar, a group of TV reporters were getting loud and drunk. At the moment the big media interest had passed on temporarily to events in Colombia and El Salvador, and the reporters stuck in Nicaragua looked marooned. Like Nicky, they were waiting for something to happen.

Nicky was on his third cup of coffee when he saw Kitty come back into the hotel from outside. She was dressed in a rather formal skirt and blouse, and she walked briskly toward the elevator—which opened and deposited her forever youthful husband, Cory Heard. This time there was no mistaking the fact that Hollywood's most liberal couple were having a hell of a go-round. Cory took her by the arm and pulled her from the elevators toward the newsstand in a far corner of the lobby, where they made angry faces at each other and didactic gestures with their arms.

Curiosity got the better of Nicky Rachmaninoff. He left his coffee and ambled over toward the newsstand, picking up a copy of the *International Herald Tribune,* the newspaper of spies. He opened the paper to sports and eased around the newsstand, closer to Kitty and Cory, keeping the paper in front of his face. Kitty was talking in low urgent tones.

"You do this, it's all over between us, I want you to know that," she said.

Cory seemed to be humoring her. "Pussycat! Let me tell you something, you gotta think *big.* You gotta expand your imagination. There's a whole world out there to conquer!"

Nicky had a feeling he had heard this speech before. So had Kitty, apparently.

"Oh, grow up!" she said suddenly, and stormed off away from him across the lobby toward a side wing. Cory looked as though he was about to follow after her, but then he swore softly and hurried off by himself toward the main exit. Nicky debated briefly which one of this glamorous couple he wished to follow most, husband or wife, and decided at this moment it was the little woman. He tucked the *Trib* under his arm and followed quickly in her wake, crossing the lobby toward a side wing of the hotel.

She was striding down a long, empty corridor. They were long, angry strides, the heels of her shoes making a bright *click-clack* against the marble floor. Nicky followed her to a side door, where she stepped out onto a wide terrace overlooking the city and an edge of the swimming pool below. Kitty came to a stop against a railing, and her shoulder heaved in a convulsive sob. Nicky came up behind her. Without warning, she spun around to face him. There were tears running down her cheek, and her lovely face was a little red.

"What do *you* want, Rachmaninoff?" she asked, wiping a few tears away with the back of her hand.

"I'm just your shadow," said he. "I saw you walking along and I said to myself, 'Why not practice your super-duper detective routine and find out where pretty Kitty is off to with such a sorrowful face?' "

"Well, get lost, okay? I just don't need the hassle right now."

"Vatever," said Rachmaninoff. "The lady vants to be alone, I vill vapidly vanish."

The lady did not smile. One thing Rachmaninoff had always found: people in the midst of marital squabblings rarely had a sense of humor, though a sense of humor was generally what they needed most.

Nicky shrugged his shoulders and turned to leave, but she stopped him.

"Wait a minute. Maybe you can be useful after all."

Nicky waited while Kitty took a handkerchief from her handbag and blew her nose. It was the most human act he had ever seen Kitty Hall perform.

"Marriage!" he told her in sympathy. "It sure can be the pits."

"How would *you* know, Rachmaninoff? From what Susan tells me, you were never home long enough to give it much of a chance."

"Ah, well! I was destined to be a lonely bumblebee, buzzing hither and thither upon the great poppy field of life, occasionally sucking some little honey—but that's a story for another time and place."

The smoky gray eyes stared at him, not amused. "You're disgusting," she said. "Look, Cory's about to do something really stupid. Do you think you could try to talk with him, Rachmaninoff?"

"I could talk. I doubt if he'll listen. What's this all about?"

"That jerk is about to screw up this whole trip, and probably get us thrown out of the country or killed."

"Maybe you should start from the beginning," said he.

"It's the money," said she. "He's not planning to turn it over to Daniel Ortega like he said."

"Oh-ho! He's going to keep it, is he?"

She shook her head.

"He's going to give it to Octavio Morales, maybe?"

She shook her head again. "He's going to use it to finance a coup d'etat," she told him.

"*What?*"

"He's going to try to overthrow Violeta Chamorro with an armed uprising. Ricardo told me about it last night."

"Good God! Major Aivas?"

"That's right. Cory and Ricardo have been scheming this to-gether. Apparently there is a group of hard-core Sandinista army officers who are just waiting for the signal, but Ricardo is getting cold feet."

"I should imagine! But why would Major Aivas come and tell you?"

Kitty stared at him steadily. "Look," she said, "Cory and I were down here last year for nearly a month. We met Ricardo at a party and we all became friends. I was feeling a little vulnerable, I suppose—my damned husband was having affairs with his students at UCLA, and I needed some reassurance I was still attractive. So Ricardo and I, well . . ."

"Ah!" said Nicky wisely.

"It was dumb," said Kitty, "and Ricardo still thinks he's in love with me, which is dumber still. Anyway, that's why he came to the hotel last night to warn me what Cory's planning to do."

"Sounds cozy," said Rachmaninoff.

"Cory doesn't know about Ricardo and me," said Kitty defensively. "And since they are close friends, I'd appreciate it if you didn't tell anyone."

"Friendship is indeed a heavy burden," said Nicky Rachmaninoff with a sigh.

"Look, there's not a lot of time to stand around and make stupid remarks. Cory's going to dig up the money today, and you've got to stop him, Rachmaninoff."

"How do you know it's today?"

"I think it's going to be during the luncheon this afternoon for the poet Santiago Borges. I heard Cory ask Susan to put him near the door in case he needs to make a quick exit."

Nicky frowned. He happened to know a little about this particular luncheon for a famous left-wing poet; Susan was organizing the affair and had been talking nervously of its outcome for several days. She certainly wouldn't be pleased if Cory did something to make it less than Beverly Hills perfect.

"He's going to sneak out of there, don't you see? But you could follow him, Rachmaninoff—isn't that the sort of thing you're good at? Cory will lead you to where he's going to dig up the money, and then maybe you could take it from him. Or better still, you could persuade him to give it to Daniel Ortega and forget this ridiculous coup d'etat that's going to get us all killed."

Nicky was beginning to feel dubious about this entire scenario. "Kitty, first of all, maybe there's some utterly ordinary reason Cory asked Susan to put him near the door—like he has a case of the *turistas*, or something. Second, to be perfectly frank, the idea of some UCLA professor trying to pull off an armed uprising in Nicaragua is a little fantastic."

"No, you don't know Cory like I do. He never does *anything* ordinary, believe me. For him, this is probably like some wonderful movie in his head—*Indiana Heard and the Lost Revolution!* So even if you're a creep and put my best friend in psychoanalysis for ten years, you've simply got to help. Will you do it? *Please?*"

"Since you put it so nicely, Kitty—how can I refuse? Now, this luncheon for the poet . . ."

"It starts in forty-five minutes—we've got to hurry if we're going to stop Cory in time!"

"I guess," said Rachmaninoff wearily. Kitty hurried up to her room to change clothes, leaving Nicky on the terrace by himself with a vague feeling that none of this added up right. He couldn't quite put his finger on what was wrong, but this story Kitty was spinning was definitely dicey, leading to the nasty suspicion that Hollywood's most fun couple was setting him up for something. Unfortunately he was curious, and the only way to discover what this was all about, he supposed, was to take the bait and follow Cory from the luncheon—though this presented a few problems of its own.

Nicky walked quickly back into the lobby of the hotel, where he noticed José and Tanya still in deep conversation, sitting on a little sofa behind a potted palm. Venus apparently had moved into a better position in the sky, because José and Tanya were now holding hands. They looked cute together, but Nicky made a mental note to speak to Susan about this—hand-holding was okay, he supposed, but his innocent daughter must be warned against the diabolical cunning of lustful young men! Tanya and José looked up in alarm at the way he was bearing down upon them.

"José, I would like to have a word with you," said Nicky.

"Dad! Don't hurt him!" cried Tanya.

"What are you talking about?"

"I am not afraid to talk with your father," said José. He followed Tanya's father a dozen feet across the lobby. "Señor Nicky, I think I must tell you about my feelings for your daughter."

"Another time, José. Right now, if you don't mind, I'm rather more interested in the use of your car."

19

THE LUNCHEON FOR THE LEFT-WING POET SANTIAGO BORGES BEGAN at one o'clock and was held in a private banquet room in the hotel, set with long tables. Nicky dressed for the occasion in khaki slacks and a blue oxford shirt. He arrived a few minutes early to find Susan frantically overseeing last-minute preparations.

"Nicky! I wasn't expecting you. I thought you *hated* things like this."

"This is the new me, Susan—lusting after culture. Why not squeeze me in next to Cory?"

"I can't put you next to Cory," she told him. "But if you behave yourself, you may sit next to me."

"I'll be a model luncheoneer," he promised, "though I may molest you just a little beneath the table."

"Promise?" She flashed him an inscrutably feminine look. "You know, Nicky, one of these days we're going to have to talk about *us.*"

This was pretty scary, but fortunately Susan was too busy with arriving guests to talk about *us* right now. The private dining room became noisy with Hollywood fact-finders trying out well-phrased descriptions of Nicaragua on each other. Cory arrived and soon was in his natural element, passing among groups of friends with provocative little epigrams about life in Central America. Everyone agreed the food was ghastly and the accommodations in the hotel not really up to par.

Lunch was served. There was soup, hearts-of-palm salad, and then a fish that had been baked with tomatoes and cilantro. Susan had done a good job getting this party together, and when at last she was able to sit down, Nicky kept his promise to molest her beneath the table, feeling up a long and lovely left leg discreetly out of view. By the time the fish course had arrived, he had managed to make his way clear to the inner thigh. Nicky was beginning to think he might start going to luncheons like this more often.

After the food was served, Kitty gave a short, angry speech denouncing U.S. foreign policy in Central America. The speech was served with spumoni ice cream and coffee and was well received. Nicky used the opportunity to slip a wandering finger into Susan's undies.

Next came the guest of honor, the famous poet himself, a small fat man wearing glasses, a heavy dark stubble on his chin. His theme was "Nicaragua, Land of Living Poetry." He told the stirring story of Rigoberto López Pérez, a young poet from the city of León, who assassinated Somoza the First in 1956. Unlike their counterparts in the United States, poets in Nicaragua apparently actually *did* things. At last the great man treated his audience to a few verses he had written for the occasion, speaking in thunderous and florid Spanish while an interpreter translated line for line:

> *"Oh, shame of social inequity!*
> *Northern neighbor, love lies famished in your*
> *Credit card soul!*
> *Why serve an empty pizza, no toppings, and not the*
>   *tasty tortilla of Truth? . . ."*

This was the first stanza, and it was followed by many more. At the end, the poem was greeted with loud applause.

"Glorious!" said Susan. "And I bet it was even better in Spanish."

"I'd like to hear it in Chinese," remarked Nicky. Unfortunately he looked across the table and noticed that while he had been so sportingly engaged, Cory Heard had managed to disappear.

Nicky jumped up from the table and darted out of the private banquet room. Things like this always happened when you started feeling too pleased with yourself. He looked through the main dining room, the lobby, and the bar, but Cory was nowhere to be found. He ran outside the hotel to the parking lot and found José sitting in his mongrelized Mercedes-Benz, waiting just where he said he would, munching on a plate of food Nicky had managed to send out from the luncheon.

"Did Cory come out this way?"

"He just came from the hotel. He's in that Volkswagen van, Señor Nicky."

Señor Nicky looked to where José was pointing. Up ahead in the parking lot, a light beige VW van was driving down the hill to the city below.

"Lunch is over, José. Follow that van."

Nicky was about to jump into the passenger's seat when he felt a hand on his shoulder.

"Where is that bastard? Did you let him get away, for chrissake?" came an angry voice.

It was Kitty. Her eyes were dark and furious, her skin pale.

"Which bastard are you referring to, Ms. Hall?"

"My husband, damn it! Where is that fucker?"

Nicky was about to say golly, he didn't know, but José spoke first and could not tell a lie.

"He is in that van," said honest José, "the van that is driving away."

"Well, let's get after him, then!" commanded Kitty. To Nicky's dismay, she slipped into the backseat of José's car.

"God damn it, let's go!" she cried. "He's getting away!"

"Hell's bells!" muttered Rachmaninoff, getting in front next to José. This was not as he would have planned it, but then few things were. The old Mercedes lurched forward to the chase.

20

THEY HAD NOT DRIVEN FAR WHEN THE GRAY TROPICAL SKIES ABOVE Managua unleashed a torrent of rain. José's car had only one functional windshield wiper, which made erratic but heroic moves against the onslaught of water. With the windows raised, the air inside the old Mercedes became hot and claustrophobic. Nicky began to feel he was in a submarine instead of an automobile.

On the road ahead, the beige VW van was only just visible through the curtain of water, making its way through the plazas and haphazard boulevards of Managua.

"Am I doing good, Señor Nicky?"

"Great, José. But look, kid, 'Señor Nicky' makes me sound a little too much like a headwaiter at the Copacabana, so why don't you just call me Rachmaninoff."

Rachmaninoff glanced back to the actress in the rear of the car. Kitty made an incongruous sight, perched between a soccer ball and José's empty beer bottles—a little too Technicolor-perfect in the white silk skirt and blouse she had worn to the luncheon, her lovely rich brown hair spilling over her shoulders, framing her small angry face.

Kitty lit a nervous cigarette and sucked in the smoke noisily.

"That's a nasty habit," he told her. "What you're doing, Kitty, you're polluting your inner environment—fucking up the macrocosm with your microcosm, if you see what I mean."

"Shut up, Rachmaninoff."

"At least I don't pollute myself. Not with cigarettes, anyway."

She blew smoke into his face. This wasn't exactly turning into a beautiful friendship. Nicky returned his eyes to the road. They were on the outskirts of town now. Outside the rain-streaked windows there were small wooden shanties and donkeys and half-naked children playing in mud puddles. The inside of the car was steaming hot, and Nicky opened his window a little to let out Kitty's smoke and the smell of all their perspiration. Before long, the town ended and they were in the country. There were no more wooden shacks, just a green forest beneath a wet gray sky. The vegetation along the sides of the narrow road seemed overgrown and chaotic. José let the beige VW van remain about two hundred feet ahead.

"'Rachmaninoff, why do we follow Cory?" José asked thoughtfully. "Is he not a friend?"

"Sure, he's a friend," Nicky told him vaguely, not wanting to get into too many details. "Hell, we're all friends here, José—but we like to keep an eye on each other, you know. Actually, what this is, is a little personal, son. Probably you'd have to be a Californian to completely understand."

"I'd very much like to go to California," José admitted. "I have a cousin who lives in East Los Angeles. Is this a good place, Rachmaninoff?"

"East L.A.? Well, if you ever go there, remember to bring your AK-47 along."

"Shut up!" Kitty cried suddenly, with a great deal of vehemence. Then she cried it again three times more, nearly out of breath: "Shut up! Shut up! Shut up!"

Nicky could take a hint. He turned his attention back to the green-gray landscape out the front window. The road was becoming worse the farther they drove from Managua, until they were being bounced torturously over a moonscape of small potholes. After a time the highway began to climb up into the hills, and still the VW van ahead of them kept going. After what seemed an endless, kidney-jarring ride, the van turned off the main highway onto a smaller road which disappeared into the jungle.

"Pull over a second," said Nicky. "Where does that road go, José?"

"It leads to a very old hacienda that was owned by a tree of the Somoza family."

"A *branch*," Nicky corrected. "This branch of the Somoza family—their name didn't happen to be Morales, did it?"

"Yes, it was!" José seemed stunned by this remarkable feat of clairvoyance. "The house is owned by Joaquim Morales now—he was the only member of the family who stayed behind after the revolution."

"Have you ever been here before, José?"

"Oh yes. The Morales hacienda is very famous. Once upon a time, there used to be big parties here where the officers of the Guardia Nacional would meet their girlfriends."

"How far is the house from the main highway?"

"Maybe five minutes' drive."

"What about walking?"

"Not long. Ten, fifteen minutes. But there is a shortcut through the trees."

"Good," said Rachmaninoff. "I feel like a bit of exercise. Ms. Hall, if you'll just remain in this fine automobile, we'll be back almost before you can miss us."

"I'm coming with you, Rachmaninoff."

"I'm afraid I must insist. If you got a chest cold in the rain, your public would never forgive me."

But Kitty wasn't about to be ordered about by a low-life reactionary like Rachmaninoff. She stepped out of the car, and Nicky and José joined her in the rain. It was a warm rain, at least, nearly skin temperature, but coming down hard. Before long, Nicky felt a small river making like a waterfall off his nose.

José was a gallant lad. "I have a rain poncho in the back," he offered Kitty. "You should wear it, please."

"You have just one poncho?" she asked.

"Yes, but you are the woman—you should wear it, please, so you don't get wet."

"I know you mean well, but you're buying into a whole sexist scenario, José. Thanks, but I think you should give the poncho to Rachmaninoff—unless that would be too threatening to his manhood."

Nicky grinned. "My manhood's not afraid of a little tropical moisture, Miz Hall."

Kitty seemed disgusted with the two of them. She turned and led the way up the muddy road, though it was tough going in her dainty white high-heeled shoes. After a few minutes, she stopped and flung her shoes angrily into a ditch, continuing barefoot. Nicky picked up the shoes after her. "For my Imelda Marcos collection," he said.

They trudged up the road in silence. It was an uncomfortable procession: Kitty in the lead, then José with his AK-47 slung across his shoulder, and Nicky a few steps behind. It wasn't long before they were drenched to the skin.

The rain did one strange and miraculous thing: it turned Kitty's white skirt and blouse completely transparent. José looked back at Nicky and grinned. Nicky grinned too. After a while they both began to giggle, softly at first, then louder.

Kitty ignored them as long as she could. "What's wrong with you two *men?*" she finally asked, laying heavy sarcasm upon the word "men."

"You really should have accepted the poncho, Kitty," Nicky told her, smirking.

She stopped and looked down at her transparent clothing. "Oh," she said. But this was a lady who was far from being embarrassed by simple nudity. She turned toward Nicky and offered herself for a better view.

"Does it turn you on, Rachmaninoff?"

"About an eighth of an inch," he admitted.

"With you, that probably passes for an erection."

"I don't think she likes me," Nicky confided to José.

They trudged along with no more giggles. The road began to snake upward in a series of switchbacks to a place where José showed them they could cut through the jungle. Under the trees the rain was not as bad, but in a few minutes they passed on through to a clearing on the other side. Climbing a slight rise, they came out upon a hilltop that looked down upon the Morales hacienda below.

It was a big old house protected behind high adobe walls topped by red tile roofs, with a small private chapel off to one side. Nicky had seen architecture like this imitated in Southern California—but this was the real thing, the sort of place that might even have a dungeon in the basement, an architectural frill generally frowned upon in California.

Nicky told everyone to lie out flat on the wet grass so they wouldn't be seen from the hacienda. About a hundred fifty feet below them, Cory's VW van was parked at the side of the house near a small family cemetery. Two men in muddy clothes, with shovels in hand, were digging up two separate graves while Cory looked on with a somber expression. The whole thing looked to Nicky like some kind of macabre funeral in reverse. Cory seemed impatient. He grabbed a shovel from one of the gravediggers and began to dig himself, sending the muddy earth flying through the air in quick motions.

"I guess this is it," said Kitty softly. "I don't want you to hurt him, Rachmaninoff—that's the only thing I ask."

Nicky didn't answer. Now that he was here, he didn't know what the hell he was going to do. On his side, he had a goofy teenager who happened to be his daughter's boyfriend, a spoiled Hollywood actress of the liberal persuasion, and a .38 automatic strapped to his ankle.

Down below, Cory and the two gravediggers had managed to get a rope around one of the exposed coffins, and they were attempting to haul it up from the rectangular hole. This was such a fascinating spectacle that Nicky missed something very important happening at his rear.

"Turn around—slowly," came a voice from behind. Nicky, José, and Kitty all obeyed the command. They were startled to see two men standing beneath the protection of a large black umbrella. One of the men had big ears, thick glasses, and a pair of binoculars around his neck. He was wearing a shirt with little sailboats on it, Bermuda shorts, and shoes with black socks. It was Bob Arnold of the CIA.

The second man was Rip Beasley, towering above little Bob so that the single umbrella could barely encompass them both. Together the two men would have made quite a laughable sight, except that Bob held a nasty little pistol in his free hand, and Rip delicately fingered an Uzi submachine gun cradled in his arms.

"Well, well," said Rip. "I believe we have arrived at the moment of truth."

21

"PUT DOWN THAT RIDICULOUS GUN THIS INSTANT," COMMANDED Kitty Hall, glaring at Rip Beasley.

"Or what? You'll tell the Academy on me?" replied Rip with a dangerous smile. This seemed to be a moment he had been looking forward to.

Kitty was a lady used to getting her own way. When Rip refused to lower his weapon, she turned to Rachmaninoff for some kind of explanation.

"He's an undercover cop," Nicky explained as gently as possible. "FBI. Bob over there is CIA. Together they are attempting to guard the American way from nymphomaniac liberals in see-through clothes."

Kitty was stunned. "Then Cory was right—months ago he said Rip was a cop, but I thought he was joking."

"Even jokers occasionally hit the mark," said Rachmaninoff.

"Why is the CIA here?" José asked angrily, after Bob Arnold had relieved him of his AK-47. There was a dark look on his face, for the CIA was not exactly popular with Sandinista sympathizers.

"We're all a little anxious about Cory, José," Nicky tried to explain. "We're afraid he might be going off on a rather serious midlife crisis."

"Shut up," said Rip. "Bob, keep an eye on these people while I suss out the scene."

Rip took the binoculars, leaving Bob with the umbrella. The wind was picking up and holding a frail black umbrella against a Nicaraguan rainstorm seemed a gesture of heroic folly. "I hate this weather," muttered Bob, as gusts of rain swirled about his legs and feet. "Reminds me of 'Nam."

"I bet!" fumed Kitty.

Rip meanwhile crawled the short distance to the top of the rise, and stretched out on his stomach with the binoculars held up to his eyes. He quietly surveyed the gravedigging action down below.

"Jesus!" he said after a moment. "Come here, Rachmaninoff."

Nicky crawled muddily back up the rise and lay alongside Rip in the rain. Down below in the Morales family cemetery, Cory and his two assistants had managed to get the first coffin out of the ground and into the back of the VW van, and were now working on the second. Rip was flushed and very excited.

"Do you know what's going on down there?" he whispered. "This is *it*, boy! The big one!"

"The big what, Rip?"

"Somoza's treasure, for crying out loud! Don't you know what this is all about, Rachmaninoff? I thought you were supposed to be a smart cop."

Nicky smiled. "You're talking about the billion dollars, are you, that got left behind in the last chaotic days of the Somoza dictatorship?"

"Holy shit, Rachmaninoff! We've been looking for this money for more than ten years. Don't you see what's happening here? That damn liberal's going to hand over the dough to the Sandinistas."

Nicky rubbed his chin thoughtfully. "I see what you mean, Rip. Of course, you and I don't have any authority down here to stop him."

"Are you crazy? We've *got* to stop him—with enough money, the Sandinistas could buy their way back into power. And you let the Marxist-Leninists get a new foothold in this hemisphere and before you know it—Guatemala, El Salvador, Honduras, Panama, even Mexico—they'll all go down like a leveraged takeover in hell, one after another. And then they'll be on our doorstep, marching into Southern California!"

Nicky tried to give Rip a calming smile. "Look, Rip, if the Sandinistas want Southern California—let them have it, that's what I say. Can they really do any worse with it than we have?"

"Very funny," said Rip, giving Nicky quite a disgusted look. He brought the binoculars back up to his eyes to follow the progress of the second coffin being hoisted up from the earth with ropes. "You know what we got to do, don't you, Lieutenant?" he asked quietly.

"Actually, no, I do not," admitted Nicky unhappily.

Rip glanced to where Bob was guarding Kitty and José, and then back to Nicky. "Well, it's fairly simple," he said. "We got to get our hands on that money, and we can't leave behind any witnesses to talk about it—you got a knife, Lieutenant?"

"Only nail clippers," said Nicky with difficulty, for his mouth had suddenly gone very dry. "Look, if I understand you correctly, I'm beginning to get a very bad feeling about this, Rip."

"We don't got any choice," said Rip. "The soldier will tell his superiors, the actress will squawk to the press. Before you know it, we'll be up in front of some damn Senate hearing, all of those bastards wanting to know why we're killing people in Central America."

"But that's a good point," said Nicky urgently. "Why the hell *are* we killing people in Central America?"

Rip gave Nicky a long look. "For freedom, Lieutenant. And if you don't have the guts to stand up and be counted for democracy, then I'll do this myself."

Rip was starting to rise, but Nicky held on to his arm. "Listen to me, Rip—this kind of democracy you kill women and children for—it's really a contradiction in terms. In fact, I'd say you're one crazy son of a bitch."

Rip had managed to get to his feet. "You disappoint me, Lieutenant," he said, and then Nicky saw the butt of the Uzi coming down hard upon his head. Just in time, he ducked to the side as the weight of the gun hit his shoulder with a shock of pain. Rip apparently was planning to do for Rachmaninoff what he was going to do for Kitty and José. Kneeling in the mud, Nicky grabbed at one of Rip's legs and pulled it out from under him. Rip let out a little cry and fell backward onto the ground, losing his hold on the Uzi. Rachmaninoff sprang upon the gun before Rip could recover, and gave it a toss into the jungle. This seemed a clever move, but Rip jumped on him from behind and rode piggyback, trying to get a stranglehold around his neck. Nicky spun around like an enraged bear until they both fell backward into the mud.

It was the worst kind of fighting—fingers clawing at eyes, palms against nostrils, arms and legs intertwined, seeking any vulnerable spot. The mud made little oozing, smacking sounds as they rolled over on each other in a close embrace. Rip Beasley had bad breath. Nicky grabbed hold of his long black curls and yanked backward. It wasn't what a gentleman would do, but this was fighting at its dirtiest.

A pistol shot cracked loudly nearby, making the two figures in the mud pause to look around. José had managed to kick out with his foot at Bob Arnold's gun hand; the hand jerked upward involuntarily, pulling the trigger and sending off a bullet into the wet skies. At the sound of the shot, there was a cry of alarm from the gravediggers below. José didn't give Bob a chance to recover, but rammed

Bob's stomach with his head, driving the elfish little man backwards against a tree.

While the menfolk were busily engaged, Kitty calmly stood up and walked over the rise of the hill toward her husband in the graveyard.

"Cory!" she shouted, and then again: "Co-ree!"

Nicky succeeded in landing a solid uppercut into Rip's chin, sending the FBI agent onto his back. Rip groaned once and then was still. Nicky took the opportunity to turn his attention to Kitty, deciding she possibly posed the graver threat. The situation was deteriorating fast. Reaching down to his ankle for his .38 automatic, he followed her over the rise of the hill trying to catch up—she was a dozen feet ahead in her white, transparent, rain-soaked clothes, floating like a disembodied spirit down the long meadow toward her husband and the two gravediggers below. The gravediggers meanwhile had exchanged their shovels for AK-47s and now stared at the wet woman in horror, as if they had just seen Ophelia rise from her watery grave.

"Cory, God damn you—I'm *not* going to let you get away with this, you son of a bitch!" she screamed.

"It was going to be a surprise, hon," Cory called back. "Wait till you hear what I'm going to do with all this money!"

"I know what you're going to do, you bastard!"

It was a strange time and place for a domestic quarrel. Kitty was moving fast, rushing down upon her husband like an avenging fury. Nicky was still a dozen feet behind her, not able to catch up. Down at the bottom, Cory and one of his helpers quickly carried the second coffin into the back of the VW van, laid it to rest alongside the first, and shut the door. The remaining gravedigger raised his automatic weapon and let loose a burst of fire that cut up the ground a few feet in front of Kitty.

"Son of a bitch!" cried Kitty. "Stop shooting at me, you idiot!"

"Get down!" Nicky shouted at her. Would she be sensible for a change? It didn't appear so. The gravedigger raised his rifle once more—but there was a single shot from the top of the hill. Nicky saw the gravedigger throw up his arms in surprise, collapse forward onto the ground, and lie perfectly still. Nicky turned to see young

José with the barrel of his AK-47 still smoking from the shot. Nicky was taken aback that a goofy young kid like that, seventeen years old, could kill so easily—but he supposed that was what growing up in a land at war did to you.

"Don't anyone come closer!" Cory cried to the figures on the hill. He too was armed now, holding an automatic weapon he had picked up from inside the van. For a moment there seemed to be a stalemate, but then there was a wild Comanche yell, and Rip Beasley, apparently recovered from Nicky's blow, came rushing down the hill as if this were Custer's Last Stand. Rip had a pistol in his hand that he had managed to materialize from somewhere on his body, and he was firing methodically at Cory, shot after shot, the gun making funny little pops and sending up small puffs of smoke into the cloudy sky.

A line of dirt was kicked up by automatic fire close to Nicky's side—where it came from, he could not immediately say. Nicky fell down into a crouch, but the slope of the hill was steep enough to turn the crouch into an ongoing somersault. Head over heels, Nicky cascaded down the hill like a bowling ball out of control. He kept hearing gunfire all around him, mixed with the sound of Kitty's screaming. He sure wished Kitty would shut up.

When Nicky hit the bottom, he stood up disoriented and muddy. The earth was still spinning around. He was getting a crazy aim on the remaining gravedigger, but before he could fire, the man simply turned and ran into the woods. Nicky heard an engine start up behind him—it was Cory, and he was in the front seat of the Volkswagen, trying to get away.

"Hold it, Cory!" Nicky shouted, spinning about with his gun raised.

"Hey, amigo!" said Cory with an apologetic smile. "Look, I'm almost home free."

"Get out of the van."

"Come on, you wouldn't shoot your old jogging buddy, would you?"

Nicky was still dizzy from somersaulting down the hill, and his gun arm wavered. Cory took advantage of the moment; he pressed down hard on the accelerator and the Volkswagen lurched forward.

"Stop!" shouted Nicky. He raised his gun—there was still a clear shot. But before he could pull the trigger, something in white jumped on him from behind. He was caught off balance and went face-forward back into the mud.

It took him a moment to realize this savage thing in white was Kitty Hall. Nicky felt teeth sink into the calf of his leg. He screamed. This was his idea of sheer nightmare—to be attacked by an actress out of control.

Fortunately, José rushed over and managed to pull Kitty off him. Nicky raised himself on one knee and wiped the mud out of his eyes with the backs of his hands, just as Bob and Rip came running up, angry and out of breath.

They all stood in a sad wet group and watched the VW van tear across the gravel road toward the edge of the forest. Just as the van was about to be swallowed by the green Nicaraguan jungle, Cory honked twice—funny little Volkswagen beeps—as if saying good-bye.

22

IT WAS A SILENT GROUP OF ADVENTURERS WHO MADE THEIR WAY BACK to Managua that night, wet and weary.

Rip and Bob departed quickly in their station wagon without a word, and José drove his old Mercedes with Nicky in the passenger seat and Kitty in the rear—just as before, but now there were no giggles, no smartass comments, no conversation at all. Just a heavy silence in the car.

Nicky experienced small bursts of uncontrollable shivering. Blood was still oozing down his ankle where Kitty had bitten him, and he could hardly remember ever having felt quite so thoroughly soaked and miserable. It was long after dark by the time José pulled up in front of the Hotel Intercontinental.

"After this, I don't think maybe I'll be seeing you again, Señor Rachmaninoff," José said sadly, just as Nicky was about to get out.

"I understand, kid. Thanks for everything. I mean it."

José reached out and took Nicky's arm for a second. "Tell Tanya good-bye for me. You must tell her that politics make too strange a bedfellow, I think."

As exhausted as he was, Nicky felt the hairs on the back of his neck rise in anger. But then, looking at José's hangdog expression, he convinced himself the kid didn't understand the language well enough to know what he was saying. Nicky sighed and got out of the old Mercedes-Benz. He found he was so stiff he could hardly walk.

"I don't think I'm going to be seeing you again, either," Kitty told him as they moved up the front steps to the hotel. "Not if I can help it, *that's* for sure!"

"Believe me, you're not exactly my idea of a good time, either."

They had been out in the rain so long that Nicky had forgotten what they looked like. He was reminded the moment they walked into the hotel lobby and all eyes turned their way. Nicky's tennis shoes made little soggy indentations on the carpet. Fortunately for Kitty, her white dress was so covered with mud, it was no longer transparent—except for one glorious left nipple.

Susan Merril was at the reception desk, making inquiries about the whereabouts of her ex-husband. She looked up to see the two muddy apparitions enter the lobby, and she let out a small gasp.

"*Where* have you been, Nicky Rachmaninoff? And *what* have you been doing to Kitty?" she demanded.

"Us silly gringos got caught in the rain," he explained. "Why don't you get Kitty upstairs into a hot shower, dear? I'll be up after a while."

Susan's blue eyes were big and full of concern. "Where are you going?"

"I have something I have to do, dear."

Nicky Rachmaninoff made his soggy way across the lobby and into the bar. All the journalists, spies, and curiosity-seekers from the north looked up as he entered. The bartender approached him with a cautious smile.

At least this trip had not been a total waste. Nicky could order a drink in Spanish.

"*Una margarita*," he managed, "*por favor.*"

"Salt?" asked the bartender.

"Sure," said Nicky Rachmaninoff. "Just rub it in."

Part Two

THE VANISHING
LIBERAL

1

KITTY HALL SAT IN LOTUS POSITION, SPINE STRAIGHT, THE CUPS OF her hands facing upward, attempting to make Beverly Hills disappear.

It wasn't easy. Illusory though it might be, Beverly Hills was a hard town to erase. It was seven-thirty in the morning, a fragrant dampness in the air, the beginning of a spring day in the middle of March. In the next yard over, Kitty could hear the rubbery slap of tennis balls against a racket as her neighbor worked out with an automatic ball machine. Farther in the distance, lawn mowers mowed, cars swished up and down Rexford Drive, a rock star practiced pentatonic scales on a guitar, and two maids chattered in Spanish about their employer losing his job at the studio—wondering how this would affect their own job security.

Kitty sat in the yoga room overlooking her swimming pool, trying to still the rumblings of her mind. She was not alone; meditating nearby were Esther, her personal assistant; two female bodyguards built like Amazons; her agent, Sally Barnes; a lady executive from Warner Brothers; and Susan Merril, who dropped in on Kitty's morning yoga from time to time. Together, this particular group of ladies was often referred to by Hollywood wags as "the Mafiettes." Leading the morning ritual was Cathy Krishna Cohen, a remarkably bright-eyed young woman in an orange leotard who had made a fortune as a personal yoga instructor to the stars.

"Om!" chanted Cathy Krishna Cohen, and the rest of the group joined in: "Om mani padme hum. . . ."

This was the end of an hour of rigorous exercise in which the ladies had twisted into human pretzels, stood on their heads, and breathed like dragons—followed by a few minutes of quiet meditation in which one was to pass beyond the nagging questions of the day: box office receipts, husbands, lovers, and trying to find (and keep) decent domestic help. Kitty was having no luck this morning.

Above the distracting sounds of tennis balls and lawn mowers and guitar scales, her mind was occupied with one loud and disturbing doubt that left her with no peace: *Where was Nicky Rachmaninoff? And when the hell was he coming back to Beverly Hills?*

Kitty tried to let it go. She closed her eyes and imagined a perfect flame burning somewhere a little beyond the bridge of her nose. A flame like this had no room for an obnoxious, slightly overweight, semi-alcoholic cop named Rachmaninoff.

Later, when they were changing out of their leotards, Kitty managed to engage Susan in seemingly casual conversation.

"Any word from your ex?"

"Nicky? He's still in Nicaragua, as far as I know," answered Susan. "You know how persistent he is—honestly, Kitty, he'll find Cory if anyone can."

"You think so? But he only knows a few words of Spanish, and every one of them has something to do with getting himself another drink!"

Susan scowled, annoyed. "Honestly, Nicky is more together than he seems. That's just a pose, you know, pretending to be a drunk—he thinks it's very ironic and clever."

"Well, you could have fooled me!" said Kitty, and then, when she saw the look on Susan's face she added, "Look, I'm sorry. I know he's your ex-husband and all, but *really*, Susan, how did you ever manage to live with someone like that?"

"Believe it or not, he was the *best* of my husbands," said Susan with a sigh.

"Look, if you *do* hear from Rachmaninoff, let me know, okay?" asked Kitty. There was a troubled cast to her eye, and for the first time since they had been friends, Susan thought Kitty was beginning to look her age.

Susan squeezed Kitty's hand. "Of course I will! Oh, you must be *terribly* worried about Cory, aren't you, darling?"

"Sure," said Kitty Hall. "Worried to death, darling."

After her fellow yogis had departed, Kitty showered and then joined Esther, her personal assistant, in the downstairs office. Esther was sorting through a pile of scripts that had arrived in the morning mail.

"Put that shit aside," said Kitty, "and get me Octavio Morales."

2

OCTAVIO MORALES LIVED NOT FAR FROM THE BEVERLY HILLS HOTEL on Sunset Boulevard, in an elaborate old Moorish mansion from the Silent Era that sat on two acres of land behind a high wall. They didn't build homes like this anymore, not even in Hollywood. There were Greek statues around the pool, mosaic fountains surrounded by formal gardens, a private screening room big enough to host the Academy Awards, and enough bedrooms to sleep a small army of tycoons.

Octavio's mansion had changed owners seven times in the past fifteen years: possessed briefly by a TV star who had great success for two seasons; a real-estate developer who eventually relocated from Beverly Hills to a federal prison; a Saudi prince whose excessive behavior caused his father to recall him home on threat of disinheritance; a film producer who was murdered by a male prostitute; a hotel magnate who was forced to declare bankruptcy and had now returned to Sydney, Australia, from whence he came; a rock star who lost the house in a divorce settlement—and now Octavio Morales, who authorities believed (but could not prove) laundered money for a South American drug cartel. This was not wealth built on the rock of generations, but Hollywood wealth—there for a momentary dazzle and flash, a thing of dreams.

Octavio Morales, the present owner, had jet black hair slicked back from his forehead, and a tidy little mustache. He was a small man with frail shoulders and intense small brown eyes that seemed long strained by staring at columns of numbers. An enemy once said he looked like a salsa version of Adolf Hitler. Like many of the most successful men about town, Octavio Morales made it a point always to do several things at once. At the moment Kitty Hall telephoned, he was pedaling furiously on an exercise machine in his office—going nearly forty miles per hour in place—simultaneously dictating a nonstop stream of notes and ideas to a circle of people gathered around, each of whom carried a pencil and an open pad.

"Okay," he said, "on the day I take over Yankee International, I want full-page ads in *The New York Times*, the *L.A. Times* and the trades. You people come up with the right wording—that's what I pay you for, right? The point I want to make is that Yankee Pictures is going to be committed to quality product, the kind of entertainment that made us the greatest movie studio in the Golden Era of Hollywood. You got that? Emphasize 'Golden Era,' my friends, for we are going to bring it back."

Pencils were scratching hurriedly across notepads.

"Now here's something else. A week after we make the announcement, I've decided to throw a party to celebrate the takeover, and I mean a *major* party like this town hasn't seen for twenty years! We'll give it at my Palm Springs place, and get this—I'm going to provide helicopter service back and forth from Beverly Hills just so no one will have to worry about transportation. Isn't that a killer?"

"Wonderful, Mr. Morales!"

"You think so? I don't want to overdo it, of course, like I'm *trying* too hard. I'm visualizing this whole thing as a costume party, you see—being down in the desert, I thought it would be fun to have a theme—the *Arabian Nights*! Everybody has to wear a costume or they can't come. I'll put up tents all over my golf course and we'll have camels and belly dancers—the kind of orgy this town hasn't seen since Cecil B. DeMille."

Ivan Lansky, president of the Lansky Public Relations Group, who had been hired at great expense to turn the name Octavio Morales into a household word, cautiously cleared his throat.

"Ah, Mr. Morales, this idea of yours, the *Arabian Nights*—are you saying that everyone has to get dressed up like an Arab?"

"Sure. What's wrong with that?"

"It's the Jews, sir. The Jews won't like getting dressed up like Arabs."

Octavio Morales stopped pedaling and rose from his machine. He began doing some cool-down exercises on the floor.

"Look, friend, when I own the oldest and most prestigious movie studio in Hollywood, the Jews will dress any way I God damn tell them to dress. Anything else?"

"Do you have a timetable yet, Mr. Morales?" asked Cynthia Lipman, who was Ivan Lansky's assistant. "'It would he helpful if you could give us *some* idea when your takeover will be complete, so that we can get all the aspects of the publicity campaign in motion."

There was silence in the room as Octavio stared moodily at Cynthia Lipman. She was an attractive girl, twenty-three years old, recently graduated from Vassar, and certainly hadn't been hired for her brains.

"Soon," said Octavio Morales gently. "I will let you know in plenty of time."

Unfortunately, there was a big problem connected with his "timetable," as the girl so nicely put it, in taking over Yankee International. Quite simply, with the studio so deliciously close for the taking, he was stalled. He had run out of money and people who might lend it to him. He was broke.

It was an absurd situation for a man of the world. He had been captivated beyond reason by the grand old studio, seduced by the faded yellow sound stages. Oh Lord, a Hollywood movie studio could swallow *huge* sums of money! Unfortunately, his friends in South America with whom he had had such a long and profitable association—for whom he had bought shopping malls, hotels, stadiums, auto dealerships—had balked at this, a mere billion dollars that would allow them a grand entrance into Hollywood. It was unbelievable, really! His South American friends had told Octavio that the entertainment business was too *risky* for their taste!

"Listen to me," he had pleaded. "These Hollywood dreams, these movies and television shows, are just like drugs. They are pure escape, a narcotic beyond anything the world has seen. If you want to talk about powerful addiction, just remember that the average American household has its TV set on for six hours a day!"

"Yes," they had replied, "but unfortunately it is perfectly legal. Let the *yanqui* Congress pass a law making movies and television against the law, and then you will see us appear, quick as little bunny rabbits—for as you know, it is prohibition, not drugs, that is the source of great profit."

Octavio knew they were correct on this one issue. But the men from Medellin did not understand that this was more than mere dollars, more than common sense—this was magic and romance, this was Show Business. So when his old partners wouldn't join him, Octavio decided to go it alone, putting his own personal fortune on the line, setting up a number of shell companies to purchase the company's stock. Now, after six months of careful maneuvering, he was ready to orchestrate his final raid, but the cost of the seduction had been greater than imagined: he could not make his final raid. Without a new infusion of capital, he could do nothing at all. Despite the mansion in Beverly Hills, the house in Palm Springs, the yacht at Marina del Rey—everything was mortgaged that could be mortgaged, and he was hurting for money as he had never hurt before.

"Very soon, my dear," he repeated, hoping to convince himself as well as the people in the room. "By hook or by crook!" he added, forcing a harsh little laugh.

And this was the moment Kitty Hall chose to call. The call was buzzed into the private office by a secretary in an outer room. Octavio scowled. "I'll take it in the shower," he said. He was feeling sweaty from his workout, and he wished some privacy to talk.

"Darling, how are you? Did you enjoy yourself in my old homeland?" cried Octavio as a deluge of hot water beat down upon his neck and shoulders. The telephone speaker was built into the wall a few inches above the nozzle, and though it would pick up sound anywhere within a five-foot radius, Octavio tended to shout at it.

"Jesus, it sounds like you're in a tropical rainstorm," Kitty complained.

"My darling, you caught me in the shower. But never mind. I'm *always* at your disposal, day or night—I want you to know that."

"Look, Octavio, just so we have this straight—I think you're a disgusting gonzoid motherfucker fascist creep who would probably molest your own children. So let's stop the 'darling' bullshit. You know damn well why I'm calling."

"Kitty, I can assure you I do not know to what I owe the pleasure of this call."

"Think about it a moment," said Kitty.

"Is it my dearest old friend, Cory?"

"That's right. And I have a message for you."

Octavio was vigorously shampooing his hair. "What is this strange rumor," he asked cautiously, "that Cory has not come back to his lovely home in Beverly Hills, but was last seen disappearing into the jungles of my native land?"

"Oh, he's on his way home, all right," replied Kitty. "But he's taking a circuitous route, a *safe* route, so that you or anybody else won't find him."

Octavio fantasized Kitty in the shower with him, lathering his body. "My dear, you really have me at a loss. I can't imagine what you're talking about," he said breathlessly.

"Bullshit! You *know* what I'm talking about. Cory has something you want, and he's willing to make a deal."

Octavio stood very still. There was no sound from the speaker above the water nozzle.

"Er, Kitty . . . if Cory has in his possession what I think he has, what could he possibly want from me? Kitty, are you there?"

"I'll be in touch," said Kitty. "I just wanted to leave you with something to think about, Octavio."

"Kitty! Don't hang up," he shouted, a little desperate now. Of course, he had been following every move Cory had made since the day his old friend had come to him with an outrageously unbeliev- able story, seeking information for a supposed "research project"— oh, Octavio knew what he was up to, all right! Very cleverly he had allowed Cory to lead him to his uncle's lost fortune, but then his spies had let Cory slip away into the jungle at the very worst possible moment, when the prize should have been theirs.

"Kitty," he said reasonably, "we must work at this together, you and I, to save Cory from himself. You must ask yourself, can a man really steal away the dinner from a pack of hungry wolves and expect to survive? At this moment our beloved Cory even has the law after him—that cop, that ridiculous Lieutenant Rachmaninoff, is still down there looking for him, I understand."

"Don't worry about some Beverly Hills cop—we'll turn Zsa Zsa Gabor loose on him if he gives us any trouble. Just worry about *me*, Octavio, unless you do exactly what I say."

"Kitty, my dear . . . *Kitty!*"

He heard a click on the line as she hung up.

"Damn!" he screamed, but then remembered his blood pressure. Octavio stood for a moment thoughtfully in the shower, and then stepped out of the stall into a huge towel that was held open for him by a very lovely redhead who was his confidential secretary.

"Tell Martin and Pedro to find out everything they can about a Lieutenant Rachmaninoff of the Beverly Hills police," he said as she dried his back. "I want to know what he likes, what he hates, where his children go to school. Who knows? Maybe we'll even invite that son-of-a-bitch policeman to our party . . . oh yes, you may dry me in the front, my love."

3

LOS ANGELES IS A PERILOUS CITY, FULL OF DANGERS THAT ARE KNOWN, and others that lie lurking beneath the surface. Of the lurking variety, Lieutenant Nicholas Rachmaninoff found none quite as insidious as the cellular car phone.

"Look out for the BMW!" Nicky shouted at Sergeant Charles Katz. "He looks like he's talking to London!"

"Relax," said Charlie Cat. "Just let me drive, okay?"

"*Relax!*" repeated Nicky gloomily. It was incredible no one worried about killer car phones except himself. This was a city addicted to the telephone, and now, with the advance of technology, one could remain talking while driving down the freeway at seventy miles per hour—wheeling, dealing, breaking up with your girlfriend, making reservations at your favorite restaurant, doing everything in the world except paying attention to the traffic around you.

"Madness!" murmured Nicky.

It was a wet Sunday night, and Charlie had just picked him up at the airport. Driving toward the Hollywood Hills, Nicky stared in amazement out the car window at the wet neon swirl of passing L.A. Fresh from Managua, to him Los Angeles appeared like some glowing behemoth rising from the earth, a city from hell.

"And then what happened?" asked Charlie Cat.

"What do you mean, 'What happened?'"

"Nicky, for chrissake, you started telling me about your trip and then you got sidetracked with car phones. You've left me in a tropical rainstorm with a half-naked Hollywood sex goddess, a teen-age soldier, a nerdy CIA agent, an FBI plant masquerading as a record producer, and a student leader from the sixties who's just disappeared into the Nicaraguan jungle with maybe a billion dollars of Somoza's lost loot in a coupla coffins. . . . Now, Nicky, *something* must have happened next."

"Actually, if you were paying attention, Charlie, I left you in the bar of the Hotel Intercontinental, where I had just ordered a margarita in flawless Spanish."

"Okay, I'm real impressed, Nick."

Nicky shrugged. "By accident, I caught a good long look at myself in a mirror behind the bar just as I was raising the margarita to my lips. I looked terrible, Charlie, wet to the skin, covered with mud, dark circles under my eyes. I mean, I could hardly believe it was me. So I looked from the mirror to the margarita in my hand and I asked myself, 'Will this really help the situation?' And you know what, Charlie? The answer was no, booze would not help. Booze was part of the problem, not part of the solution. So I put down the margarita untouched on the bar, and I haven't touched a drop of alcohol from that day to this—nearly two weeks now."

"Just what we need," said Charlie gloomily. "A sober cop."

"I've also begun jogging every morning."

"No! Not that!"

"Absolutely. I'm getting in shape. I don't know what the hell for, exactly, but there it is."

They arrived at Nicky's ramshackle country cabin, high in the Hollywood Hills. Soon there was a fire going in the big stone fire-place, and the two policemen sat in comfortable chairs in the living room and listened to the rain beating against the roof—cold California rain that came sweeping into the Los Angeles Basin from the ocean.

There was a lot of culture shock in coming home. Everything seemed familiar, yet strangely brand-new: the ratty sofa in need of a new cover, the big wooden rocking chair, the old Steinway upright piano, the giant potted fern that had been slowly dying for the past two years. Nicky wandered over to his piano and struck up an impressionistic version of "Old Man River." He was a self-taught piano player, and he didn't really know the chords.

"Nicky, stop playing the piano, for God's sake, and tell me the rest of the story."

"There's nothing to tell, Charlie. I got called into the embassy the next day for a debriefing with this guy Bob Arnold. He told me not to talk to the press—I should just forget what happened."

"What about Rip Beasley, that sneaky bastard?"

"He wouldn't talk with me at all. I think the guy blames me that his cover is blown and he can't act like a Hollywood big shot anymore."

"What about the local authorities? Someone must have heard all that gunfire and wondered what it was all about."

"Apparently not," said Nicky with a shrug. "Or if they did, they didn't talk about it. As far as everybody's concerned, the whole thing just didn't happen."

"But Nicky, Cory disappeared, for chrissake, under very strange circumstances, and he's still missing, as a matter of fact. You can't just bury something like that."

"In Central America you can," Nicky informed him. "Did you read anything about this in the paper?"

"Just a small paragraph, page seventeen of the *Examiner*. Professor Cory Heard of UCLA, husband of famous actress, was missing on a trip to Nicaragua. They made it sound like he was holed up with a local *señorita*."

"See what I mean? When people have a reason to put a lid on a story, it becomes a nonevent."

Nicky had meanwhile improvised his way out of "Old Man River" and into "Georgia on My Mind." He played through a verse and a bridge while his partner continued to study him with grave interest.

It would be hard to find two cops more dissimilar than Sergeant Katz and Lieutenant Rachmaninoff. Charlie didn't worry about things; he loved food, women, wine, and song, and had his fill of all this and more without an apparent iota of guilt. Rachmaninoff found this fascinating. In his whole life he had never met a guilt-free individual except Charlie Cat. The good life had left him as round as a ball, happy and healthy, with a ridiculously bushy brown mustache. Charlie had an apartment in Westwood full of every electronic gadget known to man, but he had been staying in Nicky's rustic cabin in the hills, looking after things while Nicky was gone.

"So everyone told you to forget about this little incident in the rain," said Charlie. "But of course, *they* didn't know Rachmaninoff—tell him to forget and he remembers, just so he can get into trouble and be depressed. Am I right?"

"Well, I was worried about Cory. I could imagine a whole lot of people wanting him dead."

"A situation he created himself, naturally."

"Yeah, but the funny thing is, I kinda liked the guy. I mean, he was a real asshole, but the sort of asshole that made you feel good about life."

Charlie rolled his eyes. "You express yourself so well," said the sergeant. "So tell me, you stayed on in Nicaragua—okay, what did you find out? Whatever became of the charismatic Cory Heard?"

Nicky stared into the flames of his fireplace. "Maybe he's in some fancy mansion in Rio de Janeiro, or on a beach in Bali. Or maybe he's lying in a shallow grave outside of Managua. Who knows?"

"Not a trace of a mad yuppie *gringo* in a small, war-torn country like Nicaragua? Wherever he's hiding, he must stick out, I should think."

Nicky looked up from the fire. "'Have you ever tried to conduct an investigation someplace where you didn't have any authority? Where you didn't even speak the language or know the lay of the land? Man, I couldn't even find my way back to the hotel most of the time—believe it or not, they haven't gotten around to putting up street signs in Managua since the big earthquake. The way you're supposed to find things, people tell you, 'Oh, *sí, señor,* the place you want is three doors down from the old movie theater that *used* to stand before the earthquake.' That was just *one* of the hassles I had to contend with."

"Hey," said Charlie, "it's not easy to be a stranger in a strange land. Look at me—I grew up in Philadelphia."

"I was humbled," admitted Nicky Rachmaninoff. "What I learned was that without the fancy computers, without the forensic labs and the fingerprint experts and the whole network of law-enforcement agencies behind us, we are totally helpless."

"I think we'd better keep this a well-guarded secret," suggested

Charlie. "So you're saying you didn't find hide or hair of him, is that it?"

"I didn't even *begin* to find him. José wouldn't see me, his father was gone someplace, and the U.S. Embassy wouldn't return my calls. My big brainstorm was to hire a taxi and an interpreter, but that didn't lead anywhere, either, except spending a lot of my own money and having several near heart attacks on some of those roads down there. Eventually, hell, I decided I might as well come home."

So here he was—he could hardly believe it himself—back in his cabin in California, with the fire burning low and the rain playing loud and soft rhythms on the roof. Charlie, convinced at last of Nicky's failure, took another tack.

"Well, you just gotta live with a certain percentage of unsolved cases. That's the way it is, buddy—you know that."

"Sure, Charlie, we all know that."

"Look, Nicky, this thing about jogging every day, being on the wagon—you're not going through yet another midlife crisis, are you?"

"No, I'm past all that, Charlie. What I'm into now is atonement."

Charlie was getting worried. "Look, why don't you let me pour you a glass of red wine? It scares me a little to see you like this."

"I'm fine," said Nicky, though he didn't *look* fine. He stood up from the piano and walked moodily across his living room to a large plate-glass window that looked out onto the rain and the distant twinkly lights of Los Angeles far below.

"Did you remember to feed the raccoons while I was gone?"

"Sure," said Charlie. "I put out the organic garbage in a bowl every night, and sugar doughnuts twice a week. Just like you told me."

"They like sugar doughnuts," Nicky admitted with a heavy sigh. "Though, God knows, the cholesterol can't be good for them."

"You think maybe the coons need some atonement in their lives too?" Charlie asked him.

Nicky gave his partner a disapproving look. Taking care of the few remaining raccoons in the Hollywood Hills was no laughing matter. Nicky's cabin was a last outpost of rural ways, at the end of a treacherous little road called Sunshine Terrace, which wove up into the hills from Laurel Canyon. His father had built it here in the forties, and the son stayed on, protecting his half-acre of meadow and trees from would-be developers and movie moguls who would build glitzy mansions upon his country funk. The raccoons relied greatly upon Nicky Rachmaninoff, and with all the other guilt in his life—love lost, noble deeds undone, cases unsolved—he certainly didn't want the extinction of a species on his conscience as well.

"I'm going to cut the sugar doughnuts down to once a week," he said thoughtfully. "We're entering a new age of healthy living."

"Sure, Nicky. Look, I think I'll go off somewhere and get drunk and laid. I'll see you tomorrow at the office."

Charlie left Nicky standing by the big front window, staring out at the rain and the carpet of city lights below. There were people down there who were even more dangerous than cholesterol, but Nicky was thinking only about a woman with wild brown hair and dark smoky eyes.

Kitty Hall was out there somewhere in the Los Angeles night. Nicky couldn't figure her out. Did she love her husband, did she hate him, what? Her behavior didn't make sense. She was a proud woman, a woman used to getting her way. Nicky had certainly expected her to go to the U.S. Embassy and the local authorities and raise total hell until they found her missing husband—but three days after Cory's disappearance, Kitty quietly boarded a commercial flight and returned to Los Angeles via Costa Rica.

Yes, this was a mystery. Even if they were having domestic squabbles, the lady should have stayed to find her husband. But the lady did not do that—the lady left.

4

AFTER A FEW DAYS HOME, NICKY RACHMANINOFF FELT HE HAD NEVER been away. This was the way it was with vacations, even bad vacations in which you ran around in the rain and people sank teeth into your leg. Nicky's job and the city of Los Angeles seemed to engulf him, leaving Nicaragua as a kind of bright Technicolor memory that grew more and more unreal with the passage of time.

To his surprise, he rather missed the place. He missed the warm, sunny faces and the way people seemed to enjoy themselves, though life was hard. By comparison, the citizens of Beverly Hills appeared both hardened and self-indulgent. It was ironic that here, where life was soft, everyone complained endlessly—himself included. On Rodeo Drive, you might easily see a driver in a Rolls-Royce have a tantrum if a parking spot could not be found—and then pass by a homeless family on the street with an angry shrug. Beverly Hills was absorbed in its own small pleasures and ambitions, but for all this it did not seem a particularly happy place. Nicky saw few smiles that were anything deeper than a glamorous pose, and there was not a friendly *buenos días* to be heard anywhere in town—except perhaps in the servants' quarters.

Nicky felt stale and bored. Chief McGroder kept his promise and offered vacation time now that he was home, but Nicky declined. It seemed best to simply get on with things. Before long he was caught up in a routine. Each morning he went jogging for his health and atonement. Each night he refrained from alcohol. He took Tanya out to dinner on Tuesday, saw a foreign movie with Charlie on Wednesday, and Thursday he spent his lunch hour giving a talk at a local elementary school on how children might best minimize the risk of abduction by strangers.

He felt he was slogging his way through life—trying to be a good father, a good cop, a good friend, and a member of the community. It was dull, dull, dull. Even the cases that passed his desk had little interest: An elderly woman (rich) with a young husband had died in suspicious circumstances, but an investigation showed the death to be quite natural after all. A retired baseball star had choked to death on a wad of chewing gum. A young Hispanic man, believed to be a burglar, was shot trying to enter a house on Bedford Drive late at night; it turned out he was the boyfriend of the live-in maid, with nothing more sinister on his mind than a night of love.

And so it went. Nicky had seen all this before. He and Charlie did a competent job of establishing the facts and filling out the required forms. That was all there was to it. Occasionally, in odd moments, his mind would wander back to Nicaragua, and when he picked up the morning paper he found himself glancing through for news of Central America. Had a billion dollars of Somoza's stolen money suddenly been found? Had a missing professor from UCLA, husband of a well-known actress, turned up dead or alive in some unlikely corner of the jungle?

The answer was a constant and nagging *no*. No news, no word. When Cory had driven his VW van off into the Nicaraguan jungle, he might as well have disappeared off the face of the earth. Nicky brooded on this, though he knew it was really none of his concern. Charlie would find him sitting at his desk in the small cubicle that comprised the Homicide Division with a faraway look in his eye and an unfinished report on his desk.

On Thursday afternoon, after giving his talk to the children at the local elementary school, Nicky gave in to an obscure urge and picked up his phone to call an acquaintance, Inspector Lombardo of the FBI. The inspector's first name was Benjamin, but for some reason people called him Bunny.

"Hey, Nick! How's life among the rich and famous?" asked Bunny on the phone. Everyone thought working in Beverly Hills must be a real lark.

"Bunny, I'm looking for some information. One of our local millionaires is a Nicaraguan exile by the name of Octavio Morales. I'm betting you have a file on him. We sure do, though we can't prove a thing against the guy. What I'm hoping is that we can get together sometime—you show me yours, I show you mine, sort of thing."

There was a long, empty pause on the phone. Bunny was a nice guy, but FBI agents were always a little paranoid. Finally he said,

"Let's meet in person—name some nice romantic and lonely spot, Nick."

They met forty-five minutes later at the top of the City Hall tower, beneath the arabesque dome. The tower was the most photographed object in Beverly Hills, but few people knew you could actually get to the top. Nicky came up here often when he was in the mood, to get away from the overcrowded police station in the basement below. He liked to see Beverly Hills stretched at his feet: the mansions and the palm trees and the gaudy shops where you could pay three times what anything was worth, simply for the pleasure of saying you bought it in Beverly Hills.

The FBI inspector was a stringbean of a man whose cadaverous body seemed lost inside a voluminous tan raincoat he wore, though it was a warm and sunny day. Nicky liked Bunny Lombardo because he always looked gloomy and he made no concessions to living in Southern California; he dressed, talked, walked, and acted in every way as though he were still in Chicago living in a kind of eternal midnight rain.

Bunny raised his coat collar against the California sun and peered skeptically over the edge of the tower to the construction area directly at their feet.

"When you guys ever going to finish this thing, anyway?"

"Who's in a hurry?" asked Rachmaninoff. "It's only ten years past schedule. With city government the way it is, what do you expect?"

"But it's still hardly more than a hole in the ground," said Bunny. "You people must be nuts."

Rachmaninoff shrugged. "It's not easy, Bunny. Beverly Hills is a city struggling to catch up with its image—these things take time."

What they were talking about was the new Beverly Hills Civic Center, whose humble construction site lay at their feet beneath the present City Hall tower. The men and women of the BHPD were particularly anxious for the complex to be finished. At the moment, visitors to the police station were terribly dismayed to discover an overcrowded basement warren that bore no resemblance to the spiffy high-tech version they had all seen in the big-budget movies that satirized Beverly Hills. It was really a little embarrassing. The BHPD had a policy of not allowing film companies to work inside the real interior of the station, and so Hollywood had built its own version of how the thing should look—to which the BHPD was now in the absurd position of having to catch up.

The ten-year delay in the construction of the new Civic Center had to do mostly with a curious change of design. In the original plans, there was supposed to be a cultural center at the very heart of the complex, but for unfathomed reasons—and at a late date—the cultural center was discarded in favor of a large indoor parking lot instead. This caused major design problems, since the original center required no automobile access to the street, while a parking lot, of course, must. Eventually, elaborate tunnels were dug deep into the earth so that cars could come and go. It was a lot of work, but in the end the building would stand as a true symbol of Beverly Hills: hollow in the center. Where culture should have been, the world's most expensive parking lot for the world's most expensive cars!

Bunny lit an enormously ugly cigar and tossed his match carelessly down into the construction pit. This was another thing Nicky Rachmaninoff liked about Bunny Lombardo—he was certainly no yuppie.

"Well, what about Octavio Morales?" asked Nicky, after they had done enough sightseeing.

"Forget Octavio Morales," said Bunny Lombardo. "You're not going to nail a guy like that—and neither am I, if you gotta know the hard truth. You know who's going to nail a guy like that?"

"Who?" Nicky asked dutifully.

"A fuckin' *team* of accountants and lawyers, that's who, with the help of maybe a few countries like Panama and Switzerland who might be so kind as to let us look at some of their closed banking records. But since that's not going to happen, you might as well forget it. The only thing you can hope for is Octavio Morales slips in the bathtub and cracks his nasty skull."

"I can see you're an optimist, Bunny."

"Here's something funny for you—we've been getting rumors the guy's attempting an unfriendly buyout of one of the big movie studios, Yankee International. The SEC turned us on to this—they're trying to build a case about some of the shell companies he's been using to conceal his moves, but they're striking out. It's the same old problem. All trails lead to a big dead end in places like Panama. But what I'm wondering is why the hell would a smart guy

110

like that want to get involved in something as quirky as show business?"

Nicky didn't really have an answer for this. "People think show business has glamour and romance and opportunities to get laid, I suppose."

"Just like being a cop!" said Bunny with a smirk. "Now here's something to think about. *Mister* Morales has heavy protection—and I'm talking about the United States government. The CIA and this guy are like snuggled in bed together. The name of this romance is drug profits that went to arm the *contras* to get rid of the dirty Marxists in Central America. Believe me, all rumors you've heard are true, and there are a lot of people don't want Octavio busted for fear he'll talk."

"*I* can bust him," said Rachmaninoff. "He's in my jurisdiction and I don't give a fuck about the CIA."

"Do yourself a favor, Nick. Don't get involved in this."

"Sure, Bunny. What about Cory Heard? Is he back in the country?"

Bunny gave Nicky a sad look with his sad brown eyes. "You know, there's an agent you used to know by the name of Rip Beasley who doesn't like you at all, Rachmaninoff. He comes out of deep cover because he thinks he's about to make the ultimate snatch of his career, but the thing fizzles, and now Rip has to cut his hair and wear a suit and tie and work downtown in a crummy office like the rest of us slobs."

"What about Cory Heard?" Nicky insisted. "He disappeared in Nicaragua—do you know anything about that?"

"He's gone, man—I don't know where. We've been watching him twenty years now, along with all those other radical jerkoffs from the sixties. I don't know why we do it anymore. Originally the order came from the old man himself, J. Edgar Hoover. Believe me, if only for old times' sake, we'd feel more comfortable knowing where Cory is too—but we don't."

"Have you checked with Immigration?"

"Naturally. This gonif hasn't come back into this country legally, anyway—though that doesn't mean he hasn't done what the wetbacks do and snuck through a hole in the fence."

"Will you let me know if you hear anything?"

111

Bunny Lombardo gathered a gob of phlegm in his throat and spat it out in a graceful arc down onto the new Beverly Hills Civic Center below. It hit the ground with a fat kiss.

"You know what I'd like, Rachmaninoff?"

"What, Bunny?"

"I want to meet me a real live movie star, one of those sexy little chickens. Whad'ya think of that?"

"I'm sure there are many glamorous women out there just waiting for a chance to meet someone like you, Bunny. Whom do you have in mind?"

"Kim Basinger," he grinned, sucking obscenely on his cigar.

"I'll see what I can do," said Nicky.

"Hey, really?"

"What are friends for?" said Rachmaninoff. "You'll keep an eye out for Cory and let me know if you hear any more rumors about Octavio Morales?"

"Hey, no problem. But you think she'll like me?" asked Bunny. He stood taller in his raincoat, looking almost handsome for a moment.

"Bunny, she's going to love you—you'll get married and have quintuplets, and they'll all have big cigars sticking out of their cute little mouths."

As far as Nicky was concerned, stranger things than that had happened in Beverly Hills.

5

ON HIS SECOND TUESDAY HOME, NICKY WOKE EARLY AND JOGGED through the narrow series of parks bordering Santa Monica Boulevard, his old sneakers making a crunchy sound on the gravel paths as he moved through the gray morning mist. Each day he was feeling more in shape.

These small connecting parks were known collectively as Park Way, and except for the fact you had to keep crossing streets, it was a jogger's paradise, busy with elegant health fiends in boutique sportswear trying to work off the effects of the good life. This was a city that had declared war against hips and thighs and sagging bellies—in Southern California, only poor people were fat—and jogging had become as close to a communal ritual as Beverly Hills could boast.

Nicky passed women with handsome faces set in narcissistic determination, loping along the paths. Sometimes they ran with a dog on a leash trotting alongside; generally they wore earphones and leg warmers. The men, on the other hand, often jogged with a business acquaintance or two, striking up deals as they went—talking above the line and below the line, points and percentages and bankable stars.

Nicky Rachmaninoff didn't really belong here, except for the fact that the Beverly Hills police station was conveniently across the street. The fashionable joggers tended to give him a wide berth; he was not dressed right (today he wore gray sweatpants that were cut off above the knees) and he was running too hard—actually *running*, not jogging—with little rivers of sweat dripping down his face.

He ran east to the far border of Beverly Hills on Doheny Drive, and then turned around westward, back toward City Hall. This might be healthy, but it was boring as hell.

"Lieutenant Rachmaninoff! What a coincidence!" called a pleasant voice with just a trace of a foreign accent.

Nicky glanced to his side to see a compact little man with slick black hair. The man was dressed in a tidy white gym suit that had a gold stripe down the sides of the legs. There was an instrument on his wrist to record his pulse rate. This was a scientific jogger, Beverly Hills perfect, running alongside Nicky without a trace of effort.

"Octavio Morales," said the man, introducing himself. "I can't believe we've never run into each other before, when we have such a good friend in common."

Nicky had not been paying attention to what was going on around him, but he came out of dreamland fast. He noticed there was a yellow Rolls-Royce on Santa Monica Boulevard that was keeping pace with them. Behind the Rolls was a black BMW with tinted windows.

"We don't have any friends in common, Octavio," said Nicky definitely.

"Oh, but indeed we do—Cory Heard!"

"I wouldn't describe Cory as a friend. More like an annoying acquaintance."

Octavio laughed as if this were quite the joke. He seemed determined not to take offense.

"Myself, I've known Cory since college," said Octavio pleasantly. "And he was wonderful in those days, a real charmer, believe me. In New York in 1967, if you wanted to know what was happening around town, Cory was the person to know. I was just a foreign student myself, very naive, but he took me under his wing, and showed me all the wonderful things one could see in those days."

Nicky only shrugged. For the hell of it, he began to jog a little faster. So did Octavio, and so did the Rolls and the BMW.

"You see, I was a bit of a rebel myself in those days," Octavio went on chattily. "Every male in my family had graduated from Princeton since time immemorial, but I refused to be stuck out there in New Jersey—I had to go to Columbia so I could be in the Big Apple and learn what America was all about! My Uncle Tachito Somoza quite disapproved—though he, as a matter of fact, went to West Point, not Princeton. You know what they said about him, don't you? Uncle Tachito was the only cadet ever to leave West Point with an entire army as a graduation present!"

"Bully for Uncle Tachito," said Nicky Rachmaninoff.

Octavio smiled pleasantly, and checked the device on his wrist to make certain blood was still pulsing through his veins.

"Of course, Cory's youthful charisma did not age very well, don't you agree, Lieutenant? What is the old proverb? 'There are no second acts to American lives.' So true, so true! Cory seemed strangely to drift into an adolescent middle age. The Peter Pan syndrome, I think you call it. As for me, after college I returned to my country and I *had* to grow up, Lieutenant, because in Nicaragua, in order to survive, it was impossible to remain a child. And so now I look at my old friend Cory, whom I used to admire so, and I find him rather pathetic and sad."

114

"What is the point of this conversation, Morales?"

"The point, Lieutenant, is that I am trying to find him. He has quite vanished, it seems. You were there on the trip to Nicaragua; I was hoping you could tell me where he is."

Nicky smiled. "Let me take a wild guess. Your interest has to do with two coffins he happened to dig up right before he disappeared?"

Octavio Morales's smile finally faltered. "Whatever is inside those coffins belongs to my family, Lieutenant. Believe me, it is not the money I am interested in so much as the desire to reinter the remains of Somoza the First and Somoza the Second in the free democratic soil of the United States. This is a sentimental quest."

Nicky laughed. "So it's true, then? Your Uncle Tachito brought the wrong two bodies with him to Miami when he fled in '79?"

"Yes, it is true," said Octavio sadly, huffing slightly. "And the only reason Cory knew about this was that I was foolish enough to tell him. By the time my uncle decided he truly must flee the country, the Communist guerrillas had the capital completely surrounded. Quite simply, the soldiers Tachito sent to dig up the coffins were afraid to leave Managua, so they shot two peasants and put them in some fancy coffins they stole from a local mortuary. Tachito didn't discover the substitution until he had reached Miami. As you can imagine, he was not pleased."

"Isn't history fascinating?" said Nicky Rachmaninoff. "But if there was so much money hidden in these coffins, I can't understand why someone from your family didn't return for them before now."

"You must understand, my uncle was very secretive about his money, even with those who were close to him. None of us knew what was really in those boxes—Tachito would have been afraid we would steal from him. I think he believed the Sandinistas were a temporary phenomenon and he would be returned to Nicaragua by the spontaneous will of his loving people, where his treasure would be waiting for him."

"That's like Jack the Ripper hoping to be invited to join a nunnery," remarked Rachmaninoff. "So how did Cory find this treasure, if no one knew where it was?"

Octavio sighed. "This was my foolishness again. I thought he was doing research for a book—he kept coming to me for notes of introduction to various members of my family and the old ruling circle who were still alive in the United States and Paraguay. Cory did his work too well. A good historian, as you might appreciate, is a kind of detective. Cory was able to gather all the information each of us knew, and put the pieces together to figure out the whole. It was quite brilliant of him; even I could not have done it, and I have suspected there was money left behind somewhere in Nicaragua for years. Unfortunately, I am still persona non grata in my homeland, even with the new government, so I was not able to join this treasure hunt myself. I made the mistake of trusting my old friend, Lieutenant. Now he must give me that money."

"Finders keepers, Octavio!" Nicky said. "Anyway, the way I see it, if there was any loot in those two coffins, it really doesn't belong to either of you guys, but to the people of Nicaragua."

Octavio's eyes became very hard slits. "I can be very generous to my friends, Lieutenant," he said. "All I want is to find Cory, to reason with him, and if you were able to help me with this little task, I think you would find my gratitude worth your while."

"Gee, are you trying to bribe a police officer, Mr. Morales?"

"Absolutely not, Lieutenant!" cried Octavio in shocked innocence. "I simply thought that your interests and mine might collide in a rather friendly way—that's all."

"Somehow I rather doubt that," said Nicky Rachmaninoff.

"Well, think about it, won't you? Meanwhile, I'd very much like to invite you to a little party I'm throwing this Saturday at my Palm Springs house. I'd be delighted if you could come—and please bring Susan, if you'd like, and your lovely daughter, Tanya. I'll send the invitation to your home on Sunshine Terrace, shall I?"

Nicky stopped dead in his tracks and gave Octavio Morales a cold stare. The man had just told him he had his number—his home, his ex-wife, his daughter, the works. This was a threat, not an invitation.

"So good-bye for now, Lieutenant. Perhaps we shall be seeing each other again soon," he added—and with a cheerful wave, Octavio Morales cut across the grass to the yellow Rolls that had been driving alongside. Two men in dark suits stepped out of the following black BMW to open Octavio's door. Nicky was supposed to be impressed.

He stood in the gravel path, watching the two-car convoy make a right turn up Rexford Drive toward Sunset. Nicky was deep in thought when he heard a woman screaming nearby. It was not a scream of delight.

It took Nicky a moment to find the source. Not far from where he was standing, a woman in a pink gym suit was standing in front of a green garbage bin where an alley touched the edge of the park. The lady's dog had apparently led her here. The dog was a full-sized standard white poodle in a pink sweater, barking every bit as loud as his mistress could scream. Nicky felt he should probably go over to see what was wrong.

"I'm a policeman, ma'am—what seems to be the trouble?"

The lady in pink pointed to a human hand protruding from the top of the garbage bin.

"Well, well!" said Nicky Rachmaninoff.

He carefully opened the lid of the garbage bin, using the sleeve of his sweatshirt as a glove so as not to disturb possible prints. There was a man inside—a Japanese man who was dressed in a nice blue suit. There seemed to be a bullet hole in the middle of his forehead.

This was a sudden appearance of that archenemy of the good life in Beverly Hills: Death.

6

NICKY COLLARED TWO LADY JOGGERS AND SENT THEM ACROSS THE street to the police station for help. In any other place in the world, a crowd of spectators might be expected to gather around the scene of the crime—but not in Beverly Hills. As far as Nicky could determine, there was an inverse relationship between wealth and casual curiosity. Rich people truly didn't want to know what was going on in the street—it might cost them something to find out.

Within a few minutes, police cars from the station began arriving, sirens blaring for the hundred-yard sprint from City Hall, then coming to a stop on the gravel path. Nicky took a roll of bright orange tape from one of the squad cars and closed off a perimeter around the fatal garbage bin. Next he sent off two teams of uniformed officers to question the nearby neighbors to learn whether anyone had information about a Japanese gentleman in their alley next to the park.

Sergeant Charlie Katz came jogging across Santa Monica Boulevard, panting for breath.

"You're out of shape, Charlie," Nicky told him.

"Screw you, Rachmaninoff."

"That's *Lieutenant* Rachmaninoff, if you please, Sergeant. This is a homicide investigation, and one of us must pretend to be in charge."

"All right—screw you, Lieutenant Rachmaninoff!"

Nicky sighed. He felt at a decided disadvantage, conducting a criminal investigation in his jogging attire, and he could use all the props of his trade.

More official vehicles were arriving by the moment. There were medical examiners and lab technicians, police photographers, and even a few secretaries from the station, who had walked over to see what was going on. Last of all, sniffing out a story, came the press with TV cameras and microphones.

"No more sushi for this guy, I guess," Charlie observed with a shake of his head, peering over the busy lab technicians into the green garbage bin. Death was very cruel.

"First thing, we'll have to find out if he was a visitor to our fair shores or an inmate," said Rachmaninoff.

"*Citizen*, I believe, is the word you are looking for, Lieutenant. *Not* inmate," came a disapproving voice from behind. It was Police Chief Wesley McGroder. "And is this an appropriate mode of attire, Rachmaninoff?" he added, eyeing Nicky's jogging costume with grave distaste.

"Mode of attire" was a real McGroderism. The Chief was a straight arrow, tall and military, with a square jaw and close-cropped gray hair. Nicky could feel Charlie storing away the phrase "mode of attire" for future comment.

"Well, Lieutenant? *Is* this how a police officer should dress here in the hills of Beverly?"

"No, sir. Of course not, sir. Actually, I'm off duty, sir, getting in some jogging before work."

The Chief made a vague sound: "Hmpf!" Charlie was smirking into his hand. "The hills of Beverly," of course, was the most classic McGroderism of all. The men and women of the BHPD took obscene delight in this phrase, changing it around to things like "the tits of Beverly," "the pussy of Beverly," et cetera—puerile humor, naturally, that was terrifically funny only if you were a bored or overworked cop.

"I understand you were the one who found the victim, is that right, Lieutenant?" McGroder sighed, as if somehow this had to be Rachmaninoff's fault.

"It was the poodle in pink that found the stiff, sir," Nicky mentioned for the record.

The Chief was gazing back mournfully across Santa Monica Boulevard. "Good Lord!" he cried. "You can actually *see* City Hall from here! Do you know how that's going to make us look?"

"Not good, I imagine," admitted the head of homicide.

"This is an insult to the hills of Beverly," the Chief said darkly. "And I want you to give this top priority with daily progress reports on my desk each morning. Is that clear?"

"Perfectly, sir. Sergeant Katz, please make a note of that—'daily progress reports.' "

McGroder gave them each a narrow look. "All right, all right," he said. "Let me know if you need more men."

The lab people had made a preliminary study of the corpse, and Nicky was informed he could now make his own visual inspection.

"Would you like to look first, sir?" Nicky offered the Chief, with only a glint of sarcasm.

The Chief said no, he must unfortunately leave details like this to "my men," as he always called his police force, though indeed many of his "men" these days were actually women. The Chief left them to cross the police line toward the waiting television cameras. He was very good at giving what he generally termed "an impromptu briefing of the press."

Nicky and Charlie giggled at each other a little wildly before immersing themselves in the gore waiting for them in the Beverly Hills alley.

7

NICKY TOOK A QUICK SHOWER DOWN IN THE LOCKER ROOM, AND GOT himself into a more appropriate mode of attire for murder: dark brown slacks, loafers, beige corduroy jacket, white shirt, and tie. This was the essential Rachmaninoff uniform. He had been wearing a beige corduroy jacket as long as anyone could remember. When one wore out, he purchased another exactly like it—though sometimes in a slightly larger size. Charlie gave him a hard time about this, which Nicky did not understand. As far as he was concerned, the world was a perilous place in which it was necessary to anchor oneself with comfortable habits. Some people had wives; Rachmaninoff had beige sport jackets. It was as simple as that. He sometimes asked Charlie, "Which do you think is the easiest to maintain?"

Charlie was waiting for him back at their office, hanging up the phone just as Nicky stepped into the cubicle. They had succeeded in identifying the dead man.

"The Beverly Wilshire confirms they have a Yoshiro Miyaji," said Charlie. "He came in from Tokyo a week ago with two other Japanese businessmen. The manager is standing by to show us his room."

"Good," said Rachmaninoff. Searching through the dead man's pocket, they had found a key to room 706 at the Beverly Wilshire Hotel. There had also been a wallet with a driver's license in Japanese, and several platinum and gold credit cards made out to the name Yoshiro Miyaji. They were coming along at a stunning pace. They could safely conclude the motive for murder had not been simple robbery.

"Hey, Nicky, I almost forgot—there was a call for you this morning from a girl with a breathy little voice. I think she may be a damsel in distress. Get a load of her name—Epiphany Moore!"

"Sounds like a character in a soap opera," said Rachmaninoff. "Or an actress," he added more ominously.

"I think just your average yuppie puppy about town. She had a kind of sweet little lisp. She wouldn't leave her number, though, or say what it was about—she's going to call you back."

And she did call back—just as they were about to leave the office for the Beverly Wilshire Hotel. Charlie answered with a leer and put her on hold. "It's the yuppie puppy. Shall I tell her you'll talk to her later?"

"No, I might as well get this out of the way." Nicky took the receiver. "This is Lieutenant Rachmaninoff—may I help you?"

"You don't know me," said a tentative young voice.

"Yes?" Rachmaninoff prodded. "I'm a little busy today, I'm afraid."

"You see . . . this is about Cory . . . and these men, these *horrible* men. They're looking for him, you see. . . ."

Epiphany Moore burst into inconsolable sobs.

"There, there," said Nicky Rachmaninoff. "What is your relationship to Cory Heard, Miz Moroe?"

"He was my professor," she managed. "At UCLA."

"I see."

" 'Central America in Transition' . . . I took his course. I knew he was married, but, well, you know. . . ."

"Ah," said Rachmaninoff gently. He could quite well imagine the *you know.* "Now tell me if you can, who has been looking for Cory?"

"They had cold eyes, oh, and cruel, *cruel* mouths!" she cried. The girl seemed on the verge of a semi-hysterical breakdown of the English language. "And they had guns too," she added. "*Real* guns."

"Those are the worst kind," Nicky said. He succeeded in learning her address in Westwood. He told Epiphany to make herself a good cup of hot tea and wait for him. He'd be right over.

"Nicky, you don't have time now for a damsel in distress," Charlie pleaded when his partner had hung up the phone. "You heard what McGroder said. It's the stiff in the alley that gets top priority, *not* some sweet soap opera in Westwood, tempting as that might be."

Nicky was gazing out the window with a faraway look that Charlie knew too well. "You go over to the Beverly Wilshire," he suggested. "I'm sure you'll know all the right questions to ask."

"Nicky, for chrissake! This is important—an insult to the very hills of Beverly! Epiphany pussycat can wait."

Rachmaninoff turned back around from the window. "No," he said thoughtfully, "I don't think she can."

8

THE GIRL WITH THE SOAP-OPERA NAME LIVED ON A QUIET STREET behind UCLA that seemed as if it had been mysteriously preserved in a time warp from the fifties. Flags with Greek letters waved serenely outside fraternity houses. Clean-cut young men with short hair tossed footballs on narrow patches of lawn and washed their cars in driveways. This was Ozzie-and-Harriet America making a grand retro comeback. There was not a protest march in sight. Cory must have taken this as a personal affront to his own rebellious youth. Still, he had managed to seduce at least one student body.

Epiphany Moore was a pretty girl, fresh as toothpaste. The only thing Nicky could say against her was that her cheeks were just a little too large, giving her a kind of pouty chipmunk look. Other than that, she had a pert little figure and big brown eyes and an air of being nineteen years old.

Nicky found her in a second-floor apartment in a white stucco building. In her living room was a ten-speed bicycle that she moved aside so that Nicky could sit down.

"I guess Cory never told you about me," she mentioned.

"Cory never told me a lot of things, Epiphany. That's a sweet name, by the way."

"Cory calls me Pip," she admitted, giggling for some reason. Pip seemed nervous. Her eyes were red from recent weeping, but she was trying to pretend she was very chipper. A chipper little chipmunk—that was Epiphany Moore.

"Can I ask you something, Lieutenant? By any chance, have you heard from him? From Cory, I mean?"

"Not since a certain wet afternoon outside of Managua. How about you, Pip?"

She shook her head almost violently. "That's what *they* wanted to know—but I haven't, I swear. Cory promised he would call me after . . . well, afterwards, you know, but he hasn't. That's why I'm starting to get so worried."

Nicky nodded judiciously. *They*, he assumed, were the men with cold eyes and cruel mouths and real guns. He thought he might come back to them a little later.

"Did you know what Cory was planning to do in Nicaragua?" he asked.

"Do you mean . . . the money?"

"Yes, my dear, the money."

Epiphany nodded sagely. "Of course I knew about the money—that was the whole point of the trip, after all. It was quite a challenging problem, you know—how to use a billion dollars to get rid of Violeta Chamorro *and* Daniel Ortega *and* get the Sandinista revolution back on track."

"What do you mean, get rid of Daniel Ortega? I thought giving the money to Ortega was the whole point."

"Oh no!" said Pip. "Ortega's not fit to rule Nicaragua—he screwed up the revolution, didn't you know that? All his mismanagement and demagoguery led to the election defeat."

Nicky was surprised. "But I thought Cory was wild about Ortega—he kept telling me he's a poet, for chrissake."

"Of *course* he's a poet," Epiphany Moore explained patiently. "*That's* just the problem, naturally—Nicaragua doesn't need a poet, it needs a politician."

Nicky was feeling slightly stunned by this revelation. And here he thought poetry was everything in Nicaragua!

Pip took the opportunity to lecture him. "Ortega's *really* stuck in ideology, you know—I mean, it's quite sad. But that's one of the problems with communism, don't you agree? You get these very mental types who want society to behave in a neat and theoretical manner. In a sense, they become seduced by their own models."

"I was seduced by a model once," Nicky admitted.

"Were *you* a socialist too?" Pip asked.

"Let's just say I've flirted with it in one body or another," said Rachmaninoff. "But maybe we should get back to the revolution."

"Well," said Pip, "naturally we decided to use Somoza's fortune to finance a coup d'etat—wipe the slate clean and start all over again. That was the idea, of course."

Nicky nodded. "Of course," he told her.

"So we spent all last semester in class—that's 'Central America in Transition,' you know—drawing up a new constitution for Nicaragua. We devised a very interesting sort of democratic socialism, a real two-party system we felt would not only work in Central America, but might become a model for the Soviet Union and the East Bloc countries as well."

"Now, wait a second! Are you telling me this whole damn thing was planned in a political-science class at UCLA?"

"It was the best class I ever had," she told him firmly. "Of course, I was the only one besides Cory who knew we were doing the constitution for real. The others thought it was only an exercise."

Pip stood up and brought over a stack of papers from her desk. "Would you like to see it? The new constitution of Nicaragua, I mean?"

Numbly, Nicky took the manuscript in his hands. Indeed, on the front page, in bold letters, were written the words, A PROPOSED CONSTITUTION FOR THE NATION OF NICARAGUA. Underneath was the subtitle: "A Model for Communist Reform in the Era of Perestroika."

"Some school project!" muttered Rachmaninoff. "But how was Cory going to put it into effect?"

"You mean the coup? Oh, Cory has friends in the Nicaraguan army," she explained offhandedly, as if the actual military operation was the easy part, once these eager young minds at UCLA had provided the blueprint. "There's a terrible amount of disenchantment with both Chamorro *and* Ortega, you know—a lot of people just waiting for the kind of bold new thinking Cory has to offer."

"But he didn't tell his wife about this part of it, did he? Kitty only began to suspect something when they were already in Nicaragua, and she wasn't too happy."

"Cory's wife? Oh God, he wouldn't tell her a thing!" Pip laughed. "*She* thinks Daniel Ortega's like totally fabulous. . . . I mean, Kitty's okay for an *actress*, I suppose, but she *does* have her limitations. Of course, her position in the public eye is very useful for Cory— that's why he's put up with her so long, even though she's extremely shallow, of course, and they haven't been in love for ages."

"I see," said a weary Rachmaninoff. "And yet this brilliant coup d'etat has apparently not yet come to pass?"

"Yes, I'm worried about that," Pip admitted—and she looked worried, too. "I've been reading the paper every day, and there's absolutely *no* mention of *any*thing going on in Nicaragua at all! I just can't imagine what could have gone wrong."

"Well, sometimes these armed insurrections prove a little tricky to pull off," Nicky assured her. "Even for clever minds at UCLA."

"But we had it all so perfectly planned!" she protested.

"And I'm sure it was a very good plan too, my dear. Now, Pip, tell me this—did Cory ever mention Octavio Morales?"

"Of course. Octavio is Somoza's nephew. When Cory realized a big part of the Somoza fortune must still be hidden in Nicaragua, he went to him for help in making inquiries among his family."

"Wasn't this unwise, like the fox going to the hounds for help?"

"Oh, Octavio didn't know what Cory was *really* looking for! Gosh, no! Cory was pretending he was doing research for a book."

"Well, my dear, believe it or not, I don't think Octavio was greatly fooled. He seems to know pretty much everything about what Cory was up to down there. I suspect he's been keeping an eye on this situation very closely for some time."

Pip's eyes opened a little wider. "Really?" she asked. "But that's terrible!"

"Hell, everyone knew he was up to *something*. The CIA was watching him, the FBI, his wife, even me. It was a lot of fun down there, Pip. You really should have been there."

"Well, I asked if I could come, of course—but he thought his wife might mind."

"I was just joking, Pip. I was being sarcastic."

"Sarcastic?" she repeated, as if it were a dim foreign word.

"Now, Pip, let's get back to these men with the cruel mouths. I imagine they were sent by Mr. Morales, who is most anxious to locate his old college pal."

Her manner changed at once. Nicky had the impression she

would much rather be talking about *perestroika* than about L.A. hoodlums. He didn't blame her much. Pip stood up, walked to her window, then came around in his direction. Nicky noticed she had gone very red in the face. She was no longer a very chipper chipmunk.

"Pip, if these were Octavio's guys, Cory's in real trouble—and so are you. It might have been a good idea to worry about this earlier."

"I told them I didn't know where he was, but they didn't believe me."

"Did they mention their names?"

"I don't know! I was too frightened to remember."

"Well, what did they look like, then?"

"They were Nicaraguan, I'm almost certain. They both wore dark blue suits, and their shoes were shined like mirrors. I don't know why I noticed something like that when . . . when . . ."

Rachmaninoff was starting to get a bad feeling about why Pip was having trouble telling him her story. "Pip, would this be easier to say to a woman? I could have a policewoman here in five minutes."

She nodded without looking at him. "Please," she said in a small voice. Nicky telephoned Officer Cathy Kaminsky at the Beverly Hills station and told her to get over to Westwood as fast as possible. Epiphany had just put her head between her knees and was letting out long, wrenching sobs.

"There, there," said Rachmaninoff bleakly. "This is a mess, all right, but I'll see what I can do."

9

RACHMANINOFF SAT IN THE NARROW HOMICIDE SQUAD ROOM, TRYING to force himself to listen to Charlie's recapitulation of the coroner's report on Yoshiro Miyaji. He sat so still that Charlie looked up now and then to make certain he was still there.

"Death was due to a small-caliber bullet entering almost exactly the center of the forehead, with an exit wound at the base of the skull. We haven't found the slug yet, but maybe we'll get lucky. . . . Let's see, the shot came from above at about a forty-five-degree angle, with the gun two to three inches away. As if he were kneeling, Nicky. Execution style . . . time of death, between eleven-thirty Sunday night and maybe two A.M. Monday morning. Body was put in the garbage can approximately half an hour *after* death. . . . Nicky, are you listening to any of this?"

"Sure I am, Charlie."

Actually, Rachmaninoff was so bitterly angry he was hardly following any of this at all. He wanted to bash heads—specifically, he wanted to find and destroy the two men in dark suits, with cold mouths and cruel eyes, who had stripped Epiphany Moore naked on her living-room floor, jammed the barrel of a pistol up inside her, and threatened to pull the trigger if she did not tell them the whereabouts of Cory Heard. Nicky had had a thicker skin about violence of this sort when he was young. Age brought a whole new range of compassion and fury.

After some brooding, Nicky managed to transfer a good part of his wrath to Cory Heard. *You set her up for this, you bastard! You got Pip involved in your juvenile intrigue, and you left her behind to take the rap!*

Yes, this was Cory's fault, the negative side of Peter Pan. It was cute to be a kid forever, except for the mess you left behind.

"Now this is kinda interesting, Nicky. Check out the contents of the stomach—white rice, avocado, bits of crab, sesame seeds, and seaweed. What does that make you think of, Nicky?"

"A picnic at Malibu?"

"*Sushi*, for chrissake! To be specific, California rolls. Hey, whad'ya say we eat Japanese tonight? Makes me hungry just thinking about it."

"It makes me want to throw up," said Rachmaninoff.

Charlie put down the report and looked at his partner closely. "Come on—what the hell's bugging you? You gotta have a sense of humor about homicide or it's gonna end up killing you, Nicky—you know that."

"Ha-ha," said Rachmaninoff. "See, I'm laughing my heart out. Now tell me what you found at the Beverly Wilshire."

"So glad you asked. I met Yoshiro's two business associates, a certain Hideo Ibuse and Kenichi Yamamoto, who were extremely polite and civilized compared to your average Californian. They told me Yoshiro Miyaji was married and led a blameless life. For recreation he grew bonsai trees and had quite a lovely rock garden in his house outside of Tokyo. Fortunately, I took that extension course at UCLA last year, 'Zen and the Japanese Garden,' so I was able to converse on this subject with some fluidity. . . . Nicky, are you listening? What am I talking about?"

"California rolls?"

"No, that is the wrong answer—we moved on from California rolls some time ago."

Nicky sighed. "Son of a bitch," he swore, "I hate God damn sex crimes on women. I'll never get used to them. They make me feel God damn embarrassed just to be a man!"

Charlie opened his mouth in sheer stupefaction. "How the hell did we get from sushi to sex crimes?"

"Easy," said Rachmaninoff angrily. "But just forget it, okay, and tell me what Yoshiro whatever his name was doing in fucking Los Angeles. Somehow I don't imagine he came here for California rolls!"

Charlie shook his head in bewilderment. Though he had spent much of his life trying to understand Rachmaninoff, he still considered himself a beginner. He decided it was wise in these circumstances simply to answer Nicky's question.

"It's a bit sensitive. Hideo and Kenichi were reluctant to tell me what they were doing here until I reminded them that this was a murder investigation and that we in Beverly Hills are no pussycats. It turns out they're part of a new Japanese incursion into Hollywood. In brief, they've come to make a bid on one of our major movie studios."

"What?"

Nicky Rachmaninoff finally appeared to be paying complete attention to what Charlie was telling him.

"The victim, Yoshiro Miyaji, was the leader of their group. They

128

represent a Tokyo-based group of financiers—they've been buying up blocks of stock, Nicky. They want to own a Hollywood studio."

Nicky was silent for a moment, trying to remember who had been talking about a studio takeover recently. Then it came to him—his conversation with Bunny Lombardo the other day. "Let me guess which studio the Japanese are after!" he said triumphantly to Charlie. "Yankee International, right?"

"Right," said Charlie with a big grin. Rachmaninoff might be eccentric, but Charlie had absolute faith in him as a detective.

"Son of a bitch!" cried Nicky, standing up from his desk with noisy energy. He took his beige corduroy jacket from where it was hanging on a pair of deer antlers in a musty corner of the office, and adjusted his tie in a small and slightly greasy mirror. Charlie took this as a definite sign of important developments. Rachmaninoff *never* worried whether his tie was straight except when he was moving in for the kill.

"Jesus, Nicky, where the hell are you going?"

Like a charging bull, Nicky had lowered his head and was moving with dangerous speed along the corridor past Burglary and Traffic. A secretary with a box of pastries and coffee from Nat 'n' Al's had to move out of the way quickly as Nicky bore down upon her.

"Wait up, for chrissake. Fucking *mad*man!" muttered Charlie, racing down the hall in pursuit. "Where are we going?" he managed to ask one more time.

Nicky turned to him in surprise. "To the studio, of course." Then he added, "Don't be so slow on the uptake, Charlie. We've solved this stupid little homicide!"

10

THERE WERE OIL WELLS NOW ON THE BACK LOT; PART OF THE WEST-
ern town had been sold off to make a shopping center. Still, Yankee
International was an impressive movie studio—street after street of
sound stages, as vast as airplane hangars, from which dreams had
been launched outward into the world.

"I gotta admit it makes me a little sad," said Charlie, "to think of
this old studio being sold to foreigners. I mean, the movies made
here back in the thirties and forties just about defined what America
was all about."

"Sure, but the guys who made those films were mostly from
places like Poland and Bavaria and spoke with thick accents you
could hardly understand. Hollywood was created by immigrants,
Charlie, who made their fantasy of America come alive on
screen. We took the fantasy to be real, and called it the American
Dream."

Yankee International was the last major studio that was not yet a
subsidiary of some mammoth business conglomerate. The man
Nicky was trying to see, Mel Donovitch, was the grandson of the
founder, Sol C. Donovitch, who had been born in a small town in
Czechoslovakia and had come to America to make his fortune. Sol
C. Donovitch had owned this entire studio outright, and had ruled
it as his personal fief. His son, Sol Donovitch, Jr., had been forced
to incorporate, selling off shares and ruling at the shareholders'
pleasure. The third generation—Mel—hardly ruled at all, but was
merely a figurehead while the great power brokers behind the scenes
called the shots.

Though humbled by time, Mel Donovitch was still a hard man
to see. Nicky and Charlie talked their way through a platoon of
secretaries and personal assistants, and then had to cool their heels
for more than an hour, waiting for a board meeting to end.

Eventually, Nicky and Charlie were led into an office that was
the size of a tennis court. At the far, far end, a small man with wild

gray hair sat behind an enormous desk. This was Sol C. Donovitch's old office, and it was said that half the supplicants who came here lost their nerve while crossing the vast carpet on the way to the desk. The grandson looked up at them with red, owlish eyes. He had been drinking. He wore an expensive suit that seemed vaguely disheveled. There was a half-full bottle of tequila on the enormous desk among a rubble of papers.

"Lieutenant Rachmaninoff, Sergeant . . . welcome!" Mel Donovitch tried unsuccessfully to rise from his massive chair to shake hands, but gravity was working too well today. "Excuse me for being drunk, but this has been a long, hard lifetime of a day."

"Let me guess—have you lost your studio, Mr. Donovitch?" asked Rachmaninoff.

Two red eyes surveyed Nicky unsteadily, like searchlights on a foggy day. "For a cop, the guy's a soothsayer," said Mel to an imaginary audience. "*Will* lose my studio—future tense, but coming soon enough, they tell me. Hey, don't I know you? You're married to some actress, aren't you?"

"I *was* married to Susan Merril," Nicky admitted. "A long time ago."

"For chrissake—*never* marry an actress!" Mel advised solemnly. "My fourth and fifth wives were *both* actresses—so believe me, I know."

"I'll keep that in mind, Mr. Donovitch. Meanwhile, I'm hoping you can tell me about Octavio Morales—he's the guy making the takeover bid against you, isn't he, Mr. Donovitch?"

"How the hell do you know that, Lieutenant? Nobody knows that yet!"

"I assume this is a hostile takeover, is that right, Mr. Donovitch?"

Mel Donovitch glared at Rachmaninoff. "What are you talking about, hostile takeover? What else *is* there? It's the God damn American way, right?"

"Mr. Donovitch, I'm interested in any information you can give me about Octavio Morales. Perhaps if any laws have been broken . . ."

"Morales? Forget that bum, will you! Let's talk about the God damn Indians, okay?"

"Mr. Donovitch—"

131

"Don't 'Mr. Donovitch' *me*, you son of a bitch! I'm asking you who was in this country first? The God damn Indians, am I right? Now let me ask you something else, wise guy—when's the last time you saw a Miwok Indian strolling up Rodeo Drive? Huh? Or maybe a Navajo at Spago? How about a bunch of fucking Apaches having a power lunch at the Polo Lounge? You see what I'm getting at, don't you?"

"Frankly, no, I don't see what you're getting at, Mr. Donovitch."

"I'm talking about hostile takeovers, for crying out loud! This country was *founded* on the hostile takeover, so I don't want any smartass cop giving me a hard time just because I'm losing my studio to some Nicaraguan pimp."

"I see. Now, Mr. Donovitch, I understand there was a Japanese group bidding for the studio as well."

Mel Donovitch took a swig of tequila straight from the bottle, then leaned forward across his immense desk. "Japanese, Nicaraguan—what difference does it make? Let me give you an example. I was in Jurgensen's market the other day on North Beverly Drive—and I go up to this guy in the produce section to ask him about the avocados and he doesn't speak a word of English! An Iranian, for chrissake! . . . That's right, Iranians in the avocados! You see what I mean? Me, I'm gonna move to Wyoming and go live on an Indian reservation or something. . . . Hostile takeover, my ass!"

Nicky could be extremely patient when occasion demanded, and this was indeed turning into a very demanding occasion.

"Mr. Donovitch, I think perhaps I can help you. Octavio Morales is someone we've had under investigation for some time. With your help—"

The third generation of Yankee International Studios threw up his hands. "Christ, you think Octavio Morales is the *first* gangster ever come to Hollywood? Why don't you just get the fuck out of here and leave me alone?"

"How much did he pay for the studio, Mr. Donovitch?"

"A billion dollars," said Mel Donovitch, leaning back with an alcoholic imitation of a smug smile. "That's right, a cool billion."

"Jesus!" said Nicky. "Isn't that a lot?"

"Lieutenant—get hip. A billion dollars is like total diddly-squat these days. For that you can hardly buy an apartment in Westwood. The only reason that greasy bastard bought us up for some dinky little diddly-squat sum like a billion bucks was we happened to lose maybe a few hundred million dollars at the box office last year. So what! My grandfather should have lived to see the day!"

Mel Donovitch was fading fast. "What we should do is have a party," he said vaguely, "We should have a party for the Last of the Mohicans, or something . . . only who the fuck cares?"

It seemed the party would have to wait. The president of Yankee International, in the twilight hours of his tenure, rather suddenly put his head down on his grandfather's desk and fell asleep.

11

CHARLIE DROVE THEIR UNMARKED SQUAD CAR INTO AN IMPRESSIVE driveway off Sunset Boulevard and came to a halt before a massive wrought-iron gate. There was high-tech security here. A television camera peered down at them from the top of a stone wall.

"*Buenos días,*" Charlie said into a small speaker on a pole. "We'll have two Jumbo Jacks, large fries, and a side of Pepto-Bismol, please."

"I beg your pardon?" replied the metal box.

"Stop fucking around," Nicky muttered from the passenger seat.

"Hey, Nicky, police work's supposed to be fun!"

"State your business, please," said the box.

"Sergeant Katz and Lieutenant Rachmaninoff from the Hills of Beverly Police Department would like to have a few words with Octavio Morales, if you will be so kind as to open this oh-too-solid gate."

"Please wait," said the voice.

Charlie turned toward Nicky in the car. "That box has got no sense of humor," he complained. "You know, I'm not certain this

is such a good idea coming here, Nicky. I mean, what have you got
on Señor Morales except a lot of dire misgivings?"

"I'm going to breathe heavily down his neck," said Rachmaninoff
heavily. "I'm going to make him a little nervous."

"Sure, Nicky—you'll scare him to death."

After a few minutes the metal box told them they could proceed
to the house. The heavy iron gate swung laboriously open, then
shut behind them as they passed through. Through the trees at the
end of the driveway, they could see, sitting grandly on a hill, a
Moorish palace with elaborate red-tiled roofs, pseudo-minarets, and
balconies. Off to the side were a tennis court, a swimming pool, and
a small Greek temple that housed either an oracle of the gods or a
dressing room for people to change for the pool. The main house
itself looked as though it had forty or fifty rooms.

"Ah, money!" said Charlie with a sigh. They parked near a fountain, alongside the yellow Rolls-Royce. The fountain was slightly
obscene, dominated by a statue of a naked satyr with a humongous
erection, from the end of which issued forth an arch of water into
the pool. A young man in a dark blue suit was waiting for them by
a rococo front door of dark heavy wood. The young man had cold
eyes and a cruel mouth, and his black shoes were shined as brightly
as mirrors. His nose was shaped like a tomahawk.

"Señor Morales will see you in the sun room," said the young
man.

"What is your name, son?" asked Nicky with a benevolent, grand-
fatherly smile, as though he might wish to adopt a thug for his
very own.

"Martin de Vega, señor—won't you follow me?"

Martin de Vega led the way into a living room that was three
stories high, with balconies overlooking the open space in the center. At the far end of the room was a window made out of hundreds
of small panes of heavy leaded glass, rising from floor to ceiling in
the shape of a Moorish arch.

"Quaint," said Charlie. "But I bet you have a heart attack when
little kids start playing baseball outside."

This was only a figure of speech; there were no children playing
on the lawns of Beverly Hills. Nicky and Charlie followed Martin de

Vega across a rich oriental carpet and then down a long corridor with windows looking out into an interior courtyard. They arrived at a closed door that was guarded by another young man who might have been Martin's twin. The second young man also was dressed in a dark blue suit; he had black shoes shined to a high gloss, and he had a cruel mouth and cold eyes. The only dissimilarity was a deep scar across his right cheek that looked as if it might be an old knife wound.

"Gee, and what's *your* name?" asked Nicky.

The young man hesitated, looking first to Martin and then back reluctantly to the two policemen. "Pedro de Vega," he replied sullenly.

"Pedro and Martin! How about that, the de Vega brothers!" cried Nicky. "Isn't that swell, Charlie? Wouldn't you like to have guys like this working for you? Probably better than having a whole kennel of pit bulls!"

Charlie cleared his throat uncomfortably, sensing trouble.

Martin was about to knock on the closed door, but Nicky stopped him by taking his arm.

"So tell me, you guys like California, or what?"

"Yes, *señor*," said Martin stonily.

"Lots of pretty girls, huh?"

"Yes, *señor*."

"Big scary guys like you—I bet you like to fool around a little, maybe stick your pistols places they don't belong, scare some little *gringo* girl to death?"

"I don't understand, *señor*."

"Don't you?" Nicky noticed a small line of perspiration appearing on Martin's upper lip. "You know, I understand big scary guys like you. You see, it's all compensation. It's always the guys with the very little dicks who like to act tough."

Martin and Pedro had become very tense. Their eyes grew colder, their mouths more cruel. Charlie was looking as though he wished he could disappear. His idea of an interrogation was to discuss Zen and the art of the rock garden with visiting Japanese.

"No balls," Nicky was explaining patiently. "*Nada cojones*," he tried in his pidgin Spanish.

"I think Señor Morales is expecting you now," said Martin in a low and dangerous voice. "And he is a man who does not like to be kept waiting."

Martin knocked on the closed door and waited for a response from inside.

Charlie put his hand on Nicky's arm. "Stop fucking around, for chrissake!" he pleaded close. "Jesus, you're going to get us killed."

"Relax, Charlie. Don't you remember?—police work's supposed to be fun!"

12

OCTAVIO MORALES WAS SITTING IN A ROCKING CHAIR AMONG A JUNGLE of indoor plants and potted trees in his sun room. There was a small indoor fountain, and just in case you didn't get the idea this was supposed to be some kind of Shangri-la, there was a brightly colored parrot perched on the branch of a rubber tree.

"*Cocaine!*" squawked the parrot indiscreetly.

"Cute," said Nicky.

"So nice to see you again, Lieutenant," said Octavio, rising. "And you must be Sergeant Katz."

Octavio was wearing his best Old World manners. He was also wearing a white silk tropical suit, a purple ascot, and brown loafers without socks. He looked very dapper, his black hair neatly in place. When he smiled, two rows of small, predatory teeth fairly sparkled.

"Have a seat, please. Can I get you anything to drink? A glass of champagne, perhaps? Coffee?"

Without answering, Nicky circled the indoor jungle with his hands behind his back, as if he were gathering observations for a field seminar. Charlie took out a pad of paper and got ready to write down anything of importance.

"Tell me something, Mr. Morales. You let this clever little parrot fly around loose in here—doesn't he ever shit on your head?"

"No, Lieutenant, I must disappoint you— such a thing has never happened."

"Personally, I like to keep my little birds in cages," said Nicky gravely.

"Well, that's your job, isn't it? Of course, you have to catch them first."

Nicky turned around and regarded Octavio more sternly. "Where were you Sunday night between eleven and two, Mr. Morales?"

Octavio sighed. "God, this is such a cliché, Lieutenant! Am I *really* required to give you an alibi?"

"You are required to tell me the truth."

"Ah, well, let's see . . . eleven o'clock, I suppose I was just arriving home from my house in Palm Springs, where I had spent the weekend."

"Who can vouch for this?"

"My chauffeur, of course. And my associates Martin and Pedro, whom I believe you have met."

"These people work for you. Can't you give me the name of someone else?"

Octavio smiled. "I'm afraid you have me, Lieutenant! Sunday night I spent entirely with my employees. We are like a small family together. It was a quiet weekend."

"This could be a problem, Mr. Morales."

Octavio merely shrugged. He sat down once again in his chair and rocked back and forth in a most unconcerned manner while Nicky and Charlie hovered over him.

"What time did you meet Yoshiro Miyaji on Sunday night?"

"Who?"

"Yoshiro Miyaji. He was the leader of a group of Japanese investors who were bidding against you to buy Yankee International. It was very convenient for you that he was murdered, wasn't it?"

"Ah! This is the gentleman who was discovered in the garbage can! *Not* a terribly dignified end, I think, and within sight of the police station, or so the papers said—that must have been a touch embarrassing for you, Lieutenant."

"I know that you had him killed, Morales, so why don't we not waste a lot of time bullshitting? You didn't want any competition, so you had Martin and Pedro shoot Mr. Miyaji in the head and dump him in a garbage can. What gets me, though, is why a guy like you would want to own a movie studio in the first place. What do you want to do, make gangster pictures or something?"

"Ah, goodness me, Lieutenant!" said Octavio with a laugh. "This really is quite amusing."

"Is it? Actually, I know all about you, Morales. Your two little de Vega twins were busy little beavers last weekend, killing off the Japanese competition and messing up little Epiphany Moore, hoping they'd get her to tell you where Cory is. You've been clever up to now, sticking to the money end of things. So maybe you're a little desperate, taking such chances all of a sudden—killing people in Beverly Hills, molesting young girls?"

"Do I look desperate, Rachmaninoff?"

"What you look like is a piece of shit who's headed to San Quentin. I'm warning you, Octavio, we're going to be looking into this very closely indeed. I just wanted to drop by and tell you, so it wouldn't come as a surprise or anything. We're going to trace your telephone calls, we're going to follow you, we're going to know everything you've done—everything you've even *thought* of doing— this past week. It may take a little time, but I'm going to nail you—you can count on it."

"I'm quaking, Lieutenant! But now I think I'll summon Martin and ask you gentlemen to leave. Perhaps, in the future, you will be so kind as to bring a warrant with you if you wish to enter my house, and allow me the opportunity to have a lawyer present. After all . . . this is America!"

Nicky had enjoyed his little game of intimidation, but he had accomplished nothing. Octavio Morales did not seem exactly terrified of the Beverly Hills police.

Martin de Vega came into the sun room, summoned by some method Nicky did not know. Mental telephathy, perhaps. Martin stood solidly by the door, the bulge of a pistol beneath his left arm, waiting to escort the two policemen away. Nicky eased closer to him until he was only a few inches away. Martin stared back without expression. This close, Nicky could smell the sickly aroma of hair spray and see individual whiskers growing from his chin. This close, the young man's dark eyes broke up into a mosaic of yellows, greens, and browns.

"I would like to see your permit to carry a concealed weapon, please," Nicky said softly.

"I'm sorry, I don't understand."

"To carry a concealed weapon in the state of California, it is necessary to have a special permit. If you have this piece of paper, I would like to see it—now."

Martin looked past Rachmaninoff to his boss. Some rapid Spanish passed back and forth.

"Lieutenant Rachmaninoff, one moment, please!" said Octavio, stepping forward. "I have many political enemies from my previous life in Nicaragua. This man carries his weapon to protect me."

"Too bad, Octavio. You're in California now."

"But Martin is from Nicaragua—he does not know all your laws. We will, of course, apply for this permit first thing tomorrow morning."

"Sergeant Katz," said Rachmaninoff in his most official basso profundo. "Will you please disarm this man and arrest him for the unlawful possession of a concealed firearm."

Charlie flashed Nicky only the briefest raised eyebrow. Octavio moved one step closer. "You are making a big mistake to be my enemy, Rachmaninoff," he said harshly. Nicky was pleased to see some of the beautiful Old World charm fading away.

"I'm quaking," quoted Rachmaninoff.

Octavio Morales was a man who didn't like to be mocked and there was a tense moment where he and Martin looked like they might do something wild, like kill everybody in sight. But then, at a nod from Octavio, Martin allowed himself to be turned against the wall, searched, and disarmed.

"A very *big* mistake," whispered Octavio. Nicky smiled happily as they led Martin out of the room with his wrists in handcuffs behind his back. Pedro was in the hallway, and they took him too, for good luck. It was only a small victory, but if Pip could identify them as the two men who attacked her, maybe it would lead to sundry confessions and betrayals. Drive a small wedge into Octavio's empire, and maybe it would collapse.

13

BACK AT THE BEVERLY HILLS STATION, NICKY SAT AT HIS DESK WHILE Charlie booked Martin and Pedro de Vega into the jail upstairs. Officer Cathy Kaminsky was telling him some kind of riddle.

"Hey, Loo, listen to this. If storks bring white babies, and crows bring black babies, what kind of bird brings no babies at all?"

"I beg your pardon?"

"This is a joke, Loo!" she told him, and then repeated it, about the white babies and the black babies and the bird that brought no babies at all.

Nicky Rachmaninoff couldn't even begin to imagine the solution to such a riddle. He didn't like jokes that promised to be both racist and obscene, and it didn't help that Officer Kaminsky was a young woman, twenty-five years old. Rachmaninoff supposed she was attractive enough in a California sort of way: blond hair, pert little nose, the usual kind of figure. But why was she trying so hard to be one of the boys, calling him "Loo" for "lieutenant"—telling the kind of squad-room joke he had always detested?

"Well, what's the answer, then?" he conceded for the sake of morale. "What kind of bird brings no babies at all?"

"A swallow!" she told him with a smirk.

Rachmaninoff sighed. He wasn't certain what to make of the Cathy Kaminskys of this world—a lady cop in all her equal-rights glory, blue uniform bulky in the middle with service revolver, handcuffs, flashlight, and nightstick. As far as Nicky was concerned, this was not a feminist victory—this was a make-believe man, everything that true feminism should have abolished forever. Why a pretty young woman like Cathy Kaminsky would want to be a cop was beyond comprehension. If he had a chance to redo his life, *he* certainly would be something else—a jazz piano player, for instance. Or a gardener. Or a school bus driver. Anything at all.

"Please," said Rachmaninoff, "I want you to call Epiphany Moore and tell her we have two suspects we would like to see if she can identify out of a lineup. Be gentle. Make sure she understands she'll be protected behind one-way glass and they won't be able to see her. Then drive over to Westwood and pick her up."

This was the reason Nicky had summoned Officer Kaminsky into his office, but it was proving a slow process to get her into gear. She sat down confidentially on the edge of Nicky's desk, knocking over a cup of pencils with her nightstick.

"You know, Loo, I sure would like to be part of the Homicide Squad. I mean, on a permanent basis."

Nicky sighed again. "Officer, I would like you to make that phone call *now*. I'd make it myself, but after what this girl's been through, I feel it's best she talk with a woman."

Officer Kaminsky grinned. "Hey, you're kind of old-fashioned, aren't you?"

She used the phone on Charlie's desk while Nicky waited impatiently. Eventually she put the phone down and shook her head.

"There's no answer."

Nicky was getting a bad feeling about this.

"When did you leave her this afternoon, Cathy?"

"Twelve-forty-five, Loo—you'll see it in my report. After the police artist left, I offered to stay longer, but she said she was okay. She said she was going to take a nap."

It was nearly a quarter to six, according to the clock on the office wall. Pip had been alone for five hours.

"Did she say she was going anyplace later this afternoon?"

"She didn't mention it, Loo."

Nicky told Officer Kaminsky to try the number again, but there was still no answer. He tried to persuade himself there was no reason she should be at home. Epiphany Moore could be shopping for dinner. She could be out jogging. She could be studying in the library. She could be doing anything.

Nicky stood up and began pacing back and forth in his small office. The two young men in the jail upstairs would be in real trouble if Pip could identify them—and by extension, so would

141

Octavio Morales. But without Pip, the tender beginnings of his case simply fell apart. By the time Charlie came down from the jail, Nicky had managed to work himself up into a real panic.

"Come on, let's get going—to Westwood, as fast as we can. Jesus, I should have put that girl in protective custody this morning!"

"Nicky, for chrissake! I'm *hungry*," said Charlie. "I hardly even had lunch today!"

Nicky took his partner by the arm and hurried him out of the office.

"What about me?" cried Officer Kaminsky, running after.

"You'd better come along too. Let's move it, everyone. Go! Go! Go!"

Charlie was a fast driver even under normal circumstances. With the siren screaming and the red light flashing, the squad car lurched out of the police parking lot and left a trail of rubber floating through a left turn on Santa Monica. Nicky hung on to his seat belt as they fishtailed through the intersection at Wilshire, narrowly avoiding a truck from Saks Fifth Avenue. They veered right on Wilshire, past the Beverly Hilton, speeding toward Westwood Village.

Nicky began to sweat. He hated going fast unless he was driving himself. Charlie hit eighty going down the center of Wilshire, with cars in both directions scattering out of their way.

"Charlie, the Volvo doesn't see us . . . Charlie!"

"He sees us."

"*Watch out!*"

Charlie skidded sideways around a powder blue Volvo station wagon. They missed by inches. For a moment the squad car floated out of control—they were about to collide with an oncoming Jaguar—but then the tires seemed to regain their tenuous grip on reality.

"Fun, huh?" said Charlie. He really enjoyed this. So did Officer Kaminsky. The cellular telephone—that instrument of the damned—rang in the front seat, and Officer Kaminsky answered as calmly as if they were back at the office.

"Homicide," she said. "This is mobile unit Able-three-one. . . . It's for you, Loo. Your daughter."

"My daughter!" Officer Kaminsky passed the phone to him in the backseat. "Tanya?" he asked. "Are you all right?"

142

"Sure, Dad. I just wanted to ask you something, okay?"

"Well, Tanya, right at the moment . . ."

"Dad, is it all right if I come and live with you awhile? I mean, Susan's beginning to drive me up a wall, if you wanna know the truth."

Calling her mother "Susan" was definitely a new phase. Tanya and Susan had been living "temporarily" at a bungalow at the Beverly Hills Hotel for over a year now, due to her third divorce, and it was not working out well.

"Honey, look, I'll have to talk to Susan about this. . . . Charlie! Do you see the truck—*the truck, Charlie!*"

"Dad, will you pay attention? I was thinking of moving up to Sunshine Terrace this weekend, maybe. I thought I could cook for you and clean house and stuff—it'll be like we're a real family for a change."

"Darling, it sounds wonderful, but I don't know about this weekend. Look, I'll have to talk with your mother and call you back. Maybe this summer . . ."

"This *summer!*" cried Tanya.

"Honey, at the moment I'm going eighty miles an hour down Wilshire Boulevard. I'll call you tonight—no, better make that tomorrow night. We'll have a good long talk."

"Oh, Christ—never mind. I mean, if you're too busy, let's just forget it."

"Tanya . . ."

But she wasn't there anymore. His daughter had hung up on him!

"Everything all right with the munchkin?" asked Charlie from the front seat.

"Who the hell knows?" growled Nicky. "Just keep your eye on the road, for chrissake!"

Nicky was exhausted by the time they pulled up in front of Epiphany's white stucco apartment building on the quiet street behind the university. His fingers could hardly undo the seat belt, and there was a cramp in his toes from the tension of applying imaginary brakes.

"Six and a half minutes from the hills of Beverly," Charlie said, looking at his watch. "Not too shabby!"

Nicky's legs felt like pudding. He ordered Officer Kaminsky to guard the squad car, and then forced himself up the stairs to Epiphany's second-floor apartment, with Charlie at his side. He rang the doorbell and waited. When there was no answer, he rang again. Then he knocked on the door with his fist. There was still no answer. Nicky tried to turn the doorknob, but it was locked.

"Let's break in," said Nicky to Charlie.

"Nicky! Nicky! Read my lips: We . . . can't . . . do . . . that . . .without . . . a . . . warrant."

"Come on, come on!"

Charlie was the one who was clever with credit cards and picks; Nicky would not have been able to open a locked door if his life depended on it.

"You're going to have to give me your Visa card, Nicky. Mine is maxed to the limit—I've been leaving it at home to avoid temptation."

Nicky took out his wallet.

"How about Macy's?"

"*That* won't open any doors. Ah, is that an American Express card I see? Hand it over, Rachmaninoff."

"Okay, but be careful. I just got it."

Charlie slipped the card along the doorjamb, and in a moment they were inside. Like magic. The apartment was dark, and Nicky flicked on the hall light. The ten-speed bicycle was still leaning against the living-room wall, and an assortment of girlish clutter was spread out on the sofa—textbooks, novels, cassette tapes, a fluffy yellow sweater, a bra. Nicky wandered into the bedroom, which he had not seen on his first visit. The bed was unmade, with a menagerie of stuffed animals propped up against the pillows.

"Her diaphragm's gone," Charlie called from the bathroom.

"How do you know she uses one?"

"There's a new cardboard box for the spermicide gel on top of her wastebasket. Probably she's just off on a hot date."

Nicky might have agreed, but the dresser drawers were in disarray in the bedroom, as if someone had quickly packed for a sudden trip. An open suitcase was leaning up against the closet; perhaps it had been rejected for one either smaller or larger. Nicky could not find either a wallet or keys.

Nicky and Charlie meandered through the apartment in silence for several minutes. In the kitchen, a can of tuna fish had been opened and then left untouched on the counter next to a red onion and a jar of mayonnaise. Nicky didn't like it. Everything here looked as if it had been suddenly interrupted.

"Let's see if the neighbors can tell us anything," he suggested.

They spent the next forty-five minutes going from door to door. It was a small, friendly building, and except for one married couple, nearly all the tenants seemed under the age of twenty-one. In a place like this, everyone knew everyone else. A young man remembered seeing Pip on the stairs this morning; a girl had run into her in the Village in the early afternoon. But no one had seen her this evening.

It was a Korean boy named Kim who gave them their break. Kim had been writing a physics paper this afternoon at a desk that stood by a window looking out upon the street. He had just come to a conclusion about nuclear fusion and was staring out his window in deep contemplation when he noticed what he described as an "outstanding car" pulling up in front. It was a car anyone might remember: a red 1959 Cadillac convertible with rocketship fins. As soon as the car parked, he saw Epiphany run out of the apartment building and slip into the passenger's seat. She was carrying a small suitcase. The red Cadillac convertible took off quickly and did not come back.

"Did you see the driver, Kim?"

"Not well. It was a man with dark hair, but he stayed in the car."

"Was the top up or down?"

"Down, but he was a little far away. Actually, I had my reading glasses on, which makes things a little blurry in the distance."

"And what time was this?"

"Three-thirty. I remember that, because my physics paper is due tomorrow, and I've been keeping a careful eye on the clock."

"Three-thirty!" repeated Rachmaninoff dubiously. This was about the time he and Charlie were just arriving at Octavio's place on Sunset. At three-thirty this afternoon, Octavio would not yet have known that the great detective Rachmaninoff was about to arrest the de Vega brothers and drive a wedge into his empire.

"This doesn't quite add up for me," Nicky admitted to Charlie as they were walking toward the squad car.

"Look, it's probably just a date. If Octavio's guys had come for her, they would *not* have been driving a '59 Caddy convertible— face it, that's a kid's car, Nicky. A student-mobile."

"Yeah, but when I saw her this morning, the girl was upset. She was worried about Cory, and those guys with cold eyes and cruel mouths. . . . I just don't see her dropping everything and going off on a date with some young stud in a slick car."

Nicky and Charlie sat in the squad car for a few minutes without going anywhere. Nicky had a peculiar, half-hypnotized look on his face, as if a bomb might go off and he would not know.

"Well?" Charlie asked at last. "What now?"

"We'll leave Officer Kaminsky here in case she comes back. If Pip's not home tomorrow morning, I'll put out an APB."

"Okay, but relax, Nick—she wouldn't have taken her new tube of spermicide gel if she was expecting anything except a pleasant time."

"Sure, a pleasant time," said Rachmaninoff, with a long sigh. After a brief bout with optimism earlier in the evening, pessimism had now taken its crushing hold. Pip was gone, maybe forever.

14

KITTY WAS HAVING AN EARLY DINNER AT CHASEN'S, ON THE EASTERN edge of Beverly Hills. Chasen's was one of the Hollywood hot spots from the old days, dimly lit, with red leather booths and knotty-pine walls. Except that you nearly needed a flashlight to find your table, this could be a respectable restaurant back East. Kitty was here with her press agent—or "publicist," as they liked to be called these days— and a journalist from New York. The journalist had disheveled hair and kept trying to peer down the front of Kitty's dress. He was drinking Bloody Marys as fast as he could order them from the bar.

This was not Kitty's idea of a good time, but six months ago she had made a film that was due to be released at the end of the month;

now she must meet the press and show the studio how cooperative she could be.

"Actually, it's a thriller," Kitty was telling the journalist. She leaned a little forward so he could get a better view of her breasts. "It's really a lot of fun. There are no politics in it at all, I promise you!"

"No redeeming social message?" asked the journalist in mock horror.

"Quite honestly, I had some back taxes due, and I did it for the money," admitted Kitty Hall.

The journalist laughed immoderately. Meanwhile, Kitty's publicist was flashing her a little look: *Careful, darling, the studio won't like this!*

Kitty didn't care. She was feeling a little dangerous tonight.

"Tell me, Kitty, there are rumors going round about your marriage," said the journalist. "I understand Cory didn't come back from a trip to Central America. Have you two separated, perhaps?"

Kitty smiled. She wasn't certain whether the journalist was flirting or trying to get a scoop. Probably both. "You know I never discuss my personal life in interviews, Richard."

"Call me Dick, won't you?"

"Well, Dick, I always feel the movie should stand alone without the gossip. Have another Bloody Mary, Dick."

It was a mistake to come to Chasen's, Kitty could see that. This restaurant held old memories. She had come here too often in her childhood with her parents, suffering through endlessly boring meals while being utterly ignored by the celebrities hobnobbing all around. In those days she had been simply the daughter of famous parents, hardly visible, having no real identity of her own. She would sit through the dinners in silent humiliation, vowing to herself, "When I grow up I will be *somebody*. When I grow up I will be noticed!"

For the first time in years, Kitty had a cocktail, a vodka martini, that gave her a little buzz. All around her she heard the sound of money, rich people plotting ways to gather still more money to their breasts. (This was Ronald Reagan's favorite restaurant in Los Angeles, God forbid—enemy territory!) It took all her discipline not to throw her drink in Dick's disheveled face, and stand up and run.

147

At least she kept the dinner short, begging a busy day tomorrow. By eight-thirty she was in her Mercedes-Benz station wagon, driving back into Beverly Hills, kicking off her heels at an intersection, playing loud rock and roll on the radio.

"Christ! I am never going to have a dinner like that again!" she swore, though she knew she probably would. Kitty raced home to her house on Rexford Drive and walked inside barefoot, already struggling to get out of her hatefully proper dress and bra and stockings. She left a line of clothes along the upstairs hallway to her bedroom, and by the time she reached her dressing room she was completely naked.

At the back of her closet was a one-piece black leather jumpsuit lined inside with fur. Kitty stepped into this naked—it fit her like a second skin—pulling up the zipper from crotch to neck, careful not to snag her pubic hair. When this was done, she had to sit down to get into a pair of high black motorcycle boots that came up over the leather leggings of her jumpsuit. An outfit like this made you feel different. A little dangerous. Ready for anything.

The motorcycle was in the garage, a big BMW, 750cc—not a lady's bike. Kitty straddled the machine and slipped the helmet over her head. With the visor down, she was no longer Katherine Hall, famous person, but just a black shadow in the night, anonymous—anyone at all. She was ready for a ride on the wild side.

Kitty cruised up Rexford to Sunset, and then turned west toward the beach. She rode low, feeling the vibrating power between her legs, leaning into the deep curves of Sunset. The dinner at Chasen's was forgotten. Fame and fortune and middle age slipped away. Kitty drove a little too fast, taking a chance on the CHP. On the motorcycle she felt as free as the wind.

She drove like this down Sunset and then up the Pacific Coast Highway, all the way to the Malibu pier, where she pulled up alongside a car that was parked in the small shopping complex across the street. The driver in the car didn't recognize her until she pulled off her helmet and let her luxuriant long brown hair shake free.

"Well?" she asked. "What have you decided?"

"I've decided yes," said the man. "As long as we can work out the details, of course. What the hell, let's deal!"

Kitty nodded. "That's a wise decision. However, I'm just a little worried about the cop—Rachmaninoff. He could get in the way."

Sitting in his yellow Rolls-Royce, Octavio Morales treated Kitty Hall to his most charmingly dangerous smile.

"Don't worry about Rachmaninoff," he suggested. "Why don't you just leave him to me?"

15

IT WAS A DARK NIGHT UP ON SUNSHINE TERRACE. THE COLD BLACK glass of the front windows reflected the flickering light of his fireplace. A Mozart piano concerto came softly over the radio.

Nicky Rachmaninoff sat in a rocking chair with his feet up on a coffee table. In his lap was a forty-page forensic report on Yoshiro Miyaji. For the past twenty minutes he had been trying to follow a fiber analysis of minute particles of material found beneath Miyaji's fingernails. It wasn't exactly fascinating late-night reading, and Nicky's mind had been wandering.

He was thinking he should call Kitty Hall. If Octavio was on the warpath, looking for Cory, he might come to her the way he had come to Pip—hard and ugly. No matter what he thought about the lady—and he thought many and various conflicting things—she should be warned she might be in danger.

At last, Nicky put down the forty-page report on Yoshiro Miyaji on the coffee table, and picked up his telephone. Kitty's unlisted number in Beverly Hills was answered by an efficient-sounding lady by the name of Esther. Nicky wasted nearly ten minutes trying to convince this person it was extremely important he be put through to Ms. Hall. However, Esther gave the impression that nothing he could say could be of much importance.

"Look, I'm the chief homicide investigator for the Beverly Hills Police Department," he finally had to say.

"Yes, I *know* who you are, Lieutenant Rachmaninoff." In fact, she seemed to know only *too* well. "I'll leave a message you called, and that's all I can do at this hour. Are you aware it's nearly eleven o'clock . . . at *night?*" she felt compelled to add.

"My dear, I'm aware it's not the morning. But I have reason to believe Kitty may be in danger."

"First of all, I am not your dear. And second, we are well accustomed to all kinds of crypto-fascists making threats upon Ms. Hall's life. So I appreciate your concern, but I assure you we are all quite safe, thank you, without your patronizing help."

"Esther, listen to me—is she home? If you just tell her I'm on the phone and that it's important, I'm sure she'll want to talk with me."

"Somehow I rather doubt that. Good night, Lieutenant."

Nicky was left with a dead telephone in his hand. It reminded him of another female who had hung up on him today—his daughter. He was thinking what a lousy father he was, when a familiar movement at his front window made him look up and smile. There was a raccoon pressing her small black nose against the glass, looking in at him with her bandit eyes. It was Agatha, an old friend, and after an unpleasant day of human beings, she was a welcome sight. Agatha rather cleverly managed to stand up on her hind legs, with her front paws on the window, so that Nicky could see the striped and furry softness of her stomach. She was trying to tell him she was hungry.

"You're too fat, Agatha," Nicky told her. "I shouldn't really feed you."

But Nicky was a soft touch where his raccoons were concerned. He stood up from his rocking chair, glad for a chance to stretch. He had brought home a pizza in a box for dinner, but had left most of it uneaten at the thought of all the cholesterol and calories. Probably he shouldn't give it to Agatha either, though he knew raccoons were particularly fond of pizza, and on a cold night like this, Nicky just didn't have the heart to say no.

"Okay," he said, going toward the kitchen for the box. "But from now on it's raw vegetables and brown rice, my friend. We're going to get in shape together, you and I."

Nicky was carrying the flat cardboard pizza box from his kitchen to the back door when several inexplicable things began to happen. First, Agatha jerked her head to the side, looking off somewhere into the yard. Then there was a shot, the whiplike crack of a pistol.

Agatha spun around violently, set in motion by some invisible force. She came to a rest, rolled on her side, twitched once, and was still.

It happened so fast, Nicky hadn't quite taken it in. He was still moving uncertainly from the kitchen, pizza box in hand.

"What the—"

He was racing now, running toward the back door, flinging himself out into the night. Agatha didn't move when he approached and knelt by her side. Gently he reached out and touched her soft fur. When he drew his hand back, it was covered with raccoon blood.

He still couldn't quite believe this was happening. "Agatha," he said dumbly, "you've been shot!"

He became aware of a roaring in his ears—it was his heartbeat pounding in his ears like an ocean. He stood up, clenching his fists, breathing hard, peering out wildly into the dark brush at the side of his house. He was beginning to believe it now.

"You motherfucker!" he screamed. "Where the hell are you?"

There was no answer from the brush. Nicky was so savagely angry, he did not stop to consider that the gun that had killed Agatha might now be trained on him. His own voice was nearly unrecognizable to him.

"*Motherfucker!*" he howled again.

At the front of the house he heard a car door slam and an engine come to life. Nicky raced through the brush toward the road, not noticing when a tree limb scratched against his cheek, drawing blood. He ran as fast as his legs would take him, but he was too late. He came out by his carport only to see the last red glow of a taillight disappear down Sunshine Terrace toward Laurel Canyon.

"You killed my raccoon!" he bellowed.

Nicky's old two-seater Austin-Healey was standing in the carport, and he flung himself into the front seat, ready to race off in pursuit. But he wasn't thinking clearly—he didn't have his car keys, but only a flat pizza box in his hand.

You can't start a car with a pizza box, no matter how angry you are.

"Damn!" He flung the box onto the ground and ran to the front door to fetch his keys from the top of his bedroom dresser, but here was another obstacle—the front door was locked for the night! How could he be so stupid, so slow? Nicky had to retrace his steps around

151

to the back of the house, and by the time he found his keys, he knew, even in the white blur of anger, that it was too late to catch the fleeing car.

Nicky stood nearly rigid with rage. Then he did what responsible citizens were told to do in emergencies of this kind: he dialed 911.

"This is Lieutenant Rachmaninoff of the BHPD." He had to force himself to speak slowly. "I would like to report a shooting at my house."

Nicky heard the beep of a tape recorder taking this in for future reference.

"Your address, please?"

"Seven ninety-four Sunshine Terrace," he managed. "That's at the very end of the road."

The operator had a lot of questions. She wanted to know his telephone number, she wanted him to describe the shooting. Operators at 911 were trained to keep the caller on the phone as long as possible.

"Damn it, it's Agatha!" Nicky cried. "She's been shot, I tell you. Just get the Sheriff's Department up here as fast as you can. Tell them to block off Laurel Canyon and get me a God damn chopper— they can land on my back lawn. I'll direct the search from the air."

"Lieutenant Rachmaninoff . . ."

"I don't have time for this shit," he screamed, slamming down the phone. He was out of breath. He hurried into his bedroom and found an off-duty gun among his underwear, a 9-mm automatic. The full clip, loaded with hollow-point shells, was kept separate from the gun, among his socks. Nicky's hands were shaking so badly it took him three tries to get the metal clip into the butt of the gun. He stuffed the pistol into his pants and walked outside to wait for help to come.

"Come on! Get here already!"

It seemed to take forever before he heard the wailing of police sirens coming from a long way off, converging upon the house on Sunshine Terrace. The sirens grew steadily louder, a symphony of death and disaster. Overhead, Nicky heard the rotary blades of a helicopter beating the air. A spotlight flashed down on him from the sky, catching him in a bright circle.

Cars now were pulling up fast into his driveway, just as the helicopter was setting down. Two men in sheriff's uniforms came running up to him, holding on to their hats to keep them from being blown away by the helicopter wash.

"Where's the victim, Loo?"

"Behind me on the lawn. It's Agatha," he told them, unable to look himself.

"Where?"

Couldn't they understand English? An ambulance had arrived, and two attendants came running over with a stretcher.

"Who's been shot?"

"It's Agatha," said Rachmaninoff again, more wearily with every repetition. "Behind me on the lawn."

"I don't see anyone," said one of the sheriffs. And then, in a moment, came a significant: "Oh!"

All the sheriffs and paramedics came to a confused halt. One sheriff gave another sheriff a meaningful look. Then they all turned to stare at Nicky Rachmaninoff.

16

BY MIDNIGHT IT WAS CLEAR THAT WHOEVER HAD SHOT AGATHA HAD disappeared into one of the many twisty canyon roads in the Hollywood Hills. The sheriffs gave the search their best effort once the initial misunderstanding was cleared up, but there was simply nothing to go on. Nicky couldn't even tell them what kind of car the gunman was driving.

He sat by himself in his darkened living room after everyone had left. A few embers burned in the stone fireplace. He suddenly had a very clear idea that he had to get out of his house. If he stayed here another moment, he was going to start smashing furniture.

He found the keys he wished he had had earlier, and started up the Austin-Healey in the carport. The engine came to life with a deep growl that was more like an old airplane than a sports car. The Austin-Healey had been around even longer than he had been wearing beige corduroy jackets; he had kept it in mint condition over the years, at much greater expense than it would have cost to buy something new. But Rachmaninoff didn't want something new. Rachmaninoff was drawn to old familiar ways.

He drove down the canyon curves hard and fast, slowing only when he hit Sunset going west into Beverly Hills. The neon glitter of the Strip looked sad and lonely this time of night, like a mournful jazz ballad. Nicky had a feeling that what he was about to do was not a good idea, but he did it anyway—he drove straight to the Beverly Hills Hotel.

He let the valet take his car, and walked up the long ramp to the lobby, and then through the lobby toward the bungalows in back. A security guard was about to stop him, but then nodded instead. Nicky didn't look like a guest, particularly tonight, but hotel people know their local police, and they let him through.

Susan's bungalow was on a path behind the swimming pool. It had once been occupied by Howard Hughes in one of his more eccentric periods; he had come here to hide, leaving messages for people in a nearby tree. Nicky paused before Susan's door. He had already decided that if her bungalow was dark, he would turn around and walk away—he would take it as a sign from heaven. But there was a warm yellowish light creeping out from behind the curtains in the living room, and so Nicky rang the bell.

"Who is it?" Susan called from inside.

"It's me."

There was the sound of flurried motion from inside. In a moment, Susan opened the door a little, but she very pointedly did not invite him in. She was wearing a thin robe with clearly nothing underneath. Her hair had a tossed look to it.

"Nicky, *what* are you doing here at this time of night? You should have called first!"

Through the half-open door, Rachmaninoff had an unfortunate glimpse of a man on Susan's sofa who was not wearing a shirt. It was a young man with this year's famous face—an actor who could not have been more than twenty-five.

"What is it, Nicky? What's wrong?"

"It's okay, Susan. Look, I'm sorry to disturb you this late. Maybe I'll give you a call tomorrow."

"Is it Tanya? She's staying at Kirsten's tonight." There was a little edge of panic in Susan's voice.

"No, no—Tanya's fine, as far as I know. I just wanted to talk, but it's not important. I'll call you, Susan."

Nicky waved halfheartedly, turned, and walked away.

"Damn it, Nicky! *You should have called first!*"

He walked slowly back along the path. Little yellow lights among the trees lit the way. From somewhere in the main part of the hotel, a woman's silvery laughter floated across the night. Rachmaninoff fought back an overwhelming urge to sit down on the path and cry.

Behind him, he heard the sound of bare feet running after him on the path. It was Susan, wearing a raincoat that she had thrown around her.

"Damn it, stop a second—I have something to tell you."

"Susan, it's okay. I know I don't have any hold on you. You should get back to your guest."

"Listen to me, Nicky. It's Cory—he called today. I was out, but he left a message on my answering machine."

"Cory—are you sure? Is the message still on your machine?"

"I think so, Nicky. I thought you'd want to know."

Without another word, Nicky ran back along the path toward Susan's bungalow. She had left the door unlocked, and he walked right in. The young man with the famous face leaped up from the sofa and spilled the glass of wine in his hand.

"Easy," he said. "Don't do anything foolish. I can explain this, I really can!"

Nicky hardly glanced at him but went directly to the answering machine on the kitchen counter. He rewound the tape, listened to a quick message from Susan's agent, and then was startled to hear a familiar voice:

"Hey, babe! I guess you must be surprised to hear from me after everything that's gone down and all, but you know us bad pennies turn up eventually. So I hope you're not mad or anything . . . just wanted to let you know I was okay, and I'll be in touch real soon. *Ciao!*"

Nicky reversed the tape and played the message again. There was something strange about this that he couldn't quite pin down, but there was no doubt about the voice.

Hollywood's most elusive liberal was back in town.

Part Three

LOVE IN A CACTUS GARDEN

1

TANYA RACHMANINOFF TOOK ANOTHER SIP OF COGNAC FROM A HUGE snifter and watched Sunset Boulevard pass by the tinted glass of her limousine window.

"Boring Beverly Hills!" she thought gloomily. "Land of eternal bad taste!"

Tanya and her friend Bunky Baker were still in their school uniforms—white blouse, blue skirt, knee socks, and loafers—coming home from school with a cigarette in one hand and a glass of Hennessey's VSOP in the other, reclining in the rear of a white Lincoln Continental limousine that had everything a young girl could want: bar, television, stereo, and telephone. The car belonged to Bunky's father, who owned a chain of department stores. At the moment, the young ladies hoped this man of commerce would not notice the lower level of the bottle of cognac they had discovered in the small cabinet next to the TV. Both girls had imagined cognac was something like wine, and now were trying not to cough or grimace, pretending this was exactly what they had in mind.

The backseat telephone beeped. It was Kirsten Cooleridge calling from her father's Rolls, heading home from school in the opposite direction. Kirsten was full of news about Dwight Worthington III, whose parents had just given him a new Ferrari for his sixteenth birthday. The car was totally rad, but did not entirely compensate for the fact that Dwight Worthington the Third (as Kirsten had been telling everybody all week) had the smallest penis in Bel Air.

"Kirsten should know," muttered Tanya, handing the phone over to Bunky. In the mood she was in, she couldn't deal with Kirsten right now. Tanya Rachmaninoff stared moodily at the great silent houses along Sunset Boulevard. Everything seemed oppressive, rich, and still.

"God, who cares about any of this, anyway?" said Tanya suddenly.

"What?" asked Bunky, putting down the phone a moment.

"Look at all these dumb mansions!" said Tanya. "I mean, why should some people have so much more money than they'll ever possibly spend, while the rest of the world is like *totally* starving? Honestly, Bunks! Beverly Hills is *embarrassing*, that's what it is. I can't wait to get out of here and go live someplace *real.*"

"Listen, I'd better call you back," said Bunky to Kirsten, sensing a crisis.

"I mean, why doesn't Dwight Worthington sell his stupid Ferrari and give the money to poor children in the inner-city ghettos? That's what *I* would do," said Tanya. "Personally, I'm going to give away all *my* money the moment I'm twenty-one."

"You know, you'd better think about that," warned Bunky, who had inherited at least some of her father's mercantile sense. "You've got to have *some* money, Tanya, or how will you go to concerts and things?"

"I don't care about concerts and things," said Tanya with a slightly martyred sigh.

The limousine dropped her off at the Beverly Hills Hotel, which appeared unspeakably gauche to her today; if her mother had any class about hotels, they would be residing at the Bel Air, at least. But an actual home would be the best of all.

Her mother, thank God, was not back from the studio yet; she was finishing up another dumb TV movie. Tanya changed out of her school uniform into blue-jean cutoffs so short they barely covered her hips, an oversized T-shirt, and dark glasses with pink speckled teardrop frames. Barefoot, she ventured out of the bungalow and along the back paths of the hotel, toward the swimming pool. She stretched out sullenly on a deck chair, lit a cigarette, and watched the world go by.

The Beverly Hills Hotel was certainly full of tourists these days. To Tanya it seemed as though any overdressed couple from Kalamazoo who could come up with the price of a room could check in here and live out their Hollywood fantasies for a few days. They all thought they were going to be hobnobbing with the stars at the Polo Lounge, for chrissake, but all they saw, of course, were gawkers like themselves.

"Gaucheness *hardly* even describes it!" said Tanya Rachmaninoff to herself, blowing out smoke. From behind her dark glasses she watched a yuppie couple on deck chairs next to her gaping at a lady in a bikini swimming laps in the pool.

"Isn't she the one on 'Falcon Crest'?" whispered the yuppie woman to the yuppie man.

"I think so," whispered back the man. They looked as though they were about to have an orgasm.

Tanya knew exactly why she was in such a bad mood. Boy, was she angry at herself! After being back now from Nicaragua more than two weeks, none of her friends had even noticed the mysterious and semi-tragic gleam in her eye; they had missed the new womanly grace with which she moved. Finally, today, in the hall between Latin and lunch, she had been forced to break down and tell them: "Guess what? I *did it* in Nicaragua."

"Did what?" asked Bunky Baker.

"Jesus! I screwed, for chrissake! I got laid—I went to bed with this really good-looking soldier."

"What kind of car did he drive?" asked Kirsten Cooleridge.

Could you believe it? This was the depth of romantic involvement in Beverly Hills: *What kind of car did he drive?* Of course, what made Tanya *really* mad was that she had played right into the whole trip.

"A Mercedes," she replied airily—and since José's car *had* been a Mercedes (once), this wasn't a complete fabrication. Unfortunately, Tanya had gone on to tell some real whoppers about the sex, padding her descriptions with a letter she had once read in *Penthouse.*

Boy, I'm a terrible person! she admitted to herself glumly. "Giorgio, bring me a Bloody Mary, for God's sake," she said wearily to her favorite waiter, who was cruising past the pool.

"Are you twenty-one yet, Miss Tanya?" Giorgio asked with a good-natured grin. They had been through this before. "I think maybe I should bring you a *Virgin* Mary."

"I'm old enough," she told him, posing a little, flirting like hell. Giorgio was actually terrifically good looking, and there were all kinds of rumors about his room-service specials for rich older ladies.

Giorgio laughed at Tanya and said he would bring her a cherry Coke. Tanya lit another Marlboro. The couple on the deck chairs next to her had been unable to reserve a table at Spago's or The Palm, and were now studying a guidebook, trying to choose between La Scala and Mr. Chow's for dinner.

Where did these people come from?

Giorgio returned with a Coke that had no less than five maraschino cherries and a paper umbrella sticking out of the glass.

"You'd better be nice to me," he said, "or I won't give you your note."

"What note?"

"I got a nice note for you from a boy who's in the park across the street."

Giorgio held out the note like bait. Tanya snatched it out of his hands, read it hurriedly—read it a second time—and then jumped up from her deck chair.

"Hey, you forgot to sign the tab, Miss Tanya," Giorgio called after her.

"You sign it for me," Tanya called back. "And give yourself twenty-five percent!"

Tanya dashed in the side door to the Polo Lounge and then through the main lobby, toward the street. One of the assistant managers—a stuffy one she didn't like—stared in obvious disapproval at her blue-jean cutoffs and bare feet, but Tanya was moving too fast to receive a lecture. She went out the front door, down the long, awning-covered entrance, said hello to the boys who were parking the cars—*they* didn't mind if she was barefoot—and took a shortcut across a flower bed to Sunset Boulevard below. Most likely the assistant manager would complain to her mother about her lack of proper attire, and not using the hotel paths and all that, but Tanya really didn't have time for the bullshit right now.

Across Sunset Boulevard from the hotel, Will Rogers Park was an island of green, sitting in the middle of the complex intersection where North Canon, Beverly, Lomitas, and Sunset all came together. Tanya was narrowly missed by a Porsche as she did a quick sprint from the flower beds on one side of Sunset to the park on the other.

Her heart was pounding. She didn't see him at first. There was a nanny in a white uniform, pushing a baby carriage. Two joggers were on the grass, doing warm-up exercises. Tanya circled the entire island . . . and there he was, dressed in jeans and flip-flops and a really gaudy surfer shirt.

He was grinning at her, leaning against a car that was as gaudy as his shirt—a red 1959 Cadillac convertible with rocket fins and tail-lights like afterburners.

"Oh my God, I don't believe it!" she said, her voice just a little unsteady.

"*José!*"

2

WEDNESDAY MORNING, RACHMANINOFF'S EYES WERE BURNING FROM lack of sleep. He sat in the narrow cubicle that was the Beverly Hills Homicide squad room, drinking black coffee and trying to wake up.

Epiphany Moore had not returned to her Westwood apartment last night, and at nine o'clock this morning he was forced to release Martin and Pedro de Vega from the jail upstairs. At nine-thirty, Nicky sent out an all-points bulletin to every police station in the state of California describing the missing girl, who was last seen entering a red '59 Cadillac convertible.

Once the APB was on the wire, Nicky attempted once again to telephone Kitty Hall, and discovered she was no easier to reach this morning than she had been last night. Various assistants and maids took his name and promised to inform Ms. Hall he had called. Nicky had a surrealistic sense they gleefully tossed his messages into the garbage the moment they hung up the phone.

In midmorning, Charlie went out to Nat 'n' Al's and brought back more coffee, pastries, and *The Hollywood Reporter*. He tossed the trade paper onto Nicky's desk.

"Better take a look," he advised.

On the front page, in trade-paper jargon, Nicky read the head-line: NEW PREZ IN YANKEE TAKEOVER.

Skimming through the article, Nicky learned that in a surprise move, Octavio Morales—described as "a California real-estate

162

tycoon"—had made a successful takeover bid against Yankee International Studios, buying the company for a rumored one billion dollars, which was nearly twice the face value of the stock. The move was particularly surprising, Nicky read, in that until two days ago a Japanese investment consortium had been expected to buy the financially ailing studio, which had lost $130 million in the past fiscal year through a string of big-budget summer blockbusters that had gone bust without going around the block.

"Take a peek at the gossip column on page five," Charlie told him. "Octavio's giving a big bash this Saturday in Palm Springs to celebrate his new life as a studio boss. He's flying all his guests down from Beverly Hills in a fleet of helicopters. They say it's going to be the party of the year."

"Well, bully for Octavio! What did you do, Charlie—read *The Hollywood Reporter* cover to cover?"

"Hey, look, man—it pays to be informed. Who knows? Maybe *I'll* own a studio one day."

Rachmaninoff was in a deep grouch when the watch officer, Lieutenant Lewis Bryant, stopped by with a problem: there was a demonstration under way at the South African consulate on Wilshire Boulevard, which unfortunately was just inside Beverly Hills city limits. Every cop in Beverly Hills wished fervently that South Africa had had the tact to set up shop in far-off Cucamonga, or perhaps even glamorous Tarzana, a town named after the King of the Apes, where they might feel more at home. As it stood, nearly three hundred demonstrators were presently blocking the hallway so that no one could get in or out of the building, and the BHPD was required to go in there and enforce the law.

It was a damnable situation. Apartheid was an unpopular policy, there were TV cameras everywhere, and there were some famous faces among the protesters—God forbid the BHPD should start beating up movie stars on network TV! Nicky's mission, should he choose to accept, was to clear the hallway in front of the consulate without making the Beverly Hills police look like a bunch of racist slime.

"I don't know, Lew," said Nicky to the watch officer. "I got a top-priority homicide case and I really don't have time for this."

"Rachmaninoff, my man, this is the kind of situation in which we all must help out. You want to see the hills of Beverly overrun by a bunch of dangerous liberals? Where's your team spirit?"

Nicky got a very bright idea. "Speaking of dangerous liberals, is Kitty Hall involved in this demonstration, by any chance?"

Lieutenant Bryant perched on the edge of Nicky's desk. "You must be psychic, Rachmaninoff. She's one of the leaders."

"Psychotic's more the word," he grumbled.

"Well, pretty Kitty's inside the building, blocking access to the consulate door. South Africa has complained to the State Department, which has passed on the complaint to us. So what do you say, Nick? Probably you even know the lady."

"Well . . . this is little inconvenient, Lew. I have a witness in Westwood who disappeared last night. . . ."

"You want some detectives, for chrissake, to give you a hand? How many, Nick? Gimme a number, and they're yours!"

"Four detectives would be an awfully nice gesture, Lew. The witness is a UCLA student—I need you to check out all her friends and places she might go. In particular, I want to know if she's been seeing a guy who drives a red '59 Cadillac convertible."

"A deal," said Lieutenant Bryant. "*If* you can get Kitty Hall away from blocking the consulate door without making the BHPD look like the Ku Klux Klan."

"Relax, Lew—Kitty and I are inseparable," Nicky assured him. "This is a lady who hardly makes a move without coming to me for advice."

3

OUTSIDE THE SOUTH AFRICAN CONSULATE ON WILSHIRE BOULEVARD, Nicky found a classic sixties sit-in in progress. Kitty Hall, dressed in jeans and a baggy sweater, was sitting in the hallway, leading several hundred voices in a rousing chorus of "We Shall Overcome."

Nicky had to step carefully over the bodies to make his way

through the crowd toward her. "We Shall Overcome" happened to be one of his favorite songs, and he had to overcome an urge to sing along. He was glad he was in plain clothes—beige corduroy jacket, of course, and slacks—not looking particularly like anyone's idea of a cop. Even so, he heard someone say the oink-oink word as he passed—it was a well-known screenwriter who was probably congratulating himself for his fine liberal views.

"Pig!"

"Hack!" Nicky returned in kind—for two could play this game.

Rachmaninoff found it slow going, wading through this crowd of limousine liberals toward Kitty Hall. He was careful not to step on a single toe, fearful of lawsuits and charges of police brutality. The singing was over by the time he reached her.

"Rachmaninoff!" she said scornfully. "Have you come to arrest me?" Her beautiful face expressed unlimited disdain, as if this were exactly the sort of thing one might expect from Rachmaninoff.

Kitty was in a rather meditative position, with her spine straight, palms facing upward on her knees, as if she were doing yoga. Nicky lowered himself onto one knee by her side.

"You didn't return my call," he chided her. "I've been trying to get you all last night, all this morning. I think Cory's back in town—he left a message on Susan's answering machine. I wanted to know if you've seen him."

"What does Cory have to do with apartheid?"

"Nothing, as far as I know. Kitty, there are conservative right-wing assholes and there are liberal left-wing assholes. It's an equal-opportunity field, and I'm beginning to think Cory belongs in the second category."

"This is supposed to be profound, Rachmaninoff?"

"Profound's too big a word for a simple policeman," said Nicky. "So tell me—have you seen him?"

"I didn't *see* him, if you must know. I *talked* with him on the phone Sunday morning."

"Did he say where he was?"

"He was at a pay phone at the bus station in Hollywood. He tried to hit me up for money."

"*Money?*" asked Rachmaninoff in surprise. "Now, money's something I thought Cory would have plenty of!"

"Not cash, apparently."

"Well, did you say yes or no?"

"Is this really any of your business, I wonder?"

"I think so, unfortunately. Good buddy Octavio is shaking up this town plenty, trying to find the old college pal who took the bodies and ran. Me, I got a little midnight visit last night I didn't like at all. Somehow, when Cory got his swell idea to play Robin Hood, he forgot about those of us left behind to pay the price. But that's idealism for you, I guess."

"What would *you* know about idealism?" asked Kitty Hall.

"Please, can't you just tell me if you're planning to see Cory and help him out with his cash flow?"

"No way, Rachmaninoff. I'm a little sensitive about the money issue with men—I've been burned a few times."

"Did he make any arrangements to call you or see you again?"

"No—and if you don't mind now, I'd like to get back to the matter at hand, which is apartheid."

"I'm sure that's very noble," said Nicky, "but do you think if Cory calls again, you could convince him to get in touch with me?"

"Why should I?"

"Because he can help me out with a little problem I have, and in return maybe I can help him stay alive. I think he'll want to talk to me when he hears what I have in mind."

Kitty appeared curious, despite herself. "What *do* you have in mind?"

What Nicky had in mind was to use Cory as bait. It was quite simple, really: Octavio wanted Cory, and seemed prepared to commit rash deeds to get him. Nicky wanted to be around when these rash deeds were being done, catching the bastard *in flagrante*. Though this plan might be ingenious, he felt he must give it a softer edge for the anxious wife.

"Cory knows a lot about Octavio Morales; I could use his help in nailing the guy. All I'm asking is for you to pass on the message to Cory that I want to see him—see if you can arrange a meeting between him and me."

Kitty had been staring at him impassively while he spoke. "I tell you what, Rachmaninoff—maybe we can talk about Octavio and

Cory another time. Right now, everyone's waiting for you to do your thing, you dig?"

"My thing?"

"*Arrest* me, for chrissake! What kind of cop are you, anyway?"

"Well, I was hoping we could avoid this," said Nicky unhappily. "Couldn't you maybe convince everybody to move out of the hall, into the street? Out there, Kitty, you could protest into the next century—have a hunger strike, even, whatever you want."

She shook her head in astonishment. "Jesus, don't you get the picture? I *want* you to arrest me—I *want* to go to jail, for chrissake!"

Nicky was scratching his chin. "Gee, I get it. You think maybe if you go to jail, this little protest will get a lot more publicity, huh?"

"This is *incredible!*" said Kitty Hall.

"I tell you what," said Nicky. "I'll make *you* a deal now—I'll arrest you in a manner guaranteed to attract *maximum* publicity, if afterwards you pass on my offer to your husband. What do you say?"

She looked doubtful. "Well, I guess so. Of course, Cory has his own idea about things—I'm not guaranteeing he won't turn you down."

Nicky offered his hand. "A deal, then," he said. Kitty looked around to make sure no one was looking, and then she shook hands so briefly it seemed almost an illusion.

"Now let's just get this over with, okay? Look, I'm going to go limp now. This is a nonviolent demonstration, and none of us are going to resist. So do your bit, Rachmaninoff—it should make you feel macho as hell."

Kitty lay back on the hall floor in front of the South African consulate in a nonviolent position she had probably learned in the sixties. The others all around her saw what Kitty had done and went limp as well, going down like a line of dominoes. Rachmaninoff sighed. He was the only non-limp person in sight.

"Okay," he said, "but this is *not* going to be pleasant."

Nicky leaned forward and put one arm under Kitty's legs, the other beneath her back. He had never touched her before. Her body was surprisingly light and supple.

"Tell me if I'm hurting you, okay?"

"I don't *believe* this!" she mourned.

He picked her up gently, like a baby in his arms. She closed her eyes and folded her arms rather primly across her breast as he began to carry her carefully over the sea of prostrate bodies. Nicky was feeling a little lightheaded. He liked the natural way she felt in his arms. A lady like this could be carried off into the sunset with hardly a grunt of effort.

"God damn it, this is *not* the way you're supposed to arrest me," she hissed at him. "Can't you do anything right, Rachmaninoff?"

"I guess not."

She had opened her eyes and was studying him severely.

"King Kong," she whispered finally. "*That's* what you look like right now."

"Shall we find the Empire State Building?" he suggested.

Nicky couldn't quite believe what happened next: she smiled. She didn't mean to, she didn't even want to—but nonetheless, the ghost of a smile more or less escaped her lips.

"The Empire State Building, huh?"

Right now she seemed to be trying very hard not to let the smile turn into a laugh, though the corners of her mouth were definitely twitching. Her dark eyes were shining up at him with a soft quality Nicky had never seen before. Then she giggled—just a small giggle at first, but there seemed to be more giggles inside that were trying to get out. All of a sudden—out of nowhere—Rachmaninoff was carrying her down the hall and she was giving him a smile that didn't have any limits on it at all.

It was strange how that smile changed everything about Kitty Hall. Where there had been cold and perfect beauty, now there was dancing sunlight. For the first time, Nicky noticed she had freckles on her nose, and her lips were just a little cracked from the sun.

They were coming around the bend in the hall, toward the photographers who were waiting behind police lines. Nicky wasn't looking where he was going. "Whoops," he said—he had stumbled slightly against the body of a limp protester, and Kitty had to put her arms around his neck for support.

They were gazing into each other's eyes with giddy astonishment when the flashguns of a dozen press cameras began exploding like the Fourth of July.

"Okay, here goes maximum publicity," said Rachmaninoff, keeping his promise. And he leaned forward to kiss her slightly cracked lips.

4

THE PHOTOGRAPH ON THE FRONT PAGE OF THE *EXAMINER* HAD A CUTE caption: A PRISONER OF LOVE? Probably it was the question mark that transformed the arrest of actress Kitty Hall from a news item into tabloid gossip.

Tanya Rachmaninoff happened to see the photograph while sitting at a Burger King on Santa Monica Boulevard. José had just left her to buy his third double Whopper with cheese when her eye was caught by the front page of a discarded newspaper on the next table. Tanya couldn't help noticing a strangely bearlike familiarity about the way the man in the photograph was holding a terrifically beautiful woman in his arms.

"Oh my God!" she cried. "It's Dad!"

"What's the matter?" José asked, coming back to the table with his plastic tray.

"Look at my dad! Jesus, *what's* he doing?"

"I think maybe they are on their way to bed," José suggested.

"God, look what it says—he's *arresting* her!"

"Your father's a funny sort of guy."

"*That's* the understatement of the year!" Tanya tossed the newspaper back onto the next table and returned her attention to José. She still couldn't get used to the idea that he was actually *here* in L.A., and driving a totally bitchin' red convertible '59 Caddy—though apparently without a cent in his pocket. Tanya didn't say anything, but she had registered the fact that he didn't offer any change from the twenty-dollar bill she had just given him for his third Whopper.

"God, José, you sure are hungry."

"I haven't eaten for two days," he admitted, mouth full.

And here she was, thinking about mere money, when some people in the world were practically starving! She watched the Whopper disappear, fascinated by the way he tore it apart. José had changed since she saw him last; he seemed older, thinner, less boyishly goofy. He had not shaved for a few days, which gave him a desperado look that was actually extremely sexy. She just wished he had at least *offered* to give her some change back from the twenty.

"So *tell* me," she prodded, "I mean, how did you get here, José? You really haven't told me a thing, you know."

"Aren't you glad to see me?"

"Of *course* I'm glad to see you, but I'm totally *dying* of curiosity."

José wiped his mouth with the back of his hand and sat back in his orange plastic Burger King bucket seat.

"You heard what happened in Nicaragua, of course?"

"You mean about Cory digging up those two coffins and disappearing into the jungle and all that? I overheard little pieces of it from my father talking to my mother—but nobody tells me anything," Tanya complained. "I mean, I'm just like the *furniture*, for chrissake!"

"Then I will tell you. Cory discovered where Somoza hid much of his money before he had to run away to Miami. This is a long story. . . ."

"I just want to hear about *you*, José. You can tell me all the other stuff later."

"Okay then . . . my father was helping Cory, you understand. That's why they were in the house that night—do you remember?"

Tanya gave him a look. *That night*, as he put it, was the night she had lost her virginity—a slightly unforgettable event. "Go on," she told him frostily.

"It's a little complicated. My father and Cory wanted the money to help the Sandinistas, but when they opened the two coffins there was a surprise."

"There was no money?"

"Yes and no. There was a little jewelry, but there was no cash, you see. What they found was a piece of paper with bank numbers

170

on it, probably for a Swiss account. So you see, they found Somoza's treasure—but they can't get at it."

"Can't they just go to Switzerland?"

"No, unfortunately we don't know exactly which Swiss bank these numbers are for. In fact, even Switzerland is only a guess—Cory says maybe the numbers are for a bank in Panama or even the Caymans. It is impossible for us to know."

"Gosh, how much money do you think there is?"

José leaned closer over the table. "Maybe one billion dollars. Maybe a lot more."

"Wow! But are you sure, José? That sure sounds like a lot."

"It *is* a lot, but Somoza was such a thief, you see, it is really impossible to say. Certainly he was very, very rich, and why should he go to the trouble to bury these numbers underground if it wasn't a very big fortune?"

"I can see that," Tanya agreed. "But how are you going to get it?"

José smiled. "We have it worked out."

"Yes, but how?"

"We are going to sell the piece of paper with the numbers to Octavio Morales, this man who is Somoza's nephew. He will know which bank these numbers are for, and will pay much for this piece of paper—perhaps a hundred million dollars. This is better than nothing, I think—and it is still enough to help the Sandinistas return to power."

"My God, José! Are you sure he'll pay that much?"

"Wouldn't you, if you could turn a hundred million dollars into a billion dollars? This is arithmetic everyone would love to do!"

"Gosh, I guess so," Tanya said uncertainly.

"Of course you would. This is all very easy, Tanya—we have it all worked out."

Tanya wasn't sure why, but it didn't seem particularly easy to her. It took only a moment to find at least one flaw with José's scenario.

"But look," she said, "isn't this awfully dangerous? I mean, what if Octavio just tries to kill you or something?"

José laughed. "You have had a very safe life, I think, growing up in Beverly Hills, where things are so nice. But me, I grew up in Nicaragua, and believe me, this does not seem so dangerous after what I have been through."

He had gotten at her weak spot. If you grew up in Beverly Hills, what could you possibly know about the real world?

"This money is like the blood of my country, Tanya. You can see I must try to help my father get it back. Even a hundred million dollars—well, it is not much when you think of all the money Somoza stole, but it is something at least."

"I see that, José, but still . . . I just don't know."

"What don't you know, my darling?" José took one of her bare feet under the table and began to massage it in a way that made it very difficult to think.

"Well . . . how did you get to California, for instance?" she managed.

"This part was easy," he confided. "When we decided we must come here to see Señor Morales, we stole an airplane from a military field outside of Managua. . . ."

"Gosh!" said Tanya. "That doesn't sound so easy to me!"

"It was nothing. The hard part was flying very low on the water so the radar wouldn't see us—we were so low you could water-ski behind us, I think! Unfortunately, we ran out of fuel and had to crash in the Mojave desert—now *that* could have been a problem, but my father of course is a very wonderful pilot and no one was hurt."

"Gosh!" she said again.

"And so here I am!" he said with a big grin. "Today my father and Cory are busy making their deal with Octavio—and so I said to myself, 'I will go visit the girl I love.' "

"But what about the Cadillac?" Tanya insisted. She sensed there must be more to this than José was letting on, and she was not willing to be sweet-talked quite so fast.

"Oh, that—well, I told you there were some jewels in the coffin. Cory gave them to me, and I was able to trade a necklace for the Cadillac with these Iranian people who own a motel in the desert. A pity it uses so much gas."

José was giving her a look that Tanya understood was a prelude to asking for money.

"Can't you pawn the rest of the jewels for gas money?" she asked him.

José shrugged. "Unfortunately, the pawn shops want all kinds of identification we do not have. In fact, I need to ask you—do you think you can lend me a few hundred dollars, Tanya? It is for a very good cause, and of course I will pay you back."

Some people were embarrassed by sex; with Tanya it was money. She found she was blushing furiously.

"Well, I don't have much cash—actually, that was my last twenty I gave you for the Whopper. Of course . . ."

"Yes?"

"Well, I could always get a cash advance on my Visa card."

José blinked and let his hand wander farther up her leg. "You have a Visa card?"

"It's my mother's account," Tanya explained hurriedly, "and naturally I have a limit—I'm only allowed to spend a thousand dollars a month."

José threw back his head and laughed loudly. "A thousand dollars a month!" he cried. "Do you know, many people in Nicaragua don't make that much in an entire year?"

Tanya was feeling more and more miserable. "Look, I gotta pay for my own lunches out of that, you know. *And* buy my own clothes."

"Oh, I know, I know!" José took her bare foot and moved it suggestively between his legs. He gave her a sexy, unshaved-desperado look that sent shivers up the back of her spine.

"You know, my little *yanqui* darling, I think we will bring social justice to Central America—just on your lunch money!"

5

NICKY RACHMANINOFF KNEW HE HAD BLOWN IT. THERE SEEMED A very good chance Kitty Hall would never smile at him again.

He sat at his piano on Sunshine Terrace, playing through a slow blues progression. Earlier in the evening he had watched the television news to discover that his promise of maximum publicity had gone further than he could have imagined—clear to Dan Rather, who used the Beverly Hills arrest as his final story of the night. Immediately afterward, his phone started ringing like crazy and he had to use his answering machine to screen out the dozens of journalists hoping for an interview with the kissing policeman.

Dan Rather had given it a cute twist—contrasting the incident to the arrest of Zsa Zsa Gabor last year. Was Beverly Hills having a crisis with its local celebrities? Zsa Zsa, of course, had been convicted of assaulting a BHPD officer who stopped her for a traffic offense in her Rolls-Royce. Perhaps this new approach indicated a softening attitude toward crime? All in all, "a very arresting moment," said Dan—who was wearing a sweater tonight and trying hard to be perceived as human. "And that's a piece of your world tonight."

Nicky knew he was never going to hear the end of this. Mixed in with all the calls from the press came an angry message from Chief McGroder, who wished to know the meaning of this latest outrage upon the hills of Beverly. As for Kitty, she had been taken to the station but never booked. There was a feeling among the brass that the Beverly Hills case had been seriously compromised.

Nicky kept the volume of his answering machine turned up loud enough to hear if Charlie called in with news of the still-missing Epiphany Moore. Meanwhile, he played the blues. A few minutes after ten, he heard his phone ring and then a graceful feminine voice coming through the little speaker.

"Nicholas? I bet you're there! Hiding, aren't you? Me too, as a matter of fact."

It was Kitty. He didn't recognize her voice immediately, since he had never spoken with her on the phone, and she had certainly never addressed him as anything except Rachmaninoff. After a brief internal debate, he turned off the machine and picked up the phone.

"Kitty? Look, I'm sorry. I hope I haven't caused you a lot of embarrassment. I admit I got a little carried away."

"Carried away?" she posed rhetorically. "I was the one who got carried away, I think!"

Was she laughing? Nicky thought he heard something of a repressed giggle coming over the line.

174

"Anyway," she said, "you kept your part of the deal—that was a 'maximum publicity' arrest, if I ever saw one. So now I'm going to keep mine. If you want to talk about Cory, I'm ready to help."

"Are you? I'd be very grateful, really."

"The question is, would you like to talk on the phone or in person?" she asked him. "Which would you think is best?"

"Oh, in person," Nicky suggested hastily. "Quite definitely."

"And when would you like to have this interview, Nicholas?"

"Let's see," said Nicky a bit wildly. "Let me think for a moment. How about tomorrow sometime?"

"Tomorrow is good," she told him. "Unless, of course, you'd rather make it tonight?"

"Tonight?"

"Well, I *am* alone. You could come over right now, for instance. Unless it's too late, of course."

"Oh no! . . . I'd say tonight was *very* good."

She *was* laughing. A throaty little chuckle.

"I'd say tonight was very good too, Nicholas," she told him. "I'll leave the outside light on for you."

6

KITTY'S BED WAS SURROUNDED BY CACTI. AN UNUSUAL FETISH, thought Rachmaninoff. There was a noteworthy phallic cactus nearly five feet tall, standing alongside an exotic puffball cactus with prickly little spines. There was a cactus that looked like elephant ears, a cactus with strange little flowers growing from the top. Cactus, cactus, everywhere he looked.

"But I'm still the biggest prick in your garden," he boasted gently.

"You're a hard man," she admitted.

They had not done a lot of talking about her husband, Cory Heard. At the moment they were lying naked on top of Kitty's giant four-poster bed, which was an old-fashioned touch in an otherwise modern home. Kitty had eclectic tastes. The room had tinted sky-lights, antique wooden rocking chairs, handwoven Navajo rugs, futuristic Swedish lamps, a Renoir, a Degas, a Georgia O'Keeffe—and enough cacti covering every available surface and free floor space to make one a tad careful when tiptoeing to the bathroom in the middle of the night.

Nicky was wallowing in the moment—as Charlie was always telling him he should do—living the big erotic *now* without thought of what this might mean or where it would lead him tomorrow. Kitty's head was resting on his chest, a leg thrown across his thigh, a hand lightly upon his stomach—sometimes moving lower for a friendly little stroke. It was like having a very lithe and sexy little moonbeam playing across his body.

"Isn't this strange?" she asked him. "I *hated* you, Nicholas, I really did."

"Lust is a complex emotion," he told her wisely.

"Most of all, I couldn't *stand* your sarcastic attitude about our trip to Nicaragua," she told him. "It really bugged me—I mean, *who* could make fun of the Hollywood Committee for Justice in Nica-ragua? We were so fucking earnest."

"It's important to be earnest," he admitted.

"But you *must* stop making bad puns, Nicholas."

"Or what?"

"Or . . . I'm going to tickle you to death!"

Oh, what a lovely homicide. As Kitty sat on his stomach tickling him, Nicky defended himself bravely, but there was a look of pure mischief on her face, a wild glee that could not be denied. Even-tually she succeeded in pinning him down, sitting on top of him with her knees against his arms. This brought a rather interesting part of Kitty's body close to his mouth.

"I won!" she said. "Now you're my prisoner and you have to do everything I tell you."

"What do you have in mind, my dear?"

Kitty had a lot of things in mind, apparently. To begin with, she lowered herself onto his mouth and let out a little gasp of pleasure, holding on to the backboard of the bed for support.

"Now it's your turn," she whispered at last. "Now I'll be *your* prisoner."

"You're sure about this?"

"Try me," she said.

And he did.

7

NICKY WAS LOOKING UPSIDE DOWN AT A LARGE GEORGIA O'KEEFFE painting above the bed that seemed to show a honeybee's delight at being inside a juicy blue flower. A nifty painting, he thought, even upside down—and he knew just what that honeybee felt like, sticky but satisfied, lulled into a languid peace.

"You know, maybe you shouldn't tell Susan about this," Kitty mentioned, and there it was: reality, the past and the future, their ordinary lives moving in upon them.

"Susan won't mind," he said. "Hell, she's always telling me I shouldn't be staying home nights, playing the piano and brooding about things."

"She'll mind about this, Nicholas, believe me. Susie's so damn competitive all the time. It's subtle, you know, but there it is. She'd feel very threatened by the idea of us being together like this."

"What about you?" he asked, propping himself up on one elbow so he could look at her better. "Are you the jealous type?"

She laughed at the idea. "*Me?* God forbid! I think I'm just too independent to care. When people are with me, they're with me— when they're on their own, what they do is their own business."

"So when Cory had his little flings, you didn't particularly mind?"

"Maybe the first time it happened, sure. It came as a shock. But then I was able to say to myself, 'Okay, this is Cory, the way he is. It's not really sex he's looking for outside of the home, but nice little ego strokes.' "

"And all the young girls, his various adoring students—they didn't make you feel . . . well, old?"

The smoky gray eyes settled on him for a moment in a hard stare. "Do I seem old to you, Nicholas?"

"Not at all!" he assured her. "Listen, personally I can barely keep up with even the middle-aged women—but I was just curious, that's all."

"Well, I began to find Cory's adventures slightly pathetic, if you want to know the truth. It was embarrassing to be married to someone so immature. But jealousy per se—no, that's not my style."

"So it's definitely over between you and Cory?"

"Definitely!" she told him with a bright, hard laugh. "Let someone else be his nursemaid for a change."

"And you don't care what he does, or what happens to him?"

"I can't afford to care, Nicholas. There are some people you can't help because they refuse to help themselves, and after a while you simply have to cut them loose."

"I guess so," said Nicky. He had been prodding because there was something about her attitude he couldn't quite fathom. There was a false chord here somewhere.

He was curious to throw a pebble into the pool and see what kind of ripples he might make, and unfortunately he had the exact pebble with which to proceed. It was more of a rock than a pebble, as a matter of fact, and it meant betraying a confidence.

"In my profession," he said, "I rarely meet wives who are not jealous. It's one of the great motives of crime."

"Well, not me," she said.

"So you didn't mind when Cory had that affair with Susan last year?"

Kitty's eyes opened a little wider; her mouth went slack. *She didn't know!*

"What . . . are . . . you . . . saying?"

"Jesus, Kitty! I thought you knew! I'd never . . . ."

"God damn it! Did Cory . . . did Cory fucking sleep with that neurotic bitch ex-wife of yours?"

"Your best friend!" Nicky added sadly, shaking his head. "But you know, I never would have told you. . . ."

"How do you know about this?" Kitty demanded. She had lit a

178

cigarette and was standing near the foot of the bed, looking as though she wanted to kill someone.

"Well, Susan told me, actually. As a matter of fact, she feels deeply guilty about the whole thing."

"God damn cunt!" swore Kitty Hall. "She'd *better* feel guilty! How long did this go on, Rachmaninoff? Tell me, for chrissake!"

"Gee, I don't know exactly. Probably not more than six months or so."

"*Six months!*"

"Well, I'm glad you're not the jealous type, at least."

Kitty sighed and sat down again tensely on the bed. Nicky put a friendly hand on her back.

"Hey," he said, "you're free now. You've cut him loose."

She stubbed out her cigarette and spun around to face him.

"Let's not talk about our exes anymore, all right?"

"Whatever," he told her mildly. "I mean, I'm sorry I brought it up."

"Just take me, Rachmaninoff. Okay? Take me really good!"

"Again?" he asked nervously, wondering if the old bones could stand another rattle.

"Sure," she said. "Just lie back, Nicholas—believe me, the mood I'm in, I could raise Lazarus from the grave."

8

NICKY SAT UP CAUTIOUSLY AND LOOKED AROUND. HE WAS STRETCHING his toes, almost ready to make the big move out of bed, when Kitty came into the room carrying a tray. She was already dressed, wearing jeans and a man's soft flannel shirt that still managed to cling to her body in a terrific way. She wore no makeup, and her hair was pulled back simply with an elastic band. She looked as elegant and fresh and clean as the sunlight pouring into the room.

"I let you sleep, darling. You seemed so exhausted."

"What time is it?"

"Almost eleven," she told him.

"Jesus!" He jumped out of bed in earnest now. "I'm late for work!"

"Relax, Nicholas. Your Sergeant Katz already called and I told him you were going to be late."

Nicky moaned a little and sat back on the bed. This was going to be hard to live down.

"Can I see you this weekend?" he asked.

"Sorry, Nicholas, but this weekend I must be in Palm Springs."

He tried not to feel disappointed. After all, why should she drop all her plans just because a terribly sexy, witty, and penetrating police lieutenant had entered her life?

He picked up the phone on her bedside table and dialed the direct number to his office at the Beverly Hills station. Charlie answered on the first ring.

"Ah! Have you awakened from your sweet repose?" asked Charlie. "I trust you are refreshed!"

"Why the hell did you call me here?"

"Well, at nine A.M. when there was no Rachmaninoff, I began to suspect foul play. I asked myself, 'Where could the great Rachmaninoff be sleeping while Sergeant Katz is busy at work?' Then I looked at yesterday's headlines and the truth began to dawn."

"Yeah, yeah, Charlie—now what's up?"

"What's up is I've got a line on Epiphany Moore."

"You found her?"

"Not quite. What I found are some friends of hers, a nice little married couple named Biff and Terry, who live in Santa Monica. I saw them yesterday, trying to locate our missing coed, and they called back early this morning. It seems Epiphany telephoned late last night in a bit of a jam, asking if she could borrow a couple of hundred dollars and their VW bug for a few days. They said yes, but then they talked it over between themselves and decided they were worried—so they gave me a call."

"Biff and Terry?"

"Yeah. Biff is the girl, by the way. A terrific young couple. I guess I left an impression of quiet strength and coolness under fire—they think whatever their friend is up to, she's way over her head and needs to be bailed out fast."

"What she needs is a good spanking."

"Nicky! The young are *supposed* to make mistakes. Where do you think babies come from?"

"When is the girl supposed to pick up the money and the car?"

"Today at three. She's coming to their place in Santa Monica."

"Good," said Nicky. He found a notepad on Kitty's bedside table and scribbled down the address Charlie gave him.

"Anything else, Charlie?"

"Here's something interesting. I'm getting some information on Octavio's finances. It turns out he owes money everywhere. Jurgensen's market threatened to take him to court last month if he didn't pay his grocery bill, and now they're taking his business on a cash-only basis."

"My, my—a busted billionaire," mused Rachmaninoff. "Of course, some of these rich people are neurotic about paying small bills."

"I think this is more than neurotic, Nicky. I think Hollywood's newest tycoon is broke."

"See if you can get a peek at his bank records, Charlie."

"Sure. And before I forget, Nicky, McGroder's calling a big pow-wow for one o'clock this afternoon. It appears Japanese business is too important to the hills of Beverly to allow the murder of Yoshiro Miyaji to go unsolved another day—I believe we are to get a pep talk."

"I tell you what, Charlie—I'm going to make you the official representative of the homicide squad at McGroder's meeting. Be sure to take lots of notes."

"Nicky, *no!* Don't do this to me!"

"Charlie, I'd love to be there, but I'm going to be tied up. Tell the Chief I'm about to break this case wide open—he'll like that."

"Nicky . . ."

" 'Bye, Charlie."

Kitty was sitting in one of her rocking chairs, glancing through a script, looking as if she had to get on with the business of her day.

"Do you have a razor I can use?"

"You can use Cory's—it's in the cabinet above the sink. I haven't quite cleared him out yet."

Kitty wandered into the bathroom to watch him shave, sitting on the toilet seat with her legs daintily crossed. There was something frighteningly domestic about this action that made Rachmaninoff considerably nervous. Sex was one thing—but anything resembling shared housekeeping scared him to death.

"You know, I still need to talk with him," said Nicky.

"Talk with who?"

"You know who. The same person I needed to talk with yesterday in front of the South African consulate."

"I told you, Cory didn't leave a number, Nicholas. I'm not sure he'll call again—he was pissed I wouldn't give him any money. But if he does call, I'll see that he gets in touch with you. All right?"

"Kitty," he said after a moment, "do you know a girl named Epiphany Moore?"

"No, should I?"

"She was one of Cory's students."

"Ah! Then let me guess. She was part of Cory's quest to stay forever young. One of his girlies."

"That's correct. As a matter of fact, she was his most recent girlie. Didn't he talk about her at all?"

"Look, Nicholas—as I told you last night, I knew there were girls, but I went out of my way to avoid the specifics. You might call this the ostrich approach to modern marriage. Little did I suspect that my good friend Susan was getting in on the act too!"

Nicky finished shaving, rinsed his face, and started getting dressed.

"What about this Epiphany Moore?" she asked finally. "Is Cory with her now, do you suppose?"

"I think she's trying to help him in some way—I don't know exactly how. Probably she thinks this is fun-and-games time in college, but the kid's headed for some bad times. Two of Octavio's henchmen have already messed her up a little, trying to get a line on Cory."

"Jesus! You think she's in danger?"

"You kidding? Anyone who even gets *close* to Cory right now is

asking for it. The guy's to be avoided like an open jar of nitroglyc-
erine."

"Poor Pip!" said Kitty with a shake of her head.

Nicky gave her a sharp look.

"What's the matter?"

"Nothing," he told her. He sighed without apparent reason. "Just
nothing at all."

9

NICKY SAT IN HIS AUSTIN-HEALEY ACROSS THE STREET FROM A SMALL
gray apartment building on a side street in Santa Monica. The
building had only four apartments—two upstairs, two down. Terry
and Biff Bingham had the upstairs corner, with a view of a trendy
Santa Fe Bar and Grill and a small sliver of the Pacific Ocean a few
blocks away.

Nicky was here half an hour early for the three-o'clock rendezvous with Epiphany Moore, not taking any chances on missing her.
He waited with a dull ache in his heart. A stakeout is generally a
long and lonely ordeal in which it is impossible to avoid the long
and lonely thoughts of one's life. There came a time when Nicky
had to take out and examine the two words that had left him in such
a state of agitation since earlier this morning.

Poor Pip! she had said. With those two words, an evening of love
had come tumbling down around his head.

He replayed every conversation he had ever had with Kitty
Hall, hoping to remember whether he had ever mentioned Epiphany Moore or used her nickname. But he had not—he was quite
certain.

Poor Pip!

There was no doubt about it: if Kitty had never heard of Epiphany, then she would not have known the nickname Pip. Thus it was

logical: Kitty had lied to him. How many times had they made love? Nicky could not even remember. A night like that made one hope that something might come of it—but it all ended in a lie. Never had Nicky known love gained and love lost to come so terrifyingly fast.

God damn you, Kitty!

He was hurt; he was furious. How could she allow him intimate access to every nook and cranny of her body and then . . . *lie to him!* He should have confronted her the moment those two fatal words had slipped out, but the transition had been too abrupt between trust and deceit.

But why should a celebrated film goddess go to bed with a middle-aged cop unless she had an ulterior motive? Nicky stepped out of his car and went to a phone booth at the end of the block, from where he could still keep an eye on Biff and Terry's building. It was time to call the sheriff's forensic laboratory about another deceit. Earlier in the day he had dropped off the tape from Susan's answering machine, which he had slipped into his pocket the night he was at her bungalow. There was something wrong about Cory's phone message—he knew it in his bones.

"It's a copy," said the technician at the forensic lab.

"What do you mean, a copy?"

"It was recorded earlier on another answering machine, and then played back over the phone onto your ex-wife's machine, Lieutenant."

"You're sure of that?"

"Absolutely. Not only is there too much background noise for it to be an original, but with enough amplification I was able to hear the beep of the first machine."

"Can you tell how long ago the message was originally recorded?"

"No, that's impossible," said the technician. "You think we're magicians?"

Nicky hung up the phone slowly, wondering what kind of game was afoot to make someone leave a fake message on Susan's answering machine—someone, he reminded himself, who must be on an intimate footing with Cory herself—for it was a woman Cory had originally called, of that Nicky was certain.

Nicky began wandering back toward his car, full of dire suspicions about the deceitful lady whose bed he had vacated only hours before. He hesitated, then turned and headed back into the phone booth.

He dialed the business office of the telephone company and asked for one of the managers there, a man by the name of Dennis Graves. Nicky Rachmaninoff had never actually met Dennis Graves, but he had had a telephone relationship with him for a number of years.

"Dennis, I have a phone number in Westwood in the name of Epiphany Moore—can you give me a readout of her outgoing and incoming calls from, say, last Friday to Tuesday morning?"

"*Out* I can give you right away. *In* will take a few hours of computer time."

"I understand, Dennis. Listen, I really appreciate this."

In fact, what Dennis was doing could cost him his job, for there was a definite set of procedures for telephone officials to follow in giving information like this to the police. Nicky hung on to the phone, and in a moment he heard Dennis's voice coming back on the line, reading off a list of Epiphany's outgoing calls from his computer screen. Nicky had a notebook open, and he was scribbling as fast as he could.

For a young woman, Epiphany was not particularly telephone-active—still, the list of calls from Friday to Tuesday morning covered three pages in Nicky's notebook. Most of the numbers had no meaning for him and would have to be investigated. There were two intriguing collect calls from a place called Twenty-nine Palms, and one from Palm Springs; being collect, they were listed with the outgoing calls, since they would be charged to Pip's number. And finally there were the calls Nicky had expected, to a number he had already memorized since he had dialed it repeatedly himself—the unlisted Beverly Hills number of Kitty Hall.

Poor Pip, in fact, had telephoned Kitty's house on Friday evening for twenty-three minutes, twice on Sunday for a combination of nearly an hour, and once Monday afternoon at 3:10, which was exactly twenty minutes before she had driven off in the red Cadillac convertible.

So there it was: Kitty had apparently spent a total of nearly two hours in the last few days, talking on the phone with someone she claimed never to have heard of. The lie was revealed, yet this new indication of her deceit did not cut nearly as deeply as had the first *Poor Pip*.

It all came back to Kitty. She could easily have replayed an old message from Cory on her answering machine over the phone to Susan's machine. And why would she do such a thing? Because Susan would tell Nicky, and it would seem as if Cory were alive and well in California, while indeed the opposite must be true. And if the opposite *was* true . . .

Nicky gave a sharp and bitter laugh, startling an old lady who was passing by with a shopping cart.

"Damn it, Kitty!" he said aloud to the street. "You murdered your husband, didn't you?"

10

PIP APPEARED ON FOOT NEARLY AN HOUR LATE, WALKING FROM THE direction of Santa Monica Boulevard. She was wearing tan jeans and a turtleneck, and her brown hair was pulled back in a ponytail, away from her chipmunk cheeks. She seemed preoccupied, worried. From the way she was walking, she looked as though she might stumble through a plate-glass window without particularly noticing.

Even so, Nicky slumped discreetly down in the front seat of his car, so she wouldn't see him. He watched Pip stop a moment to inspect a bright yellow VW bug parked at the curb, then continue on inside the apartment building to see her friends.

Was young Pip going to lead him to Cory Heard in her newly borrowed VW bug, and prove his murder theory all wrong? Nicky was dying to find out. At the moment he was parked across the street from the VW bug, facing the wrong direction. He decided it would be a good idea to get himself into a better starting position. As soon as Pip disappeared inside the building, he made a U-turn and headed toward a free space four cars back from the Volkswagen—

but a brown Ford Taurus pulled into the spot just before he got there. This was exactly the sort of minor incident from which wonderfully planned police operations so often began to unravel. Nicky took out his shield and was about to demand that the Ford get out of his way, but there was another surprise in store for him. The driver of the Ford Taurus was a funny little man with big ears and short hair, wearing a baseball cap; clip-on shades were attached to his regular glasses.

"Bob!" cried Nicky. "My God, it's Bob Arnold!"

"Sh!" said Bob, looking around nervously. "Get out of here, Rachmaninoff! The girl's going to come down and see us double-parked and you're going to blow the whole thing!"

"But what are you doing here?"

"The same thing you are. Now beat it, for crying out loud!"

Nicky was a little stunned. The last time he had seen Bob Arnold was in the rain outside of Managua, and he had certainly never expected to run into him in Santa Monica. Bob kept making shooing gestures with his hand, telling Nicky to get lost. Nicky obliged by driving his Austin-Healey a dozen feet ahead of the Ford Taurus, finding an illegal parking spot next to a fire hydrant only one car back from the VW bug. He hoped that Pip would be too wrapped up in her thoughts to notice him, and that a meter maid would not appear at some crucial moment and start to write him a ticket.

Nicky Rachmaninoff concentrated on being optimistic. He supposed the CIA had reason enough to hope Epiphany Moore would lead them to Cory Heard. Possibly they were all on the same side, the good guys against the bad. He and Bob against the evils of the world.

Pip was upstairs for nearly half an hour. To kill time, Nicky played a little game with himself of counting all the actions in his life that he now regretted. He was working backward, beginning with going to bed with Kitty Hall. He had arrived at the very big mistake of not flossing his teeth more carefully when he was young, when Pip came down the steps from the building and unlocked the yellow VW bug. She had a small overnight bag that she threw in the backseat. Nicky put a newspaper in front of his face—it happened to be the issue with his own photograph on the front page holding Kitty Hall in his arms, which might one day make a swell souvenir. When he heard the VW engine sputter to life, he put down the paper, started his Austin-Healey, and followed Epiphany out into the traffic heading toward Santa Monica Boulevard.

Behind Nicky Rachmaninoff, Bob Arnold of the CIA pulled his brown Ford Taurus away from the curb to join in the procession. As he passed an alley, Bob gave a hand signal to two men parked in a black BMW who came out into the traffic after him. The two men wore blue suits. They had cruel mouths. They had cold eyes.

It was a merry chase: Pip in the lead, then Nicky, then Bob—Innocence, Guile, and Intrigue, followed close behind by Death and Fear in a sleek black car.

11

AS SURVEILLANCE GOES, TAILING A YELLOW VOLKSWAGEN BUG WAS about as optimal a situation as you could get: the car was bright and it was slow, leaving Nicky with lots of time to think about murderous movie stars who took unsuspecting policemen into their beds.

From Santa Monica Boulevard, Pip drove toward the coast highway and then took the tunnel from the beach onto the Santa Monica Freeway, heading east. Nicky settled back two cars behind her. Occasionally he studied his rearview mirror for a sign of Bob Arnold in the brown Ford Taurus, which he generally found close on his tail. Nicky didn't like this very much, but there wasn't a lot he could do. All together they made a courtly kind of procession, with Pip leading the way at exactly fifty-five miles per hour.

Nicky was beginning to think the girl was going to get off the freeway at one of the Beverly Hills exits, but she kept heading east on Interstate 10 toward downtown Los Angeles. It was nearly five-thirty by now, and the great asphalt arteries of L.A. were clogged and moving slowly. By the time Interstate 10 changed its name from the Santa Monica Freeway to the San Barnardino Freeway, Nicky was driving in second gear at twenty miles an hour, coming to a complete stop every fifty feet. Eight lanes of stalled automobiles, bumper to bumper, were doing little more than spewing out toxic chemicals into the atmosphere. This was the kind of traffic in which frustrated Angelenos had been known to pull out pistols and shotguns and let loose a hail of gunfire against anyone who tried to cut into their lane.

By six o'clock the gray shroud of pollution above the city began to dim into a premature twilight. People were switching on their head-lights, and if Bob Arnold in his Ford Taurus was still among the million automobiles behind him, Nicky did not see him. Maybe Bob had gotten lost or decided no surveillance was worth the hassles of L.A. traffic. Nicky concentrated on keeping the VW bug in sight not more than two cars ahead, and not giving an inch to the huge diesel trucks that occasionally tried to cut him off from his prey.

Pip led him on and on, passing through West Covina and Po-mona, through a tedious landscape of shopping malls, car lots, and industrial parks. This was a part of L.A. that wouldn't quit. Where once, in Nicky's childhood, there had been mile after mile of sweet-smelling orange groves, now there were gas stations and miniature-golf courses and still another shopping mall, another retirement community with little flags flying over half-finished homes. And still Pip led the way eastward on Interstate 10.

Nighttime fell, a darkness lit by an infinity of electric lights that left a milky shroud above the city. Not far past Pomona, Nicky began thinking once more about lovely Kitty with her lithe, catlike body and predatory eyes. Why, he wondered, would a lady with everything decide to kill her husband? A motive, after all, was essential to a crime.

There was money, of course—something Kitty apparently had plenty of. Susan had once mentioned that although she kept a low profile, Katherine Hall was worth perhaps fifty million dollars. Not only had she invested wisely, but she had inherited a large fortune from her parents. It was peachy for Kitty to be so fabulously wealthy, except for one nasty thing: *What if she wanted a divorce?* With California's community-property laws, she might theoretically be forced to give Cory as much as half of her fortune. How convenient in such circumstances that her husband should disappear forever in the Nicaraguan jungle! Twenty-five million dollars was as good a motive for murder as Nicky had ever seen.

But maybe it wasn't money—maybe it was passion. What if her

liberal Prince Charming refused to stop having affairs with younger women? Kitty was so used to getting her own way—could she stand to have a man she loved slip out of her control? Murder, in a sense, was an ultimate attempt to reestablish control.

There were lots of intriguing possibilities and more than a few loose ends. What should he make, for instance, of the fact that Pip and Kitty had been in nearly constant communication last weekend? This was something that made little sense at all.

"Okay then, lead me to Cory," said Nicky to the yellow VW bug ahead of him. "Show me I'm wrong, Pip. Show me Cory's still alive!"

After Redlands, the traffic at last began to ease up. In another ten miles, Nicky managed to get his Austin-Healey into fifth gear and he was trailing the Volkswagen once again at a steady fifty-five. Occasionally he glanced in his rearview mirror, trying to decide if any of the anonymous headlights behind him on the road might belong to a brown Ford Taurus—but it was impossible now to say.

Twenty minutes later, Pip took the freeway exit onto Highway 111, which headed toward Palm Springs. The night air grew warmer as the two-lane road made a gradual descent into the desert. Up ahead, the lights of Palm Springs sparkled like a thousand little jewels, and there was a half moon hanging fat in the sky, turning the desert into a phosphorescent carpet of sand. On the right side of the highway, the San Jacinto mountains rose abruptly from the desert floor nine thousand feet to snow-covered pine forests on the top. It was a dramatic landscape, full of contrasts and the crazy exaggerations of California nature.

Nicky rolled down the windows of his car to let in a wind that was hot and dry and restless. Pip kept going until the two-lane highway turned into Palm Canyon Drive on the edge of town. The desert here became immediately better groomed—even the palm trees were lit decoratively from below with orange spotlights, lending the fronds a gentle neon glow as they danced in the night wind.

As he came into Palm Springs, the traffic slowed to a crawl and Nicky found himself directly behind the yellow VW bug. He hoped Epiphany would not remember a rusty red Austin-Healey that had been following her since Santa Monica. They inched their way along Palm Canyon Drive, past small motels with names that suggested vaguely Arabian delights of dancing girls and pleasures that might come to pass on king-size waterbeds. Unfortunately, paradise was full up this evening. Every motel on the outskirts of town had its NO VACANCY sign sorrowfully lit.

Stalled in traffic, Nicky began to sense the stirring of some wild carnival to which all the cars around him seemed to be heading. He heard loud rock music drifting up Palm Canyon from some point ahead. A siren was wailing not far in the distance. From a nearby convertible came a festive scream.

He couldn't imagine what was happening to disturb the usual geriatric quiet of wealthy Palm Springs, a town to which Republican Presidents came for golf. But the night was full of riot and young people everywhere—they were hanging out of car windows, crowding the sidewalks, sitting in the beds of pickup trucks drinking beer. Two blond giants in swimming trunks crossed the street by climbing over the hoods of stalled cars. Directly ahead, four boys walked up to Pip's yellow bug and tried to pick it up by the fenders and carry it away—but fortunately they were too drunk, and they gave up quickly.

Worst of all, there was not another adult in sight. Rachmaninoff had a curious feeling of being the last remaining grownup in a teenage land. This was not a good feeling. At the next intersection, a frantic policeman in a riot helmet was trying to direct traffic. Nicky flashed his own shield at the officer as he was driving past.

"What's going on here, Officer?" he shouted above the carnival din.

The answer made Nicky's blood run cold—two words designed to strike terror into the heart of any human being past the age of twenty-one:

"Spring Break!"

12

RACHMANINOFF HAD A GOOD LONG LAUGH AT HIMSELF. IT ALL MADE sense now: the wild Mardi Gras mood of the streets, even Pip's long drive to the desert. She was the right age—probably this had nothing to do with Cory at all. She had merely answered the same primal party urge as the rest of her tribe.

Spring Break! Where the beer is, and the boys and girls do play! He hoped Bob Arnold had a sense of humor too—if Bob had indeed managed to make his way here. Nicky had lost him miles back.

The hot desert wind was whipping up the hormonal madness, mixed with the smell of stale beer. Nicky found himself surrounded by a cacophony of shouting, swearing, horns honking, and radios playing full blast. Meanwhile, the traffic was dead in the street. He was thinking he would take the next right turn, circle back to the highway, and head home. If this was her destination, Pip could party without him.

But then she did something to change his mind. Without warning—as if she couldn't stand being stuck in traffic a moment longer—she drove her yellow VW bug over the curb onto the side-walk. Teenage pedestrians scattered in all directions, whistling and yelling their approval of such flagrant irresponsibility. Pip drove across the sidewalk and a patch of lawn, into a 7-Eleven parking lot. She left her car without bothering to lock it, and began walking quickly up Palm Canyon Drive.

This was curious. Was Pip really in such a hurry to party? Nicky decided he had better find out. He followed her tracks from the road, across the sidewalk and over the lawn, to double-park illegally next to the abandoned bug. He put an OFFICIAL POLICE BUSINESS card on his dashboard, hoping it would keep away the tow trucks. Then he tried to find Pip again on the crowded sidewalks.

Unfortunately, a young girl with chipmunk cheeks and a cute ponytail was nearly indistinguishable from a thousand other cute girls, each of whom probably spent every waking hour trying to dress and look exactly like everybody else. Nicky forced his way through a monolithic crowd, butting aside young bodies with his elbows and shoulders. There were no blacks here, no browns—Spring Break in Palm Springs was a last holdout of a white America gung-ho on youth, and no one seemed too pleased to find a grouchy middle-aged person in their midst.

Toward the center of town, automobile traffic had been diverted onto the side streets, and Palm Canyon Drive was a solid mass of writhing bodies. Probably Nicky would never have found Epiphany in this crowd if she hadn't been detained by a small pack of fun-loving college boys who thought it might be fun to take her bra for a souvenir. Nicky heard a scream as two boys held her arms and another ripped open her turtleneck shirt and tried to remove her bra with his teeth. Other young people gathered to watch, shouting their approval. Then, without warning, the blond kid with his mouth full of Epiphany's bra screamed and sank to the sidewalk, his hands between his legs. Pip had just kicked him in the balls. Hard.

Good going, Pip! cheered Nicky Rachmaninoff. He didn't know she had it in her.

Unfortunately, the situation was getting worse. The group of young men seemed to feel collectively threatened.

"Fucking Jew!" said one of the guys. Certainly he was mistaken—Epiphany was as Protestant as you can get—but racism had made a fashionable return to the college campus, along with such pranks as swallowing live goldfish and accosting stray girls. All the boys were very drunk, they didn't like Epiphany whatever her religion, and they began to drag her off into an alley to teach her a lesson. Nicky Rachmaninoff decided he had remained a spectator long enough. He took out his pistol and forced his way into the alley, bringing down the butt of the gun hard on the back of a blond crewcut who was busy holding down Pip's arms. The blond crewcut let her go and sagged forward onto his knees, but two other boys were on Nicky right away. Nicky ducked a wild punch, then lashed out at an exposed stomach. There was a groan and the stomach disappeared—but now someone was coming up from behind. Nicky swung around fast with his gun hand and shoved the barrel of his .38 service revolver up a freckly young nostril. The boy cried out, but didn't dare move. Seeing the gun out in the open, the others began to back off.

"Go back to school and learn some manners, young men!" Rachmaninoff told them. They stared at him in astonishment. Nicky pulled back the hammer of his revolver and pointed the barrel between the freckly kid's legs.

"And now, on the count of three, I believe I'm going to blow your dick off," he said quite calmly. "One . . . two . . ."

The whole group turned and ran screaming out of the alley. Rarely did a cop feel so securely on the side of justice, but while he was playing the White Knight, Pip had managed to disappear. Nicky made his way back to the sidewalk, but couldn't see her anywhere.

Nicky was carried along by a moving ocean of humanity down Palm Canyon Drive. Someone threw a beer bottle at him, but it shattered harmlessly against the hood of a car. Rachmaninoff was beginning to suspect this was the college generation he had read about, the one that was losing out in test scores against the Japanese.

He decided it was thirsty work, ducking beer bottles and saving young maidens from rape. He had been dry too long, and was wondering if any of the local bars would serve a patron of his advanced age, when he noticed a patio restaurant where people were sitting with food and drinks. To his surprise, he immediately saw Pip at one of the tables—yes, it was Chipmunk Cheeks herself, clutching her torn shirt to keep herself decent. She was talking with a woman seated next to her at the table. The second woman was wearing big round dark glasses and a wide-brimmed straw hat—in fact, there wasn't much of her that was not hidden from view. Probably Nicky wouldn't have recognized her if he had not spent most of last night exploring every nook and cranny of her memorable body.

Nicky shook his head in grief. So Pip had not come to Palm Springs to meet Cory, but instead to see Cory's wife. Silly Nicky. He was so depressed, he simply stood and stared. Kitty and Pip were deep in conversation, but there must have been something in the way Nicky was staring that made Kitty turn his way.

Did she see him? Or did she see only the general mayhem of the streets? The face behind the dark glasses gave nothing away. Nicky was about to go inside the restaurant when he felt someone take hold of his shoulder in a most unfriendly manner.

"You're dead meat, Jack," said a voice in his ear. And then a dozen strong young arms picked him up and carried him away.

13

MIRACLES DO HAPPEN. TANYA RACHMANINOFF EXPERIENCED DIVINE intervention just when she least expected it, between Algebra and World History, in the form of a message from the school office telling her to call home.

She used the pay phone outside the gym to dial the private line that went direct to her mother's bungalow at the hotel.

"Darling, I'm so glad I got you!" cried Susan; she seemed a little out of breath. "Look, sweetheart, I'm frantic—something's come up—I absolutely have to go to New York for a few days."

"Like when?"

"Like right *now*, darling—I mean, the limousine's waiting for me and everything. I've been asked to read for a Broadway play—aren't you excited for me? Thank God I finished that dumb TV movie! I have a meeting with the producer and director first thing tomorrow morning. I've been trying to reach your father all morning to see if you could stay with him, but I can't find him anywhere."

"Mom, I'll be fine at the hotel by myself."

"Are you sure? I was thinking of staying in New York until Sunday—maybe take in a few plays and do some shopping. You won't be lonely, will you?"

"Mom, how could I be lonely at the Beverly Hills Hotel, for chrissake?"

"Tanya, don't get sarcastic—you know I don't like that."

"I wasn't being sarcastic, I was just being *factual*. I mean, there are *thousands* of people making ga-ga eyes at each other, just about *hanging* out the windows of the Polo Lounge!"

"Maybe I should cancel my trip?" Susan wondered.

Tanya knew her mother damn well wasn't going to cancel her trip. For a chance to star in a Broadway play, Susan was heading to New York whether Tanya was lonely or not. These last-minute histrionics were only an exercise in guilt. Tanya knew she had to play the middle ground, neither *too* glad her mother was leaving nor too sad to be left behind—keeping in mind always that this was Thursday morning, and that if Susan was gone until Sunday, she would have three totally radical nights alone!

Of course, her mom had to go on and on about the stupid Broadway play, a musical about a prostitute with AIDS, which was supposed to win all kinds of awards. Quite miraculously, the actress originally hired for the role had just broken her collarbone falling off a horse in Central Park, giving Susan a chance in a lifetime finally to be taken *seriously* as an actress.

"The funny thing is I *saw* this coming in my horoscope just last Sunday. 'The time is ripe for artistic endeavors and business opportunities to go hand in hand, Sag.' Do you remember? I showed it to you."

"Sure, Mom."

"But are you *sure* you're going to be all right?" Susan had to ask—not once, but at least a dozen more times. It was beginning to get wearisome. "I feel terrible, abandoning you like this, darling—I just wish I could reach your father."

"Mom, I'm going to be fine!"

"Will you keep trying to get your father? You could spend the weekend with him."

"Sure, Mom, I'll keep trying."

"Of course, I could get Wayne to stay with you if you'd like."

Wayne was her mother's agent, a six-foot-three-inch homosexual with an orange tan and a toupee. Tanya would rather hang out with Jack the Ripper.

"Mom, *please!* I'd really prefer to be on my own."

"Well, all right. I'll leave a few hundred-dollar bills on your dresser—and you can sign for everything at the hotel, of course."

"Mom! I'll survive for a couple of days. I mean, you can relax and just forget about me, okay?"

"Well, I worry, darling. You won't go out and do anything . . . well, *wild?*"

"Je-sus!" Tanya sighed. This was getting stressful. Standing in the phone booth with the receiver cradled between shoulder and ear, she began searching through her bag for a cigarette, wading through vials of eyeliner, a box of condoms, a bag of marijuana, and a fake ID that claimed Tanya Rachmaninoff was twenty-one years of age. She found her Marlboros, lit up with her Zippo, and took a few furtive puffs while keeping an eye out for any passing teachers.

"I mean, *really*, Mom—what can happen to me in a few days on my own at the Beverly Hills Hotel?"

14

BY NIGHTFALL, TANYA WAS STANDING UNDER THE CANOPY IN FRONT of the hotel, ready for action—dressed in shredded jeans and a faded jacket covered with a mosaic of peace symbols and emblems for the Grateful Dead.

José was a few minutes late picking her up, and Tanya drew some disapproving looks from people going in and out of the hotel. They seemed to think that for all the money they were paying to stay at the Beverly Hills Hotel, everybody should look like a movie star. It was really unbelievable how uptight people could be—and here she was, even wearing shoes tonight!

Fortunately, the boys who parked the cars grinned and greeted her by name and made up for all the uptight tourists. *They* approved of Tanya Rachmaninoff, and they were all very impressed, of course, when José finally pulled up the driveway in his red 1959 Cadillac convertible, which was badly in need of a new muffler. Greg—who happened to be Tanya's most favorite parking valet—made a big production of opening the door for her and bowing very low.

"I hope Madame has an exceptional evening," said Greg.

"Boy, me too!" said Tanya, slipping him one of her mother's hundred-dollar bills that had been left on her dresser—for Tanya was a practicing socialist and believed in sharing the wealth.

José drove out onto Sunset, heading toward the Strip, giving her attire a quick and skeptical look out of the corner of his eye.

"Tell me, is it okay to dress this way for such a fancy hotel?"

"Dress *what* way?"

"You know—like a hippie."

Tanya was stunned. "Like a hippie!" she cried. "Christ, I'm just being *myself*, José—I gotta be *me*. And when you think about it, it's like totally pathetic *not* to be yourself when you're paying the kind of prices they ask in fucking Beverly Hills!"

"Tanya," he said coolly, "I don't like it when you use these words like 'fucking' all the time—you sound like someone from the gutter."

Tanya could only gape at him in astonishment. She took a few deep breaths, and then asked—in an actressy sort of voice she borrowed from her mother—"And here I thought you were *supposed* to be a revolutionary, José! I never dreamed you could be so utterly bourgeois!"

He sighed. "Look, I'm sorry," he said quickly. "The last few days, I've been stressed to the max."

As a matter of fact, Tanya had never seen José look so exhausted. There were dark circles under his eyes. The fact that he didn't look in such good shape drained away a lot of her anger. One nice word from him, and she might forgive him all the way.

"What's the matter, José?"

"Oh, who knows? Maybe I should have just stayed in Nicaragua."

"Isn't your plan working—I mean, to get the money back from what's-his-name and all?" Tanya was always vague on details of anything having to do with money.

"Octavio Morales? We're working on it," he said, "me and my father and Cory. But it's difficult—this is a tough man, and I think maybe he would rather kill all three of us than pay a hundred million dollars!"

"Well, what does he say, José? Is he going to buy the Swiss bank numbers or what?"

José shook his head. "This is very difficult to know. Octavio Morales is a man who can say yes and no at the same time. He wants to see proof we actually have these numbers, and of course we can't give him proof without giving the numbers away. Besides that, this takes much time back and forth because we cannot meet with him in person for fear he just grabs us and kills us, maybe."

"So how do you talk with him?"

"Oh, we have a negotiator," José said proudly. He seemed to like the word a lot. "You see, our negotiator goes back and forth from Octavio to us, trying to work out a deal. But it is very difficult, very slow. And meanwhile I am out of money again for gas."

Tanya felt his eyes give her a questioning look. She stared straight ahead. They were driving west on Sunset, through the Strip, into Hollywood.

"I've got money," she said at last, not looking at him. "Where are we going?"

"Hey, it's a surprise," he told her. "But I promise you, it will be someplace nice and hot where we can fuck like crazy."

Tanya's shoulders went rigid. "I don't like it when you talk about fucking that way."

"But you say this word all the time!"

"Look, I only say 'fucking' when I'm *not* talking about fucking—when I talk about *fucking*, I like to be just a little more romantic, okay?"

José pulled over. California girls were a very big mystery, but he could see they weren't going anyplace until they cleared the air.

"You must teach me what to call it, then."

"Making love," Tanya said defiantly.

"Okay, making love. You see, my English gets better every day. So let's not fight—let's go to a motel and get into a big bed and I will make love to you all over."

When he talked this way, Tanya found herself melting fast. But she wasn't going to give in too easily. "I don't know," she said moodily. "Look, can we put up the top? I'm getting cold."

"The top's broken," he said. "You will just have to sit very close to me."

"Not until you start being nice to me!"

Tanya reached into the back and found a green army jacket on the floor, but she gave a little scream when she tried to pick it up. Hidden beneath the jacket was José's AK-47 automatic rifle, with an extra banana clip and a box of ammunition.

"Jesus, José—you *can't* just drive around Los Angeles with an AK-47 in your backseat! I mean, this isn't Nicaragua, you know!"

José smiled at her innocence.

"I think maybe there are more AK-47s in Los Angeles than in my entire country," he told her. "The trouble is, you have led a very protective life here."

Tanya didn't like to be reminded about her protected life. "Okay," she said, "let's go to a motel, then. Let's just stop talking about it, okay?"

It was disappointing, after such a big buildup, that José didn't take her anyplace fun, like East L.A. They headed out of town into the desert to just another Hollywood hangout, almost as boring as Beverly Hills—Palm Springs.

15

NICKY RACHMANINOFF OPENED HIS EYES TO THE FIRST TRACES OF dawn in the eastern sky. It was a beautiful sight, though Nicky couldn't imagine what he was doing here, lying on his back with a scruffy cactus at his feet and some lonely sagebrush by his head. He stank as if someone had peed on him and then emptied a bottle of bourbon over his head for good luck. Each minute part of his body throbbed with a vivid and lively pain that made him want to close his eyes and die.

A jackrabbit hopped by close to his head, gazed at him in astonishment, then took off fast. The rabbit reminded him of Easter, and Easter reminded him of Spring Break—and soon he remembered it all.

Nicky sat up very gingerly. Despite the various pains, he didn't think he had broken anything too vital. He was in a vacant lot between two motels, and the world looked as if it had a very big hangover. A green and white Palm Springs police car cruised by, and Nicky tried to wave at it. The cops pulled over and stepped out of their car.

"My, my," said one, "aren't you a little old to be partying with the kids?"

"Jesus, this fella stinks!" said the second.

Nicky tried to tell them he was a policeman, but his lips were bruised and swollen and his words were incomprehensible. He tried to sit up a little more and discovered to his horror that his beige corduroy jacket was ripped up the side. This was worse than his second discovery, which was that his gun and wallet were missing.

"Mm . . . goon," he managed.

"What's he saying?"

"My . . . gun," he got out with tremendous effort. The two cops understood him this time, but unfortunately *gun* was not the word they wished to hear. Before Nicky knew what was happening, the cops had him rolled over, face pushed down into the desert sand, handcuffs tight on his wrists behind his back.

They threw him roughly into the back of their cruiser and hauled him down to the station, where he was booked for public drunkenness, vagrancy, and disorderly conduct. He once again tried to tell the sergeant at the desk he was a cop, but had no better luck than he'd had the first time.

He fell asleep while they were taking his fingerprints, and woke up some time later in the drunk tank, alongside twenty stupefied college kids, half of whom were unconscious on the floor, with the other, more lively half shouting and moaning and throwing up every now and then upon whatever or whoever happened to be beneath them.

This was decidedly the unglamorous side of Palm Springs. Nicky gratefully fell asleep on the concrete floor, and when he awoke there was a hallucinatory vision staring at him from the other side of the bars: a slim, graceful woman—oh, such a lovely woman!—dressed entirely in the most dazzling white—loose muslin pants and a coarse Greek cotton top with a gold belt around her slim waist. Nicky could only sigh with the wonderment of it all—the lady wasn't even wearing a bra! As it happened, Nicky would recognize those perky nipples anywhere, even if the rest of her was incognito behind big round dark glasses.

"Nipples," he said, reaching out through the bars. He was still having trouble articulating his words.

"That's him all right," said Kitty Hall to a cop by her side.

"What do you want to do with him, Miss Hall?" asked the cop in his best cop-to-movie-star manner.

"Wrap him up," she said. "I'll take him home."

16

"DON'T CROWD ME, RACHMANINOFF," SAID KITTY HALL. "JUST BE-cause we've been to bed together doesn't mean I owe you any explanations."

"Inshamissy i'bid aw mooshual trush," he told her cryptically.

"What?"

He was trying to tell her that intimacy was built on mutual trust and understanding, and if she wanted to keep on enjoying his fab-ulous body, she'd better start dishing out the God damn truth. Unfortunately his lips and tongue were swollen so badly she could barely understand a word he said.

They were sitting in her car outside the Palm Springs Police Station, next to the airport. Kitty's car was a Mercedes-Benz station wagon—not a cheap car, but not the usual Rolls or Ferrari that movie people generally favored to achieve maximum glitz and envy. Kitty apparently had more subtle uses for money. She lit a cigarette and blew a cloud of smoke in his direction, and then used a master switch on her side of the automobile to open all the windows and the sun roof to let out both smoke and smell of Rachmaninoff.

"That was silly of me, wasn't it? The moment I said 'Poor Pip,' I knew you had me."

Nicky stared at her angrily. "How you fine' me?" he managed.

"Look, I'm sorry, Rachmaninoff, I really am—but I thought you could take care of yourself, for chrissake," she told him defensively. "Okay, I saw those college kids pick you up and carry you away, but I was right in the middle of something important. Jesus, why didn't you pull out your badge and tell them you were a cop? Or did you think you're so damn macho you could handle them without that?"

"I'm matho all rith," he said.

"You need to put some ice on that swelling," she told him. "Anyway, this morning I started worrying about you. Actually, I didn't sleep all that well last night, wondering if you were okay, and as soon as it was light I started calling the hospitals and police stations."

Nicky was glad he had at least troubled her sleep. "Tell me about Pish," he said.

"Who? Oh, *Pip* . . . well, okay, so I lied to you about her, but what *you* did was worse."

"Whash I do?"

"You concealed the fact that you *knew* I was lying. You just turned and walked away. I was really hurt by that, you know."

Nicky sighed so deeply it hurt his ribs. They seemed to be at an impasse.

"I'm going to take you to a doctor. You look terrible, you know that?"

Nicky reached over and pulled the keys out of the ignition.

"Tell me about Pip," he said once again, pronouncing the words carefully. He found he could speak all right if he kept his mouth open wide and his tongue away from his teeth. "What in God's name have you two ladies been up to?"

Kitty sucked on her cigarette. "Okay," she said, "I'll tell you. Pip telephoned when Cory didn't come back from Nicaragua. I felt sorry for her, I guess—I can't really blame *her* for the fact that Cory has to seduce every girl in sight. She's been worried sick about him."

"Hash she . . . *has* she seen him?" he asked, greatly interested in this single fact.

"Naturally. Cory called her Monday, I guess just a short time after you left her apartment in Westwood. They made a date. He came by and picked her up later in the afternoon. They spent a night in a motel, catching up on old times, and then he came back to the desert without her."

"He's in Palm Springs?"

Kitty looked at him a moment before she answered.

"Has he broken any laws, Nicholas? Are you going to arrest him if you find him, or what?"

"All I want is to see him with my own eyes and talk with him awhile," said Rachmaninoff, then added, "He hasn't broken any laws in this country at least, not that I know of."

"Well," she went on reluctantly, "he's been staying at a motel in Twenty-nine Palms—that's a little town about ninety miles southeast of here. But I don't think he's there anymore."

"Where is he now?"

"I don't know, Nicholas. I'm telling you the truth."

"Have *you* seen him, Kitty?"

She shook her head, not looking at him directly. "I've only talked to him on the phone a few times. I feel I owe him that. He's in trouble, for chrissake."

"How does he sound? Chipper? Depressed?"

"Oh, you know Cory, always the optimist. He thinks this is all fun and games."

Nicky leaned closer, so that Kitty winced at the way he smelled. "You know what I think? I think he's dead, Kitty. I think you're lying to me."

"What the hell are you talking about?"

"Cory's dead. Everything you've been telling me's just a lot of bullshit."

Kitty sat up rigidly behind the steering wheel and stared straight ahead. Apparently she was not accustomed to people doubting her word.

"I told you, *I* have talked with him on the phone—Pip has seen him, spent the fucking night with him! Or you may reverse that order—spent the night *fucking* with him, if you please."

"Cross your heart and hope to die?"

"Are you calling me a liar?"

Nicky laughed as well as he could with a swollen lip and tongue.

"Look, if you don't believe me, you can see him for yourself," said Kitty.

"That's exactly what I want. I keep telling you this, Kitty—I want to see him."

"Well, I shouldn't be telling you this, but I guess I will," said Kitty, stopping to light one of her eternal cigarettes. "Pip's meeting Cory today at five o'clock at the top of the Aerial Tramway. If you want to be really obnoxious, I suppose you could show up and put a damper on their little rendezvous."

"Where's this Aerial Tramway?"

"It's a cable car, a big tourist attraction. It goes from Palm Springs up into the mountains. Pip's supposed to meet him at one of the lookout points."

"They're going to all this trouble so they can make lovey-dovey with a view?"

She flashed him a dirty look. "You think I care? I don't. But that's not the reason they're meeting."

"Well?"

"Jesus, you stink! Do you mind staying over on your side of the car?"

"Kitty, so help me, I'm going to put you over my knee and spank you if you don't tell me what this is all about."

The smoky eyes flashed. "Promise?" she asked.

Nicky sighed.

"Hey, just kidding, Rachmaninoff. Okay, I'll tell you. I don't know *why* I'm telling you, but I guess I've got to trust you. Cory's giving Pip the bank numbers so she can give them to me."

"Wait a minute. What bank numbers?"

"Oh, you don't know about those, do you? This is the big treasure—what Cory found in the two coffins he dug up outside of Managua—just a list of bank numbers. We don't even know if they're for banks in Switzerland or Panama or what, but we figure Octavio will know or can find out."

"You're going to give these numbers to Octavio?"

"Nicholas, I'm going to *sell* the numbers to Octavio. That's what this is all about—a salvage operation."

"Sweet Jesus!" mourned Rachmaninoff. "And I thought you were a smart lady!"

"Well, what's not smart about it? Sure, I wish there had been a billion dollars in gold bullion in those coffins—then we wouldn't have to deal with a scuzzball like Octavio Morales—but there wasn't. It just turned out to be a bunch of God damn bank numbers. So we sell and he buys. It's only logical."

"When you say *we*, Kitty—who all are involved in this little plot?"

"Just Cory and Pip and me."

"Now *that's* a cozy little triangle."

"Nicholas, listen to me—I don't care about Cory and Pip. Once this is over, Cory can ride off into the sunset with all the teenage girls he wants. All I want is to get back just *some* of the money Somoza stole from the people of Nicaragua. I don't know if you can understand this or not, but it's something I have to do. It's a moral obligation."

"Ah, it's moral, is it? Well, exactly how much money are you trying to extort from poor Señor Morales?"

"Nicholas, first of all, it's *not* extortion—it's just a salvage operation, like someone finding an abandoned boat on the high seas and returning it to its owner. Our selling price happens to be a hundred million dollars."

"Jesus!"

"It's not for us, it's for the Sandinistas, like I keep telling you. Octavio's actually getting a hell of a deal—there must be at least a billion dollars in those numbered accounts. Somoza was a very greedy man."

"Who worked out this deal with Octavio? You or Cory?"

"I did." Kitty looked just a little bit pleased with herself. "I've been on the phone with that fascist greaseball every day for the past week. Octavio's tricky as hell, but he's also unbelievably greedy, and he wants those numbers so badly I can almost hear him salivating on the phone."

"You're playing with fire, you know."

"You think I'm a fool, for chrissake? Octavio would like to bump us off and get those numbers without paying a cent."

"Doesn't that worry you a tad?"

"You can relax, Nicholas," she told him smugly. "I have a plan."

Nicholas sighed. "I must tell you something, Kitty, from some years of experience in this area—plans generally don't work. Do you know the Greek word *hubris*? The gods are jealous of clever human conceits and throw a monkey wrench into the works just when you least expect it."

"We've thought of everything," she said. "Believe me."

"Sure," he said gloomily.

"It's basically simple—we're going to make the exchange at Octavio's big party tomorrow night. I'm going to bring the numbers and Octavio will have the cash. We'll do the deal right out in the open—half of Hollywood's going to be there, and he won't dare try anything underhanded."

Nicky shook his head. "Look, you're going to be on *his* turf, Kitty. Do you really think he's going to let you walk away with a hundred million of his money?"

"He's not going to have any choice. We're providing a few little surprises just in case he decides to act up."

"Like what?"

"Like maybe I'm not going to tell you everything, Nicholas. You'll just have to trust me on this."

"Trust you!" said Rachmaninoff mournfully. He was trying to keep this impersonal and forget that for a few hours he had trusted Katherine Hall too much.

She reached from her bucket seat to his and took his hand. "*Please*, Nicholas. Just trust me until tomorrow night. Look, if you're worried, why don't you come to the party as my date? Octavio's not going to try anything with a police lieutenant standing by my side. Remember, he owns a movie studio now, and he has to be able to live in this town once this deal's over."

"I'm glad I can be so useful."

"Say you'll come, Nicholas? You'll be the extra bit of insurance I need to pull this off. If you won't do it for me, then do it for Nicaragua."

"Nicaragua!" he repeated bitterly. "Land of living poetry!"

"Well?"

"Well, I'm thinking. Shut up a moment, all right?"

Whatever the merits of Kitty's plan, there was one very large problem of which she seemed blissfully unaware: As far as Nicky could tell, Octavio Morales was broke—he was having enough trouble paying his grocery bills at Jurgensen's, much less coming up with a hundred million dollars to buy some numbers whose worth was a matter of speculation. But a clever policeman could conceivably use this situation to snag one raccoon killer *in flagrante*—as long as he lived to tell the tale.

"Are you still there, Nicholas? You look like you're on a spaceship to Pluto."

"Yeah, I'll come to the party," he said. "Sounds like a real ball."

"It's a costume ball," she told him with a thin smile. "You'll have to dress up like a character from the *Arabian Nights*."

"Well, what the hell. The way my nights are going, maybe it'll be an improvement."

Having come at last to an agreement, Nicky asked if she would drive him across town to the 7-Eleven on Palm Canyon Drive, where he had left his car last night. It was midmorning, and there were signs of college youth coming to life and getting themselves worked up for another day of wild and crazy fun. Kitty and Nicky drove in silence across the flat residential blocks of small apartment buildings and small businesses. Empty beer cans and broken bottles littered the sun-drenched streets. Palm Springs would certainly need a good cleaning before any more Republican Presidents came to play golf.

The 7-Eleven was where he remembered it, but it took Nicky a few minutes to find his car. The Austin-Healey had been moved—it looked as if a hurricane had picked it up, or perhaps just a dozen drunk giants, and carried it twenty feet down the road. Nicky got out of Kitty's Mercedes and limped down the road. When he reached his familiar old machine he sighed, leaned forward, and put his cheek against the warm metal of the hood.

"For chrissake, Rachmaninoff, it's only a car," called Kitty from her sleek Mercedes. "Hell, how long have you owned that thing, anyway? It's time you bought something new."

Nicky was too sick at heart to answer. Together, he and his car made quite a ruined pair: The windshield was smashed, the headlights broken, and the canvas top had been torn with a knife. He also had four slashed tires, a crushed fender, and a pink ticket on the remains of the windshield, citing him for illegal parking. Last but not least, someone had used a can of spray paint to write the word PIG in giant letters across the hood.

Nicky found his eyes were stinging with tears. This was getting to be a lot of abuse, even for a guy as tough as Rachmaninoff. First he had lost his favorite raccoon, then his favorite beige corduroy jacket, and now his old Austin-Healey looked ready for the junkyard. These had been the cornerstones of Nicky's life, and he was starting to get a little bit mad.

17

TANYA RACHMANINOFF KNEW SHE WAS GOING TO LOVE THE GARDEN of Allah Motel in Twenty-nine Palms from the moment she saw the parking lot full of exotic cars one would never see in Beverly Hills—cars with strange names like Buick, Oldsmobile, and Chevrolet.

Twenty-nine Palms itself was little more than a patch of highway through the desert, with motels, gas stations, and stores on either side. There were also, naturally, twenty-nine thick and bushy palm trees surrounding an oasis on one end of town. Tanya and José had come here because every motel in Palm Springs was full, and this was fine with Tanya. The Garden of Allah really had tons of atmosphere. It was run by an Iranian couple with four small children who occasionally poked their faces out from a dark bedroom behind the office, which smelled of incense and Middle Eastern cooking. The sign in the window said OPAN. The pool was shaped like an hourglass, and there were green plastic lounge chairs set out on top of a synthetic material that was supposed to resemble grass. Tanya felt she should be taking notes. This was all so interesting—such obvious material for her future memoirs—that she found herself constantly writing in an imaginary journal.

Our room has no less than two king-size beds, she wrote. *For orgies, I imagine! We have a television set chained to the wall, a picture between our beds of the Champs-Elysées in the snow, and two plastic drinking glasses in sanitary wrap. Most of all, we have each other!*

"It is not quite the Beverly Hills Hotel, I think," José admitted.

"José, this is like absolutely totally romantic," Tanya gushed.

And it was. They made love on both beds, jumping from one to the other whenever the mood struck them. *Blissfully seeking lips, tongues and arms and legs intertwined*, wrote Tanya. *He is gentle, strong, and horny. Ah, Man! Ah, Woman! We will fill the dry desert with our love. . . .*

It was true that José snored loudly, and around one in the morning, the couple in the next room had an orgasm that shook the very foundations of the motel. But Tanya lay in the dark, watching the glowing end of her cigarette, thinking her romantic thoughts and writing poetry to the beauty of the night.

In the morning there was more lovemaking. *Coffee-flavored kisses,* she wrote, *Upon my creamy thighs./ And will he know that this is/ Like totally awesome in my eyes?*

The Garden of Allah was almost paradise. But paradise was lost in the late morning when José left her to drive to Palm Springs to meet up with his father and Cory Heard. Tanya asked if she could go along, but José said absolutely not.

"My baby, this is like business," he told her.

As if she couldn't deal with business! What did he think, she was an airhead or something? Actually, although she pretended to be hurt, she was glad to be left on her own for a while. There were too many new impressions to sift through and classify.

Tanya took a shower, watched some television, and then, in the early afternoon, decided to venture out to the swimming pool to have some interesting conversations with the people she found there. She always imagined that outside of Beverly Hills there existed *real* people who laughed a lot, spent hours each day with their children, and worked at *real* jobs. Although Tanya had not actually met many of these mythical beings, she vastly looked forward to it. The swimming pool at the Garden of Allah Motel seemed a very good place to start.

She stretched out on one of the green lounge chairs, dressed in her blue-jean cutoffs, halter top, and dark glasses. The pool did not appear entirely clean, which perhaps explained why there were so few people sitting at its side—just a mother with two small children and a very tanned middle-aged man who was glistening in oil and wearing a slightly obscene European swimsuit.

"Hi!" said Tanya.

The mother with two children regarded her suspiciously; the well-oiled middle-aged man leered.

"I'm going to beat the shit out of you if you do that again!" the mother suddenly screamed at one of her children.

"Wanna have a drink with me, honey?" asked the middle-aged man. "Up in my room?"

Tanya excused herself quickly and said she might be down a little later *when her boyfriend got back*. By the time she had locked herself in her room, the first rosy blush of life at the Garden of Allah Motel had somehow paled. The Champs-Elysées looked sadly inappropriate on the wall of their room, the TV had only soap operas and quiz shows, and Tanya was beginning to feel this was a very big mistake. José had told her he would be back by two, but at four o'clock he had still not returned. Tanya was getting hungry, but she didn't dare venture out past the middle-aged man at the pool, who she was convinced was waiting to leap upon her the moment she emerged.

By five o'clock, Tanya was angry. By six o'clock, she had started imagining José in some terrible automobile accident, splattered across the road. Tanya started playing out the scene in her imagination, the crash, his dying words—"Tell Tanya I love her!"—and her own tragic grief, of course. After a while this became so sad she forced herself to think about other worries—like what her mother would say if she ever found out about this little escapade! Susan always pretended to be very liberal about sex, but Tanya wasn't fooled—checking into a motel with José would cause some awesome shit to hit the fan!

By seven o'clock, when José had still not returned, Tanya was about ready to call her father in Los Angeles and ask him to pick her up; he would be angry, naturally, but she knew Nicholas would eventually forgive her anything.

Unfortunately, there was no phone in her room; and if Tanya wanted to call she would have to go out. She thought about this for nearly another hour, changing her mind back and forth. Tanya was not feeling brave, but she was becoming aware she had to do *something*. Eventually she left the room, walked down the outdoor hallway, and made her way carefully around the side of the motel, circumventing the pool, to a phone booth near the office. The desert twilight had faded into a dark night, and Tanya had never felt lonelier in her life.

She dialed her father's number, and even the sound of his ringing telephone brought a sense of comfort. But after four rings, she heard the electronic whir of the answering machine and then her father's slightly stilted voice: "This is the Rachmaninoff residence. No one can come to the phone just now, but if you leave a message at the sound of the tone, I'll get back to you as soon as possible."

"Dad! This is Tanya!" she said. She fought against a great desire to break down and cry. "Look, I've been kinda stupid and like I'm *totally* stuck at this *really* sleazy motel in the middle of God knows where . . . and I was hoping like maybe you could come and get me. Can you, Dad? So I guess what I'll do, I'll call you later on. 'Bye. I love you."

She had begun walking dejectedly back toward her room when she saw the red Cadillac convertible pull into the parking lot. José sat in the car without moving after he turned off the ignition. Tanya felt a rush of relief that quickly turned to anger. She rushed from the phone booth across the parking lot and bore down upon him.

"Where the fucking hell have you been all day? Do you know how long you've been gone?"

José was very pale. He smiled wanly, the strangest and palest smile she had ever seen. He raised his hand and she saw there was blood running down his sleeve.

"Oh my God!" Tanya screamed. "What's happened to you?"

"You must help me to the room," he told her softly. "Quickly now."

"But what's wrong?"

José didn't tell her, but when she got him inside, she was covered with his blood and she could easily see the problem for herself.

The problem was José had been shot.

18

BY THREE O'CLOCK THAT SAME AFTERNOON, NICKY RACHMANINOFF was standing in a gas station, watching his Austin-Healey being towed to a temporary resting place at the rear of the building, near the garbage cans. At the moment, he was looking in better shape than his car. The Palm Springs Police Department, eager to atone for their error of arresting the head of the BHPD Homicide Squad, had let him use their facilities to shower and shave. One of the sergeants had loaned him a silver jogging suit, and a doctor had been called in to dress his wounds. Except for a case of lasting grouchiness, it was considered likely that Lieutenant Rachmaninoff would survive his encounter with Spring Break.

The man from the tow truck was shaking his head. "This old thing is totaled, I'm afraid. You're going to have to buy yourself a new one, Lieutenant."

Jesus! What else can go wrong? he wondered. And then it hit him, something much worse than losing a raccoon or a sport coat or an old car.

"I gotta use your phone," he said urgently, striding into the gas station office. "This is a police emergency. Don't worry, I'll pay the charges."

He telephoned the private number at Susan's Beverly Hills bungalow, but got no answer. At this time of the afternoon, Susan could be at work or giving an interview—or doing anything at all—and Tanya should be still at school. To put his mind at rest, Nicky phoned the school office, only to learn that Tanya Rachmaninoff had not come in today. This did not put his mind at rest at all. He put down the phone with a deep scowl on his face.

After a moment he phoned the Beverly Hills Hotel a second time and asked to be put through to the front desk. It was unfortunate he reached the one assistant manager who most disapproved of fourteen-year-old girls who ran barefoot through the lobby: Mr. Marsh, a small man, prematurely bald, who believed he had a holy mission to preserve the city's oldest and most glamorous institution from the desecration of the young.

"Mr. Marsh, this is Lieutenant Rachmaninoff. I'm trying to get hold of Susan or Tanya. I'm a little concerned, actually. I can't reach them."

"Don't you know?"

"Don't I know *what*?" For a moment Nicky could barely breathe.

"Miss Merril left for New York yesterday—she won't be back until Sunday afternoon. She's staying at the Plaza, in case you want to reach her."

"She took Tanya?"

"No, your daughter remained with us. Miss Merril asked if we would keep an eye on her. As a matter of fact, I was hoping you would have a word with her—Tanya really *mustn't* be allowed to walk through the lobby barefoot, I'm sure you understand."

"Yes, but when did you see her last?"

"Lieutenant, it's impossible to keep track of *one* teenage girl in a hotel of this size. I tried explaining that to Miss Merril when she left. . . ."

"Mr. Marsh, *please*—when did you see Tanya last?"

"I believe it was yesterday afternoon. I had to ask her *not* to put out her cigarette in the potted palm by the reception desk."

"That couldn't be Tanya," Nicky said. "I'm sure she doesn't smoke—she's only fourteen, you know."

The assistant manager chuckled nastily. "It's like the old saying," he said inexplicably. " 'Where there's smoke, there's fire!' "

Nicky asked if housecleaning could check whether Tanya slept in her bed last night. The assistant manager told him this might take a little time, but if he wished he could call back later in the afternoon. Nicky put down the telephone and stared for a moment at a calendar on the wall with a photograph of a half-naked woman. Then he called Charlie in Beverly Hills.

"Aha!" said Charlie. "Could it be the missing Rachmaninoff? Where are you, pray tell?"

"Palm Springs."

"Are you singing duets with Sonny Bono?"

"Charlie, you wouldn't believe me if I told you. Listen, I want you to drop everything and see if you can find Tanya for me.

214

Susan's gone to New York, and Tanya didn't show up at school today. If you want to know the truth, I'm worried as hell. You might try her friends Bunky and Kirsten, see if they know anything about this."

"Nicky, is this really police business?"

"I don't trust Octavio. Shooting Agatha was his way of telling me he can get at the things I love."

"Okay, I see your point. But relax, Nicky—the chances are Tanya's just having fun somewhere."

"Yeah, sure. Look, once you find her, see if Officer Kaminsky can stay with her until I get back. I just can't imagine why the hell Susan left her alone!"

"Hey, Nicky, I'll find her. Meanwhile, you can just go back to playing golf, and all those fun things you're doing in glamorous Palm Springs."

Nicky snorted contemptuously over the wires. "What's going on in the office?" he asked.

"Listen to this—I got a witness, Nicky, a witness who can place Yoshiro Miyaji at Octavio Morales's house in Beverly Hills just a few hours before he was killed. What do you think of that?"

"Who's your witness?"

"It's a maid—she's a Mexican girl, and I was able to lean on her a little because she doesn't have a green card. She said Octavio had a Japanese *señor* over for dinner that night—she didn't know his name, but she was able to identify Miyaji from a photograph."

"That's swell, but will she tell her story in court, or will she mysteriously change her mind when she realizes Octavio can make her life a lot more miserable than our immigration service can?"

"We can isolate her, Nicky—put her and her family in our Special Witness program. Maybe we can even promise her a green card at the end of it all."

"Okay," said Nicky, without a great deal of enthusiasm. "Get her off the streets and make sure we can keep her safe. Did you get anything else?"

"Only that Octavio is broke, like we thought. And I mean *really* broke. He has a few balloon payments due next month, and could lose his house in Beverly Hills if he doesn't come up with some hard cash. The feeling about town is that he got seduced into this movie

215

deal because he wants to be a Hollywood player so bad. He paid more than twice face value of the stock for Yankee International, and he's so deep in debt he's a pretty good prospect for a hostile takeover himself. The rumors are the Japanese are reorganizing for another bid, and there are some local raiders getting into the action as well. Octavio may turn out to be Hollywood's briefest tycoon."

"Good," said Nicky. "But forget about all this now, Charlie, and just find Tanya. Find her and tell her that as soon as I take care of this one last case, I'm going to stop all this bullshit and make some time for her . . . I swear to God!"

19

THE PALM SPRINGS AERIAL TRAMWAY, NICKY DECIDED, WAS REALLY an oversized breadbox dangling on a wire. The breadbox took off from the valley station with a vertiginous swoop and with cute little screams from all the people packed in like muffins. These people were only pretending to be frightened, of course—they were not *really* frightened, like Rachmaninoff.

As the cable car went up the face of the mountain, video cameras protruded from every window, filming everything in sight. A pre-adolescent boy in the front of the car began jumping up and down to try to make it bounce. Nicky leaned forward to whisper into the child's ear, "Listen, kid, if you don't stop that jumping, I'm going to pick you up and throw you out the fucking window!"

They arrived at the first tower, passed over a series of small wheels, and swung out dizzily into the open space beyond. Beneath them, the land changed from desert to sheer granite cliffs, and they still kept climbing. Nicky closed his eyes. As far as he was concerned, this was a trip for eagles—not tourists.

"Nicholas, you're looking a little pale," said Kitty. "You're not afraid of heights, are you?"

"What ever gave you that idea?" he murmured.

Kitty was in deep disguise so her fans wouldn't recognize her, dressed as an aging hippie in a big leather hat, dark glasses that had an iridescent rainbow sheen, old jeans, and Birkenstock sandals. This was method acting at its finest; she even had a patch on the rear of her jeans that said MAKE LOVE, NOT WAR. Nicky had agreed Kitty could come to the top of the mountain, but she was to wait for him in the bar while he took the trail to the rendezvous point with Cory. Nicky wanted to have a good long talk with Cory alone. Unfortunately, he had had no idea this mountain above Palm Springs would be so large, or the cable car so insubstantial.

He opened his eyes only when the door opened and the Aerial Tramway disgorged its passengers onto the top of the mountain. The air was twenty degrees cooler here than eight thousand feet below, on the desert floor. There was a resinous smell of pine. Nicky dared one quick glance down to the desert below, and then he was shuffled off with all the others into the mountain station with all its little gift shops and cafeterias and telescopes that gave you three minutes for twenty-five cents. As far as Nicky was concerned, it seemed a prodigious waste of energy to conquer a mountain of this size for the sake of camcorders and postcards and pricy hot dogs with a view.

Nicky left Kitty in the bar with instructions not to go anywhere, and then he made his way out of the rear of the building into the woods. A number of trails converged at the end of a short concrete path; Nicky was to take the self-guided nature loop, which went past a series of vista points where brave souls might gaze down to the desert below. According to Kitty, Cory and Pip were meeting at the second vista point along the path; she said he couldn't miss it as long as he followed the trail. Nicky was not so optimistic. He was no Daniel Boone, and this mountain, he quickly observed, made the hills of Beverly look like a very small molehill indeed.

It was already a quarter to five, and Nicky was afraid he would be late. He ignored the assorted aches and pains of his battered body, and broke into a slow, masochistic jog along the dirt path, passing through an ancient pine forest where huge trees towered above his head. It was still more than an hour before sunset, but the forest lay in a hushed twilight broken only by the sound of parents shouting at their children and a distant Swiss polka coming over the loud-speakers from the tram station.

After a while, Nicky passed beyond the sphere of the polka, and the only people he saw were isolated groups of hikers heading back toward the station. He was unprepared for the immensity of this forest; there were patches of snow beneath the trees, and a cool wind was moving through the upper branches. He wished he had his beige corduroy jacket. Probably wild animals—raccoons, even— would start coming out as soon as the last tourists were down the mountain and safely in their Palm Springs motels.

It was ten past five when Nicky reached the first vista point. He forced himself to keep jogging, discovering that after enough abuse, a body becomes simply numb. The second vista point was ten minutes farther down the trail. He was now twenty minutes late for the rendezvous, but maybe Cory and Pip would have a lot to talk about—old times in the classroom, conspiracies, sex—anything at all, please God, as long as he didn't miss this meeting.

The trail to the second vista point led off steeply from the main path and passed around the side of a large boulder. Nicky approached more cautiously, keeping an eye out for vanishing liberals and their teenage girlfriends, but he came to the end of the path a few minutes later without seeing a soul. The path simply ended in a small clearing and a sheer drop that seemed to fall off thousands of feet to the brown carpet of desert below. There was no guardrail to keep tourists and stray policemen from falling to their doom.

The sense of height was dizzying. Fingers of the wind seemed to reach out for him and pull him toward the edge. Nicky backed against a boulder, as far from the abyss as he could get. He wondered if this was the right vista point. Had Cory and Pip already come and gone? Nicky's fear of heights made it nearly impossible to think clearly. Standing very still, he began to hear subtle forest noises above his heartbeat—the creaking of trees in the wind, the lonely cry of birds. Somewhere beyond the edge of the cliff, a stone came loose and fell. Nicky could not hear it land, which he knew was not a good sign.

The wind was coming up stronger now, shaking the trees. As

Nicky stood with his back against the boulder, he began to hear a soft moaning coming from somewhere below him. It sounded as if the wind were crying in pain.

His teeth began to chatter. The sky was turning into a deepening twilight, and he knew that if he didn't start moving soon, he might be stuck here all night. For the first time in fifteen years, Nicky wished fervently for a cigarette. He promised himself that the moment he returned to civilization, he would rediscover some old and comforting vice. Life was too short and dangerous to live clean.

The wind was still moaning. Now it sounded like actual words: "Co-o-ory!" cried the wind. "Co-o-ory! . . ."

"Hello!" shouted Rachmaninoff. He didn't shout too loud, however, for fear it might somehow blow him off the edge of the mountain. He forced himself to call again: "Hello! . . . Who . . . is . . . there?"

For a moment there was nothing. Then he heard it again: "Co-o-ory! . . . Co-o-ory!"

The voice, Nicky judged, could not be far away. To his horror, he realized it must be coming from over the side of the cliff, out where there was nothing but empty air.

"Is anyone out there?" he asked. Shivers were creeping up his spine.

"Cory!" said the voice, more clearly.

"This is Lieutenant Rachmaninoff," he called out. "Where are you?"

But there was no answer now. Nicky waited a few minutes, but the voice did not come again. His heart was beating loudly in his ears.

"Epiphany, is that you? This is Lieutenant Rachmaninoff—can you hear me?"

There was still no answer. Nicky figured he had two choices. Either he could investigate further—he could force himself to look out over the edge of the cliff and see who was there—or he could make his way back to the main path and run as fast as his bruised body could take him to get help.

Meanwhile, it was getting darker by the minute, and something must be done soon. Nicky told himself he was being very childish to be scared witless by a mere drop of eight thousand feet straight down. He lowered himself carefully onto his hands and knees and crawled, hand over hand, to the edge of the cliff. Very cautiously he peered over the side.

He was relieved to find that the cliff did not fall off as abruptly into the void as he had feared. About twenty feet below was a small ledge protruding from the side of the mountain, and that was where he saw the girl. Epiphany Moore, dressed in shorts and a blue T-shirt, was lying on the ledge, on her side. She looked hurt, but she was still alive. As he watched, Pip moved a little, opened her eyes, and looked about a bit wildly.

"Don't . . . move," he told her cautiously, afraid the words themselves might jar her loose and send her cascading over the side of the cliff.

"Cory?"

"This is Nicky Rachmaninoff. Don't you remember me? You telephoned and I came to your apartment."

There was blood on her face, and perhaps the girl had received a knock on her head, because she didn't look entirely all there. Nicky wondered if he could lower himself to her, but the twenty feet of cliff face that separated them was too steep to climb—and worse, beyond the small ledge on which she lay, the cliff really did drop off in one majestic and terrifying sweep, clear to the desert below.

"Pip, can you hear me? Don't move—I'm going to go for help."

"Cory, don't leave me!" she cried with a sudden strength.

"It's Nicky Rachmaninoff," he told her again gently, leaning farther out so she could see him. "I can't get down to you, so I'm going to go for help. Can you understand me?"

"You're not Cory!" she cried with alarm.

"Sh! It's going to be all right. I'm a friend."

Meanwhile, Pip had managed to sit up on her narrow ledge and raise an arm. At the end of the arm was a solid object Nicky did not immediately recognize in the dwindling light, but then he realized—*she had a gun!*

"Pip, just relax now—I'm here to help you."

The girl pointed the gun generally in his direction and pulled the trigger. There was a dry click, nearly as dry as Nicky's mouth: a hammer striking an empty chamber. She tried to fire again, but had the same results. The gun was empty.

"Pip, I think you should stay very . . . very still," he suggested in the most soothing voice he could summon. "Look, this is kind of ridiculous, you on that ledge trying to shoot me with an empty gun, and me up here afraid of heights, but if we both just stop and think about this, I'm sure we can work something out."

Pip seemed to be getting bored. Maybe there was something in his voice she found soothing. With a little sigh, she lowered her head to the hard stone and seemed to fall asleep. It was an odd place to sleep, Nicky thought—*he* certainly wouldn't sleep there so close to the edge. A bad dream, the slightest movement, and she could roll off and fall thousands of feet to her death.

Nicky didn't know what to do. If he left to go for help, he was certain she would not be alive on the ledge when he returned. On the other hand, there wasn't much he could do for her here.

Nicky studied more closely the twenty feet that separated him from the girl. About five feet below him was a gnarly root sticking out of the ground and descending along the side of the cliff to nearly six feet above the girl. Theoretically—if he was brave and the root was strong—he might climb down the root and lower himself to the ledge. The biggest problem was getting down the first five feet to where the root began.

Nicky really didn't want to do this, but what kind of man would he be if he walked away from a maiden in distress? He began by turning over on his stomach and dangling his legs over the side. Inching his way backward, he let his feet swing down and search for some kind of foothold. After a moment his right foot was able to wedge against a small protruding rock. He put some weight on it and found it would hold.

Nicky used his arms to push off farther from safety, and his left foot found another hold. Bit by bit—feeling more like a spider than a man—he lowered himself so that he was at eye level with where he had started, his body clinging to the side of the mountain. He felt he must be close to the root by now. He moved his right foot and found some kind of toehold an inch farther down. Gradually he let his weight settle—and then the inconceivable happened. To Nicky's ultimate horror, the ground beneath his right foot broke away. There seemed to be a small avalanche and then he was falling, grasping at the side of the cliff, reaching out wildly for anything

221

solid to grab on to. His body gave a violent lurch and his arms nearly pulled out of their sockets as he managed to catch hold of the root he had seen from up above. For a moment his feet swung crazily in the air, but then found something solid—a crevice in the rock wide enough to stand on.

Nicky was breathing hard. There was something sticky on his arm, which he discovered was blood. The moon was rising. A coyote howled nearby to give things a little atmosphere. He heard another sound, and was amazed to discover it was himself laughing.

"Cory?"

Apparently the girl had woken from her sleep. "It's just me, Nicky Rachmaninoff," he told her, clinging to the side of the cliff.

"What are *you* doing here?"

He tried to stop laughing. He was close to hysteria.

"It's a long story," he assured her with only a small giggle. From where he was dangling, he couldn't actually see her, but the girl's voice sounded stronger than before, and she seemed cognizant of what was going on around her.

"Are you hurt?" he asked.

"I think I bumped my head. I feel a little dozey."

"Stay awake," he told her. *"Please!"*

"Where's Cory?" she asked again, her old refrain.

"I thought you were seeing him at five."

"He didn't show up. José came instead."

"José?" Nicky asked in surprise. "Do you mean goofy José? The kid from Nicaragua? Black hair? About seventeen years old?"

"I think so."

"Listen, stay tight. I'm coming down to get you."

"But why did he try to kill me?" she asked plaintively.

"Who tried to kill you, Pip?"

"José! He tried to push me off the cliff! It was so scary! But you know what? I got *him* instead. I'm tired of being a victim, Lieutenant Rachmaninoff. So I shot him with my gun."

Nicky sighed.

"I shot him, but he still came after me, and then I slipped and fell down here onto this ledge. I pretended I was dead so he would go away."

"*José!*" said Nicky mournfully, resting his cheek against smooth rock. "You rotten son of a bitch!"

"And you know the funny thing?" said Epiphany from below. "When I first met him, I thought he was so cute."

20

TANYA HAD JOSÉ'S BLOOD ALL OVER HER CLOTHES.

"José, for God's sake, let me call a doctor!"

With his right hand he took hold of her arm and held on hard. His left hand was useless because there was a bullet embedded in the fleshy part of the arm near the shoulder joint.

"This is not a bad wound, Tanya. Believe me, I have seen much worse in battle. See, put your hand here—you can feel where the bullet is, just under the skin. It was a lucky shot from far away. All you must do is cut it out with my knife and make sure everything is clean."

"I can't do it, José—don't you understand, I just *can't!*"

Tanya was feeling a little hysterical. In her entire life, no one had ever asked her to cut a bullet out of an arm before. José was lying on the bed in their motel room, and with his good hand he held on to Tanya and would not let her go.

"Listen to me. Don't be a spoiled rich girl who feels sick at the sight of blood. This is nothing, I tell you. Once in the war when I was fourteen, I myself was forced to cut off a man's leg with a bayonet—now *that* was something. This will take only a minute. You can get me a bottle of whiskey, maybe, so I don't feel the pain."

Tanya began to cry. "I can't buy a bottle of whiskey, honestly, José, they won't let me—*I'm only fourteen!*"

He looked at her scornfully. "Then for chrissake just turn on the TV set loud—in case I scream."

"A doctor," she told him. "We've got to get you to a doctor."

He shook his head. "I told you why we can't, Tanya. Now do this for me," he said. "Just shut up and do it!"

"But what *happened*, José? I really gotta know!"

He sighed. California girls asked a lot of questions.

"Okay," he said, "I'll tell you. I was with my father, and out of nowhere a whole bunch of Octavio Morales's gunmen started shooting at us. It was very bad. We were up in the mountains, at the top of the Palm Springs tramway. My father and I had to separate."

"Gosh, is he all right?"

"Who?"

"Your *father*, of course!"

"Yes, yes, I think so. We were in an ambush, but he got away. I caught this bullet just as I was running into the woods."

"But what were you doing at the top of the Aerial Tramway, for chrissake?"

"Tanya! I'm bleeding to death! But I will tell you quickly—we were there to meet Cory, but he never showed up."

Tanya was getting used to the sight of blood, and was beginning to understand that the wound was not as bad as it looked. She studied José's face closely.

"But how did you get down the mountain?"

"Holy Mother! What are you talking about? I got on the cable car and down, down it went."

"No, I mean with your arm all bleeding and all. Someone must have noticed all that blood and said something. I mean, they wouldn't just let you walk away like that."

José leaned back on the bed and moaned. "Tanya, I will tell you how this happened. I used a jacket, you see, to put around me so that no one could see the blood. Now I am in some pain—so please just do this for me."

Tanya had a terrible feeling José wasn't telling her the truth. "But you didn't *have* a jacket when you left here, José."

"Are you a policeman now, like your father? Listen to me carefully, Tanya, for it is a little hard for me to talk. What I did, I actually stole a jacket some man had left on a rock. I didn't want to tell you this for fear you think I am a bad person. When I was almost back to the motel, I threw the jacket out of the car into the desert so you wouldn't find out."

"But why did they shoot at you in the first place? I mean, *that's* what doesn't make sense. Octavio wouldn't want you dead until *after* you'd given him the bank numbers. You see what I mean?"

José moaned in pain and clutched his wounded arm. "God, you are going to kill me! How do I know why Octavio Morales should do the things he does? But this bullet, I think you must agree, is not a fantasy. And if you love me, Tanya—if you care for me at all— you will get this thing out."

"Okay," she said grimly. "Look, there's a 7-Eleven across the street. I've got to get some Band-Aids and some First Aid Cream or something—maybe some hydrogen peroxide. Otherwise it's going to get all infected."

He nodded. There was a gleam of sweat on his face, and he lay back on the bed, looking very pale. Tanya took her handbag and ran out the door of their motel room, down the hall, and across the street. The convenience store was next to a gas station, and she walked inside the brightly lit interior, past teenagers playing video games and a man buying a twelve-pack of beer, amazed that people were still doing normal things. She found the Band-Aids next to potato chips and nuts on a shelf with toothpaste and deodorant. Tanya wasn't sure exactly what she would need, so she scooped up five boxes of Band-Aids and three tubes of Johnson's first aid cream. On the way to the checkout counter, she picked up a bottle of Paul Masson Cream Sherry for good luck.

The man at the checkout counter was old and as leathery as a snake. He looked as if he had been in the desert a thousand years, gazing at Tanya mutely with watery blue eyes as she poured out the contents of her shopping basket onto the counter.

"Well, that's everything!" she said merrily—and then she remembered she was covered with José's blood and must look an absolute mess. "Oh, I cut myself shaving my legs—that's what all the Band-Aids are for!"

The old man was looking her over. "I gotta see an ID for the alcohol," he said slowly.

"Oh, is that *alcohol*?" she cried in astonishment. "Gosh, I thought it was cream *soda*, for chrissake! I tell you what, why don't I just take the Band-Aids and first aid cream and maybe forget all about the alcohol."

"I think maybe that's a good idea," he told her. Tanya paid for her medical supplies and ran with them back toward the Garden of Allah Motel. Crossing the road, she turned around suddenly and saw the old geezer staring at her through the window of his store. There was a telephone up against his ear.

Tanya knew there was about a ninety-percent chance he was phoning the police. Her feet stopped moving. Her first thought was *Thank God!* The police were safety—her father was a cop—maybe even her father would come and take care of things. But this wasn't Beverly Hills, the cop who would come to the 7-Eleven would not be her father, and good God, was her mom going to be mad!—holedup in a sleazy motel with a wounded outlaw, an AK-47 in the backseat of their car. This was more incredible even than losing her virginity—Tanya felt as if she had been marooned in a Humphrey Bogart movie.

Tanya made her choice fast. She ran quickly into their room.

"José, we gotta get out of here. Like *right now!*"

"What are you talking about?"

"Listen, the cops are coming—we've got to leave fast."

José wanted just to lie there, but she made him move. He put his good arm over her shoulder, and she helped him to the parking lot and into the passenger seat of the car. Across the road, she watched a police cruiser pull up in front of the 7-Eleven. She had been right about the phone call. Tanya was afraid they weren't moving fast enough. The officer would go inside the store, question the old man, and then come over to the motel, looking for the underage girl covered in blood who had tried to buy a bottle of booze.

"Hurry up! Gimme your keys, José."

"They're in the ignition."

Tanya thought it might be a good idea not to tell him she had never driven a car before. She turned the keys in the steering column, but nothing happened.

"Damn! It's broken, José! Maybe you're out of gas."

"You must put the gear to Park."

"I knew that, I guess I just forgot."

At least it was an automatic. Across the street, the police officer was still inside the store, and Tanya had a momentary impulse to stop all this, go to the nice officer, and ask for help.

But it was too late. Way too late. José was shot and she must help him. She must be the strong one now, take care of things where he could not.

Tanya fired up the red '59 Cadillac convertible. Reverse was a little tricky—the car shot backward, and one of the rocketship fins slammed into the side of a parked Buick. There was a sound of breaking glass she didn't dare investigate. Fortunately, it was easier to go forward. Tanya Rachmaninoff pressed down on the accelerator and gunned forth into the night—cigarette between her lips, rock and roll on the radio, her blond hair blowing wild in the wind, and José bleeding by her side.

By the time they hit the freeway heading south, she knew this was about the most fun thing she had ever done in her entire life.

21

NICKY RACHMANINOFF WATCHED THE MOON RISE HIGHER IN THE SKY. Under ordinary circumstances it would have been a very lovely crystal-cool mountain night.

He had managed very carefully to lower himself down onto Pip's ledge, which was approximately four feet wide and six feet long. Pip looked freezing cold. She was wearing shorts and a T-shirt, dressed for the desert, not a mountaintop at night. There was dried blood on her forehead, and her teeth were chattering. Nicky gave her the top of his borrowed silver jogging outfit. This left him cold himself, dressed only in jogging pants and a light T-shirt, but at least he was living up to a heroic image of himself.

"How are you feeling?"

"Still cold—but better, thanks," she told him. "I guess I hit my head and was kinda out of it for a while. But you must be freezing, Lieutenant Rachmaninoff!"

"A little," he admitted, rubbing himself for warmth. "Let's hope we get rescued soon."

"Gosh," she said, "this sure is a predicament!"

"All we need is an eagle to come along," said Rachmaninoff, "and peck on our livers."

"What do you mean?" she asked nervously.

"That's just an allusion to a Greek myth," he assured her. "Believe me, our present problems are not nearly so metaphorical."

"You think maybe we could huddle closer together—for warmth, I mean?" she suggested.

It seemed a good idea. The ledge was not wide enough to sit side by side, so Nicky knelt in front and wrapped his arms around her, rubbing her back vigorously so she wouldn't get the wrong idea. Her body was shaking in small bursts of shivers.

"Gosh, my legs are so cold. Do you think . . . ?"

It was awkward finding a position in which they could huddle together for warmth and he could manage to rub her legs as well. Eventually he sat in a kind of lotus position, with her legs wrapped around his waist. She held him tightly as he vigorously rubbed the bare skin pressed into his sides. Her skin felt a little rubbery and brand-new.

"Does that feel better?" he asked.

"Mm, yes! Please don't stop! I'm sorry to be such a pest."

She was clinging to him as though her life depended on it, her cheek nuzzled into the hollow of his neck, rubbing his back just as vigorously as he was rubbing hers. It was working. Nicky was definitely beginning to warm up from the heat of her body, and the girl's teeth were no longer chattering. He had a feeling that if they rubbed long enough, they could almost start a fire.

"Who told you Cory was going to meet you here at five?" he asked, while they continued to hug and rub. "Did Cory call you himself?"

"Gosh, no, Lieutenant Rachmaninoff—actually, it was Kitty. But she told me four o'clock, not five."

"Four? Are you sure?"

"Positive. I even wrote it down."

"Well, well," said Rachmaninoff. "When was the last time you actually saw Cory, then?"

"A couple of days before he went to Nicaragua, like I told you before. He came over because, you know . . . he wanted to make love."

"But Kitty mentioned he picked you up after I came to your apartment the other day. She said you and Cory spent the night together in a motel."

Pip stopped rubbing long enough to sit back and give him a curious look. "Gee, I don't know why Kitty would say something like that."

"Do you mean you haven't seen him at all?"

Pip settled back into his arms, snuggling closer. Her mouth was close to his ear, tickling him a little as she spoke.

"Not since before Nicaragua—just like I keep telling you, Lieutenant. That's why I was so excited when Kitty told me he wanted to meet me up here at four."

"Why did you bring a gun?"

"Well, it's my little security blanket, you see—I usually keep it in my desk. My parents gave it to me when I decided to come to college in L.A. I mean I'm *really* a pacifist, of course, but after those men the other day, I thought I should just have it along in my bag."

"Probably a wise idea," said Rachmaninoff with a deep sigh. The girl wasn't shivering at all anymore. In fact, she was so closely wrapped around him that he could feel her breasts pressing into his chest and her thighs rubbing against his thighs in a very intimate way. He felt her warm breath on his neck. Despite himself, Nicky was getting excited.

He talked quickly, trying to get his mind on other things. "So who picked you up in the red Cadillac convertible?"

"That was José."

"José!"

"Sure. He said he was going to take me to Cory, but he didn't. We went to some dumb motel to wait, but Cory never showed up. I just can't imagine where he is!"

Nicky was beginning to imagine all too well. "Son of a bitch!" he muttered, thinking mostly of the untruthful Kitty Hall. "And Kitty—did you telephone her when Cory didn't come back from Central America?"

"Gee, I *never* would have had the nerve to call Cory's wife, Lieutenant—she called me and suggested we get together to talk."

"And she told you that Cory was back and wanted to see you?"

"That's right. She said José would come by in his car and take me to him."

While they were talking, Pip had managed to move her body slightly forward so that she was sitting on his lap. She put one of her hands under his T-shirt and began massaging his bare chest.

"Pip, I don't think . . ."

"Please, Lieutenant Rachmaninoff. Just keep on holding me. I'm so frightened and cold. Do you think we'll have to be here all night?"

"I bet help is on the way right now," he told her soothingly, not sure at all. "Now tell me, my dear, why do you think José tried to kill you?"

"I wish I knew. He just showed up, and when I asked him where Cory was, he laughed and he grabbed me and tried to push me over the side. I was so frightened! If I hadn't been able to get to my gun . . ."

She was beginning to cry again, and Nicky didn't have the heart to continue his questions.

"Sh!" he said. "It's going to be all right."

He held her until very gradually the tears stopped and she lay closely against him. For a moment he thought perhaps she had gone to sleep, but then she spoke.

"Can I tell you something?" she asked.

"Of course, Pip. Anything you want."

"You know, I saw you in Palm Springs last night—when you saved me from those horrible boys on the street. I don't want you to think I'm ungrateful. I mean, no one's ever saved me before, Lieutenant Rachmaninoff."

"Well, it's just part of my job," he assured her.

'Oh no! I think you're a *very* brave man—and here you are, saving me again! But aren't you uncomfortable with me on your lap?"

"A little, my dear. A little."

"You can take down your pants if you want. I mean, if you would be more comfortable that way."

"Pip . . ."

"You see, the thing is, when I'm feeling really cold and miserable, there's just *one* way I can get myself relaxed."

"But surely not when you're dangling on a ledge eight thousand feet above a certain death?"

Loose jogging pants with a drawstring cord were no protection against Pip's busy little hands. In a flash she had reached into his pants.

"Pip, this is crazy."

"Please! You can close your eyes and pretend I'm someone else. Honestly, I'll try not to kill us or anything, Lieutenant Rachmaninoff."

"But you *have* to stop calling me Lieutenant Rachmaninoff!"

She had to stand up to rid herself of her shorts, which fell carelessly over the side, floating down, down, down gently to the desert, carried on a wind that was as arbitrary as love—landing at last upon an insignificant piece of cactus below.

"You know, I think this could be the start of something," said Epiphany Moore, sitting down securely upon his lap.

Part Four

THE GUILTY PARTY

1

ON THE MORNING OF HIS BIG PARTY, OCTAVIO MORALES WAS HOVER-
ing on the verge of a nervous breakdown. It wasn't so easy trans-
forming a fifteen-acre Palm Springs estate into a living fantasy of the
Arabian Nights. By midmorning the champagne had not yet
arrived, Octavio was seriously considering murdering the caterer,
and shortly before noon two camels had broken loose from their
ropes, pulling down a white Arabian tent and nearly destroying the
third hole of his nine-hole golf course before being brought under
control.

Then there was his dwindling guest list. At one o'clock, Rona
Barrett's office called to say she would be unable to attend, and the
list of refusals was growing with each passing minute: Barbra Strei-
sand, Robert Redford, Michael Jackson, Bill Murray, Johnny Carson, Michelle Pfeiffer, Billy Crystal, and Mr. and Mrs. Ronald
Reagan—to name just a few—were also unable to attend tonight's
festivities. Apparently, movie studios were bought and sold with
such rapidity these days that the mere owning of one did not auto-
matically confer A-list status. Octavio retreated into his meditation
room for half an hour of yoga. When he emerged he was nearly
calm—but there was a new disaster. He had left the matter of the
second course of the banquet entirely in the caterer's hands, only to
discover the man had really screwed up.

"Lobster cocktails!" Octavio hissed with vicious sarcasm. "You
shithead, lobster cocktail's been *dead* a trillion years. Are you trying
to make me look old-fashioned?"

The caterer was a swarthy man who described himself as Persian,
which in Southern California was a euphemism for "another God
damn Iranian."

"But lobster cocktail is a very lovely dish, very traditional, Mr.
Morales," protested the sweating Iranian.

"Yes, but we despise tradition here, you moron! What do you

think California cuisine is all about? It must be brand-new, never before tried—you must astonish the senses with novelty!"

This was turning into a nightmare—one thousand and one unfashionable lobster cocktails had already been prepared, each in its own champagne flute, and it was too late to change. Octavio quickly decided they might save the day by adding a sliver of avocado and an edible flower to the top of each cocktail—a narrow escape from the embarrassment of culinary obsolescence.

Octavio had to stop a moment to let one of his bodyguards take his blood pressure. He had an unreasonable fear of heart failure. Unfortunately, he had good reason to be upset. He had been foolish—oh, how he knew that now! In order to buy his lovely movie studio, he had been forced to borrow a final three hundred million dollars on a short-term loan from his old associates in Medellin, Colombia. The loan plus interest was due to be repaid in six weeks' time, and the men from Medellin took a very grim view of those who defaulted on their debts. Octavio had allowed himself to get into this ridiculous situation only because lust for his beautiful movie studio had clouded his mind; he had let himself believe he would be able to repay the loan easily, once he had recovered his Uncle Tachito's long-lost fortune.

"And where is that bitch, Katherine Hall?" he asked his bodyguard Martin de Vega.

"She is at her house, sunbathing naked by her swimming pool. We have two very happy men watching her every move."

"Let's hope they don't become *too* happy and forget what they are doing," grumbled Octavio. "And what about Cory? Have you managed to find that son of a whore?"

"We are still hopeful, Señor Morales," said Martin circumspectly. "But he has eluded us so far."

Octavio let loose a long, florid stream of invective in his native tongue against Cory Heard and his whore bitch of a wife who were playing such games with his peace of mind.

"They will not dare double-cross you," said Martin soothingly. "You must let yourself enjoy your great moment of triumph, Señor Morales."

And so the preparations continued. By midafternoon Octavio

was beginning to relax, when there was yet a new problem: the caviar had arrived from Beverly Hills, but the driver would not leave it off without first collecting ten thousand dollars in cash. Octavio offered to write a check, but apparently the first check he had written for the deposit—two thousand dollars—had already bounced at the bank.

"This is outrageous!" cried Octavio to the driver. "How dare you question my good credit! I promise you, heads are going to roll first thing Monday morning! Meanwhile, I will write you a new check."

"I'm sorry, Mr. Morales. My instructions are clear—no cash, no caviar."

Octavio was nearly speechless. "Do you realize I own a movie studio?" he gasped. "My guest list tonight includes the cream of Hollywood! Do you *really* believe my check for a measly ten thousand dollars will not be honored at the bank?"

The driver shrugged. "I don't really believe anything, Mr. Morales. I just follow my instructions."

Octavio sighed. "Very well," he said. "The caviar is actually here, I presume?"

"In the truck," said the driver, nodding toward a van in the driveway.

"Well, you'd better let Martin take you into the house. We keep a little mad money in my office."

Before Martin left, Octavio took him by the arm and said softly in Spanish, "Beat him up a little and lock him in a closet until tomorrow, eh? Try not to get any blood on the carpet."

As soon as the driver from Beverly Hills had disappeared inside the house, Octavio told his head caterer to begin unloading the truck. If the driver was smart, he'd stay quiet about his overnight accommodations; if not, a new disaster would befall him. It was unfortunate, really, but there it was: Here in the Promised Land, life was cheap, but caviar most assuredly was not.

2

THE POLICE HELICOPTER FLEW LOW OVER DOWNTOWN LOS ANGELES, beating its way out of the sunrise from Palm Springs to Beverly Hills. Nicky dozed fitfully in the passenger seat, occasionally opening his eyes blearily, surprised to see canyons of boulevards below him, rather than canyons of granite cliffs.

The helicopter came down upon the landing pad at City Hall, forcing Charlie and Officer Cathy Kaminsky to step backward from the wash of wind.

"Too much, dude!" said the young Palm Springs police pilot with a big grin, as Nicky was about to disembark. "You're like a legend in your lifetime, Lieutenant."

Nicky sighed. In the parking lot, Charlie and Officer Kaminsky were also grinning at him. Unfortunately, the police grapevine was a miracle of efficiency, and this had been the juiciest rescue in years. The Palm Springs helicopter Kitty Hall had finally alerted to look for the lost Rachmaninoff, had found an unforgettably X-rated sight in their spotlight, and the news had been quickly passed on.

"Don't say a word," a grouchy Rachmaninoff warned his subordinates. "We were merely keeping warm in a critical situation. Now, Charlie, you get back to Palm Springs in this miserable helicopter. Kaminsky, you come with me."

Officer Kaminsky drove Nicky to Bunky Baker's home in Benedict Canyon, not far from the Beverly Hills Hotel. Bunky was Tanya's best friend, and Nicky was hoping for information. Her parents were gone for the weekend, leaving her in the charge of a butler, two maids, a chauffeur, and a gardener. Nicky found her having breakfast by the swimming pool.

"Gosh, you look terrible," said Bunky, and then was immediately embarrassed by her rudeness. "I mean . . ."

"That's all right, Bunky. What's more, I *feel* terrible. Do you think I could have a cup of coffee?"

Nicky joined her at the table, and the butler immediately appeared to pour him a cup of coffee from a silver pot.

"Bunky, Tanya hasn't gone to school the last two days, and the Beverly Hills Hotel tells me she hasn't been sleeping at the bungalow. Now, if you know anything about this, you won't be disloyal to her by telling me."

"Gosh, Lieutenant Rachmaninoff," said Bunky, "Charlie was here yesterday, asking the same thing—but I really don't know where she is."

"Maybe there's something small you've forgotten. A boy she met? A date she might have had on Thursday night? Anything at all might be a big help."

Bunky seemed lonely with her parents gone, glad to talk to somebody—anybody—but she had no information for him. Nicky's next stop was Kirsten Cooleridge, Tanya's other best friend, who lived in Bel Air in a big white house on Stone Canyon Drive. Kirsten's parents were gone like Bunky's, only they were even farther away—in Rio de Janeiro for two weeks—leaving their daughter to transform their Bel Air mansion into an ongoing teenage party. At eleven o'clock Saturday morning, young bodies were asleep on the living-room floor and in a hammock by the pool. None of these bodies, however, appeared to be Tanya Rachmaninoff. Nicky found Kirsten in a cabana behind the pool. She was in bed naked with a blond-haired boy who pulled the covers over his head and continued to snore. There were empty beer cans on every surface, ashtrays were full of cigarette butts and marijuana roaches, and a few torn condom wrappers were scattered across the floor.

So this *is what the teenagers do these days*, thought a gloomy Rachmaninoff. Kirsten sat up in bed, not bothering to cover her breasts, and lit her first cigarette of the day. This was a girl whose beauty had peaked at the age of thirteen; now, at fourteen, she seemed used up. Nicky looked at her and felt profoundly depressed. Worse, like Bunky, she also had no knowledge of where Tanya might be.

"Actually, I'm *really* pissed at your daughter, Mr. Rachmaninoff—she doesn't tell me anything anymore. I mean, she met this gorgeous boy in Nicaragua and she wouldn't even tell me all the gory details, you know, even though like we're *supposed* to be best friends!"

"Gory details?" asked the father nervously.

"I wish," said Kirsten. "Personally, as far as I'm concerned, the best part of sex is talking about it," she added, giving her sleeping partner a rueful glance.

Nicky decided he had heard enough. He fled Kirsten's house and sat quietly in the squad car as Officer Kaminsky drove them back down Stone Canyon toward Sunset.

"Where to now, Loo? Any more swell mansions on our list?" Cathy Kaminsky was very perky today, her police hat set jauntily on her blond head.

"Let's try the Beverly Hills Hotel," he told her dejectedly. "I want to take a look at the bungalow."

At the Beverly Hills Hotel, Nicky once again left Officer Kaminsky in the squad car, and persuaded one of the assistant managers to give him a key to Susan and Tanya's bungalow. The bungalow consisted of two bedrooms, a living room, and a kitchenette. The colors were muted pastels. A slant of sunlight came in through a window and cut a coffee table in half with its beam. Nicky sat down on a postmodern pastel sofa and tried to think. He had spent much of his adult life looking for people of every description, but now that it concerned his daughter, his mind had become a blank.

He felt old and tired. Guilt seized him like a vise: Why hadn't he given Tanya more of his time? There had always been an important case he was working on, excuses and defaults. If only he had been a better person, less driven by the needs of his profession.

He left the bungalow with a heavy heart. Tanya's bedroom—her record collection, her books, her clothes—all left him with an inexpressible sadness. He locked the door behind him and strolled back slowly along the flowered paths of the hotel grounds where he had walked away from Susan a few nights before. What a dismal job they had done at being parents! An actress, a cop—they had both been too busy with things that seemed vitally important at the time, but in retrospect were hardly important at all.

Nicky returned the bungalow key to the main desk, and then walked to the front of the hotel, where the valet attendants took the cars. Cathy Kaminsky was waiting for him in the black and white cruiser, tapping her nightstick against the steering wheel. Nicky was walking toward her when a thought made him retrace his steps to the carport.

"Aren't you Greg?" he asked one of the valets, a surfer type who looked not completely at home, stuffed into the dark green uniform of the Beverly Hills Hotel. "I bet you know my daughter, Tanya? She's blond. . . ."

"Hey, everyone knows your daughter around here, Lieutenant. Tanya's one of the few guests who treat us with any human dignity, like we're actual people, if you can dig where I'm coming from."

"Is that right?" said Nicky. He found himself absurdly pleased to hear his daughter praised.

"Yeah, that young lady has a lot of class," said Greg, nodding gravely. "A *lot* of class."

"Actually, I'm trying to find her, Greg. Her mother's in New York and she missed school on Friday. I'm worried sick."

"Is she in trouble, is that it?"

"No, no," Nicky said hastily. "I only want to make sure she's all right. Can you tell me the last time you saw her?"

"Well, that's easy—Thursday night around seven. I was working a night shift, subbing for one of the guys. Tanya was standing here for a while waiting for her date to show."

"Her date?"

"Yeah. Lucky guy. He came in here driving an old Cadillac convertible, a real monster."

"A red Caddy? 'Fifty-nine?"

"Sure, a real classic."

Nicky felt sick. "Did you get a look at the guy?"

"A little. Nice looking, maybe seventeen or eighteen. Dark hair. He looked maybe a little Latin."

"Had sort of a goofy expression?" asked Nicky.

"No," Greg told him. "I didn't see that."

"I guess not," Nicky sighed. "Not anymore."

3

"HEY, YOU SURE AS HELL GOT A MILLION-DOLLAR VIEW, LOO," SAID
Cathy Kaminsky, looking out Rachmaninoff's back window on Sunshine Terrace. They had come here from the Beverly Hills Hotel.
Nicky used his phone to put out an all-points bulletin for his missing daughter, while Officer Kaminsky proceeded to explore every
inch of his house, looking in the kitchen cabinets to check out his
dishes and cutlery.

"I bet you got tons of girls wanting to move into a place like
this—I mean, the rents being what they are. You should get a
microwave, though—it'd save you a ton of time."

Nicky put down the receiver, too demoralized even to tell Officer
Kaminsky to shut up. He noticed the red light of his answering
machine was on, and he ran the tape back to the beginning.

The first call was from Police Chief McGroder, wondering why
he hadn't been receiving written reports the last few days. Nicky had
almost forgotten there *was* such a thing as Chief McGroder, much
less a written report.

The second call was from Susan, saying she had been trying to
reach Tanya for two days and was getting worried. A little late! She
asked if Nicky would try to find her, then call her back in New York.

And the third call was from Tanya. Nicky had to sit down when
he heard her voice:

"Dad! This is Tanya! Look, I've been kinda stupid and like I'm
totally stuck at this *really* sleazy motel in the middle of God knows
where . . . and I was hoping like maybe you could come and get
me. Can you, Dad? So I guess what I'll do, I'll call you later on.
'Bye. I love you."

The messages ended there—Tanya had not called later on as she
had promised, and she had not left an address or phone number.
Nicky played her brief message again and again, finding new nu-
ances of fear and loneliness in her voice and always coming to the
last three words, which tore him apart: *I love you.*

He knew he had to get moving. He had to find a really sleazy motel in the middle of God knows where. Meanwhile, Officer Kaminsky was trying out his television set and saying she was like totally amazed there was *one* person left in Los Angeles who wasn't on cable. Nicky stood up and walked to the window overlooking his back meadow and stared out into space.

He had failed Tanya—failed her so completely he had lost her. *He didn't even know where she was!*

"You know, Loo—maybe I should come back and cook dinner for you some night. I mean, if you'd like that, and all." Cathy Kaminsky moved around from the television set toward Nicky, and then stopped, embarrassed.

"Jesus!" she said, "You're crying!"

4

AT BOB'S OASIS MOTEL IN INDIO, TANYA RACHMANINOFF WAS STUDY-ing herself in the full-length mirror on the bathroom door, posing with José's AK-47 rifle—which sure made a girl look sexy.

Tanya was proud of all she had accomplished. She had driven here last night without getting lost or crashing the car, deciding an obscure motel in Indio would be better than one closer to Palm Springs. As soon as they had arrived, she'd stripped naked so she wouldn't get any more blood on her clothes, and with no more hesitation than if she were brushing her teeth, she had cut out the bullet in José's arm with a knife. José said she looked like an angel of mercy if ever he saw one.

This morning Tanya had left for a while to buy a change of clothes at a nearby Salvation Army store: used olive green work pants and a brown shirt. What the outfit lacked in style, it made up for in price: two dollars and fifty cents for top and bottom. She loved the proletarian way it made her feel. With the AK-47 cradled in her arms, and her eyes narrowed in an intense scowl borrowed from early photographs of Bob Dylan, Tanya thought no one would ever imagine she had once lived in Beverly Hills.

There was a knock on the door and she hid the automatic rifle in the shower stall, closing the plastic curtain.

"Who is it?"

"It's me," said a voice from the other side.

Tanya cautiously opened the motel door and saw a woman of indeterminate years standing in the open hallway. The woman was wearing a scarf tied around her head, a baseball cap on top of the scarf, and big round dark glasses perched on her nose. She could be a bag lady or a housewife; there wasn't enough of her visible to make a positive identification one way or another.

Tanya had been expecting her.

"How is he?" asked the lady.

"He's sleeping right now," Tanya answered. "I think maybe the wound is getting infected."

"I've found a doctor in Beverly Hills," said the woman. "He should be here by two o'clock."

Tanya gave her Bob Dylan scowl. "Doctors have to report gun-shot wounds to the police—that's the law."

"Honey," said the woman, "what Beverly Hills doctors care about is making money—that's *their* law. So just leave this to me. I've also rented you a car. Don't drive the Cadillac anymore, the police know about it. I've got you a nice little Ford Mustang outside in the parking lot, but you'll have to give me a lift back to Palm Springs. Can you manage that?"

"Sure," said Tanya. More and more, she felt she could manage just about anything.

"Did José tell you about the party tonight? What we're trying to do?"

"Naturally," said Tanya coolly.

"And you . . . you're going to help us?"

"Why not?" she answered with a nonchalance she didn't quite feel. Life, Tanya was discovering, was just an imitation of the mov-ies, and as long as you kept that in mind, the lines came easy.

The woman reached into an expensive black Gucci handbag that was totally out of sync with the rest of her outfit.

"Here's the invitation for the party—you'll need it to get inside

243

the gate. The house is just off Frank Sinatra Drive in Rancho Mirage, before you get to Bob Hope. Do you think you can find that?"

"I'll just turn on my TV set and ask Johnny Carson," replied Tanya flippantly.

The woman in the baseball cap with the Gucci handbag gave Tanya a hard look. "Are you sure you can manage this, honey?"

"I was kidding. I'll look at a map, of course."

"I meant the whole deal, Tanya. You know, your parents are going to be mad as hell."

"Screw them," said Tanya. "I mean, my mother thinks she's such a big liberal and all, maybe it's time someone in our family actually *did* something more than talk."

"And your father?"

"Screw him too. I mean, when was *he* ever around to care?"

"Tanya, look, if you do exactly what I tell you, this is going to be a piece of cake. If I thought there was any real danger, I wouldn't let you get involved—you know that, don't you?"

"Let's just skip the preamble," said Tanya while lighting a cigarette in the corner of her mouth, "and get to the main event."

The lady gave the girl a long, searching look from behind her dark glasses. She sighed finally and then continued.

"Okay, then. You know it's a costume party—I left you something in the trunk of the Mustang I think you'll get a kick out of. Right now, I'm assuming José will be well enough to do his part. If the doctor says no, we'll have to make new plans."

The woman stopped speaking and came to an uncertain pause. "Look, Tanya, you know you can still change your mind about doing this. I don't want you to think I'm pressuring you."

Tanya knew damn well the woman was pressuring her. This offer of changing her mind was nothing but the babbling of guilt—and at her age, Tanya had an inner antenna fine-tuned to pick up on guilt and transform it into an instant payoff.

"So you're on?" asked the woman hopefully. "You know how much this is going to mean for the people of Nicaragua?"

"Sure," said Tanya. She wasn't sure exactly *why* she was on, except that José was helpless and she was having the time of her life actually being able to *do* things—drive cars and play doctor and outwit small-town policemen. But as for "the people of Nicaragua," she was beginning to think if she heard that phrase one more time she'd puke.

"You know something? When I was your age, I was just like you," said the woman.

"Sure you were," said Tanya—giving the lady a stunning *fuck you* look such as Hollywood celebrity Katherine Hall had not received for a long, long time.

5

NICKY RACHMANINOFF STRETCHED OUT IN THE BACKSEAT OF THE BHPD black and white cruiser while Officer Kaminsky drove along the same route he had used in following Pip two days before. They were going back to the desert. If José had last been seen at the top of the Palm Springs Aerial Tramway, then Tanya couldn't be far away. Nicky tried to worry about this for a while, but nature took over. He fell into a troubled sleep, cramped and fitful.

He awoke to Officer Kaminsky pulling on his arm. His mouth was dry and he couldn't imagine where he was or what he was doing. The sky had the look of late afternoon, and there was a golden arch standing at the edge of the desert. Could this be paradise? On closer inspection, it was revealed as only a fast-food restaurant on the edge of Palm Springs.

"Wake up, Loo. I've got you something to eat—a couple of Big Macs to keep you going. I wasn't sure if you wanted coffee or Coca-Cola, so I got you both."

The smell of fast-food burgers was like warm processed air. Officer Kaminsky waved a white bag at him with the goodies inside. She smiled in as motherly a way as a lady cop can who is all bulky in the middle with gun, nightstick, flashlight, and handcuffs dangling from her belt. Nicky forced himself to drink the coffee while struggling to keep his burning eyes open.

"What time is it?"

"Sixteen hundred hours, twenty-four minutes, and twelve seconds," she informed him, examining her digital watch. "I talked with Sergeant Katz forty-three minutes ago on the radio. He said he was checking out a lead in Twenty-nine Palms and would meet us at the Royal Sands Motel, where he's taken a room."

Nicky was too groggy to argue. It had been days since he had a decent night's sleep, and all the beatings and clinging to the sides of mountains were starting to get to him. He let Officer Kaminsky drive them from McDonald's to the motel on a side street off Palm Canyon Drive. The motel room had red wallpaper and imitation bordello decor. Nicky stretched out on one of the two king-size beds and promptly fell asleep. He awoke not certain how much time had passed. The room was dark except for a shaft of yellow light from the bathroom, and the glow of the TV set, which was showing "Wheel of Fortune" without sound. To his astonishment, an attractive young blond woman stepped out of the bathroom wearing nothing but a very skimpy motel towel that more or less covered the vital areas. Nicky had to rub his eyes.

"Whoops! Sorry, Loo—you were asleep and I thought I might get cleaned up a little."

It was Officer Kaminsky. Nicky had never seen her out of uniform and would not have recognized her if she hadn't called him "Loo." She retreated into the bathroom for a moment and came out wearing the top of her uniform, but no bottom.

"Officer Kaminsky, this is turning into an unprofessional situation," he told her. "Kindly put on your pants and tell me what time it is."

The officer giggled. "It's eighteen hundred hours, twenty-seven minutes, and thirty-four seconds," she said, flashing her eyes a little.

Nicky had to do some quick arithmetic to realize it was almost six-thirty and he was running late.

"God damn it, why didn't you wake me? I'm supposed to meet Kitty at seven. And where's Charlie, for chrissake?"

"Sergeant Katz hasn't come back yet. And I'm sorry, but you looked so wiped out I didn't have the heart to wake you."

Nicky mumbled a string of obscenities and made his way into the bathroom. "Call the Palm Springs police, see if *they* know where the hell Charlie is," he told her grumpily. "I'm going to take a fast shower."

She poked her head into the bathroom just as Nicky was drying himself. He wasn't certain if she was trying to be seductive or if this was simply coed locker time.

"Don't you knock, Officer?"

"I just wanted to tell you, Loo—the PSPD says Sergeant Katz went from Twenty-nine Palms to Indio, still checking out some lead. Indio's a town about thirty miles south of here."

"I know where Indio is, for chrissake. Charlie still hasn't called in? Damn it, I need him!"

"Maybe I can help you?" asked Officer Kaminsky hopefully.

Nicky sighed and realized he would indeed need Officer Kaminsky's assistance. He continued drying himself; there wasn't time to be modest, and if she wasn't embarrassed, what the hell.

"Do you have a pair of walkie-talkies in your car?"

"Sure. I keep 'em in the trunk alongside the tear-gas canisters and extra ammo. I'm prepared for anything."

"Okay, then. Look in my wallet—it's in the back pocket of my pants. You'll find a card with Kitty Hall's Palm Springs phone number. Give her a call and say I'm running late but I'll pick her up in half an hour."

"Katherine Hall?" she asked. "The *movie* star?"

"Just *do* it, Officer Kaminsky—and get the hell out of here so I can get dressed."

Her eyes flickered appraisingly up and down his body. "You know, you're in pretty good shape, Loo," she said, "I mean, for an old guy who's been beat up some."

6

KITTY'S DESERT RETREAT WAS A FEW MILES OUTSIDE TOWN, NEAR THE foot of the mountains, away from other homes. She owned three hundred acres of empty space all around her, just so no one could put up a shopping mall or a golf course and spoil her view. The house itself was a sprawling old adobe with thick cool walls and vines of bougainvillea creeping up the sides. Rough-cut beams held up the roof; there were more Georgia O'Keeffes on the walls, old wooden rocking chairs in every room, and a cactus garden surrounding the house that would probably discourage any wise burglar.

"Well, well," said Rachmaninoff, taking in the decor. "You could play cowboys-and-Indians all day long in a place like this and hardly even know the outside world was still there."

Kitty smiled vaguely. "Get ready for the party, Nicholas, or we'll be late."

"But tell me, my dear—have you heard from Cory?" Nicky tried to keep any subtle traces of sarcasm and bitterness from his voice. "Perhaps he telephoned again?"

"He's going to meet us there."

"At the party? How nice."

"He'll be in disguise, of course."

"Of course," said Rachmaninoff. "Knowing Cory, he'll probably fly up in a magic carpet. Or here's an idea—maybe he'll just pop out of a bottle like a genie!"

"What's with you, Rachmaninoff?"

Nicky had followed Kitty into her dressing room, where she was seated in front of a three-way mirror, applying final touches of makeup to her coldly perfect face. Nicky moved in closer from behind, watching her watching him in the glass. Only her eyes moved.

"I'll tell you what's with me," he told her. "It's poor Pip. It's the damndest thing, but poor Pip says she hasn't seen Cory for weeks and weeks. She says she didn't spend the night with him in a motel, like you told me. He didn't telephone her, he didn't even ask her to meet him up at the top of the tramway at five o'clock yesterday. You were the one who did that. You told her to meet Cory there—but at four o'clock, not five."

"So?"

"So?" cried Nicky. "What this means, my dear, is that you set her up. In fact, not to mince our words, you are a God damn liar."

Kitty stood up from the mirror and let her silk kimono float to the floor. She was wearing nothing underneath but a pair of brief panties, but this didn't do anything for Rachmaninoff, not anymore. Ignoring him, Kitty began to put on her costume for the party—white silk pantaloons and a little brocaded bikini top that showed off a good deal of flat stomach, belly button and all.

"What are you supposed to be? Some sort of Arabian whore?"

"I'm Scheherazade," she told him airily. Very *la-de-da*. "If you don't know who that is, I'll send you the book sometime."

"Oh, I know, Kitty—I know. Us cops are more literate than you'd suppose. Scheherazade is the lady who has to make up all the stories to save her life, a thousand and one of them, if I remember right. I just wonder how many stories you've told me."

"Look, I've had my reasons for doing what I've done," said Kitty. "I've never *really* lied to you, Rachmaninoff. It's just . . . well, there are different levels of truth."

"Oh-ho!" cried Nicky. "And what level are we on, my dear? Could this be the bargain basement, perchance?"

She spun around angrily from the mirror to face him. "I've been telling you what you need to know," she said, "in order for you to play your part. Now put on your costume, for chrissake, or we're going to be late."

"*My part!*" Nicky repeated vaguely, picking up a silver-handled hair brush from her dresser and running it through his thick, unruly hair. "The trouble is, I don't really *have* a part."

"Rachmaninoff! I'm losing my patience."

"Me too, honey buns. So let's stop bullshitting and talk for starters about José."

"Who?"

"You know God damn well who. The kid. Young goofball with

the goo-goo eyes for my daughter. What the fuck is he doing in California?"

"All right, Nicholas—if you must know, he's here on behalf of the Sandinistas. Naturally, the U.S. government would *not* be terribly amused by this, so we're keeping it a secret. Okay?"

"Not okay. Why did he try to push Pip off a rather nasty cliff?"

"I don't know what you're talking about. Maybe Pip imagined something—you know how young girls are, a little hysterical."

"Well, I guess we'll just have to ask José all about his adventures in Gringoland. Where is he, Kitty?"

"I'd tell you, but I honestly don't know."

Nicky chuckled. "Sure you know, honey buns. And I wouldn't use the word 'honestly,' if I were you—it'll make your nose grow."

"If you call me 'honey buns' one more time, I'm going to kick you in the balls, you . . . you male chauvinist dinosaur!"

Without warning, Nicky reached out and grabbed her hard, holding her arms so tightly she gave a small scream.

"Where's my daughter?" he demanded.

"I don't know!" she shouted back.

"Yes you do. She's with José! *Tell me!*"

He was shaking her. Shaking her so hard her head rolled around on her neck.

"God damn you!" she screamed. "Go ahead! Hit me, beat me up. Act like a pig!"

Nicky let her go as suddenly as he had grabbed her. He stood staring at her in dismay, frightened at how close he had come to violence.

"Pig!" she taunted. "Well, beat me up, Rachmaninoff! Show us what you're made of!"

"Shut up," he said quietly. "Shut your stupid mouth."

She gave him a withering look and then turned back to examine her makeup in the mirror.

"God damn you, you really piss me off," she said after a moment. "You think I'd let anything happen to Tanya? She reminds me too much of myself."

"Oh, that's swell! Everything comes back to *you*, doesn't it?"

"*You* should talk about being selfish!" Kitty hurled at him. "Fucking Susan waltzes off to New York to see about some stupid part on

Broadway, and *you're* never around—you're always off playing cops-and-robbers with the boys."

Nicky hated it that Kitty should be so right about him. "I don't give a shit about any of this anymore," he told her. "Not you, not Cory. I don't care about my job, I don't even give a shit that you've murdered your husband, Miz Hall, and I guess that's pretty bad. All I care about is getting Tanya back safe. Are you listening to me?"

Kitty was quiet for some time. "Okay, then," she said finally. "Tanya will be at the party tonight. If you do what I tell you, she'll come through fine."

"How can I believe you?"

She smiled a little. She seemed to like the idea of having Rachmaninoff in her power.

"I guess you'll just have to trust me now. Won't you?"

7

"I MURDERED MY HUSBAND," SAID KITTY. "IS THAT WHAT YOU REALLY think, Rachmaninoff?"

"Let's just skip it," said Nicky. They continued to drive in silence in Kitty's noblesse-oblige Mercedes-Benz station wagon through the warm Palm Springs night toward Octavio Morales's party in Rancho Mirage.

Nicky was in the passenger seat. Everything in Palm Springs looked unreal to him tonight—the palm trees with amber spotlights at their bases, the liquor stores with their bright, optimistic façades, the pretentious motels whose outer glamour only masked the basic shabbiness underneath. Even Kitty, dressed as Scheherazade in her silk pantaloons and chains of gold, was more the kind of Arabian princess you'd find in an old Victor Mature movie than was ever to be found in the Middle East.

At times like this, all of Southern California appeared as insubstantial as a badly made film. As for Rachmaninoff, Kitty had provided him with a Wise Man outfit—a long white robe and Arab headdress. Nicky felt pretty silly. He even had a white beard for added wisdom. At least he had managed to change in Kitty's guest bathroom, away from her watchful eyes, and the costume concealed a .38 Smith & Wesson police revolver in a shoulder holster beneath his robe, as well as a small walkie-talkie he had taped to the shoulder strap. Officer Cathy Kaminsky, he hoped, had the mate to his walkie-talkie, trailing them in the squad car at a discreet distance. It worried Nicky that his one contact with the outside world was a rookie female police officer who showed progressive signs of being a flake.

"Answer me," said Kitty after a while. "Back there in the house, you said I'd murdered Cory. I want to know why you think that."

Nicky grumbled impolitely. "I told you, I don't care."

"But why would I kill Cory? That's the dumbest thing I've ever heard."

"Is it? Well, first of all, it's obvious Cory has to be dead."

"Why?"

"Because you've been trying so hard to conceal it. That's what this whole thing is all about. I should have remembered you were an actress, Kitty. What you've done is to stage-manage this whole affair so it would look like Cory was still alive. Thus it is elementary, my dear—the opposite must be true. He is dead."

"Go on . . . I'm fascinated to witness a great detective at work."

"You see, you knew Octavio was watching Pip, hoping she'd lead him to Cory. You knew that because she called you and told you about the two guys who had come to see her. So—clever you—you decided to use that opportunity to dangle poor Pip as bait."

"How could I do a thing like that?"

Nicky smiled at her coldly. "What you did, you convinced her that Cory was out there in trouble, hiding somewhere, and he wanted to see her. You set up that fake meeting in a motel—and when Cory didn't show, you said, 'Too bad, maybe he'll try again.' Pip probably isn't too bright, and she was in love—she wanted to believe Cory was out there trying to contact her. So two days later you run the whole deal by her again. This time, you say Cory wants to meet her at the top of the Aerial Tramway at four—not five, like you told me, but we'll get to that part later."

"But why, Rachmaninoff? Why would I go to all this trouble to fool her?"

"I think it's obvious. Everyone would follow Pip, me and Octavio, even little Bob Arnold from the CIA, all of us thinking she was about to lead us to her boyfriend. This was all designed to give substance to the lie that Cory was still alive, the point of this exercise being that you needed to resurrect your husband just long enough for Octavio to go ahead with the deal."

"Wouldn't he go ahead anyway, even if Cory was dead?"

Nicky shook his head. "I doubt it. Octavio has known Cory a long time—he doesn't trust him exactly, but he knows what to expect. If Cory was dead, there would be too many variables. For starters, you wouldn't be able to make it convincing enough that you really had the bank numbers."

"Incredible!" said Kitty Hall.

"And for insurance, you left some old telephone message of Cory's on Susan's answering machine, knowing she would tell me about it. If *I* thought Cory was alive and I was running around looking for him along with everybody else, then the whole illusion would be even more solid."

Kitty popped a cigarette in her mouth and pushed in the lighter at the side of her armrest.

"Now comes the nasty part," said Nicky. "You've fooled Pip twice now, but you knew you probably wouldn't manage a third time. Like I said, Pip was supposed to meet Cory at four, not five like you told me. You see, Pip and I had a little time to talk last night, and this was one of the small details that came out. So I was left with this little puzzle: What is the meaning of this extra hour?"

Nicky paused long enough for Kitty to light her cigarette on the end of the glowing metal. "Well?" she asked. "I'm breathless with anticipation."

"The meaning of this extra hour was that you decided Pip had served her purpose and you'd best get rid of her before she caught on and blew the whistle on the whole scam. So you told José to kill her and get rid of the body before I got there at five. Probably you could have figured out something less permanent, but face it, Kitty—you hate that girl. She's younger than you, and Cory liked to screw her even more than he liked to screw you. So you decided to exact a little revenge—only Pip surprised everyone by having a gun in her bag, and José wasn't able to finish the job."

Kitty turned to him angrily. He wasn't certain whether she was flushed in the face or whether it was only the reflection of the red light at the intersection.

"I told you, I never cared about Cory's girls. They came and went, but he stayed with me."

"Sure, you cared, Kitty. You cared all the way. You see, your problem is you just gotta be top puss in Hollywood. You can't stand the idea of any competition. That's why you went to bed with me, I bet—to get one up on Susan. And that's why you killed Cory in Nicaragua."

"That's absurd. I never had to worry about girls like Pip—*or* Susan, for that matter."

"You don't think so? Actually, Pip's pretty hot stuff—don't let that innocent façade fool you."

"How would *you* know, Rachmaninoff?"

Nicky smiled at the memories. "As a matter of fact, Kitty, you're not really as hot in bed as you think you are. What you are, you're a little too mental, you see. Sex with you is this kind of voyeuristic pornography. I really think you should see a therapist and try to get into your body more, and out of your head."

Kitty laughed. "Oh, this is good! A sexual critique from a meat-and-potatoes man!"

Nicky shrugged. "Sticks and stones may break my bones, but you still murdered your husband, lady. You wanted to get rid of him without the nasty expense of a California divorce where you might have to give him half of everything you own. That would be ironic, wouldn't it, if he was able to support his young girls on *your* money? So you met Cory the night after we last saw him in the rain—or maybe it was the next day—and you shot him. Or you stabbed him. Or maybe you even slipped some poison into his beer. I could find out, but as I told you, I don't really care anymore."

Kitty shook her head in disbelief. "This is amazing! Look, Rachmaninoff, if I wanted to get rid of Cory, I could have just thrown him out. So what if I had to pay alimony and maybe he got one of the houses—I'm not such a materialist as you think."

"I know exactly what you are," said Nicky. "You're spoiled, Kitty, and you're proud. And now you're getting older—not that it shows yet, but it will. You're beginning to get a little scared. There are all these lovely young girls flitting around, and the men don't look at you quite as much as they used to, do they?"

"Shut up!" she said. "You don't understand me at all, Rachmaninoff."

"Don't I?"

Kitty gripped the wheel and they drove the rest of the way to the party in a tense silence. The desert night was opulent, with stars in the sky and sleek expensive cars drifting down quiet streets. Rancho Mirage was a wealthy corner of the desert, with enormous houses just visible behind high walls. There was a smell of flowers in the air, the soft sweet scent of plumeria carried on the night breeze.

Octavio Morales's estate was just off Frank Sinatra Drive, at the end of a small dead-end street. Kitty followed a line of limousines moving toward the front gate, where two private guards were closely checking invitations. Above them, a helicopter descended from the sky, its red and green running lights flashing in the night, landing somewhere on the other side of the high wall.

Kitty's knuckles were white around the rim of the steering wheel. "You don't understand me at all," she said a second time. "But I have to give you credit. You got *some* of it right, maybe. I would describe your effort as close, but no cigar."

Nicky shrugged. "I don't know why you keep on lying."

Kitty laughed, which bothered him a little.

"Actually, it's pathetic how backwards you've gotten everything—I'm almost tempted to give you a clue."

"Please don't bother."

"No, I will. Are you ready? Here it is: Susan once mentioned you don't follow sports much, but that's a pity. If you watched football, you might have figured this out."

"*Football?*"

There was a tap on the car window. Nicky was surprised to see Charlie standing on the street, trying to get his attention.

"Hey, don't *you* look sheik!" said Charlie. "Look, I gotta talk to you, Nick. Something's come up."

"Wait for me," Nicky told Kitty, stepping out of her car. He joined Charlie on the sidewalk, but his eyes were still on Kitty in the car.

Football!

8

CHARLIE CAT LOOKED AS SLEEK AS A SEAL TONIGHT IN A TAN SUMMER suit, blue oxford shirt, and tie. His hair was slicked back, his stomach protruding. He had been gaining weight over the past few months and was starting to look like some kind of Jewish pasha.

"Look, Nicky, I got a line on Tanya," he said. "I hope you're not going to be worried. She's all right—she's been staying with José, that's all. The people who have seen her say she looks fine. José, on the other hand—I think José has a gunshot wound."

"Yeah, Pip shot him," said Rachmaninoff sourly.

"Little Epiphany yuppie-puss? Nicky! What's the world coming to?"

"Her parents gave her a gun to bring with her to Los Angeles. So why shouldn't she shoot someone?"

Charlie was shaking his head. "Our generation invented casual sex, but it took a brave new world to create casual violence. Well, José seems to be bleeding a lot, but I guess he's still alive."

Nicky looked over his shoulder at Kitty, sitting in her Mercedes-Benz, parked to the side a few feet away.

"You'd better tell me about this quick."

Charlie told him. He had picked up Tanya's trail at the Garden of Allah Motel in Twenty-nine Palms, where a police officer had come to investigate a call about a young girl covered with blood. The manager had noticed José limping out of the motel supported by Tanya shortly before the police arrived. The car on their motel registration was a '59 Cadillac with California plates. Charlie put out an APB on the old Cadillac, and in a few hours he was lucky: an officer in Indio spotted it parked by a cheap motel. By the time Charlie arrived, however, the car was there but Tanya and José were gone. A maid had seen them drive away in a blue Ford Mustang with Tanya at the wheel.

"Christ! She's fourteen years old! What do you mean, Tanya was at the wheel? She can't drive yet!"

"Calm yourself, Nicky. These things happen with teenagers."

"Jesus! Staying in a motel, driving a car without a license—if I wasn't so worried, I'd kill that child!"

"Nicky, go easy—you gotta remember you weren't always Father Time. Meanwhile, I've told the local cops and the CHP to keep an eye out for a blue Ford Mustang."

"Hell, I think she and José are coming to the party," Nicky said grumpily. "At least that's what Lady Left tells me."

"Who?"

"Kitty, for chrissake. Tell me something, Charlie—do you think it's possible to be liberal, sexy, and rich all at the same time—and be a killer to boot?"

"Hm!" said Charlie, stroking his mustache. "This is the Dr. Spock syndrome, I believe. Babies who were brought up to expect that life would grant their every wish, and then found they wanted even more. Yes, I would say rich, liberal, and sexy add up to a hell of a lot of self-indulgence—and self-indulgence taken a few steps too far can lead to murder."

Nicky scowled. "Tell me, Charlie, are there any, well . . . football games coming up soon?"

Charlie had a good laugh. Nicky's lack of interest in sports was proverbial among the Beverly Hills police; he was the man who called the Super Bowl the Super Bore, and a year ago had astonished the entire Burglary Division with an unwitting reference to the *Brooklyn* Dodgers. "It's April," Charlie explained patiently. "I can take you to a basketball game if you'd like to become a real American. But football, my friend, does not begin until fall."

"There are no exhibition games, nothing like that?"

"Not for months. Why?"

"Oh, it doesn't matter, I guess. Look, Charlie, I want you to go see if the Palm Springs police can get us a quickie warrant to search Octavio's estate. Tell them I have reason to believe a major drug buy is about to come down tonight—tell them anything at all. Then get back here with as much force as you can round up. Officer Kaminsky's behind me somewhere, and I'll be in touch with her by walkie-talkie. When I give the word, get your people in fast."

Kitty leaned out the window of the passenger side of the car and began to shout:

"Rachmaninoff! What are you guys doing? Jerking each other off?"

"Coming, dear," Nicky called to her. And then to Charlie: "The lady seems to require my presence."

Charlie grinned. "Careful, Nicky. If I were you, I'd guard my balls at all times!"

9

KITTY HANDED OVER HER INVITATION TO A MAN WITH A PISTOL ON his belt, and then drove on through the gate into the estate. Nicky noticed two more armed guards directly inside the property, sitting in a jeep off to one side on the grass. He had a bad feeling that getting out of here tonight could prove more difficult than getting in.

A Saracen with a jeweled dagger in his belt took the Mercedes at the main house, and tried to give Kitty a piece of ivory as a claim check.

"I don't believe in the slaughter of innocent elephants," said Kitty haughtily, handing back the piece of ivory as if it were burning her hand. The Saracen smiled, bowed, and said he would easily remember the lady and her automobile without a claim check.

"Salaam!" he said, pocketing her keys. As he bowed, Nicky had a glimpse of the butt of a pistol protruding from his robe.

"Christ, this is so tacky!" said Kitty, taking Nicky's arm. "I wouldn't be at all surprised if they're serving *pink* champagne!"

"Are you a snob, Miz Hall?"

"No, I'm *not* a snob," said the lady. "I just can't *stand* these new arrivals who try so pathetically hard to out-Hollywood Hollywood."

"Isn't that what Hollywood's all about?" asked Rachmaninoff.

White Arabian tents had been set out on Octavio's golf course. Camels were tethered to palm trees. Belly dancers wiggled, serving girls served, and a Latin band dressed up as Arabs played a samba version of "There's No Business Like Show Business."

So that everyone could see one another, the grounds were lit by burning torches stuck in the ground, which gave the whole affair a Polynesian glow. There were also small colored lights in the palm trees that might have been left over from Christmas in Beverly Hills. Two acrobats flew by, doing cartwheels and somersaults in the air. Hollywood couples in stunning costumes mingled and caroused, but seemed faintly ill at ease. At the edge of the golf course, Octavio's house stood grandly, all glass and sweeping curves of concrete, but closed to the public for the evening.

Despite the obvious expense, there was something wildly inappropriate about this fantasy Arabia imposed upon a golf course in the Mojave Desert. Nicky, however, was giving it scant attention; he was keeping an eye out for Tanya and thinking about football. It was an intolerable challenge that Kitty had actually given him a clue, and worse, he couldn't figure it out.

"I got you thinking, haven't I? Look, there's one small thing I haven't told you yet that unfortunately has nothing to do with football," said Kitty. "Actually, it's rather a big thing. I have a feeling you're going to be angry at me."

"Kitty, you've taken me beyond anger, beyond incredulity, to a state of simple numbness. So why don't you just spill the beans?"

Unfortunately, they were interrupted by a gossip writer from *People* magazine, a woman with a shrill voice.

"Kitty! How marvelous! So tell me, do you think Octavio Morales will last, or is he a fly-by-night?"

"I wouldn't even bother to learn his name, darling," said Kitty Hall.

Kitty was one of the few real celebrities here tonight, and once she was spotted she was much in demand. Nicky had to take her by the arm and lead her toward a sand trap near the fifth hole, away from the crowd.

"Oh, look at the time!" said Kitty. "At nine we're supposed to meet Octavio behind the main dining tent, just as dinner is served."

"Kitty, what is this small matter you have neglected to tell me?"

She anxiously lit a cigarette—not the most ladylike habit for an Arabian princess.

"Kitty, damn it—tell me!"

"Well," she said, "it's about the Swiss bank-account numbers."

"Yes?"

"You see, there *aren't* any. We just made the whole thing up."

Nicky stared at her, not immediately comprehending. "What are you talking about?"

"Just what I told you. When Cory opened up those two coffins in Nicaragua, there was nothing there—I mean, there were *bodies*, naturally, but no loot. So either they were the wrong coffins, or someone already dug them up and took what was in them—or maybe Somoza never left any money behind in the first place. Probably we'll never know."

Kitty explained this in such an offhand manner that it took Nicky a moment to absorb the implications. "Are you telling me there was no buried treasure?"

"None at all," admitted Kitty. "Never was, never will be."

"Then what the hell are we doing here?" demanded an irate Rachmaninoff.

"Well, of course, *I* know there's no buried treasure, and now *you* know—but the mere absence of a fictitious Swiss bank account doesn't necessarily mean we can't relieve Octavio Morales of a hundred million dollars to help the poor people in Nicaragua."

"*Fictitious* bank account!" Nicky repeated dumbly, "Do you mean . . ."

"Aren't you listening? Cory *never* knew where Somoza's fortune was buried—he wasn't even sure there *was* such a thing. Oh, sure, he suspected Somoza might have left some money behind in Nicaragua, it seemed plausible in fact. But with this particular fortune . . . well, to be frightfully honest, it's entirely imaginary."

Unbelievable really, but there it was: *This whole thing was a bluff!*

Of course, Hollywood was a town that bought and sold imagination at a great price. Still, this was the most imaginary deal Nicky had ever seen: a lost treasure that did not exist, being offered to a man who had no money to pay the price! However, Kitty did not seem to realize Octavio was almost certainly bluffing too, and for the moment Nicky thought he would not enlighten her.

"Stop shaking your head and looking so apocalyptic. We're going to pull this off, Rachmaninoff. Believe me, it's all been figured out."

"A bluff! But what the hell was Cory doing in that god-awful rainstorm digging up those damn coffins?"

"Nicholas, you're a disappointment to me. That whole charade was for *you*."

"For me?"

"Of course. Remember, I asked you to follow Cory that day? The idea was that if a highly placed police officer actually witnessed Cory removing two coffins from the ground, then Octavio would come to believe we had really found his uncle's lost fortune. Cory had been hinting about this supposed fortune for months. Octavio had already taken the bait, but you should feel honored, Rachmaninoff— you were the *pièce de résistance*."

"Do you know the line from *King Lear*, Kitty—'Nothing can come from nothing'? That's what we have here, I'm afraid, nothing at all."

"That's why you're only a cop, Rachmaninoff, and not a millionaire. You think this is so unusual, selling an imaginary product? Have you been watching Wall Street lately?"

Nicky had to laugh. This was the ultimate Hollywood deal, all right—just a fanciful cloud in which nothing was real but basic greed.

"So what about Cory?" he asked. "If you haven't murdered him, where the hell is he?"

Kitty just kept smiling.

And that was when it hit him, the thought that had been trying to arrive. The football analogy. The game plan.

This was more than a bluff, it was a fake reverse. In fact, Pip had been nothing more than a diversion, sending all the players chasing hot on her tail while the real ball carrier ran down an empty field toward a touchdown.

10

OCTAVIO MORALES WAS WEARING PETER O'TOOLE'S ORIGINAL COS-
tume from *Lawrence of Arabia*, but he was missing his own party,
sitting behind the massive marble desk in his second-story office.

"Has Nick Nolte arrived?"

"Not yet, Señor Morales," said his aide, Martin—who was
dressed in a turban and a loincloth, and was supposed to be a genie
from a bottle.

"What about Paul Newman?"

"Señor Newman is not here either."

"Steven Spielberg?"

"A secretary from the Spielberg office called a short while ago to
send his regrets. Apparently Señor Spielberg had to make an unexpected trip to London."

Octavio stood up from his desk and paced up and down near the
marble fish pond in the center of the room. Not too many private
offices had an actual fish pond like this one, filled with priceless *koi*,
but it wasn't doing him much good tonight. Octavio watched a fat
speckled fish swim serenely toward the surface, give him a sly fishy
look, and disappear.

"Jack Nicholson?" he asked wearily.

"Perhaps on the next helicopter," answered Martin judiciously.

"Who's down there, then?" Octavio cried in wounded agony. "A
lot of second-raters! People who want to sponge a free meal! I want
you to make a note of this, Martin—all these so-called big shots who
have not come to my party, they are finished in this town, as of now!
None of them will work again!"

Martin carefully made a note of his boss's words. Octavio sat
down again behind his giant desk. "I've owned one of the most
famous movie studios in Hollywood for nearly a week now," he said
softly. "Why haven't the 'A' people come to my party? Well, never
mind, Martin. Get me my gun and let's take a last look at our
money, eh?"

It took Pedro de Vega and two security guards—all dressed as slaves—to carry in the canvas sacks containing a hundred million dollars in one-hundred-dollar bills. Octavio pulled out one of the bills and examined it against the light. Ben Franklin looked all right, and the bills bore quite a good resemblance to real money except for one thing: they had been minted by a man in Panama who couldn't spell. The words ONE HUNNERT DOLLERS had been reproduced incorrectly a million times. The engraver had been tortured and shot, and Octavio had managed to pick up the counterfeits for nearly nothing at all.

"Well, it will be dark," said Octavio philosophically.

There was a camel waiting for them at a side door. The sacks of misspelled money were loaded across the animal's back and then Lawrence of Arabia, three slaves, and a well-armed genie took off across the golf course beneath the Palm Springs moon.

11

THE DINING TENT WAS BIG ENOUGH TO HOUSE A THREE-RING CIRCUS. There were a hundred round tables set out upon the lawn, each with a white tablecloth, a flower arrangement in the middle, a candle in a glass chimney, and place settings for twelve. When everyone sat down, it became obvious that only about half of the expected guests had bothered to come.

Nicky and Kitty were standing behind the big tent, near a smaller tent that was serving as a kitchen. From this position they could hear the cooks and waitresses laughing and talking about the guests. The smell of cooking food drifted across the night.

Nicky became aware of a surprising spectacle: no less than two camels were lumbering their way from different directions. The first was a real camel, coming from the main house with five men by its side, all in Arab dress. The second was only a make-believe camel—a clever costume with two pairs of human legs sticking out the bottom, front and back. The make-believe camel came within a dozen feet of where Nicky and Kitty were standing, and then veered off into the dining tent. Nicky had a strange feeling there was something familiar about the camel's rear end.

"Good evening, Miss Hall," said Octavio, coming up at the head of the real camel. Octavio made a little bow toward Kitty—a sort of *salaam*, Nicky supposed.

"Don't you adore my costume? Actually, it's the very one Alec Guinness gave Peter O'Toole in *Lawrence of Arabia*—do you remember that scene?"

"We didn't come here to talk about movies, Mr. Morales," said Kitty.

"As you wish."

Octavio turned at last toward Nicky, with a look of great expectations in his eye.

"And now, Cory, my old friend," he said—then stopped abruptly. "What kind of trick is this? *You* aren't Cory."

"That's for damn sure," said Nicky.

"You're . . ." Octavio yanked Nicky's long white beard. "My God, you're Lieutenant Rachmaninoff!"

Nicky smiled. He had never realized he was supposed to be Cory Heard—another little thing Kitty had forgotten to tell him.

"What is the meaning of this?" Octavio was asking angrily.

"Just a little extra insurance, Mr. Morales. The lieutenant is only here as an observer."

"We are doing absolutely nothing illegal—it's a very simple exchange, Lieutenant," said Octavio hastily. "But where the hell is Cory?"

Nicky had been wondering about this himself.

"The deal can go forward just as we arranged, Mr. Morales. We have the bank numbers, you have the money. Why don't we just get on with it?"

Octavio Morales gave Nicky a nervous smile. "You are just an observer, then, of our simple transaction?"

Nicky nodded briefly and kept a careful eye on the genie and the three slaves, whose hands were beneath their robes—on their weapons, he presumed. *Simple* was not the word he would have used to describe this transaction. Among Octavio's genies and slaves, Nicky recognized Martin and Pedro de Vega, the brothers he had arrested for unlawful possession of concealed weapons.

"Well," said Octavio with a sigh, "I suppose we can proceed. Why don't you show me my uncle's bank numbers, Miss Hall? And then I will allow you to inspect the money."

"Not so fast," said Kitty. "I suggest we do it the other way around—first the money, then the numbers."

Octavio smiled and turned to Nicky for support. "You see how difficult this is, Lieutenant? No one trusts anybody anymore. Here's what I suggest: Why don't you give the bank numbers to Lieutenant Rachmaninoff to hold? Just temporarily, of course. Then I will have my assistant, Martin, show you the money while Rachmaninoff lets me inspect the numbers—all at the same time. What could be simpler?"

Kitty looked at Nicky, then back at Octavio. "Lieutenant Rachmaninoff already has the numbers on his person. Well, all right, I agree—where's the money?"

Octavio flicked his eyes to Nicky. "Is that right, Lieutenant? You have these numbers that belong to my family?"

"That's what the lady said, isn't it?"

Octavio stepped closer to Nicky. "Martin," he said, "take down the bags from our friend the camel and let Miss Hall count her cash. Unfortunately, it will take you some time, Miss Hall—the bills are done up in packages of twenty-five thousand dollars, so you will have four thousand packages to inspect—unless you are willing to simply trust me, of course."

"Let's get on with this, Morales. If the money is really in the canvas bags, have Martin pull them down from the camel."

"Yes, why don't you do that, Martin? And now, Rachmaninoff, please give me these numbers I have been waiting for so long."

"The lady hasn't seen the money yet," Nicky reminded him. "Maybe your bags just have old newspapers stuffed inside."

Octavio smiled. "I tell you what—I am a reasonable man, and rather than get stuck in some boring impasse, this is what I suggest: Martin will open the three bags wide enough so that Miss Hall may see there is money inside, not newspaper. But she may not actually touch the money until I have inspected the bank numbers and can ascertain that *they* are as real as my hundred-dollar bills. And I must warn you, Lieutenant—I can recognize the authenticity of Swiss bank codes. As it happens, I have in my possession the first five digits of my uncle's account, so I will certainly be able to tell if these are real or not."

"Believe me, our bank numbers are every bit as real as your money," Nicky assured him.

"Then indulge me, please. Martin, you will open the top of each canvas bag, but do not let Miss Hall reach inside."

"It looks like money," said Kitty after she had looked inside. "But I can't see without my glasses."

"Put on your glasses, by all means!" Octavio encouraged.

Kitty reached into her purse, but instead of glasses she produced a small snub-nosed revolver. It was not a clever move. She only managed to raise the gun an inch out of her purse before Martin knocked it out of her hand with the hard edge of his palm. Kitty gave a little cry of pain and anger.

"That wasn't nice," said Octavio. Martin twisted Kitty's arm around her back and held her tight. Nicky had done nothing so far except stand exceptionally still. When he turned to Octavio, he saw the ugly end of an automatic pistol pointed his way from out of the flowing material of an Arabian sleeve.

This was what Nicky had been waiting for, he supposed: Octavio Morales was finally breaking the law in front of witnesses! He actually raised the gun to the bridge of Nicky's nose, assaulting a police officer and causing reckless endangerment. It was all looking very bad for Octavio Morales.

"I think you will give me those numbers now, Lieutenant."

"All right," said Nicky, reaching slowly beneath his robe with his left hand.

"Careful," said Octavio. "Don't do anything too fast."

Nicky felt the walkie-talkie beneath his robe. Careful not to make any sudden movement, he managed to turn it on and press the transmit button.

"Mr. Morales, I must warn you that holding a police officer at gunpoint constitutes a very serious crime in the state of California."

"What do you have under there?" Octavio demanded suddenly. "Bring your hand down slowly—very, *very* slowly."

Nicky let his hand slip downward from the transmit button. The moment he did so, there came an electronic squawk from the tiny speaker, and then the voice of Officer Cathy Kaminsky:

"Is that you, Loo? I couldn't make out that last message. Please repeat."

The two slaves took hold of Nicky's arms while Octavio ripped open the front of his robe. Nicky was feeling less wise by the second.

"What's this, you son of a bitch?" Octavio relieved him of his .38 Smith & Wesson, but it was the walkie-talkie he stared at in horror.

"We've been transmitting this entire conversation, Octavio," Nicky lied. "Half of this county's police force is outside your gate right now."

"You're bluffing, Lieutenant," said Octavio with a brave smile. "Now where the hell are my bank numbers?"

"Gee, Octavio—I can't remember right now. But I'm pretty damn sure I don't have them on me."

Octavio hit him across the cheek with the side of his gun. This would certainly add another six months to Octavio's prison sentence, though for the moment Nicky saw only a bright flash of stars.

"We will take you inside the house now, and I think you will remember rather quickly—yes, I really think you will, Lieutenant."

The slaves dragged Nicky toward the main house, while the genie took charge of Kitty. She seemed undaunted, though there was a gun in her back, and so far tonight's work had not exactly furthered the leftist cause in faraway Nicaragua.

As Nicky was dragged across the golf course, he had another glimpse of the make-believe camel with the two pairs of human legs protruding from the bottom. The camel was standing some distance away, gazing at him sadly—Nicky could almost swear—from the Oasis Bar by the fifth hole.

12

"I ALWAYS KNEW THERE WAS SOMETHING FISHY ABOUT YOU," SAID Nicky Rachmaninoff to Octavio Morales.

"This is a terrible joke," said Octavio. "And I don't think you will be making jokes for long."

Nicky was kneeling before the marble sides of the decorative indoor fish pond in the center of Octavio's office, staring at a large orange and black *koi* that seemed to find him interesting too. The fish was as fat as a small puppy, and sent little kisses through the water in his direction.

Nicky had more on his mind than fish-watching, however. His hands were tied behind his back, and he had been stripped down to his underwear. Octavio's men had searched him for any scrap of paper bearing numbers, and, finding nothing, they now held his face inches from the surface of the water.

"Are you going to force us to go through this barbarism, Lieutenant?" asked Octavio. "You can save yourself a great deal of discomfort by telling me where those numbers are."

"You'll never get them, Octavio," replied Nicky truthfully. A hand holding his head by the hair pushed him forward into the water. Nicky knew this wasn't going to be easy. The orange and black *koi* swam closer, inspecting this new addition to the decorative pond. Nicky tried not to panic. The claustrophobia grew gradually, along with the terrible inability to breathe. The body rebelled; instinctively he tried to flail his arms, pull back his head. He jerked and twisted, but the hands that held him were firm. Fingers of darkness gathered around his consciousness, and then hands were pulling him back into the bright air. Nicky had time for only two rasping breaths before he was pushed down once again into the green water.

The second time was worse. He no longer could pretend to be calm—he was in a panic from the very first second. His lungs would surely burst, his body implode—every nerve and muscle screamed for air. And then, after an eternity of pain, he was jerked back out of the water.

"Well, Lieutenant? You see how simple but effective this can be? The water method was a favorite of my Uncle Somoza. Believe me, in the end everyone talks."

Nicky took in all the air he could in wretched little breaths. Then he said, as clearly as possible, in a voice he hardly recognized, "You and your Uncle Somoza can go to hell."

Octavio seemed to find this amusing. "What about you, Miss Hall?" he asked with a chuckle. "You can end this disturbing spectacle by telling me where the bank numbers are. Spare yourselves the pain."

Kitty was tied to a chair beyond the line of Nicky's vision.

"You fascist bastard! I'll never tell you!" she cried, "no matter *what* you do to Rachmaninoff!"

13

NICKY GOT A BREATHER THANKS TO SONNY BONO, MAYOR OF PALM Springs, who arrived at Octavio's party at just this moment, accompanied by a Latin version of "I've Got You, Babe," struck up hastily by the band. Octavio wished fervently that the more glamorous Cher—Sonny's former singing partner—had come instead, but he decided he must briefly return to his party to say hello.

The guards tied Kitty and Nicky together, back to back on the floor, and then looped the end of the rope through an iron ring embedded in the marble slab of the pond. The job was professional and uncomfortable, the ropes were strong. When it was done, Octavio and his bodyguards left the office knowing Nicky and Kitty would not be going anywhere in their absence.

"This sure is clever, the way you have this all planned out," said Nicky to Kitty. "But I'm beginning to wonder when the cavalry comes to set us free?"

"Shut up, Rachmaninoff, and just try to get us undone," she told him.

"I think we *are* undone," he complained. "That's what I'm trying to tell you. Do you know why Octavio didn't bother to leave a guard in the room? It's because there's no way we can get loose from these ropes."

"Aren't you going to try, at least? I never figured you for a quitter."

"Kitty," he said, "I know you're used to getting your own precious way, but at the moment you're up shit creek without a paddle and you might as well save your breath for when they play dunk-the-apple with *your* pretty head."

Kitty Hall was a lady who did not accept the obvious. She began tugging at their bonds, trying to wiggle her way free. No matter how willful she was, their four hands were tied securely together, and all of Kitty's motion only made the ropes cut deeper into their wrists.

"Be still," said Rachmaninoff, "and listen to me a moment. The chances are Octavio won't actually kill us as long as he thinks we can tell him where those bank numbers are. So let's not confess the sordid truth, shall we?"

"What do you think I am? An idiot? You think I couldn't figure that out for myself?"

Nicky couldn't think of an adequate response. The way they were tied, he couldn't see any part of her, but could only feel her spine against his back. He could tell from her spine how tense she was.

"Since we have time to kill," said Nicky, "why don't we talk about your husband?"

"Do you need another clue?" she sneered.

"No thank you. I got the first one about football just fine. We were supposed to think Pip had the ball, so to speak—if we followed her, she'd lead us to Cory. But that was all a feint, right? You fooled all of us into looking the wrong way—and *poof!* Any minute now, Cory's supposed to appear from somewhere else!"

Kitty didn't reply.

"But what I don't understand—if Cory's going to show, don't you think this would be a good moment right now? Of course, that's assuming you haven't actually murdered him, which is a lot more likely."

270

"Shut up, Rachmaninoff," she said. "You're getting on my nerves. Anyway, what if this room is bugged? For all we know, Octavio left us alone just so we'd talk."

Nicky chuckled. "You've been watching too much television, pussycat."

"Stop calling me 'pussycat.' You're pathetically old-fashioned, do you know that?"

"Then tell me where Cory is. If you didn't kill him, *pussycat*, where the fuck is he?"

"This is a nightmare," she sighed, "being a captive victim to your chauvinistic remarks." Still, she leaned her pretty head back against his shoulder so that they were nearly cheek to cheek.

"Okay, I'll whisper it in your ear," she whispered. "Can you hear me?"

"Sure."

"Okay," she said. "You want to hear the story, here it is, asshole. After that day in the rain outside of Managua, Cory met up with Ricardo and they both went into hiding in a little village in Jinotega province in northern Nicaragua. I was to come back to California and do whatever I could to draw attention away from them."

"What about José?"

"José followed me to California on his own—he went out through Costa Rica and picked up a ticket to Los Angeles that I had left with a travel agent. No one was looking for José, so it was easy. As soon as he got to California, we started working on Pip, making her think Cory was back and wanting to get in touch with her. You were right about her—I thought I could use Pip to get the heat off me and Cory. This was only supposed to go on for a few days, but then Cory and Ricardo didn't show up in California when they were supposed to, and I had to stretch it out."

"When were they due in California?"

"More than a week ago. The plan was they were going to get out of Nicaragua to the north, into Honduras. It was a dangerous route, but Ricardo knew some of the old trails the *contras* used. As soon as they got to Honduras, they were going to pose as businessmen and make their way to Mexico City, and from there to California. When they didn't show up, I had to improvise. Obviously, if Octavio thought Cory was lost somewhere in Central America, the whole

271

deal would have fallen through, so I did a few more things to make it look like he was in L.A."

"Like copy an old telephone message onto Susan's answering machine?"

"Exactly. Octavio got a call like that, too."

"But why me, Kitty? Why was it so important *I* thought Cory was around?"

"You were the clincher, Rachmaninoff. You gave the whole thing credibility. Actually, you were important to this plan from the very beginning. If you weren't such an asshole, you'd probably feel honored."

"You mean it wasn't any accident Susan invited me on the trip to Nicaragua?"

"That's right. Susan and I had a few girlish lunches at the Bistro Gardens, where I convinced her maybe she should give you another try—you couldn't be worse than the Hollywood beauty boys she was dating. Cory and I decided you would be the final touch—you would give substance to the lie. And since Octavio was keeping a close eye on you, if *you* believed, then *he* would believe."

"Wait a second. Why would Octavio be keeping an eye on me?"

Kitty was silent for a moment.

"Kitty! How the fuck did he know about me?"

"Look, Rachmaninoff, I steered him in your direction. I told you, you were part of the plan. Octavio was led to believe you and Cory had a number of intimate conversations in Managua—we made it look like you might know a lot more than you were letting on."

"Thanks!"

"Well, I thought you could take care of yourself, for chrissake. I thought you were tough."

"So why the hell did you go to bed with me? Were you trying to see how tough I was?"

"*That* was not part of the plan. That just happened, Rachmaninoff—and believe me, I regret it as much as you do."

"Okay, we both have our regrets. Let's try a new subject. Why did José try to kill Pip on the mountain?"

"That wasn't part of the plan either. José was upset—I just told him his father was dead, and I guess he got a little carried away. You see, we'd fooled Pip twice, and dumb as she may be, we were afraid she'd catch on and do something to give us away."

Nicky was suddenly very angry. "So this is where all your political idealism ends up—you revenge yourself against a girl who's slept with your husband!"

"It wasn't like that at all, Rachmaninoff. Sure, I used her—I used you, too. That's the price you have to pay sometimes to do something important. But I only told José to put Pip on ice a few days until the transaction was over—nothing permanent. As I said, I guess news of his father's death sent him over the edge a little."

"Swell. What he did, unfortunately, was send Pip over the edge. But let's get back to Major Aivas, your ex-lover. Who killed him, I wonder—your husband?"

"Nicholas, this may seem a little incredible, but Ricardo's death had nothing to do with our plan—the *contras* got him. The forces of reaction killed him with weapons you and I paid for out of our tax dollars!"

"Kitty, you can skip the politics, since I'm not in a position to vote at the moment. Anyway, haven't the *contras* been disbanded by now?"

"Bullshit, they have! They may be mostly bandits now, but in the past year these wonderful 'freedom fighters' have managed to kill hundreds of Nicaraguans, mostly civilians. Anyway, Cory and Ricardo were in the wrong place at the wrong time—they ended up right in the middle of a raid. Ricardo was killed, Cory was captured and taken into Honduras. It was so stupid—something we didn't count on."

"Well, let's pretend I believe this for the moment. Is Cory still a prisoner in Honduras?"

"Of course not. Cory convinced one of his guards that if he set him loose and came with him to Los Angeles, Cory could make him a movie star."

"Ah, the lure of the limelight!"

"Well, Cory's a fast talker—it worked. The two of them escaped the *contra* camp and made their way on back roads into Mexico. When they reached Mexico City, Cory ditched him and telephoned me in Beverly Hills. This was only three days ago. I sent him a plane ticket to San Francisco."

"Why up there?"

"I was afraid Octavio's little helpers in the CIA would be keeping an eye on the L.A. airports. Besides, Cory could hide out at his mother's house in Tiburon a few days. No one would think of looking up there."

"So now comes the big question: When the hell's Cory going to show up and rescue us, according to your lovely little plan?"

"Relax, Rachmaninoff. Any minute now."

Nicky tensed suddenly. "Do you smell something burning?" he asked, raising his nose. There was something acrid in the air, the smell of smoke.

"I'm not sure . . . maybe it's something cooking. Jesus, it sounds like they're setting off firecrackers downstairs."

"Hope you're ready for some excitement, my dear," said Nicky Rachmaninoff. "That's automatic rifle fire."

"*Don't* call me 'my dear,' asshole!"

"Then stop called me 'asshole,' my dear."

The name-calling could have continued indefinitely, but the lights in Octavio's office flickered and then went off, leaving Nicky and Kitty tied together in the dark, listening to the harsh sounds of gunshots coming ever closer. Hot clouds of smoke billowed up to the second floor from down below.

"You know what?" said Rachmaninoff in the dark. "I think before this is over I'm going to feel nostalgic for that lovely wet fishpond."

14

BEING THE REAR END OF A CAMEL WAS NOT EXACTLY HEAVEN. TANYA could barely see what was going on at Octavio's party except through a small ventilation hole in the flanks of the costume. It was stuffy inside the heavy material, and she had to rely on José, in the front, to be her eyes and ears. Most annoying of all, the moment José was well enough to get around, he seemed to take it as his natural right that he should be in command.

"Where's my father now?" she asked.

"He's in the house with Kitty. Don't worry—this is all part of the plan."

"Sure!" said Tanya. "You know, you might have told me my *father* was going to be at this party, for chrissake. You haven't been exactly truthful, José."

"Don't be an ass," he snapped back at her. "This is a little late for second thoughts."

"I'm *never* going to get involved in anything stupid like this *ever* again," she assured him.

Tanya trudged along as the rear end of the camel for what seemed an eternity, having no idea what was going on around her, except for what José told her. At last he said they must make their way toward the main house. For all Tanya knew, they could be heading back to Beverly Hills. At least she had José's AK-47 on a strap around her shoulder, which gave her a feeling of *some* power; José's left arm was in a sling from his wound, and *he* could handle only a pistol.

"Why are we stopping?"

"Sh!" he said. "Don't say a word now."

In a moment, she heard a new voice from somewhere close. The voice was polite but firm: "I'm afraid the main house is closed for the party, Señor Camel."

"We're looking for the bathroom," said José.

"You will find rest rooms in the guest house next to the swimming pool."

"Oh yes? Will you help me out of this costume, please? It is inconvenient being a camel when you wish to go to the bathroom as badly as I do. . . . Thank you so much, if you just hold up the side, I will slip out from underneath."

Tanya wasn't certain what happened next. She heard the sound of a gasp, and then two bodies struggling in silence. José had managed to slip out of the front of the camel, and she was enveloped in the costume by herself. Without a front end, the material hung about her like a heavy tent, trapping her inside. She was struggling to free herself when she felt someone grab her from outside. Tanya screamed.

"Be still!" said José. "I am helping you get out."

Tanya crawled out from under the material while José held it up for her. To her surprise, she emerged directly behind the real camel, which smelled like wet straw and urine. At the side of the real camel, one of the "Arab slaves" was stretched out face down on the ground.

"Is he . . . is he . . . ?"

"No, he is not dead, Tanya. He is just taking a nice peaceful nap, I assure you."

Tanya wasn't so certain. She was staring in dismay at the very quiet body on the ground while José was pulling three canvas bags off the camel's back.

"Help me! For chrissake, Tanya, don't just stare at the ground. This is the money! The money we have been waiting for so long!"

"Fuck the money, José—let's just get my father and Kitty and get the hell out of here."

"Oh, fuck the money, you say! This is very easy for such a rich girl! But you will help me carry the bags inside the house, Tanya."

"Honestly, José—this can't be the money. I mean, who would leave a hundred million dollars outside with just one guard on the back of some dumb camel?"

"They were very sure of themselves, I think. But don't argue with me, Tanya—I saw Señora Hall inspect this money with my own eyes. Now you must take two bags because of my bad arm—I will take one. Help me with this, and I will make certain your father is safe."

José cared so much about the damn money! They were standing at a side door to Octavio's house, shielded from the party by the camel, which continued to chew its cud in a grouchy camel way, appearing totally bored by human affairs. Tanya didn't blame him much.

When José found the door was locked, he simply raised his pistol and shot the lock.

"Jesus, José!"

"Hurry now, inside—there is no more need to keep quiet, I think."

"José, I don't think . . ."

276

"No, you stop thinking, girl, and do exactly as I tell you! I am the man here, *I* am the one in charge."

Boy! Wait until she told Bunky about this! It was really *very* disillusioning. For a revolutionary, José was even more old-fashioned than the boys back home in Beverly Hills. She sighed and gave him her Zippo lighter when he asked, and watched him set the house on fire.

15

WHEN THE LIGHTS WENT OUT AND OCTAVIO'S SECOND-FLOOR OFFICE began filling with smoke, Nicky Rachmaninoff began to think this was it, the Big Good-bye. It seemed strange to think a person might die with so much guilt left unrepented.

Nicky was pondering these and other Great Questions when the door to Octavio's office burst open and he saw a strange sight:

A young girl in olive pants and a brown shirt, with an AK-47 cradled in her arms. She stood as still as a statue, her finger on the trigger, silhouetted by a flickering orange light behind her—her blond hair parted from her eyes to show an intense, angry flare of green. She looked to Nicky like some dark angel of the revolution. But it was only his daughter, Tanya.

"Dad!"

José was behind her, his left arm in a sling, a pistol in his right hand.

"Bring in the money," José said to the girl.

"*You* bring the money."

"God damn it, get it!" snarled José.

"God damn it, get it yourself," Tanya snarled right back.

Nicky had a sense that Venus had descended to the very basement of teenage love, which did not bother him a bit. Tanya rushed over to where he and Kitty were tied together, leaving José to trudge back and forth into the hallway for the three canvas sacks.

"Is that *it?*" Kitty was asking.

"That's it!" said José. "All of it!"

Tanya was pulling at the ropes frantically, but having no luck.

"I bet you're like *totally* furious at me," she said to her father. "Like probably you're going to spank me or something."

"You'll have to untie me first," he said mildly. "Just out of curiosity, where's all the smoke coming from?"

"Oh, we set the house on fire. Pretty clever, huh? Now Octavio will be too busy to come after us!"

Nicky sighed. "You'd better see if José has a knife, dear," he suggested. "Quickly."

José finished dragging the canvas bags into the room, and he approached cautiously.

"Hello, Señor Rachmaninoff."

"Why, hello, kid," Nicky replied with equal caution. "It's been a while, huh? You think you can cut us loose?"

Without a word, he handed Tanya a Swiss Army knife from his pocket, taking from her the AK-47. José stuffed his pistol into his belt and cradled the automatic rifle awkwardly in his good arm, keeping an eye on everything while standing very close to the money.

"I guess our whole plan hasn't worked out too well," Tanya said while she was sawing through the ropes.

"That's all right, dear—none of my plans have worked out for years," he admitted. "The truth is, we've been put on earth to ad lib."

"Will you two just shut up until we get out of here!" Kitty complained. She was yanking on the ropes while they were still only half loose, giving the impression she couldn't wait to be free of Rachmaninoff.

The moment the ropes fell free, Nicky put his arms around his daughter and felt her warm cheek against his own. It was a great relief to hold her, but he kept a wary eye on Kitty and José, who were having some kind of conference in low voices a few feet away.

"So how are we supposed to get out of here?" he whispered.

"The roof," she whispered back.

Nicky was wondering if he could arrest José for attempted murder, and Kitty for extortion, *and* save their lives as well. It was a lot to ask, but people in California were born with great expectations. Nicky stood up from the floor, walked over to Octavio's desk, and picked up a telephone.

"What are you doing?" asked José quickly, swinging around the AK-47 so that he had Nicky covered.

"Relax—I'm calling 911. It's our all-purpose emergency number, and this is an all-purpose emergency if ever I saw one."

"Put the phone down, Señor Nicky."

"José, we need the fire department! Do you want Frank Sinatra Drive to go up in flames?"

"Don't worry, Rachmaninoff. We've got an escape route," said Kitty.

"Well, I think we'd better use it, then," said Nicky, looking at the smoke billowing into the room through the crack at the bottom of the door. He put the phone back on its cradle, and watched José slightly relax his position with the gun. This was definitely not the same goofy kid he had known in Nicaragua.

"Okay, we're going out in the hall," said Kitty, all business. "Rachmaninoff—you, me, and Tanya will each carry one of the canvas bags."

"Kitty—"

"Let's get moving, everybody," said Kitty. She put a hand on the doorknob but pulled back immediately in pain. "Christ, that's hot!"

"Kitty, pay attention—we're not going to get out that way, not unless you want to be a charred star. So whad'ya say you let me call the fire department?" Rachmaninoff knew he was a voice of reason in the wilderness, but no one was listening to him.

"The window!" cried José. "We'll climb out the window and up to the roof that way."

"Are you a bird, perhaps?" asked Nicky.

"There's a ledge, Rachmaninoff," said Kitty, who was already at the far end of the room, opening one of the large windows, peering outside.

"Damn, it's pretty small," she admitted. "But if we can make our way along it to the side of the building, there's a balcony I think we can use to climb up to the roof. But, José—I don't think we're going to be able to carry the money bags."

"What do you mean, not carry the money bags? *What are you talking about?*" he cried. "You rich people! You already have everything you need for yourselves—what do you care about the poor people in Nicaragua?"

"That's *really* unfair!" replied Kitty hotly. "I've spent the past four months of my life turning down some pretty nice film offers just to help your fucking little country—so don't lay a guilt trip on me, buddy!"

"This is the problem with revolutionaries," explained Rachmaninoff to his daughter. "They always end up fighting among themselves."

16

THE LEDGE WAS THREE INCHES WIDE AND NEARLY TWENTY FEET above the ground—not as high as the top of the Palm Springs Aerial Tramway, but high enough. Rachmaninoff treaded cautiously.

"Keep moving," said José. He was the only one of them who was armed, and he seemed to think this put him in charge. "We only have seven minutes."

"Seven minutes until what?" asked Nicky patiently.

"Just keep moving."

Kitty led the way, followed by Nicky and Tanya, with José in the rear, each of them hugging the building, moving only inches at a time. To make it more difficult, Kitty, Nicky, and Tanya each had a heavy canvas bag slung uncomfortably over their shoulders, while José only carried his guns—the pistol in his belt and the AK-47 on his back. Clouds of smoke rolled about them, covering them in a thick, acrid fog, then clearing suddenly with the vagaries of the desert wind. From this side of the house, Nicky could not see the party, but from the shouts and the distant sirens he could tell that the fire and gunshots had put an end to the *Arabian Nights.*

Kitty reached the balcony first, and then helped the others over the railing to safety.

"Now what?"

"Now we will go to the roof," said José. "We will climb there." He was pointing up a gully that ran alongside a large dormer window clear to the top of the building.

"No way, José," said Nicky Rachmaninoff. "Anyway, what's on the roof? Is Cory going to fly down like a bird and carry us all away?"

"Something like that," said Kitty. "We have to hurry or we'll be late."

"Look, you two go where you want. I'm taking Tanya down to ground level and getting the hell out of here," said Nicky. It seemed a good moment to test the water and find out whether he was José's prisoner or only his future father-in-law. José stared at him fiercely, his dark Latin brows knit together, but he seemed undecided whether to go for his gun. They could have been stuck at this impasse for some time, but two men with pistols appeared down below on the lawn and began to use the figures on the balcony for target practice. José slid the AK-47 from his back, held it awkwardly with his one good hand, and strafed the lawn with a short burst of gunfire. The two men below went scurrying around the side of the house for safety.

"You still wish to go to ground level, Señor Nicky?"

"Well, kid, maybe the roof has some merits after all."

Kitty went first. She removed her shoes and used the balcony railing to get a step up onto the wooden shingles. The roof here slanted upward at about a thirty-degree angle, which was steep but not impossible to climb. Kitty made her way by using both hands and feet, crawling with her butt in the air like some large spider. José told Tanya that she should go next. As soon as Tanya was a few feet up the roof, José told Nicky to pass up the bags to her, one at a time.

"I told you, screw the money, José. If you want to waste your time dragging this shit around, that's your business, but I'm only concerned with getting Tanya out of this alive."

José casually swung the barrel of the AK-47 so that it was pointed at Nicky's chest. "Do this," he said, "and I will make certain you are both safe."

"Are you threatening me, José?"

"Dad, come on!" cried Tanya. "We have to get out of here!"

With the house on fire and the gunmen somewhere down below, Nicky had to agree this was not a good time to argue. He stood up on the balcony railing and they set up a relay. José passed the bags to him, and he handed them to Tanya, who carried them upward several more feet to Kitty—who took them to what seemed to be a level clearing at the very top of the house.

When the bags were taken care of, José used Nicky as a stepladder to get himself started, pushing off with his feet on Nicky's shoulders, then quickly scampering to the top. Nicky went next. There was more shooting from down below, and a bullet slammed into the wooden shingles near his hand as he made his way upward. José gave him some covering fire, and Tanya grabbed his arm and helped hoist him over the top, where he fell with a thud onto what appeared to be an elaborately private sun deck. Nicky lay panting a while, looking around. Probably this was where Octavio sunbathed in the nude to get that perfectly even tan. The deck was a hundred feet long, with a small wading pool, a few potted palms and flowers in boxes, and a bar at one end. Kitty seemed worried. She looked at her watch and then up into the night sky. "Where the hell is Cory?"

"Isn't *that* the eternal question?" remarked Nicky.

"He's supposed to be here," Kitty said distractedly, still searching the sky. "He hijacked the helicopter shuttle from Beverly Hills."

Nicky chuckled. "Come on," he said. "Be serious."

"I *am* serious. Cory's going to let out the passengers and the pilot on the desert somewhere, and then come and pick us up."

"Are you telling me the boy wonder can actually fly a helicopter?"

"Naturally. Do you think he would try something like this otherwise?"

Nicky didn't know what to believe. As far as he was concerned, there was still a mighty big chance Cory Heard was dead somewhere in Central America, and Kitty and José were lying to him again.

"He's late," said José, looking into the sky.

"He's always late," said Kitty.

"Maybe he got bored with Nicaragua and decided to save El Salvador instead," suggested Nicky.

This was getting a little crazy, the two of them looking up into the sky, waiting for salvation, while down below all hell was breaking lose—fire trucks and police cars speeding up the driveway, with thick black smoke pouring out one end of the house, up into the night sky. Nicky put his arm around Tanya and began to pull her casually off to one side. He was wishing fervently for a gun, when a door at the far end of the deck burst open and a squad of Octavio's security forces came out firing their weapons.

Nicky grabbed Tanya and made a fast dive with her behind the bar, which was a little bit of Hawaiian heaven—rattan stools set up against a wood counter with a thatched roof made out of palm leaves. Nicky and Tanya crouched next to a silver ice bucket behind a small refrigerator and sink, hoping no stray bullets would come their way. From his position he could hear the gun battle raging on the deck, but he couldn't see a thing.

"Dad, what's going on?"

"I don't know, dear. I'm sure Charlie's about to rescue us any moment. He probably just stopped to eat a few hors d'oeuvres."

Nicky reached into a drawer above his head, hoping to find a knife at least with which to defend themselves, but all he could come up with was a corkscrew. *Could you defend your family with a corkscrew?* he wondered. Maybe if you were being attacked by a wine bottle. It was quite a fancy and heavy corkscrew, at least. Nicky was not optimistic, but he opened it so that the curlycue of the point was ready to do some damage. Tanya was shivering so hard he squeezed her tighter.

"It's okay, Munchkin. We're going to be all right."

"Dad, you're squeezing me to death! And I'm *not* a Munchkin. I mean, honestly, I've been doing all *kinds* of grown-up things, and you'd think—"

"Don't talk a second! What's that sound?"

It was the rotor blade of a helicopter whipping up the air. Nicky risked a peek above the bar, corkscrew in hand, to see a large passenger helicopter coming down out of the sky, hovering over the roof.

The wind from the helicopter blade hit the roof with hurricane force, clearing the air of smoke. One of Octavio's gunmen began firing wildly at the chopper as it descended slowly toward them. Nicky was transfixed by the scene. The helicopter dove below the level of the roof to get away from the gunfire, and then came up slowly level to the sun deck.

And there he was: the long-missing Cory Heard in person, sitting at the controls with the joystick in hand, hovering in the air not more than twenty feet from Nicky Rachmaninoff. For a moment Nicky was not certain this was really him, but then his boyish face was lit by a sudden *whoosh* of flames coming from the house, and there could be no mistake.

Cory saw Nicky at the same time. He grinned. He waved as if this was really *fun*, meeting again in such a kinky situation.

"Hey, amigo!" he shouted. Nicky couldn't actually hear the words, but he was so close he could read Cory's lips.

Nicky Rachmaninoff was furious. "You think this is just a game?" he shouted. "Fucking idiot! See all the trouble you've caused us!"

"Dad!" called Tanya, nervously tugging on his leg. "Calm down."

"I'm not going to calm down. I'm tired of being fucked over by a bunch of egocentric Hollywood idiots."

There wasn't much Nicky could do. As a symbol of his disgust, at least, Nicky brought back his left hand, wound up like a pitcher on the mound, and threw the corkscrew with all his might toward Cory's damnably smiling face. His aim was good, but the corkscrew bounced harmlessly off the unbreakable windshield. Cory grinned and shook his head at Nicky's histrionics.

"Dad! What are you doing? Are you crazy?"

Nicky had picked up the silver ice bucket off its three-legged stand by the refrigerator. The thing was heavy, still half-full of water from some recent indulgence.

"Dad, get down!"

Crazy or not, Nicky Rachmaninoff grasped the ice bucket with two hands, pulled back his arms, and tossed the thing at Cory. This time Nicky's aim was bad. The bright metal object sailed through the air and flew directly into the moving rotor. There was a quick but terrible clang, a spray of water, and a look of disbelief on Cory's face as the helicopter tilted at a crazy angle, hovered in the air for just one more moment, and then dropped like a sack of rocks to the ground below.

Nicky was amazed that a single well-placed ice bucket could do so much damage, but he came out of his reverie fast when a line of bullets strafed the bar. He dove back down behind the refrigerator, wrapped his arms around his daughter, and listened to the battle. After a few minutes he crawled toward the end of the bar and cautiously peered out, trying to decide if there was any way he could escape with Tanya down the roof to the balcony from whence they had come. As he was looking out, he saw a fire ladder drop against the deck railing, and a figure dressed in blue came hurtling over the side, landing in a firing crouch and shooting orange flames of death in all directions.

"*Ai-eee!*" cried this terrifying apparition. In a kind of dervish dance, the figure spun and landed a karate kick on one of Octavio's men who tried to make a rush from behind.

"*Ai-eee!*" cried the figure in triumph. When the pistol at the end of the arm was empty of bullets, it was thrown at the enemy—and a new pistol appeared in hand with hardly a break.

There was no fighting such an inexorable blue demon. The firing stopped, and the cordite smoke gradually cleared. On the deck, a fallen body was reaching slowly for a fallen gun—but in one smooth gesture, Officer Cathy Kaminsky sent her wooden nightstick sailing through the air to knock the pistol out of reach.

"Take *that*, motherfucker!" said she. Officer Kaminsky turned to inspect the damage, and found Lieutenant Rachmaninoff huddled behind the bar with his daughter.

"Hey, Loo," she said in greeting. "How are things?"

17

THE HELICOPTER NICKY RACHMANINOFF HAD BROUGHT DOWN WITH AN
ice bucket was lying on its side in a croquet court. Nicky climbed
down from the roof on a fire ladder and went over to see how Cory
had fared in the crash.

The helicopter looked like a dying bug, the running lights still
blinking in a kind of death spasm. Several firemen were shooting
some kind of foam onto the engine to keep it from catching fire. In
the midst of this, the side door opened and a battered-looking Cory
Heard emerged. There seemed to be something wrong with his legs,
but he was grinning at the apocalyptic scene of destruction he had
made of Octavio's house and gardens.

"Nicholas! Long time no see, amigo!"

Nicky helped him down off the helicopter. Cory collapsed on the
ground with a small cry of pain, and two firemen hurried over with
a stretcher.

"Well, have you been having fun?" asked Nicky sternly.

"Only so-so, amigo. But, hell, at least I lived on the edge a little
while. You know, for the first time in twenty years I wasn't bored."

"Congratulations," said Nicky sourly. "You sure as hell didn't
end up doing much for Nicaragua."

Cory only shrugged. "Who cares about Nicaragua? Let me tell
you, the *real* action these days is in Eastern Europe. What I've
decided, Nicholas, is that you and I should take a little vacation in
Bucharest. . . ."

Nicky watched in disbelief as Cory Heard was strapped into a
stretcher and carried off toward a waiting ambulance, talking a blue
streak all the while about what he called "twenty-first-century demo-
socialism," which was going to combine all the best features of every
previous political system.

"Believe me," he called to Nicky from a dozen feet away, "Eastern Europe is an absolute blank page upon which men of true vision
can leave a mark!"

"You think they're ready for us in Romania?" asked Nicky with a sigh. Halfway to the ambulance, Kitty fell upon the stretcher like some half-crazed peasant woman, weeping and wrapping her arms about her husband so that the firemen eventually had to pull her away.

"They make a lovely couple, don't they?" asked Charlie Cat, materializing at Nicky's side.

Nicky only grunted, "Where's Octavio?"

"Look behind you. Officer Kaminsky has him in custody."

Turning around, Nicky watched a triumphant Cathy Kaminsky leading Octavio Morales toward a waiting patrol car. Octavio still wore his costume from *Lawrence of Arabia*, but his wrists were securely handcuffed behind his back, and on his face was a look of utter dejection.

"There goes Hollywood's briefest tycoon," said Charlie.

"Sure," said Nicky. They would book Octavio for assaulting an officer, attempted manslaughter, false imprisonment, and resisting arrest. It wasn't Murder One, but it was something at least. If Octavio could still raise the money for a slick lawyer, probably a number of the charges would be reduced or thrown out because of Lieutenant Rachmaninoff's unorthodox procedures. From Nicky's experience in these matters, he imagined Octavio would end up doing maybe six months, for in America it was only the poor and unconnected who received long prison terms—which was enough to make you a little left-wing, if you stopped to think about it too much.

Emergency vehicles of every description were pulling up into the estate. A number of the remaining guests, still dressed in their Arab finery, watched the house burn from positions of safety behind police lines. Nicky saw Rip Beasley, wearing a blue FBI windbreaker, step out of an official car. Rip was in the company of Bob Arnold, who wore the same sports shirt with little sailboats on it that Nicky had first seen in Nicaragua.

"Oh-oh, time to get out of here," said Nicky. "Where's Tanya?"

"She was on the other side of the house, talking to her boyfriend, last time I saw her," said Charlie.

Nicky looked up in alarm. "*José?* She's with José?"

"Nicky, come on—they seemed to be having kind of a personal talk. You gotta give young people some space."

"Give me your gun, Charlie."

"Nicky—"

"*Give me your gun!*"

With a drastically raised right eyebrow, Charlie handed over his pistol. Unlike Nicky, who was content with his police-issue .38, Charlie kept a real hotdog gun—a .357 with a long barrel. Nicky took the gun and ran around to the other side of the house, with Charlie close at his heels.

José and Tanya were standing at the edge of the golf course, next to the camel. The three of them together made a pretty picture—Tanya, José, and camel—the desert behind them and a nearly full moon fat in the sky, like Joseph and Mary in Egypt. Only Joseph seemed more concerned with money than with religion; he was tying the three canvas bags onto the back of the camel.

"You still after that money, kid? I think you should step away from the camel nice and slow," said Nicky, leveling Charlie's .357 at the boy's chest. "Easy now."

José turned around from the camel and scowled. Very quickly, he grabbed Tanya's wrist and pulled her in front of him. With his bad hand, he managed to get to the pistol that was stuffed in his belt and bring it up to Tanya's head.

"Don't come any closer, Señor Nicky, or I kill your daughter."

"Gently, gently," said Nicky. "Let her go, José. You sure don't want to hurt Tanya—I know that, José."

Nicky stood, offering himself as a target, lowering Charlie's pistol to his side. Tanya, with the pistol against her head, was sputtering mad.

"Boy! And I gave you money and everything!" she cried at José.

"Come on, kid—we've all been through too much together for a bad scene like this," said Nicky. "What do you say?"

"You get me out of here, Nicky, or I'll blow this rich girl away!"

"Just relax," said Nicky. "Relax and you can have whatever you want. Are you okay, Munchkin?"

Tanya nodded at him. The whites of her eyes gleamed in the moonlight.

"I want a helicopter and a pilot to take me where I say. I'll let Tanya go when I'm safe."

"Sure, José. Whatever. But be cool, kid—this may take some time to arrange."

"No time, Nicky—do it now. I am very serious. I will kill your daughter if you do not do exactly what I say."

"Don't help him, Dad," Tanya cried.

"Easy, Tanya. You too, José—you're making a very big mistake, you know. Octavio was broke. He didn't have the money, just like you didn't have the bank numbers. It was a double bluff. The only thing there was plenty of in this deal was imagination."

"You're lying for sure, Nicky. I looked in the bags—they are full of hunnert-doller bills!"

"Those bills aren't going to help anybody in Nicaragua, José. They're as fake as you are."

José laughed. "Oh, I don't think I'll take them to Nicaragua, Nicky—that is too poor a country for a rich man like me! Maybe Rio de Janeiro, maybe the south of France . . . we will see."

"You scumbag, you nerd, you fucking phony!" Tanya hurled at him. "You don't care about justice or truth or social equality, not *any* of those things—do you?"

"I did when I was poor," he told her with a grin. "But now that I am rich, I think maybe I will find new things to believe in."

José was not quick enough for a woman's wrath. Tanya didn't even bother to think about the gun against her head. Without warning, her fingernails clawed out at his face, catching him off guard. José screamed and fell away from her, against the camel. Nicky didn't risk a shot. He leaped forward, got José around the waist, and pulled him down beneath him onto the ground. Nicky's superior weight did the rest; it was a moment in which years of calories paid off. Nicky shook the pistol out of José's bad hand and was sitting on his chest, pounding his fists into the boy's face, when Tanya came up behind him and took hold of his arm.

"Don't hurt him, Dad! Please!"

Charlie was there too, helping Nicky off the dazed teenager. Charlie turned José over, face down on the ground, and got a pair of handcuffs around his wrists in back.

Tanya was crying, and Nicky took her in his arms. After a while, her cries turned to little snivels and hiccoughs.

"Will you get me a cigarette, Dad? I swear, I'm gonna *die* if I don't get some nicotine fast."

Nicky looked at her sternly. "When did you start smoking, young lady?"

"Honestly, Dad, absolute ages ago! I mean, *everyone* my age smokes."

"I didn't know that," said Nicky.

"There are lots of things you don't know," said Tanya.

"You'll have to tell me, then," said Nicky. He supposed it was time to stop the fantasies and allow for reality instead. Nicky managed to bum a cigarette off one of the firemen, and he watched Tanya light up. She had become a woman, nearly, while he wasn't looking.

"Are you really mad, Dad?"

"Furious," he said. And kissed her on the forehead.

They walked off toward a waiting police car, and Tanya saw he was limping.

"Gosh, you're hurt, Dad—and it's all my fault!"

Nicky didn't disillusion her. Hell, why not let *her* feel guilty for a change?

Epilogue

WHAT IS LEFT

ON A CLEAR AFTERNOON IN EARLY JULY, NICKY RACHMANINOFF AND his ex-wife, Susan, drove their daughter, Tanya, to the airport.

Tanya had let her hair grow longer in the past few months, and it was tied back away from her eyes with an elastic band. She was still wearing jeans—these days there were no holes in the knees—and she had a guitar in a case covered with peace symbols and emblems for her favorite band, the Grateful Dead.

Tanya was meeting eleven other teenagers and an adult from a group called Experiments in International Living in front of the Pan Am counter. One of the teenagers was Tanya's current boyfriend, Dylan. Dylan had long blond hair braided in a ponytail down his back. His father was the head of a major record label, but Dylan had an urge to renounce material things, preferring the rural funk of Sunshine Terrace, where he had been living for the past six weeks while Nicky played father to both him and Tanya.

All together, the twelve teenagers and the adult in charge were heading to the Soviet Union for a seven-week tour. They were to spend a week in Moscow and a week in Leningrad, and the rest of the time working on a collective farm alongside Russian teenagers in the Ukraine, not many miles outside of Kiev.

Tanya kissed her mother, kissed her father—and then she was gone. Nicky and Susan watched the jumbo jet pull out of its port and disappear down the runway. Then they walked slowly back along endless airport corridors and down the escalator to the garage. Nicky felt a pang of loss. Tanya had been staying with him on Sunshine Terrace ever since the day they had stood outside of Octavio Morales's burning house, and he felt a cruel stab at her going away.

They had come in Susan's Bentley, for Nicky's rebuilt Austin-Healey had not been big enough for them all. Nicky took off his beige corduroy jacket and tossed it onto her backseat—he had three corduroy jackets now, just in case he ever again suffered a sudden loss—but the raccoons that had once visited him on Sunshine Terrace had never returned.

Susan had been back in California only a week now since finishing her play in New York. There was some talk she might receive a Tony award for her portrayal of a prostitute dying of AIDS.

"Did I tell you? I saw Kitty and Cory at the Four Seasons just before I came home. They're flying off to Syria to meet with Yasir Arafat—part of a group called Hollywood Jews for Palestine."

"*That* sounds like a guilt-ridden cause if I ever heard one!" muttered Rachmaninoff. "And Kitty's not even Jewish."

"Oh, but she is—she only just found out! Her mother hid it from her all these years. As soon as Kitty found out, she told everyone, of course—she's become *very* Jewish just to make up for her mother's lying about it all these years. She's working terribly hard for the Palestinians."

"That makes sense," said Nicky. "Now she can be anti-American and anti-Israeli at the same time. It opens up brand-new areas of self-immolation."

Susan giggled. She had gained a little weight in New York, but she had never looked so pretty.

Nicky didn't like to think too often about Kitty and Cory Heard; he was glad to be back to more normal police routine, in which people committed crimes out of simple motivations of lust and greed. Out of the "Nicaraguan mess," as he tended to call it, only Octavio Morales had been sentenced to do time: five years in San Quentin. Charges against Kitty and Cory had been filed and then dropped with some persuasion from the State Department that it was best to let sleeping dogs lie. Even José had gotten off without a sentence. Pip had refused to testify against him, and with the attempted murder charge gone and Tanya's status as a possible kidnap victim a little too dubious to pursue, there wasn't much else. Kitty hired José such an expensive lawyer that the kid was even able to avoid deportation, somehow managing to claim he was a political exile who had been secretly aiding the pro-democratic forces.

It was a farce, of course. If anybody was guilty, these people were—Cory, Kitty, and José. But Nicky bore no grudge. A lot of guilty people were walking around free. José was working these days as a waiter in a chic Nicaraguan restaurant just off Melrose, and his biggest punishment probably was that Tanya cut him dead whenever he tried to call.

They were driving in silence when Susan said, "Tell me something, I've always been curious: Was Kitty good in bed?"

"Well, she *was* good in bed," Nicky admitted, "but we sure as hell couldn't talk."

Susan's Bentley was like a *Queen Mary* stateroom on wheels. Instead of heading back toward Beverly Hills, she pointed the bow toward the freeway to the beach.

"Where are we going?"

"I have a surprise for you," she said. "Something I want to show you. . . . Actually, *I* had an affair in New York," she mentioned after a while.

"Did you?"

"Mm . . . he was young and very romantic, but absolutely no sense of humor. We couldn't talk either. It became very boring."

"I can imagine."

Susan headed up the Pacific Coast Highway, past Santa Monica and Malibu, and still kept going. The sun was sinking into an explosive red and orange sunset on the western waves.

"I talked to Charlie the other day," she said after a couple of miles. "To tell the truth, I called him up to ask if you were seeing anyone these days."

"Did you?"

"Mm . . . he said you had been going out for a while with a college girl. What was her name?"

"Epiphany Moore," said Nicky. "It didn't really work out."

"May I ask you why?"

"I was looking for someone too young to understand me. Unfortunately, I succeeded too well. We didn't really have a lot to say."

Susan gave him a funny sideways look from behind the wheel. "It's difficult," she said, "to find someone you like to go to bed with and can talk to as well."

"It sure is," he agreed.

At Trancas, Susan turned off the Coast Highway onto Broad Beach Road. Half a mile up the private road, she pulled into the driveway of a two-story Cape Cod beach house that was painted white with blue trim. It was a cozy old-fashioned house with dormer windows and a nice little garden of geraniums and roses—not a cactus in sight. When Susan turned off the car engine, Nicky could hear the pulse of the ocean waves against the beach.

"Well, this is the surprise! I mean, I *bought* it, Nicky! This beach house is mine!"

"Gee, that's swell, Susan."

He was trying to feel glad for her, but he was thinking that now that Susan had a real home, she would probably want Tanya back to live with her again after she got back from the Soviet Union.

Susan took his hand as they were sitting in the car. "Do you remember, you always used to say how you wanted to live at the beach? How Los Angeles would be all right as long as every morning you could wake up and look at the ocean?"

"Sure, I remember that."

"Well, look, I've been thinking about how Tanya needs both of us right now—a real family, a mother and a father—and I've come up with this *really* interesting idea. Would you like to hear my interesting idea, Nicky?"

"Well, all right, Susan."

"It's a little complicated," she admitted. "I tell you what—why don't you come inside to bed . . . and afterwards we'll talk?"